INTO EACH LIFE

INTO EACH LIFE

SHELIA E. LIPSEY

URBAN BOOKS, LLC
www.urbanbooks.net

Urban Christian books are published by

URBAN BOOKS
10 Brennan Place
Deer Park, NY 11729

ISBN: 1-893196-90-9

First Printing January 2007
Printed in the United States of America

10   9   8   7   6   5   4   3   2   1

*This is a work of fiction. Any references or similarities to actual events, real peo-
ple, living, or dead, or to real locales are intended to give the novel a sense of reality. Any similarity to other names, characters, places, and incidents is entirely
coincidental.*

Submit Wholesale Orders to:
Kensington Publishing Corp.
C/O Penguin Group (USA) Inc.
Attention: Order Processing
405 Murray Hill Parkway
East Rutherford, NJ 07073-2316
Phone: 1-800-526-0275
Fax: 1-800-227-9604

Dedication

Life is a journey that each of us must travel. Into each person's life there will be ups and downs, sunshine and rain. Into each of our lives come pain and heartbreak, tragedy and sorrow, joy and happiness. But remember that there is always hope if we hold on and place our faith and trust in God Almighty. This book is dedicated to all those who have gone "through," yet persevered because of the people God has placed along your path and the ways of escape He has predestined for you. It is dedicated to those who share the unbreakable cord of friendship, relationships, and the power of unconditional love that holds you up.

Into each life some rain must fall . . .
Into each heart some tears must fall.
A. Roberts/D. Fisher

Acknowledgments

To God Be the Glory because, of course, I must give Him the highest praise for allowing me to write this book. To every person who played a part in assisting me with publication of *Into Each Life*—maybe you read it in its draft stage, or you encouraged me to keep on writing, or you said a prayer and wished me well—I say thank you. To Alisha Yvonne, you hold a very special place in my life. You believed in me, and my work, and showed me true love from the beginning. The friendship that has formed between us is something I am especially thankful for and will cherish for the rest of my life. To Carl Weber, thank you for giving me this opportunity of a lifetime. You are the one who has breathed life into my dream of seeing my God-inspired books in print. Carl, may the blessing you have brought upon my life spill over into yours. To my editor, Joylynn Jossel, thank you for the time and effort you put into helping me perfect my manuscript. To Memphis Rawsistaz, thank you for your support, your words of encouragement, your love, and your concern.

To all of the people who will purchase a copy of *Into Each Life*—book clubs, friends, families, strangers, all of you who will purchase a copy and who will take your valuable time to read it—I want you to know that I appreciate you already. It's because of the readers that we, the authors, become who we are in this literary world. To my sons, thank you for your untiring support and your unconditional love for me. I pray that your dreams and aspirations will come to pass and that the favor of God will always be over your lives. To my grandchildren, the Golden Child (Kevin, Jr.), the Beloved Child (Leland), and the Divine Child (Kaleb), I love you so much. The three of you make my life complete and joyous. To all of my other grandchildren by love and by blood, I thank God for you (Sabrina, Tahj, Tehja, Kassidy). To my niece Shanté, and my nephews, DeAndre and Jermon, your belief in my abilities inspires me and motivates me to keep on. To my sisters, Sandra, Yvette, and Yvonne, I thank God for the close relationship and the bond we share that can never be broken. To all who have helped me along the way, my cousin Tanglea, to my best friend, Kaye Frye, and to my deceased best friend, Eileen James (I miss you Eileen), through each of you, I have learned how to survive the storms of life because you have helped to keep me afloat. I love you and I thank God for each of you.

And finally, I must always, always say a very special thank you to my mother, Cora Ann Bell, who is forever by my side, praying for me, praying with me, believing in me, telling me that I can do it and that I will make it—I love you with every fiber of my being, Mommy.

Prologue

September 1984

It was Prodigal's first high school dance and it was off the chain. With girls scattered like bees over the giant auditorium, Prodigal found it hard to concentrate on his date. He scanned the dimly lit auditorium and marveled at the ultra-revealing clothes some of the girls wore, but he wasn't complaining.

He wasn't the best dancer, but his sister had taught him a few moves, and his best friend, Teary, had shown him some dance steps too. His eyes scanned the packed room in search of Teary.

"What's on your mind, Prodigal?" his girlfriend Faith asked, as if she didn't already know.

"I was looking for Teary, that's all. I haven't seen her for a while."

"You know Teary—she's probably out on the floor somewhere shaking her rump, I betcha. Or maybe she's outside with Debra and Chelsia. Anyway, stop worrying about Teary. We're here to have fun. I'm sure that wherever she is she's having fun."

"You're probably right." Prodigal scanned the room one last time for his best friend. "Come on, let's dance." He grabbed Faith by the hand, and the two made their way to the dance floor.

Prodigal and Faith slow danced to Anita Baker's, "No One in the World." She rested her head comfortably against his chest and listened to the soothing lyrics of love as she continually tried not to allow Prodigal and Teary's friendship to forge a rift between herself and Prodigal. Faith liked him far too much, and if she wanted to continue being his girlfriend, she had to understand and accept that Teary wasn't going anywhere.

As much as Prodigal liked Faith, he couldn't concentrate on her at the moment. He was worried about Teary. It had always been that way. Ever since the two of them were kids living across the street from each other, they had a bond that nobody could break. Not even the fine girl who held him tight around the neck.

Prodigal stopped dancing just as Anita sang, *"No one in the world can love me like you do . . ."* Hold up, Faith, I want to find Teary and make sure she's okay. I'll be right back."

Faith didn't respond to Prodigal, but inside she was seething. She stepped aside and allowed him to leave her in the middle of the dance floor.

He searched around the crowded auditorium. No Teary.

He asked a group of classmates, "Hey, have any of you seen Teary?"

Each shook his head no.

He spotted Teary's friend, Debra, in a corner of the gym. She was sipping on a punch.

"You seen Teary?" he asked her.

"She was over there talking to Chelsia a few minutes ago." Debra pointed to the other side of the room.

When Teary saw Chelsia dancing by herself, he made a detour and went outside where he saw Langston, a guy Teary used to be crazy about. Prodigal flinched—Langston was nothing but bad news. Nevertheless, he walked up to him to see if he'd seen her.

"Last I saw your girl, she was making out with dude, uh, Derrel whatshisname," Langston said, a smirk on his face. "Man, when are you going to learn? That female ain't all righteous and holy like she wants you to think. She just don't want to give you none." Langston and his friends broke out in hysterical laughter.

Prodigal balled both hands into a fist. He stormed off before he lost his composure with Langston and refocused his efforts on finding Teary. It wasn't like her to run off, especially when they were having a blast like they were tonight.

He went back inside and went through the double doors that led to the classrooms. His pounding steps were interrupted by the distressed voice coming from the senior lounge.

He heard a female voice yell. "Stop it. Stop it!"

"Who the hell do you think you are? You're not getting away that easy. Come on here," a voice demanded. "I'm getting some of this tonight."

"Derrel, no, let me go," the girl begged.

Prodigal yanked open the door and leaped at the shirtless, blonde-haired boy, punching him in the stomach and grabbing Teary underneath his arm.

"If you ever put your hands on her again, I swear, I'll break every bone in your body," Prodigal yelled. He abruptly left Derrel bent over in pain then turned and walked away with Teary safely underneath the curl of his arms.

Prodigal examined Teary. Her eyes were red, and the new dress she bought for the dance was slightly tattered. "You okay? Did that punk hurt you?"

"No, I'm okay. How did you find me?" she asked, brushing herself off.

"Girl, now you know not to even go there. Didn't I tell you that I have a special 'Teary detector' that can track your butt a-mile-a-minute? Now come on, let's go back to the dance, and this time I'm not letting you out of my sight."

Prodigal was quite protective of Teary. No one better mess with Teary Fullalove, not as long as he was around. It had been that way since the beginning, and nothing or no one was going to change that.

Part One

The Days of Youth

"Be happy, young man, while you are young, and let your
heart give you joy in the days of your youth. Follow the ways of
your heart and whatever your eyes see, but know that for all
these things God will bring you to judgment."
—Ecclesiastes 11:9 (NIV)

1

From the First Moment

"Nappy head, nappy head, go back home and go to bed!" five-year-old Prodigal yelled, bouncing around, laughing and licking his tongue out at Teary.

"Prodigal Runsome, if you don't leave me alone, I'm going to tell yo' momma," seven-year-old Teary warned.

Tucked safely away from the hustle and bustle of the world, the minuscule city of Broknfield, Oregon, barely boasted a population of 100,000, and Prodigal pledged himself among them, in more than only a headcount: he loved the breathtaking mountain views with snow-capped mountaintops; the winding back roads that indented valleys into the midst of clear, babbling brooks and streams; the massive rocks cropping up between budding juniper trees; the luscious ferns peeping out from among their hiding places; the miles of stone wall flowing graciously, yet powerfully, through the surrounding countryside.

He didn't have to venture far outside the neighborhood to find a steep pitch to climb or a private place of solitude to claim among the stars. Like many of the other kids, he used nature's pathways to escape into his own world and to find a shortcut to his friends' homes.

"I'm sick of you, boy. Now you betta get outta my face!"

Teary's voice echoed through Prodigal's mind as he reminisced about the first time he saw her, the day he spotted the orange-and-white U-Haul in front of what used to be Amos Small's house. Curiosity coaxed him to peek through his bedroom window. He stared without blinking, while movers unloaded tables, chairs, and boxes.

Maybe another boy will move in and I'll have someone else to play with. He positioned himself comfortably on the inside ledge of his window and sat there watching for hours.

Finally rewarded, he inched closer as a blue Chrysler drove up in the circular drive. A well-dressed, portly woman opened the door from the driver's side. Almost simultaneously, the passenger side of the door opened, and a girl who looked to be about the same age as his eleven-year-old sister, Fantasia, stepped out.

Shucks, this definitely is not a good sign.

His heart livened up, when he saw the back door of the car swing open. He zeroed in with intensity and watched as a jean-clad leg swung out of the car. He moved closer to the ledge and gasped with anticipation, filling his narrow chest cavity. His eyes widened, his heart raced.

Then he saw them—two dangling pigtails bouncing in the wind. Air deflated from his chest, and in its place, a heavy sigh claimed victory.

"Why couldn't she be a boy?"

She climbed out of the car and immediately looked around, surveying her new home and neighborhood. Unexpectedly, she turned directly toward Prodigal's house.

He gasped and moved with lightning speed away from the window.

After a few seconds, he inched slowly back up and reclaimed his spot, just in time to capture a perfect view of the prettiest girl he'd ever seen. Her golden-brown skin and thick, reddish hair made his young heart go pitter-patter. He wondered if she ever let her hair hang down the spine of her back, like maybe on a Sunday.

Worried she might see him before he was "ready," he took

refuge behind the printed gabardine curtains. He watched her pigtails bounce. His mouth hung open, drools of his own spittle forming on the windowsill.

Without warning, she glanced up in his direction.

He swiftly jumped from the window and raced down the stairs. *Dang! Did she see me?*

"Boy, where are you headed in such a hurry?" Prodigal's daddy grabbed his only son by the scuff of his blue plaid shirt.

"Uh, nowhere. I was just coming downstairs to fix me some bologna and crackers," Prodigal quickly lied.

"Well, slow down. You're going to hurt somebody running through the house like that, you hear me?"

"Yes, sir," he answered, proceeding to the kitchen.

Prodigal dealt the bologna and crackers out like a deck of cards and poured a glass of grape Kool-Aid for himself, sloshing it over the countertop. He was worried the pigtails would be gone by the time he'd made it back outside. He then exited the kitchen and made his way out the front door. He strategically positioned himself on the front porch, balancing the crackers on his lap and placing the Kool-Aid on the first step. *There's still a chance a boy my age is moving in too.*

After all, he hadn't given himself a chance to see if anyone else may have been getting out of the car, once his eyes fell on the pretty pigtailed little girl.

He cautiously allowed his brown, spectacle-covered eyes to zero in across the street. Neither girl was in sight. He carefully studied the two grown-ups talking to the movers and came to the conclusion that they were the parents.

Suddenly, the front door of the two-story house swung wide open, and the girls bounced out. The pigtailed one raced to the end of her driveway and stood at the edge of the sidewalk. She waved her hand back and forth in Prodigal's direction.

He turned and looked around, but there was no one else around. Awkwardly, he waved back, not knowing what to do next.

Tat, tat, tat!

Prodigal swiftly turned his head to meet the sound.

Tat, tat, tat! His daddy's towering frame peeped out the living room window, his charcoal fingers tapping against the windowpane.

Prodigal almost choked on his bologna. He acted like he'd just been caught with his hand in the cookie jar.

His daddy pointed in the direction of the U-Haul truck.

Prodigal didn't know why.

Again, his daddy pointed.

Prodigal shrugged.

Obviously exasperated, his daddy opened the oak door and joined his son on the concrete steps. "Hey, why don't you go over there and welcome our new neighbors?"

"I don't want to, Daddy. It's only two girls over there anyway, and I was hoping and praying that a boy my age would move in."

"Son, you can still be friends with girls. And look, I'm not telling you to be their friend anyway. But don't you think it would be polite and courteous if you'd at least welcome them to the neighborhood?

Reluctantly, he agreed. "Aww, okay, Daddy."

"Come on, son. If it'll make you feel better, we can walk over there together. I'll introduce the both of us, okay?"

Prodigal mumbled. He gobbled the rest of his bologna and crackers and forced it down his throat with the remaining Kool-Aid before they struck out across the street.

"Hi, I'm Solumun Runsome, and this is my son, Prodigal," Solumun said as he and his son approached their new neighbors. Solumun extended his hand. "It's nice to have you in the neighborhood."

"Thank you. I'm Brian Fullalove, and this is my wife, Cynthia." Brian grabbed his wife around the waist. "These are my daughters, Sara and Teary." He smiled at his daughters.

"Nice to meet you, Cynthia. And you too, Sara and Teary," Solumun remarked.

"It's nice to meet you too," Mrs. Fullalove stated. "I told Brian that I believe we're going to enjoy living here in Broknfield. I can just feel it."

"I'm sure you will. This is a great neighborhood, and Broknfield is a great town," Solumun assured them.

Prodigal tried to stay in the shadow of his father and said a silent prayer. *Lord, don't let these girls come near me. And please let my daddy and this man finish talking real quick.*

Prodigal allowed his thoughts to come back from when he first met Teary to now. He smiled just thinking about her again, fantasizing, like the other boys and men in town did over the women they saw every day and probably thought about every night.

Though the neighborhood residents attended Deliverance Temple of Praises Church, whose shepherd was none other than Pastor Marcus Grace, Jr., and still committed their secret little sins, all in all, Broknfield wasn't so bad. Nevertheless, the people were people, and the children were children, and life was life—the norm.

"All right, Prodigal, that's it. You've done it now." Teary lashed out as he narrowly escaped her raised fist. "I'm telling yo' momma," she yelled.

Prodigal glowed inside with the fires of friendship and first love for Teary. *She must be the ideal girl,* he thought as they rode their bikes to Willow Lake.

Without so much as a slip in his stride, he dropped his bike on the manicured lawn surrounding the lake. In less than two steps he was at her side. Before she could so much as plant her pink-and-white sneakers on the ground, Prodigal grabbed her bike handle and steadied it while she quickly hopped off.

She brushed him aside, but he didn't move away, keeping her clear of the thorn bushes around them.

"I think I like you," he whispered without looking at her.

She watched him the way a kitten watches everything that

moves. "I like you too." Her voice whipped around his face like the summer wind.

Desperate to prove his affection for her, he pulled the branches of a giant thorn bush closer and without warning pricked his thumb bravely, not making any sound of pain. He handed the branch to her.

She regarded it silently, and then quickly making up her mind, stabbed her own thumb. They stoically squeezed until tiny splatters of blood poured from each of their thumbs.

Together, they pressed their bloody thumbs together allowing their blood to mix.

"I vow to always be your friend, Teary, even when we grow old, die and go to Heaven." Prodigal's eyes innocently lingered on her cherub face. "Now it's your turn—Do you promise too?"

She slowly nodded her head up and down in agreement.

2

Predestined to Be

Prodigal's parents, Ruth and Solumun, were teenagers when they met and fell in love. It was during a neighborhood tent revival that was held every summer by Pastor Marcus Grace, Sr. that the two of them met. When Ruth laid eyes on Solumun's lean body as he waltzed under the giant white revival tent, she thought her heart would drop. She giggled as she walked alongside one of her friends underneath the hot and musty tent.

"Look, there's that boy I told you about the other night," Ruth said. "Girl, he's so good-looking, I can hardly stand to look at him."

"You're right. He is cute," her friend squealed in agreement.

"Look how tall he is. I bet he's every bit of six feet, and he's skinny just like I want my man to be."

"Ruth, you better hush before somebody hears you." Her friend giggled.

"I don't care. Look at how neat his Afro is, not a hair out of place."

"Girl, come on here. We need to find a seat before revival starts."

But Ruth ignored her. She was in a world of her own as the object of her affection made his way toward where she was standing.

"Excuse me," he said to Ruth and her friend as he walked up and eased by them to take a seat.

Ruth thought at that moment she was going to pee on herself. She tried not to stare into his soft brown eyes. And the way he moved, his broad shoulders oozed confidence without cockiness. During the three-hour revival service, other than an "Amen" or "Praise the Lord," absolute silence was shared between them.

When service ended, Ruth lingered a moment, wanting to take in the boy once more before she traipsed off to find her parents at the front of the tent.

Without warning, he asked, "Hey, what's your name?"

Ruth was tongue-tied.

"You do have a name, don't you?" His voice resonated with boldness, reminding Ruth of their youth minister's thunderous set of vocal cords.

She, in turn, responded in a shy, demure voice. "Yeah, I have a name. I'm Ruth. Ruth Peace. What's yours?"

Even though she was almost fifteen years old, she'd never had a boyfriend. Her strict parents wouldn't allow such a thing anyway, and the boys that attended their small community church were all like brothers to her. She would just about puke if she thought any of them liked her as a girlfriend. Ruth had plenty of friends at school too, but boys seldom approached her or the other girls in her group. It might have been because they were often teased and called religious freaks because they prayed before eating or taking an exam. But she couldn't care less what anyone said or thought of her.

"My name's Solumun Runsome. I haven't seen you around here since this revival started, and I've been coming here all week long."

By this time, she couldn't help herself. She stared deep into the fine-looking boy's captivating baby browns.

"Are you coming back tomorrow night?" he asked. "You know it's the last night."

He sure hoped she would say yes. He wanted to get to know her. He couldn't believe he hadn't spotted her before. He attended Benton High, but he'd never seen her around there. Of that he was sure. He could only assume that she lived across town and attended some other school.

"I'll be here. But even if I didn't wanna come, my Momma and Daddy would make me anyway."

"I know how that goes. Mine too. So, I tell you what—If you get here before me, then why don't you save me a seat? And if I get here first, I'll do the same. How about that?"

"Okay, it's a deal. But I really need to go now. I have to find my parents. I don't want to make 'em mad."

"Yeah, you do that."

"I'll see you tomorrow then." She smiled and turned to walk away.

Five years after that fateful meeting, they stood before Pastor Grace and exchanged wedding vows.

Prodigal often found it rather difficult to fathom the deep and abiding love his Momma and Daddy shared. It was a love that remained constant and very much alive—until the night their lives changed forever.

Prodigal tossed and turned night after night as visions of that evening terrorized him while he slept.

They were headed home from Sunday night praise and worship service. Like always, the drive home was full of their chattering.

"Hey, kids, do y'all want to stop and get some ice-cream?" Solumun asked.

"Yes, sir," Prodigal and his oldest sister, Fantasia, squealed in unison.

His little sister, Hope, a broad smile covering her angelic face at the mention of ice cream, said, "Yes."

Solumun drove the Chevy Celebrity into the Malt Shoppe parking lot, where they all climbed out, Ruth holding Hope's chubby body on her hip.

Prodigal surveyed the sight before him and felt like the luckiest boy alive to have such a close family. Many of the kids in his school had parents who were divorced. He thanked God every night when he said his prayers for his Momma and Daddy.

After putting in his request and receiving his order, Prodigal took a lick of his chocolate and strawberry swirl ice-cream.

"Fantasia, let me have a lick of yours," Prodigal begged his sister.

"No, I'm not giving you anything. You're always begging."

"I'm not either. I just wanted to see how green ice cream tastes. You're so stingy."

"I'm not. You're just greedy." Fantasia stuck out her tongue at her brother.

"Okay, stop it, you two. No arguing tonight," Ruth said. "Just finish your ice cream so we can go home."

Prodigal smiled when he witnessed his daddy kissing the vanilla ice cream from his Momma's lips.

After finishing up their treats, the Runsome family made their way home.

"Okay, kids, go take your baths and get ready for bed," Ruth said as they walked inside the house.

"Yes, ma'am," Fantasia answered as Prodigal mumbled something under his breath.

Hope had fallen sound asleep and was nestled in her mother's arms. Ruth studied her chocolate, smooth-as-silk skin and used the back of her work-worn hand to caress her baby girl's chubby cheeks. Her Rockwell figurine eyes were perfectly formed and reminded Ruth of Solumun. Her coarse black hair shielded her deep temples, which pounded like the beat of a drum. Solumun certainly left a piece of himself in each of them.

"Let me have her. I'll put her to bed," Solumun said.

Ruth kissed Hope's hair then passed her to Solumun.

He gingerly laid her down while Ruth lingered in the kitchen.

After Prodigal and Fantasia bathed, they kissed their parents good night and went to bed.

Within minutes Prodigal heard his parents down in the kitchen laughing and talking. Sometimes he'd see his Daddy squeeze on his Momma's booty. She'd let out a yelp, and then they would go in their bedroom, always careful to close the door behind them.

As they stood face-to-face, Solumun reached out and drew Ruth close to him. "Girl, you know you're some kind of fine to me. You still look doggone good after all these years and three babies later."

"Boy, please, I bet you say that to all the girls."

Ruth teased back.

"No girl has my eye but you." He moved his hands over the firmness of her bottom.

"Is that right?" she crooned, caressing his chest.

"Every time I look at you, I get excited, woman. You know I'm right."

"Naw, tell me about it."

"You already know what you do to me."

His voice had become heavy, and his words sounded more like moans.

"No, tell me—what do I do to you?" she asked seductively.

"I can show you better than I can tell you. Come on and give me some of that good lovin'," he commanded, a sheepish grin on his face. When Ruth moved and filled the space between them he reached out, grabbed her around the waist, and pulled her thick-hipped, shapely body against his. His wide lips pressed against hers, and he parted them with his tongue.

Ruth tasted the black walnut ice-cream on his breath. She loved him with all of her soul.

He gently hoisted her up on the Formica kitchen countertop. His hands eagerly traced the familiar outline of her body.

"Ahhh." Her moans revealed her satisfaction. She could never get enough of Solumun, and he definitely couldn't get his fill of her.

He grunted in obvious pleasure, reveling in the warm moistness nestled between his wife's Tina Turner legs.

With one hand, she fumbled with his leather belt buckle, and with the other one, she pulled down the zipper on his black polyester trousers.

Without warning, he abruptly pulled back and grabbed his sweaty forehead. "Hey, baby, I'm feeling a little lightheaded."

"Well, come on, let's go lay down." Ruth released a sexy, low-key laugh. "I told you I was always going to have that kind of an effect on you, now didn't I?"

Before either of them could take a step toward their bedroom, Solumun collapsed and landed on the cold tile floor.

"Baby, what's wrong? Solumun?"

He stared straight ahead.

Ruth screamed frantically. She reached out for him and cradled his head carefully in the palm of her small hands. "Solumun!" she screamed again, fear swiftly rising in her voice.

A faint smile crossed his face before his eyes closed.

Fantasia and Prodigal were awakened by the screams of their mother. They hopped out of their beds and bolted downstairs. The screams woke Hope, and she began to cry loudly. But no one stopped to pacify her this time.

"Call an ambulance," Ruth yelled out.

Fantasia was terrified, when she stepped in the kitchen and saw her father lying on the floor unconscious. "Momma, what's wrong?"

"Everything is going to be all right. Just do as I say and call 911 now."

Prodigal watched his mother cradle his daddy against her chest. "What's wrong with him?"

Solumun didn't move a muscle. His hands dangled from his side.

"Why isn't he getting up, Momma?"

She tried to reassure him. "Listen, Prodigal, your daddy's going to be just fine."

Fantasia ran back to where her daddy lay, tears streaming down her face. "Momma, the ambulance is on the way."

Minutes later, when the paramedics arrived at the Runsome residence, Prodigal realized that everything would not be all right. Not ever again.

3

Into Each Life

Ruth hid in her room underneath the bed covers for weeks after Solumun's death. Solumun was always the picture of perfect health. In fact, there was no sign of anything being wrong with him, so when the doctor told her that he died from a brain aneurysm, Ruth was even more devastated.

Prodigal retreated into his own private world of grief. He didn't know how he would face life without his father. Who would teach him how to be a man? Who would play catch with him now? Who would do the things with him that only a Daddy could do?

Across the street, at the Fullalove house, Teary was full of questions. She understood that Mr. Runsome was with God, but everything had changed between her and Prodigal. Teary was worried about her best friend. When he was sad, it made her sad.

"Momma, Prodigal's no fun anymore. He's always acting sad, and he hardly ever wants to hang out with me," Teary complained one evening.

"Honey, you just have to pray for Prodigal," Teary's mother told her.

Teary hated to see Prodigal going through such pain. She didn't know how to help her friend. She tried to spend extra time with him, but that was hard. He refused many times to come outside or visit her. When she went to see him, all they did was sit and stare at the TV set. He didn't even want to ride his bike to Willow Lake, their supposed favorite spot.

Teary was at a loss as to what to do about Prodigal, which is why she went to her parents for answers. "Momma, why did God take Mr. Runsome away? Prodigal and his whole family are always sad now. I thought when someone goes to Heaven to be with God that it's supposed to be a happy time." Teary looked puzzled.

"Honey, it is good to go to Heaven. But when someone we love dies, it still hurts because we love that person so much and we miss them too. That's how Prodigal and his family are feeling right now, honey." Ruth stroked Teary's hair. Sara, her only sister, sat and listened.

"Baby, we don't always understand why things happen the way they do. We just have to keep our faith."

"Yeah, your mother's right," her father interrupted. "God is in control, and everything will work out, you'll see. Prodigal is going to be just fine, just give him some time."

"Okay." Teary sighed and stood up, nodding in agreement.

Sara didn't say a word, but instead turned back toward the TV and started watching the rest of *Martin*.

Teary still didn't quite understand why Mr. Runsome was gone and why God took him. All she knew was that her best friend was sad and there was nothing she could do about it.

Prodigal stood in the foyer of their house reading his father's favorite passage of Scripture that hung on the wall—*As for me and my house, we will serve the Lord.*

Prodigal thought about how every morning before going off to work, his father gathered the family around the kitchen table and prayed. Prodigal could hear his daddy's baritone voice in his mind. He remembered the way his daddy prayed. *Lord, You are good and I thank You for waking us up this morning. Bless my family and bless me to be the man You would have me to be, dear Lord.*

Sometimes while he prayed, Prodigal and Fantasia elbowed each other to see if they could make one another holler while Hope squirmed around. Prodigal would peek out of one eye and sneak a look at Hope. If she looked his way, he'd make a funny face, and she would start giggling every time. He always managed to close his eyes before his Momma caught him.

After what seemed like forever and a day, his Daddy finished—*And so I thank You right now, Father. Amen.*

Before Solumun died, the Runsome clan attended church two or three nights every week. Now months after Solumun's death, and Prodigal and his family had been to church only a few times.

The pangs of grief were still far too great for his mother to bear. Ruth started working longer hours at the hospital. Being a registered nurse was demanding, but it helped her deal with Solumun's death by keeping her busy. Too busy for her to think of all she'd lost when he died. She tried to exercise her faith by believing that in time, everything would be all right, but she was finding it difficult. She missed her husband so much, and no matter how much she prayed, the sting of grief plagued her mentally and spiritually. Whenever she attended church, she felt a fresh dose of pain. Everywhere she turned, she imagined Solumun's towering figure, whether in the vestibule, Sunday school classroom, or the sanctuary. She couldn't bear sitting on the pew without him beside her.

Fantasia, being the oldest of the Runsome children, took over most of the daily routine of preparing meals and performing household chores. She tried to help her mother keep up her strength and maintain her sanity, but nobody seemed to realize that Fantasia missed her father too. She retreated into her own world filled with dreams of one day escaping the pain and sadness that, to her, was a part of Broknfield.

Family was precious, but friends added a stability they all needed. Sara and Trina filled that role for Fantasia. Trina lived five houses away from Fantasia and was just as smart, if not smarter. An only child, and a spoiled one at that, everything was always about her. Whenever the Popsicle truck came ringing its bell down the street, Trina made sure she was the first one to get a fudgesicle and a grape popsicle. She had to show everybody that her folks believed she was the bomb. But somehow Fantasia understood her.

Wise beyond her tender years, Fantasia saw the need in Trina's heart for love and attention. That was her reason for being so selfish. She was needy. Trina's loads of material possessions didn't take the place of affection and love she craved from her successful parents. Unlike Trina, Sara's personality was similar to Fantasia's, and they always got along.

Sometimes Fantasia would sit on the top bunk in the room she shared with her little sister, and doodle on any paper she could find, including the brown paper sacks her Momma brought in from the grocery store.

"Fantasia, what on earth are you doing with all of this paper, girl?" Ruth inquired one evening after she returning home from work. "Young lady, for the life of me, I just can't see you using this much drawing paper, plus paper bags, notebook paper or whatever else you use around here—Are you eating the paper or what?"

"Momma, stop teasing me." Fantasia laughed. "You know I'm not eating paper. I'm drawing on it. You see just about everything I draw."

Fantasia's drawings seemed to take on a life of their own after her father's death. Blood red splotches dressed her paintings. The dagger of pain could not hide behind the host of hearts splashed across the canvas. Whether round, square, cracked, abstract, or modern, each revealed the broken nature of her very own heart.

She also used her passion for school to shield her grief. When she wasn't drawing, her head was stuck between the pages of a book. Unlike Prodigal, her grades went up. College would be her ticket to a whole new way of living. She made a vow with herself that when she left Broknfield, she would never look back.

Prodigal missed his father just as much. No matter how many times well-meaning people told him that his daddy was in Heaven, the hurt still flooded his heart. At night, alone in his room, he cowered underneath the privacy of his bedspread and shed silent tears. He wept bitterly. "Lord, I don't ever want to get married—never, ever, ever."

Still, nothing compared to seeing his mother crying day after day, night after night, her eyes often swollen and puffy. The smile his daddy etched on their hearts was stolen from each of them, when he died that night. And it hurt. It hurt like hell.

4

Life Goes On

Prodigal hurried to the auditorium to register for his classes. It was the first day of high school, and already he was tired of standing in the slow-moving registration line. He didn't give much thought to what he was doing and clumsily bumped into the girl in front of him. When she abruptly turned around, his mouth quickly flew open, and his eyes locked with hers. He couldn't help staring. She was definitely one of the most beautiful creatures God had created. Her petite frame and perfectly shaped body mesmerized him, his eyes fixed on her. As if caught in a capsule, he stood paralyzed by her beauty. Her hair, the color of onyx, followed the roundness of her face, and her bob style hairdo made her look prettier than a peach.

"Excuse me, look, er, I'm sorry. I didn't mean to run you over."

"No problem," she replied, her voice childlike. "I'm okay." She continued to move forward in line.

The palms of his hands dripped sweat. He had no idea what to say next or even if he should say anything more. After all, he felt like he had already made a complete jerk out of himself anyway. Finally, he decided to take a chance and ask her name.

"Uh, uh, hey, excuse me." He touched her gently on the

shoulder. "May I ask you your name?" Prodigal wasn't used to throwing a line to a girl. When he was in middle school, occasionally he'd get a telephone number or two from silly girls in his classes, but usually they didn't give him the time of day. He wasn't bothered by it either, too hooked on Teary anyway. But somehow he hoped this girl would be different. He wanted this girl to be different.

"Yes, you may."

Silence followed. Prodigal had no idea what to say afterwards. *What is she thinking? Probably that I'm some kind of jerk.* He was frozen.

"I'm waiting," she said with a welcoming smile.

Prodigal still wore a look of confusion on his face.

"My name is Faith Meadows—that's what you just asked me, right?—my name?"

Prodigal turned beet-red. He felt stupid. "Yeah, of course. Sorry about that. I guess I'm a little . . . well, never mind. Faith is a pretty name; it fits you perfectly," he said, trying to appear a little more confident.

She didn't know what to think about him. She was just as nervous as Prodigal. What she did know was he sure was handsome. She allowed her mind to quickly envision the two of them kissing. *What's wrong with me? Why would I be thinking of something like that? God, please forgive me for that thought.* It was her turn to be in her own little world, not even hearing him continue his conversation.

"Faith—I like that name. My name is Prodigal. You live around here?"

"Excuse me, did you say something?" she asked, stumbling out of her trance.

"Yeah. I just asked if you live around here."

"Sort of. Actually, I live about six and a half blocks from here. I'll have to catch the bus over here almost every day, and I sure don't like that. When I was in middle school I could walk to school. I guess I could do the same this time, but it would just take too long, and my parents don't want me to anyway. So what about you? Do you live 'round here?"

"Yeah. Less than a block away."

He felt his nervousness quickly disappear as the line picked up its pace. Before they realized it, the two of them had finished signing up for their classes.

"Did you get all the classes you wanted?" she asked.

"Yep, all of 'em, except one. I wanted to get in the electrician apprenticeship class, but it was already full. So now I have to take computer literacy."

"Computer literacy was one of my first choices." Faith beamed. "And I got it. What period do you have it?"

"Fourth."

"Hey, how about that—so do I." Her mouth formed into a pleasant smile.

He was thrilled at the thought of them having the same class at the same time. *High school just might be all right, after all.*

Prodigal's teenage years proved to be a crucial turning point in his life. To him, it seemed like only yesterday when he was a young boy, reeling over the death of his father, nursing a huge crush on Teary, and feeling like an all-around total dork. For the first time ever, he had someone he liked other than Teary, and so far, Faith acted like she liked him too. When she agreed to go to the basketball game with him, he was elated.

The Tigers were definitely hyped up for the championship game against their rivals, the Carver Cougars. It was game day, and everyone was anxious for the pep rally that was being held the last period of the school day.

Teary and her group of friends made sure they found a good seat at the top of the gym bleachers. They waved their black-and-gold pompoms back and forth to the thunderous beat of the drummers, while the cheerleaders yelled out for everyone to join them in the school cheer.

"*T-i-g-e-r-s*—Tigers. *T-i-g-e-r-s*—Tigers. Go, Tigers, go."

They cheered and swayed to the hyped beat for over an hour.

When the pep rally ended, Teary, Prodigal, and Faith, along with all the rest of the excited students, left school in a hurry.

"Come on, y'all," Faith told them, "if we want to get some good seats for the game, we need to be back here at the school by at least six-thirty."

As they neared the bus stop, Prodigal hovered next to her. "I'll catch the bus with you to your house and make sure you get home safely," he said bashfully. "Is that all right with you?"

She blushed. "Sure. I just don't want to make you late."

"Don't worry, you won't."

The bus pulled up, and they continued to talk as they inserted their bus passes.

"As soon as I see you off the bus, I'll make a beeline for home. I know a shortcut I can take that'll get me home in record time. I could use the exercise anyway. Who knows, maybe I'll develop some of those muscles all you girls go crazy over when you see that new guy—Langston whatshisname."

"I think I know who you're talking about but, for your information, I don't go crazy over Langston what's-his-name, or any boy like him for that matter," Faith replied rather angrily. "And anyway, he's not my type."

Prodigal was pleasantly surprised. "Well, tell me, what's your type then?"

Faith didn't know what made the words come out, but she found herself saying, "You."

Did she just come on to me? Before he could answer his own question, the bus jolted him as it came to a stop.

"Hey, this is where I get off." Faith stood up and gave Prodigal a quick kiss on his cheek. She raced off the bus and hurried down the street to her house.

Prodigal sat in his seat, rubbing the side of his cheek where Faith had kissed him. He felt himself becoming flushed. He quickly leaned out the side window and yelled out loud, "Hey, wait, Faith . . . will you be my girl? Faith, will you be my girl?" He yelled even louder.

She turned around swiftly. "You bet. See you tonight. Now get home before you make me late." She took off and ran up the sidewalk that led to her house.

Prodigal hopped off the bus at the next stop and dashed home as fast as he could, took a shower, splashed on some *If you like Eternity for Men, then you'll love Everlasting for Men* cologne. He jumped into his navy-blue sweats and his black-and-blue sneakers.

By the time he finished getting dressed, it was close to five-thirty. He still had time to grab a bite to eat and say a quick hello to his sisters.

Prodigal walked through the kitchen. "Hey, sis, what's for dinner?"

Sitting at the kitchen table, Fantasia paused from drawing and glanced up at her brother. "I threw some fish sticks in the oven, and there's some corn and green beans on the stove." She turned her attention back to her drawing.

"Thanks, Fantasia. You're such a good sister." Prodigal planted a big, sloppy kiss on her forehead. Then he focused his attention on Hope, who had just come from playing outside with her friends. "Hey, pretty girl. What's happening with you?"

"Nothing. But what's wrong with you? Why are you talking like that?" Hope wore a look of confusion on her face.

"What are you talking about? There's nothing wrong with me. I'm just lucky to have such sweet, beautiful sisters, and on top of that, one who can cook her butt off too." Prodigal smiled.

"Boy, stop tripping. You musta got into something." Fantasia allowed a laugh to escape as she spoke. "'Cause there is definitely something wrong with you."

"Naw, I think I'm falling in love, that's all."

" 'Falling in love'?" Hope repeated.

"Yes, little sister, falling in love."

"Who are you falling in love with? Can't be anybody but Teary, so tell me something I don't know." Fantasia stopped drawing and furrowed her eyebrows as she looked up at her brother.

"No, it isn't Teary. You know Teary only looks at me as a brother, not the lover that I am." Prodigal grinned.

Fantasia jerked her head around, looked at him and laughed. "Ooh, aren't we cocky today? Who is this mystery girl?"

"I don't know if you know her or not since you're one of them uppity upper-class girls—you know how you seniors think you're all the fire."

"Whatever—like I said, who is she?" Fantasia asked again, impatiently.

"Her name is Faith Meadows. She's the prettiest girl in the whole wide world, besides Teary, I might add. Except, unlike Teary, this girl is crazy about me."

"Boy, puhleeze . . . I think I know who you're talking about. Doesn't she wear her hair in a short bob, and she's got a baby face, and she's sort of all right-looking?"

"Yeah, that's her, but you have one thing wrong, sis—she's better than just all right-looking; the girl is definitely a dime piece."

"Ooh, you're too much for me. Well, I'm happy for you. But just take your time and don't go getting in trouble or anything."

"Don't worry, I'm going to be extra careful. We haven't even had a real kiss yet. She just told me today that she likes me as in 'boy likes girl' kind of like."

"There's nothing wrong with that. You just take it slow. I know you call yourself half-grown now and think you know it all; but remember, you have your whole life ahead of you, Prodigal. And you're going to meet a lot of girls in your lifetime. You see, I don't let any boy get close to me. I'm not falling for all that bull. I'm trying too hard to get out of this town home free, with no babies, no holdbacks, or anything. As soon as I graduate this year, I'm off to Montserrat College of Arts. I'm going to be a famous artist, and one day I'll have my very own art gallery. Maybe once I get my career established, then and only then will I possibly have time for a relationship. But until all that happens, I'm not studying any of you horny, young boys."

"I believe you're going to do just what you said too, and I'll be behind you one hundred percent because you deserve it. And I understand where you're coming from, and I'm going to take it slow." Prodigal finished fixing his plate and sat down next to Fantasia.

"Hope, go in the bathroom and wash your hands so you can eat," Fantasia ordered.

Prodigal mumbled thanks to God for the food then looked up at Fantasia again. "Now let's talk about you—Have you sold any more of your paintings lately to the art store?"

Fantasia had made a tidy sum selling some of her paintings to the local art store. Some were even displayed in the hallways at school and a couple of her pictures she called *Jesus Ain't Got No Color* hung in their church.

"The art store manager called me just the other day to see if I had any more paintings I wanted to sell," Fantasia eagerly told him. "But I've decided that I'm not going to sell anymore. I'm building up my portfolio, and I don't want to have too much available just yet. You see, a portfolio is more than just some paintings stuck in a binder. It's one of the major factors that determine whether a person is accepted at an art college or not. It's supposed to be a representation of my best and most recent work. It's more than just drawings. It demonstrates my skills, basic elements like composition, space, color, knowledge and—"

"Okay, okay, I get it, Fantasia." Prodigal swallowed a mouthful of food. "Once you start to talk about your art, you won't let up. But I feel you, I really do." He was proud of his sister. He had no doubt that her dreams were going to come true one day. He proceeded to change the subject. "Hey, are you going to the game?"

"Nope. You know good and well that I'm not into all that sports stuff. I rented a couple of videos. Me and Hope are going to watch them, eat some popcorn, gobble soda, and just cool out until Momma gets home. Sara and Trina are going, though. You know they always have their minds on one of y'all 'hard legs.' And, like I said, I just don't have the time for that stuff right now."

"Okay, suit yourself."

Prodigal wolfed down the last bit of his fish sticks and corn and then washed it down with a cold glass of his all-time favorite grape Kool-Aid. He jumped up from the table and ran upstairs into the bathroom. He picked out his hair, patted it down, brushed his thin mustache that had finally begun to grow, brushed and flossed his teeth, and scurried back downstairs and out the door.

He ran across the street to Teary's house. He raced up to the door, ringing the doorbell and knocking at the same time.

"I know that's you, Prodigal Runsome, beating on the door like that. Wait a minute, boy," Sara hollered from the inside. She opened the door. "Come on in. Teary's still upstairs getting ready. You know how slow she is. She's going to make y'all late."

"Teary," Prodigal yelled, "come on. We're going to be late if you keep prancing around up there."

"I'm coming," she screamed back. "Sometimes you work my last nerves. You know it takes time for a star like me to get ready." Teary leaned over the upstairs railing, went into a quick tailspin, snapped her fingers at him, and disappeared.

"Prodigal, I'm out of here," Sara announced. "I'm going to stop by Trina's on the way, and me and her are going to walk to the game together. Tell Teary that if Momma and Daddy haven't come back from the grocery store by the time y'all leave to make sure she locks up."

"All right. Later, Sara." After Sara left, Prodigal yelled back up the steps, "Teary, will you hurry up?"

Teary finally came prancing down the stairs dressed in a black-and-gold jogging outfit that matched the school colors. Her long braids were pulled back with a black-and-gold hair twister. She wore only a hint of lipstick, her large gold-plated hoop earrings bobbing with her every move. She grabbed her pompoms off the table. "Come on, I'm ready since you're in such a big hurry. Is Faith still going?"

"Yeah, she's going—guess what?"

"What?"

"She told me that she likes me—She said that I'm her type. Can you believe that?"

Teary locked the door. "Of course, I can. You are quite handsome, you know. Not to mention the fact that you're really nice too. She's lucky, and she might just be the right girl for you."

He was shocked to hear Teary call him handsome. The "little-boy" crush he had on her somehow never really left his heart, and hearing her say such nice things about him stirred up feelings inside his groin that he didn't want to claim. At least not with her.

He thought to himself. *Is this my lucky day or what!*

Faith met up with them at the corner of Hodge and Sullivan, which was about a block from school. Prodigal's thoughts of Teary quickly disappeared when his eyes zeroed in on Faith. Faith's black stretch pants revealed her "knock-a-guy-off-his-feet" hips. The black-and-gold knit shirt clung to her perfectly formed breasts, and her gold locket nestled contently between them. He wanted to grab her, inhale her girly aroma, caress her secret places, and feel her lying against his hairless chest. He'd never even kissed a girl, except for the peck on the cheek he gave Teary, his momma, or sisters.

As they headed back to the school, Faith and Teary whispered and giggled all the way to the gym.

He lagged behind, watching both of their butts wiggle.

By the time they arrived, the gym was quickly filling up with Fairley Tigers on one side and the Carver Cougars on the other. Teary looked around to see if she could spot her girlfriends, Debra and Chelsia. Besides Prodigal, they were her closest friends. When she didn't see them, she yelled out over the loud crowd to Prodigal and Faith.

"Hey, you guys, I'm going to go see if I can find Debra and Chelsia before the game starts. I'll see y'all a little later."

"Okay," Prodigal replied. "Faith, you want to get some popcorn and a soda before we sit down?"

"Yeah, that'll be fine with me."

After they got their popcorn and drinks, they proceeded to climb the rows of bleachers until they found a spot at the very top.

"I like sitting up here 'cause it makes me feel like I'm close to the stars and to the heavens," Faith said.

"Yeah, I like it too, though I've never thought about it quite like you. Tell me something, Faith—"

"Whaddaya want me to tell you?"

"Did you mean what you said earlier?"

"What did I say earlier?"

"You know . . . that I'm your type, and that you like me."

"Sure. I really think you're nice, and you make me feel special."

Prodigal's chest puffed out with pride. "Really?"

"You're not like most of the other boys—always thinking about getting in somebody's panties and all. When that happens for me, it'll be with the boy I love, who loves me back. In other words, the one I marry."

They stared into each other's eyes until Teary walked up with Debra and Chelsia tagging along beside her.

"Hey, scoot over, y'all. Give us some room." Teary twisted her butt around, moving to the music.

The earsplitting beat of the drummers reverberated throughout the gymnasium as cheerleaders from both teams began to perform their routines.

"Hey, y'all, just wait," Teary remarked. "Next semester, after I try out for the cheerleaders squad, I'm going to be down there shaking my booty—Go Fairley Tigers! Yeah, that's going to be me, baby."

Just then she spotted the new guy, Langston Silverman, and a couple of his friends coming up the bleachers toward her group.

When Langston enrolled at Fairley High, girls dreamed of being his lady, and Teary was no exception.

"Ooh wee, look at that there," chimed Chelsia.

"Ain't he just the epitome of fineness?" Teary was unable to take her eyes off him.

Debra was mesmerized too. She'd had her own opinions about Mr. Silverman. "Teary and Chelsia, that boy's skin looks smooth as a baby's booty, and his charcoal-black self makes me want to give him some of this tail."

"Debra, you're too hot for me. Isn't she, Chelsia?" Teary waved her hand at Debra.

"Teary, you know good and well Debra ain't giving up no booty. She just tripping," Chelsia said.

"Yeah, I know. But, Debra, you know you telling the truth, don't you?" Teary giggled and gave a high-five to both of her friends.

His confident swagger often compared to Denzel's, Langston's triceps and biceps drew attention away from his short stature, and his deep bow legs accentuated his athletic build. His designer clothes hugged his sculpted body in all the right places. Though he was not altogether handsome, when he smiled and his heavy voice boomed forth, girls were drawn to him like a magnet. On top of all that, he could move his body across a dance floor like nobody's business. His hips and tight butt made sinful gyrations that drove the girls wild.

"Do you have room for me?" Langston asked confidently.

Teary raised her head to meet the voice in front of her. "Are you talking to me?" Her voice trembled as she spoke. She couldn't believe Langston Silverman was actually talking to her.

She heard her friends oohing and ahhing, and felt special.

"Yeah, I'm talking to you—Anybody sitting here?"

"You are, I guess." Teary shrugged her shoulders.

"I guess, I am." Langston and his friends squeezed in. He sat next to Teary. "What's your name?"

"Teary," she replied, playing coy.

"I'm Langston."

"I know who you are."

"Oh, you do? And how is that?"

"I just do, that's all."

"Well, good. Now I know who you are."

Teary couldn't find words to say anything. Langston had her spellbound. She peeked over at Debra and Chelsia, searching for some guidance as to what to say or do next.

Chelsia shrugged her shoulders; Debra followed suit.

Langston kept on with Teary. "Hey, you know you sounded real good cheering. You should be on that gym floor with the rest of the cheerleaders."

"Oh, don't worry. I'm trying out next semester. I plan on being down there."

"I don't have any doubt you'll make it, too, sweet lady." Langston looked into Teary's eyes.

When the game started they began rooting and yelling, hollering and screaming. There was no time for idle chatter. Everyone was into the game.

Suddenly Prodigal sprang to his feet and yelled, "Hey, ref, that was a foul. What's wrong with you? Call the game right."

A stream of boos from Fairley students followed, signaling agreement with Prodigal's remarks.

When the game ended some two and a half hours later, the Cougars came out victorious.

Prodigal voiced his frustration over the loss. "Man, I just knew we had that game. I can't believe that referee called a foul at the last few seconds. Man, that was wrong."

Langston agreed. "You got that right. But like they say, you win some and you lose some."

Prodigal gently reached over and grabbed Faith around her waist, holding her steady as she moved down the steep bleachers.

Langston grabbed hold of Teary's hand, just like they had been an item all along.

"Is your daddy picking you up, Faith?" Prodigal asked.

"Nope. I told my parents that a bunch of us would be walking home together. They said it was okay just as long as I wasn't alone."

"You definitely won't be alone—I guarantee that."

After saying their goodbyes, Prodigal and Faith strolled across the campus hand in hand until they reached a nearby breezeway. They paused for a moment. He reached out to Faith and looked deep into her hazel eyes longingly. "I want to kiss you so bad."

She looked back up into his spectacled eyes and removed his glasses.

Prodigal allowed his virgin hands to embrace Faith's shoulders, being extra careful not to go any further. He lifted her chin toward his and placed a sweet, innocent butterfly kiss on her lips. When his mouth touched hers, it was like tasting cotton candy. Her lips were soft, and he felt his boyhood rising. He felt nervous as he experienced unfamiliar desires and feelings.

Faith's heart pounded like it was about to jump outside of her body. She wasn't supposed to be allowing this to happen. She had made a promise to God that she wasn't going to let a boy touch her in any way, not even kiss her, until she knew for sure that he was the one, but she liked this feeling, and she definitely liked Prodigal.

Prodigal tried to remain focused. This was not the time or place for things to get out of hand. He stopped before he could no longer control himself.

They continued the long walk home, holding hands in silence.

"Where do you live, Teary?" Langston asked.

"On Parkdale." Teary's belly quivered.

"Good. Only one street over from mine. Mind if I walk you home, or are you going to walk with your girls?"

"Nope. Don't mind." She sashayed around and eyed her friends. "Hey, Debra, Chelsia, I'll talk to y'all tomorrow."

Chelsia responded first. "Okay, sure. See ya."

Debra waved and walked off with Chelsia, the two of them giggling along the way.

Butterflies continued to keep up a ruckus in Teary's stomach. She thought her heart would pop right through her chest.

"What grade are you in?" Langston inquired, as they slowly walked the distance to her house.

"Tenth. What about you?"

"I'm a senior. This is my first year at Fairley. I just moved to Broknfield a few months ago."

"Hey, I didn't know that. From where?"

"Atlanta. My dad's job was transferred here."

"Oh, I see. Any brothers and sisters?"

"Nope, just me. Do you have any?"

"Yeah, I have one older sister. Sara. She's a senior this year, so pretty soon when she graduates and goes off to college, it'll be just like I'm an only child too."

"Then I'll just have to keep you company, won't I?"

"I don't know about that. Will you?"

"I think so." He cautiously moved his arm around her teeny waist and brushed his fingers against her long, braided hair. His mind quickly visualized what his body yearned to do.

When they approached her house, Teary scanned the dimly lit street for signs of her sister or Prodigal. She didn't see either of them. A sense of relief caused her to sigh.

The night was cool and peaceful. Langston watched her with intensity without moving his arm from around her waist. He twirled his fingers through her hair.

Again, Teary began to feel funny inside. Her stomach gurgled, her throat became dry, and her body felt like it was about to jump outside of itself. *What's next? I just met this boy.*

That thought quickly rushed from her mind when Langston leaned over and kissed her on the cheek. Her eyes quickly closed, and she lifted her head toward his. He gingerly kissed her nose, then her eyelids, careful not to come on too strong. He didn't want to frighten her. When he felt her responding positively to his touch, he backed off.

Teary suddenly opened her eyes. The warmth between her legs felt surprisingly good. Somehow she knew it wasn't right for her to feel this way, but she couldn't resist Langston. She was glad to have him standing beside her doing things to her that she'd only seen on HBO.

"Hey, thanks for letting me walk you home," Langston said in a low, seductive voice.

She felt the warmth of his breath against her ear as he spoke. She didn't know what to think. *Why did he stop? He made me feel alive, like a real woman*—"Earth to Teary, are you there?"

She quickly thought of a lie. "Oh, sure, I was, uh, wondering if my sister had made it home, that's all."

"I see. Look, can I get your number so I can call you sometime?"

"Sure." She rummaged inside her black cloth shoulder bag until she pulled out a pencil and an address book. She scribbled her phone number down then tore the piece of paper from her address and gave it to him.

Langston took the piece of paper out of her hand. "Thanks. I'll give you a call, okay?"

"Okay. Good night."

He flashed a flirting smile at her. "Good night." He turned to walk away—"Oh wait, I forgot to ask you something."

"What is it?"

"Can you receive company from the opposite sex?"

"Why?"

"Because I just might want to come and see you sometime—anything wrong with that?"

"No, of course not. I'd like that." She hoped her nervousness wasn't showing too much. She didn't want to appear like a naïve little girl.

"Can you date?"

"Yep, one weekend day a month. I have a ten-thirty curfew—and no school nights under any circumstances—that includes having company, unless it's to study."

"Sounds good. I'll give you a call. Maybe I'll come over this week, meet your parents, and see if we can go check out a movie. How about that?"

Still feeling excitement rushing through her body, she answered demurely, "That's fine."

He planted another kiss on her lips and walked off. "See you, Teary."

"Good night, Langston."

Faith rushed straight to her room, yelling a quick, "I'm home," to her parents as she bolted by. She felt like a time bomb about to explode. She didn't want Prodigal to stop kissing and touching her. She'd heard about girls who'd had sex and became pregnant when they were only thirteen and fourteen years old, and she was determined not to turn out like one of them. *I've just got to pray and ask God to forgive me for tonight. Shucks, I didn't really do anything anyway.*

She flung herself across her full-sized bed. Pulling the pink satin covers up over her, she closed her eyes and re-lived the night.

She sang to herself, "Prodigal and Faith sitting in a tree, *k-i-s-s-i-n-g*." She giggled and continued thinking about him. *Prodigal, you made me feel real good, but I'm not giving up the booty*. A smile caressed her face.

Within minutes, she drifted off to sleep, before she could even remove her clothes, or even say her prayer of repentance.

Prodigal couldn't believe how one day had changed the entire course of his young, uneventful life. Of course, he wasn't a man just yet, but he still had feelings and insight. His body ached from the memories of tonight. Afraid they'd witness his excitement, he didn't want to wake his mother or sister. He sneaked quietly in the house.

"Prodigal, is that you, sweetheart?" His mom yelled out just as he entered the house. She would've had a hissy fit if she saw his manhood trying to eagerly press itself outside his jogging pants.

"Yeah, it's me, Momma." Prodigal snapped his finger and mumbled under his breath in disappointment.

"Who won the game?"

"The Cougars did . . . again. This time by two points."

"Well, I hope you had a good time, son."

Boy, was he glad she didn't bother getting out of bed and simply talked to him from her bedroom. "I did. I had a real good time. Good night. I love you, Momma."

"I love you, too, sweetheart. See you in the morning."

Whew. He breathed a sigh of relief. He just knew she was going to get up and start talking, but to his surprise, she didn't. *She must really be tired tonight.*

He hated that she had to work so hard and so much. He made up in his mind that he was going to graduate from high school, go to a trade school instead of college, get a decent job, and take care of his Momma. That way, she wouldn't have to spend her evenings working for anyone.

Yeah, everything is going to be all right. It couldn't be any other way.

Sara Fullalove had a secret of her own. His name was Anthony Chamberlain. Sara and Anthony had been seeing each other ever since she met him at the movie theatre almost eight months ago.

She and Fantasia were standing at the refreshment counter when they saw him. He stood at the counter next to her, and their eyes met at the same time. Sara shifted her brown eyes in the opposite direction, but not before answering his smile with one of her own.

They ended up in the same movie, and he took a chance and

sat beside her and introduced himself. The two of them hit it off right away.

Sara started meeting him at the movies almost every weekend. She swore Fantasia to secrecy. He became her first boyfriend, and she quickly fell head over heels for him. It wasn't long before Sara started sneaking to meet him at every opportunity.

Tonight was such an opportunity. During the championship game, Sara met Anthony in the school parking lot. They sneaked off from the game in his Honda and drove to Willow Park. They talked and watched the moon's rays skip over the lake.

She never expected to cross the line that would lead her to go against her Christian principles, but her attraction for him proved to be far too strong for her to resist the temptation.

"Sara, sooner or later, someone's going to find out about us," Anthony told her.

"Well, let it be later. The only person who knows about you and me is Fantasia, and she promised not to breathe a word to anyone."

"Why can't we tell anybody? I don't understand the big secret."

"The big secret is that I don't want my parents to know that I have a boyfriend. They're way too strict, and my daddy is so overbearing. I wouldn't be able to listen to his lectures day in and day out about what to do and not to do. Plus, you're four years older than me—My daddy would hit the roof if he found that out."

Anthony kissed Sara on her cheek and pulled her head against his muscled shoulder. "I love you, that's all. I want everyone to know it. So what if I'm a little older? Why do I have to be penalized for that? You'll be out of school in a few months, and you're old enough to have a boyfriend. Don't you love me too?"

Sara tilted her head so that her eyes met his. "What kind of question is that? You know I love you, Anthony. But we have to do everything in the right order. Just be patient a little longer, and soon we can tell everybody that we love each other."

He breathed a heavy sigh and pulled her tighter against his immensely broad chest. His tongue flickered around inside her mouth.

She enjoyed it. She didn't resist either, when his hand traveled underneath her blouse.

With his other hand, he gently lifted her skirt.

Sara pulled back, looking at him with a mixture of lust and love. "Anthony, we'd better go. I need to get back before the game is over. I don't want Teary to be looking everywhere for me."

Sara and Anthony made it back to the game during the last few minutes of the fourth quarter. She met up with Trina after the game and walked home, making it there before Teary.

When Teary went inside the house, heading for the stairwell, she met Sara coming out of the downstairs bathroom.

"Teary, where have you been, and what took you so long? I looked for you after the game, but I didn't see you," Sara said, trying to hide her own guilt.

"Shhh! I didn't see you either." Teary pressed a finger against her freshly kissed lips. She whispered cautiously, "Where are Momma and Daddy? I hope I'm not in any trouble. You know they want me and you to come home together." She was scared now. She didn't want to be grounded, and she didn't want to listen to a lecture about a *"disobedient child's days being cut off"* either. Not tonight. She had other things on her mind.

"They're upstairs—I gotcha back—I told 'em you were right behind me walking with Prodigal, Debra, and Chelsia. So tell me—Where were you? I didn't see any of y'all after the game."

"I was with Prodigal and Faith," Teary lied. "I guess we just missed each other because, like I said, I didn't see you either."

"I don't know why," Sara lied too. She turned her head quickly, so her sister wouldn't see the guilty look plastered across her face. "Maybe because it was jam-packed."

"Yeah, I'm sure that's it."

Teary didn't want to tell Sara about Langston just yet. She didn't feel like telling everything. She wanted to hurry up and get in her bed so she could dream about tonight.

She felt throbbing between her virgin legs. When it came to sex, she was green as grass. She had heard some of the girls at school talk about "doing it," but she couldn't relate to anything they said. The boys who liked her never were as bold as Langston. There was something about him, something different. Langston was the first boy who ever kissed her like a real man. When he touched her, she found herself wanting more. Her spirit told her that she had better be careful with this boy. Real careful.

5

Growing Up Young

Prodigal walked Faith to the bus stop. It was Thursday afternoon, and he was looking forward to the upcoming weekend. He and Faith had made plans to spend time together. He kissed her goodbye and headed for home. On the way, he saw Teary standing on the sidewalk, talking to Langston. As Prodigal came closer, he saw one of Langston's buddies parked at the curb.

Langston walked toward the car.

Prodigal approached Langston and Teary.

Langston threw up his hand. "What's up, dog?"

"What's up, Langston?" Prodigal replied dryly. "Hey, Teary."

Before she could respond to Prodigal, Langston kissed her on the cheek, and told her he'd call her later. He hopped in the waiting car and rode off.

"What was that all about?" Prodigal asked.

"Oh, nothing. He just dropped me off at the end of block, so Momma and Daddy wouldn't catch me riding in the car with a boy—You know how old-fashioned they are."

Prodigal was finding it hard to contain his fury. "Yeah, sure."

Teary was taking unnecessary chances and doing things she'd never done before, all since hooking up with Langston Silverman. There was a time when she would never even consider disobeying her parents; now she was lying and sneaking around like some wild girl.

Prodigal tried to push the thoughts of Teary's new attitude out of his mind. The two of them walked the rest of the short distance to their homes, barely talking to one another.

Standing in front of Teary's house, Prodigal asked, "Hey, Teary, do you want to go hang out later this afternoon? We could go to Willow Lake. It's been a while since we've been there."

"Sorry, Prodigal, I can't. Langston is supposed to be coming over later this evening. He's going to help me study for my American history exam."

"Oh, I see. No problem. Well, guess I'll talk to you later. *Dang, why can't she see me the same way she sees that punk*? Prodigal walked across the street to his house. He slammed the front door behind him and stormed into the house. He threw his books on the table and jetted toward the kitchen.

He thought about Teary and how much he liked her, but her mind was on Langston. There was something about Langston that simply rubbed Prodigal the wrong way. Something told him that he was bad news for Teary, but he didn't want to burst her bubble, or come off like he was jealous of Langston. But deep down inside, the green monster lurked, even though he and Faith were an item.

Seeing Teary with Langston this afternoon, he could tell that she was definitely sprung and couldn't see past him.

"Teary, is everything still on for my friend's birthday party next Friday night?" Langston asked her over the phone.

"Of course. My parents already said I could go with you. I know it's going to be wild up in there, and I can't wait."

"Look, I have another idea."

"What's up?"

"My parents are going to the coast for the weekend. I was hoping that after the party we could go to my house and spend some time alone."

"Is that right?"

"Hey, better still, we can just skip the party altogether. There's always going to be plenty of chances to go to some lame party."

"I don't know about that—I don't want to get in trouble."

"You know we don't ever have a chance to really have time to ourselves. How about it? Come on, Teary," he pleaded in a sing-song voice, "do it for me."

"You know I want to be with you too." Lying back on her bed, the phone drawn close to her ear, she fantasized about the two of them finally being alone together. "But I'm scared. I don't want anything to happen that will mess up our relationship."

"Hey, don't you trust me? You know I wouldn't do anything to hurt you. You're my baby, my sunshine. My parents are leaving me the car, so I'll pick you up Friday around seven."

"Okay, I'll be ready."

Friday night came quickly. At seven sharp the doorbell rang. Mrs. Fullalove appeared on the other side. "Good evening, Langston," she said after opening the door.

"Hello, Mrs. Fullalove. How are you this evening?" he said politely.

"I'm fine, honey. Come on in. Teary will be down in a few minutes." Mrs. Fullalove shook her head in wonderment. "You know that girl well enough by now to know that she's never ready on time."

"No problem. That's Teary for you, ma'am." Langston chuckled. He made sure to present himself as a perfect gentleman, whenever he was around Teary's parents.

"Go in the den and have a seat, Langston. I'm going to the kitchen to check on my muffins."

"Yes, ma'am."

A few minutes later, Teary came galloping down the stairs into the den. Her sky-blue, form-fitting skirt rested just above her knees.

He imagined unfastening the buttons streaming down the

front of her almost-sheer blouse. Her blue mules were perfect for the outfit she'd chosen. Her hair was twisted and pulled up with a blue-and-white scrunchie. She looked absolutely gorgeous to Langston.

"You ready?" Teary asked.

"Yeah. By the way, you look great."

"Thank you, Langston."

Teary and Langston headed toward the front door. She turned and yelled into the kitchen, "Mom, we're leaving, and don't worry, I'll be home by curfew."

Mrs. Fullalove came out of the kitchen, wiping her hands on a dishtowel. "You sure better, and I don't want any excuses either. Tomorrow is Sunday, and I don't want to hear you talking about you're too sleepy to go to church. And, Langston, when are you going to come to church with us?"

Teary couldn't believe her mother was bringing this up now. She just wanted to get away.

"I told Teary that I would go with her to one of the services you all have during the week, Mrs. Fullalove. You see, my parents really aren't too keen about me visiting other churches. We go together every Sunday as a family, and they won't let me out of it. I'm sure you understand how that is."

"Sure, I do. What's the name of your church again?"

"Mom, please . . . if you keep on talking, it's going to be time for me to be back home."

"Oh, okay. Get out of here, and y'all have a good time." She waved Teary and Langston off.

Langston was glad Teary interrupted when she did. He couldn't remember what church he told her that he and his family attended. He would have to make sure when he lied that he remembered the lies he told. He would definitely have to be more careful.

He opened the passenger door of the champagne Ford Taurus. "Did I tell you how pretty you look tonight?"

She blushed, easing her freshly shaved legs into the car. "Yes, you did."

"Do you want to stop and grab something to eat before we go to my place?"

"Sounds good to me. I am a little hungry." *And nervous too. I want to be alone with him, but I don't want things to get out of hand.*

When they reached Langston's house, Teary was pleasantly surprised. The inside looked like it had been professionally decorated. Everything looked expensive and plush.

"Let's go in the family room and eat, okay?"

"Okay. By the way, I like your house." Teary looked around as she followed behind him.

"Thanks, but you'll probably change your mind when you see my room." He turned on the stereo once they entered the family room.

While eating they listened to one of the local radio stations, cuddling between bites.

Langston whispered softly in Teary's ear, "What's on your mind?"

"Nothing. I'm just a little shaky, that's all." Teary shrugged her shoulders.

"I can fix that—You ever had wine?"

"I tasted it one Thanksgiving when we went to my aunt and uncle's. My parents let me have a sip. Why do you ask?"

He pointed. "See that bar over there?"

Teary looked in the direction Langston was pointing. "Yes."

"Every kind of drink you can imagine is inside. Come on, let me show you." He took hold of her arm and pulled her toward the bar. When he opened the door, her eyes almost popped out of her head when she saw all the different kinds of liquor inside.

"I hope you don't expect me to drink any of that. I have enough to repent for already without adding drinking to my list of sins."

"Teary, stop being so naïve. Do you think God is standing over you keeping a record of everything you're doing right now? I don't think so. He has robbers and murderers to judge and people doing a whole lot worse than what we're doing. Plus, he knows we're young and we're going to make mistakes, so stop worrying."

His words sounded right, but in the back of her mind, she knew better. But when it came to Langston, she found it hard, downright impossible, to say no.

"As for my parents finding out, girl, they have so much stuff in here, they won't miss it. Anyway, we're just going to try a little wine. One glass, that's all. Do it. Do it for me please . . . pretty please." He leaned toward her and planted a light kiss on her lips and nibbled on her ear lobe. "After all, we have to celebrate."

"Celebrate what?"

With him kissing her the way he was, it was getting harder for Teary to concentrate.

"What do you mean?"

"We have to celebrate you and me," he said in a deep, hypnotizing tone.

"Oh, okay. I guess we are worth celebrating," she said, hesitantly but smiling nonetheless.

"Now, that's more like it." He reached overhead and pulled two wine glasses down from the glass holder. He searched in the bottom of the bar until he found the bottle of Chardonnay.

"Let's go to my room. We can listen to the music up there."

"Okay," she said meekly.

Holding her hand in his, he led her to his bedroom.

Teary continued to peruse the house with a keen eye, trying to ignore the flittering motion in her stomach. She focused on a room arranged like a den.

Langston quickly by passed it and guided her to his room. His king-sized bed was draped in a blue chenille bedspread and had a pile of matching pillows expertly fluffed and placed against the oak headboard. Except for a few clothes scattered on the floor, the room was spotless.

He sat the wine and glasses on the night table beside the bed. "Come here. Don't be acting like you're scared. This is your man you're with." He held out his arms to her, and she took a seat on the bed.

He turned on the stereo.

While Sade sang, "Your Love is King," he poured each of them a glass of wine.

"Come on, let's have a toast," he said, picking up his glass.

"What are we toasting?"

"Our future together, baby." His eyes gleamed, and his body ached for hers. But he had to take her slow. He couldn't allow his emotions to get out of hand.

Her mouth puckered, and her eyes squinted at the taste of the bitter-sweet wine.

After a couple of sips, she felt herself relaxing.

"Come here, I'm not going to bite you; at least not yet." Langston made a face and laughed wickedly, like Dracula.

"Boy, you're so stupid." She grinned and took another swallow of wine.

They lay back on the bed listening to the soft, romantic music. He watched carefully to see when her glass was getting low and refilled it without her putting up any fuss.

After her third glass, he removed it carefully from her hand and pulled her close to him. He took this chance to make his move. When he kissed her, a light sound escaped from her lips. He felt her body arch toward his. His kisses were gentle, and she slowly succumbed to his touch.

The wine was doing its intended job. Any fear and apprehension she had was replaced with the flame of desire for him. She hungrily accepted his kisses, his firm, experienced hands caressing the length of her legs ever so softly.

When he reached around and underneath her back to undo her bra, she weakly resisted.

"No," he said hoarsely. "Let me do this. I'm going to show you how much you mean to me tonight. Just trust me, Teary. I promise not to hurt you. I want you to remember," he added raspily in her ear, "that you're my girl." His voice was like a magnet drawing her under his spell.

"My goodness, you're beautiful!" He pulled the scrunchie from her hair, allowing the thick locks of hair to blanket her shoulders.

To her amazement, she wasn't bashful when he raised himself up to look down on her intimacy. The wine had made her totally relaxed, the desire for him filling her virgin thoughts.

He was careful not to let her feel his excitement, not just yet. Langston reached for one of her hands and intertwined it into his.

She allowed his other hand to travel to secret places that only she knew of. Before she could resist, he started kissing her more forcefully.

"Langston, what are you doing?" she said, barely able to speak.

"Loving you. I want you, Teary. I need you."

"Ohhh . . ." she moaned.

And he slowly made her his.

6

First Pain

The phone rang just as Teary climbed out of the tub. "What's up, girlfriend?"

For a few seconds there was silence on the line.

"Hello. I'm standing here dripping wet, so speak up. You are still there, aren't you?"

"Yeah, I don't know how to tell you this," Debra said, "so I guess I should just come right out and say it."

"Tell me what?"

"Tell you what I saw, or should I say *who* I saw?"

"Debra, will you stop stalling and just tell me what's going on."

Debra took a deep breath. "I was coming from Chelsia's earlier this afternoon when I saw Langston and that new girl who moved down the street from me. They went into her house."

Teary plopped her wet, naked body down on the side of her bed. "Hold up a minute. Maybe there's a good reason he was with her," Teary said, on the verge of tears.

"She was grinning all up in his face. I'm telling you, I believe they're messing around."

"Do you really think so?"

"Yeah, and, anyway, what would he be doing going over her

house when her parents aren't home? Prodigal was right—
Langston ain't about nothing. In the beginning he acted like he
was so crazy about you, and now look at him. Girl, if I were you,
I'd quit him and never look back. And another thing . . ."

"What?"

"It's good you didn't do anything with him."

"Anything like what?"

"I mean, you know what I'm talking about . . . the sex thing.
'Cause even though he told you he was crazy about you, look at
his good-for-nothing tail now."

If she only knew the truth.

Teary was glad she hadn't confided in Debra about her and
Langston's sexcapade. Debra would be sure to think the worst of
her. But then again, Debra couldn't possibly think anything half
as bad as what Teary now thought about herself. She felt used
and betrayed. How could the boy she loved do her this way?
There must be a reasonable explanation for what Debra saw, and
she would get to the bottom of it once and for all.

"Debra, I have to go. I just got out of the tub. I need to dry off
and put some clothes on."

"Okay, sorry I had to be the bearer of bad news."

"Yeah, sure. Bye." Teary quickly hung up.

After she dried off and slipped on her robe, she plopped on the
window seat in her room and then dialed Langston's house.

"Hello, Mrs. Silverman, this is Teary Fullalove. Is Langston
home from his dance audition?"

" 'Dance audition'?—Honey, I don't know what you're talking
about. Langston is over at a friend's house studying."

"Oh, I see. Thanks, Mrs. Silverman." Teary hastily hung up
the phone.

A flood of tears fell from her eyes.

She called to tell Debra what happened. "Debra, I can't get
over that dog. His momma didn't know anything about a dance
audition. She said he was over at a friend's house. He told her he
was going to study."

Debra's ears perked up, and with a voice of sarcasm she said, "I know you can't be for real. He sure has some weird study habits, not to mention the study partner."

"Yeah, she's some study partner, all right, but I'm just saying, I can't believe he lied like that."

Just then, Teary's other line beeped. "Hold on a minute, Debra, let me see who this is." She clicked over. "Hello."

"Hey, what's up?"

"Hold on. Let me get off the other line." Teary clicked back over to Debra. "This is him on the other end. I'll call you back later and tell you what lie he tells me."

"Okay, girl. Bye."

"What's up?" he asked in a rather irritated voice after Teary clicked back over. "You called me?"

"Yeah, I sure did. I thought you had made it home from your so-called audition, but your momma said you were over to a friend's house studying. She didn't know anything about an audition—What's up with that, Langston?—Why you been lying to me?"

He exploded. "What are you doing checking up on me anyway? I don't need you trying to keep a leash on me."

"I'm not trying to keep a leash on you. I just want to know why you lied."

"Let me tell you something—I don't like this bullcrap. I didn't know you were going to be the possessive type. I thought what we shared was supposed to be special, but I see now that you really don't trust me."

Before she could respond, he said, "I tell you what Teary—it's over—I don't need some female who doesn't trust me. I'm done."

"Langston, what are you saying? I do trust you. And what are you talking about, 'it's over.' Don't be talking like that," she pleaded tearfully. She didn't even bother to tell him what Debra had seen.

"If I let you get away with this crap this time, all you're going to do is something else crazy. Look, I think it's time we go our separate ways. I enjoyed what we had while we had it. But now, hey, I'm outta here. Plus, I'm young, you're young, and we don't need to be in a serious relationship anyway. I'll holler back at you." With that, he slammed down the receiver.

What am I going to do? I can't confide in Sara. Teary sat there in tears. *All she'll do is lecture me, or she might even tell Momma and Daddy. I can't tell Debra any more than what I already have. God forbid that. She means well, but she's sure to tell Chelsia, and Chelsia will tell somebody else, and that somebody would tell somebody else, and before long, everybody in the school will know about me and Langston.* Teary was hurt, confused and scared.

"Teary, time for dinner," her mother called.

Teary yelled back down at her mother. "I'm not hungry. I have some homework to finish up."

She climbed up into her full-size bed, pulled her teddy bears close to her, and let her tears fall freely. Holding on to her favorite stuffed animal, she started her prayer. "God, I'm sorry. I really messed up big time. I've been so stupid. Please forgive me." She cried until her eyes were swollen and sleep took over.

7

That's What Friends Are For

The early morning sun kissed the peach curtains, casting a stream of light on Teary's swollen face. She felt the soothing heat against her skin and lazily opened one eye and then the other. She slowly climbed out of bed, but stumbled backwards when she saw the person staring at her in the mirror.

Her face was puffy, her eyes were tight, and her hair was tangled and all over her head. At first she didn't remember the past day's events, but as her mind fully awoke from her night's sleep, the dreadful memories swooshed back to their rightful place. She slowly pulled the curtains back and peered across the street at Prodigal's house to see if his porch light had been turned off. If it was, then she knew that someone was up.

The light was out, so she dialed his number. The phone rang three times.

"Boy, am I glad you answered. You up yet?" Teary sighed into the phone.

"Yeah, what's up?" He knew her like a book. Something was wrong. He heard it in her voice. *It had to be that no good punk, Langston.*

The only person Teary felt she could trust was Prodigal. No matter how bad things were, he wouldn't let her down.

"I need to talk to you. Can you meet me in about half an hour at Willow Lake?"

"Yeah, but I can meet you sooner than that if you want me to. Fantasia and Hope are still asleep, and Momma called and said she has to pull a double."

"Give me about ten minutes then, and I'll meet you outside. But don't come over here and knock on the door. I don't want to wake up anybody. You know how they like to sleep in late on Saturday. I'm just going to sneak out and be back before anyone knows I've been gone."

When he laid eyes on her, Prodigal was livid. "Look at you. What did that creep do to you? I swear, I'm going to—"

"Stop it, Prodigal. You're not going to do anything. I just need you to listen. Now, come on. Let's go before somebody sees us."

They got their bikes and rode in silence the three and a half blocks to Willow Lake. When they got there, they both headed for their favorite bench and sat down, still neither of them saying anything.

She rested her head on his shoulder and listened to the sound of the hungry ducks and pigeons beginning to surround them.

Prodigal pulled a bag of stale breadcrumbs from his pocket and began throwing them out to the ducks and pigeons. He decided to wait until she was ready to tell him what was going on. Things were serious, but he had already decided that no matter what had happened, he was going to stand by her. He loved her, and he couldn't stand the thought of anyone hurting or misusing her.

After a few minutes, she broke the silence. "I can't believe he did me like this," she cried to her best friend. "I just can't believe it. And you know what I did with him?—I went all the way with him, Prodigal. I gave him all of me. And before you pass judgment on me, before you tell me you hate me, just listen."

Disappointment and a look of utter disbelief washed over Prodigal's face. His chest tightened, and his fists began to clench, but he remained quiet. He looked like someone had stabbed him smack-dab in the center of his heart. He was hesitant to say any-thing for fear of completely going off on her for being so vulnera-ble when it came to Langston.

"Don't be angry with me. Don't hate me, and don't hate Langston. It's as much my fault as it is his. I love him, Prodigal, and I thought he loved me too."

"Sshh! It's going to be all right." Prodigal brushed her hair from her face with his hands.

"Oh my God! Suppose I'm pregnant. Suppose he has an STD and passed it on to me. Prodigal, why didn't I think about all of this before I had sex with him? How could I mess up my life like this? How?"

"Teary, stop it. Don't be so hard on yourself. What's done is done. Come here." He held her closer to him, shielding her in the warmth of his arms.

Her tears were wetting his jersey now. "That's not all, Prodi-gal."

"What else happened?" Prodigal asked, not sure he could take much more.

She lifted her head back so she could see his face. *I might as well tell him everything.* "Debra saw him with another girl the other day. When I called and tried to talk to him, he just went off. He said he didn't want to have anything else to do with me. Then he just hung up the phone in my face. I can't believe he did me like this."

A fresh stream of tears washed down her face.

Prodigal cradled her in his arms and rocked her slowly back and forth like a baby. *If she was my girl, I would never make her cry.* "Shhh. I'm here. Please don't cry." He planted a kiss on her fore-head and then kissed the salty tears running down her cheeks.

She felt safe in his arms. She wished Langston could have been more compassionate and caring like Prodigal. She thought of all the times Prodigal had stuck by her whether she was right or wrong. She nestled closer underneath the curve of his arm and listened as the beat of his heart meshed with hers.

"You know I didn't like him for you in the first place. He just came on too strong, way too strong." He eased back but still embraced her and looked into her eyes. "If he really cared for you, he wouldn't have pressured you to go all the way. Now, he's running up behind someone else, and she just doesn't know it yet, but more than likely she's in for the same thing. But you know what?—forget that. You can't worry about him anymore. You have to let it go."

"But I'm so ashamed. I feel stupid, dirty, and used."

"Look, you'll be fine." He cupped her chin in the palm of his hands, gently lifting her face up. "I know I may not go to church that often, but it doesn't mean that I don't believe in the Man up there." He glanced upwards and pointed one finger toward the sky. "My daddy used to always say, 'There's nothing too hard for God'; he used to say that all the time. And he also used to teach us that God will forgive us when we mess up."

Her tears began to subside as she listened.

"I know you think that what you did is unforgivable, but believe me, that isn't true. Langston isn't worth getting depressed about. One day you'll find someone who's really for you, okay?" He clutched her tightly, wishing he could be that someone.

"Promise me we'll always be friends. Promise me that, Prodigal," Teary pleaded.

"I promise."

A few days after their breakup, Teary saw Langston and the new girl standing together at the school bus stop.

When Langston spotted Teary, he leaned in closer to the girl and whispered in her ear.

She released a silly giggle and wiggled her butt like she had to pee or something. She gave Teary an evil, crooked smile, and eased her arm around Langston's waist.

There were times Teary sat in the bay window in her room to think about what she should have done differently. In the recesses of her mind, she heard her father's raised voice grilling her and Sara about being good Christian girls.

"Listen here, the two of you," her father would say, especially after Sunday service, "save yourselves for your husbands. Don't let any smooth-talking, mannish punk get you to give up the most precious gift you can give to your husband—your virginity. I know what I'm talking 'bout. Remember, I was once a boy myself. When I was a youngster, I tried to run game on girls myself. I even tried with your momma."

Sara and Teary covered their mouths, trying to hold back their snickering.

"But your momma didn't go for my fast talk. Every time I tried to go too far, she'd start quoting Bible scriptures, talking about the Bible says that we should abstain from fornication. I said, 'What you say, girl?—'Abstain from fornication'? Baby, I just want to make out with you, that's all. Shucks! I didn't even know what she was talking about then. 'Forni-*what*,' I asked her? This here is what she said—" Mr. Fullalove raised his voice to a high pitch, pretending like he was their mother. "Boy, you know what I'm talking about—sex is a sin if you do it and you're not married."

He couldn't hold back his laughter any longer. He looked over at his wife. "Honey, what was that Bible verse you used to quote whenever I got fresh with you?—I know you still know it too."

"I most certainly do." Mrs. Fullalove smiled at her husband's poor attempt at imitating her. "It's in the fourth chapter of First Thessalonians, around the third or fourth verse. It says, 'For this is the will of God, even your sanctification, that you should abstain from fornication.' Whenever I repeated that verse to your father, he couldn't help but take his mannish butt on somewhere else and out of my face." She moved closer to her husband, grabbed hold of him, and wrapped herself underneath his massive arm.

"Now, you hear what she just said? I want the both of you to be just like your momma, you hear? Don't be hardheaded and disobedient. The

Bible will tell you the same thing that I'm telling you. Your days will surely be cut off if you disobey your parents. I'm telling you what the Lord says. Do you hear me, Teary? Do you hear what I'm saying, Sara?"

"Yes, Daddy."

"And another thing—If you do what we say and keep your legs closed, you won't have any problems."

Teary didn't know if Sara had followed their father's teachings or not. She only knew that she hadn't. So many times she wanted to believe that Langston was the one for her, but she had been so wrong.

"Teary," Sara yelled from downstairs.

"What is it?"

"Prodigal is here."

"Here I come." Teary pulled her hair back in a ponytail, stepped in her slides, and went to see what was up with him.

"What's up?" Teary asked as she made her way down the stairs.

"What were you doing up there?" Prodigal asked her.

"Nothing, really. What are you getting ready to do?"

"I'm going to see Faith later on, but right now I wanted to see if you wanted to walk to the corner store with me." Prodigal looked for any excuse to be with Teary. He liked Faith a lot, but no girl would ever fill the space Teary had in his heart.

"You must be going to get a grape soda?"

"Now what would make you think that?" He chuckled.

"Boy, you know that I know you like the back of my hand. A grape soda is the only reason your butt will walk to the store."

"Okay, so you're right. Now, are you going with me or not?"

"Yeah, I'll go with you. Let me go get some change." She went upstairs to her room, grabbed her change purse, and hurried back downstairs. "Come on, let's go," she told him, walking past him to the door.

They took their time walking to the store.

"Are you feeling better?" Prodigal asked her.

"A little bit. But it's still just hard running into Langston at school or on the street, you know."

"It'll get easier. And you know what the old folks say—time heals all wounds."

"I sure hope so." Teary sighed. "Oh, I forgot to tell you that I got my period, so I don't have to worry about being pregnant."

"Ugh . . . spare me the details please."

"Sorry, but you're the one who told me to keep you posted." Teary grinned. "So you said that you were going over to Faith's later—what do you two have planned?"

"We'll probably watch a video or something. Do you want to go over there with me?"

"Boy, please . . . you know that wouldn't be right. That girl does not want me sitting between the two of y'all, messing up your flow."

"What flow?—We're just going to watch a movie. She won't mind if you come. She's cool, and you know it. She understands that you and I are tight."

"I hope you didn't tell her what happened, Prodigal." Teary stopped walking and squinted her eyes at him.

"Now you know me better than that—I would never betray your trust in me."

"I know. I guess I'm just still a little paranoid about things."

"Sure. I understand."

"But getting back to you and Faith. She's cool, but she wants to spend time with you, Prodigal, not me and you—Don't you get it?"

"I just want to make sure you're going to be all right, that's all."

"Thanks. I appreciate that. I really do. But you go and hang out with your girl. I'll be okay. Me, Debra, and Chelsia might go to a movie tonight anyway."

Once they arrived at the store, they went in, and Prodigal bought a grape soda for himself and a peach soda for Teary. The warm weather heightened their thirst, so they drank the ice-cold sodas on their way back home.

Prodigal managed to make Teary laugh by telling her jokes along the way. He even yanked on her hair a few times like he used to do when they were kids. She took off running after him, threatening to break every bone in his body. For a moment, she forgot about everything around her. Everything and everyone, except her and Prodigal.

When they made it to her house, they were both out of breath from their antics. Standing on the sidewalk, he told her, "Listen, if you change your mind and decide you want to go over to Faith's house with me, then give me a call. I'm going over their house around seven."

"Sure, but I'm not going to change my mind. You go and have a good time. I'll talk to you tomorrow."

"Suit yourself. I'll see you."

8

Nothing Stays the Same

Fantasia, Sara, and Trina marched across the stage proudly to receive their first rite of passage—a high school diploma. Fantasia delivered a valedictorian message that brought everyone in the audience to their feet. She couldn't wait to start the summer program at Montserrat College of Arts.

A few weeks after graduating, however, the three friends went their separate ways. Trina took off for New York to live with her uncle and his wife before starting college in the fall.

Sara's life took a surprisingly different turn. Mr. and Mrs. Fullalove had made plans to send her to Seattle to live with her Aunt Vashti.

Aunt Vashti didn't say a word, when she received the call from her brother, telling her that Sara was pregnant. When he asked if Sara could come to Seattle to live, she readily agreed for him to send her as soon as she graduated and had the baby. Knowing her brother, Brian, as well as she did, Vashti believed it was probably the best thing to do for Sara's sake. If not, Sara would've had to listen day in and day out to her father telling her about how disappointed he was in her.

Aunt Vashti was one that didn't want her two nieces to have to endure the wrath of their father. She even looked forward to

Sara's move to Seattle. Having a young person in the house would surely lift her lonely spirits. Her Aunt Vashti promised to help Sara get a job at the University of Seattle, where she was a professor of English.

No one could actually tell when Sara marched across the stage that she was already seven months pregnant. She had gained only a few pounds and was still able to wear all of her regular clothes.

Her parents were devastated when they first found out. They never even knew she was remotely interested in any boy, and for her to turn up pregnant was shocking. They felt angry and betrayed.

Even Trina acted indifferently toward her when the news got around the school that Sara was pregnant.

Sara called Fantasia on the phone late in the evening after their commencement program. She needed a shoulder to cry on, and Fantasia was the only friend who supported her. Everything around her seemed to be caving in, and she was terrified.

"Fantasia, I don't know what to do. I've screwed up my life big time," Sara said frantically.

"Sara, all I can tell you is that there are worse things that happen in life."

"That may be true, Fantasia, but for me, there's nothing worse than being young, single, and pregnant with a father who's never going to let me live this down. What am I going to do? I'm going to hell for sure."

"No, you are not going to hell, Sara," Fantasia yelled. "Everything will be fine. You're almost grown anyway. I'm so sick and tired of people talking about we have to do this or we're going to hell, or if we do this, then we're committing a sin, on and on. It's, 'God this and God that.' I say that if there really is a God, then a lot of this crazy, evil stuff in the world wouldn't be happening."

Sara was terrified at hearing her best friend's remarks. "Fantasia, don't say that. You know that you shouldn't talk like that about God. It's blasphemy."

"Well, that's how I feel, and no one's going to change it either.

All you can do is make the best of your situation. Anthony loves you, right? And you love him?"

"Yeah, I guess so, but I don't want to be with him right now. I've got to think this through." Sara's voice cracked.

Fantasia could tell she was crying. "Why don't you want to be with him?"

"I just don't, that's all. I'm leaving around the same time you leave for school. My parents are adamant about me going to Seattle to live with my aunt and raise my baby."

"How can you let them do this to you? See . . . that's what I'm talking about. How can they dictate your life and tell you that you've committed such a terrible sin? It makes no sense to me and I'm tired of living a lie, pretending that I agree with Pastor Grace and all this religious stuff. My daddy believed in God and where is he?—six feet under." Fantasia took a deep breath to calm herself down before starting up again. "But this isn't about me; it's about you, Sara. I say don't go anywhere unless you want to. We're grown now. I don't know about you, but I'm going to make my own decisions about my life and what I believe. You do what you have to do, and I'm going to do what I have to do.

"Fantasia, I don't see any other way out of this."

"Well, I hope everything turns out all right for you, Sara. Remember that I'll always be a phone call away."

"Thanks, Fantasia. You're the best friend I have. Anyway, I think I'm going to turn in. I'm exhausted. We'll talk tomorrow, okay?"

"Sure. Just try to get a good night's rest, Sara. Don't worry about a thing."

The girls hung up the phone.

Sara wiped the tears from her tear-streaked face before going over to the dresser to get her nightshirt.

At the Runsome household, Fantasia crawled up in her bed, grabbed her sketch pad and colored pencils, and began to do what she loved best.

Teary couldn't believe it either when her mother told her

about Sara's dilemma. She thought that if anybody would slip up and get pregnant, it would have been her. But Sara? Not her practical, "never-does-anything-wrong" sister, Sara. By the time Teary even found out about Anthony, her sister was quite serious about him, but she never thought Sara would go and get herself knocked up. *Oh, well. What's done is done,* Teary thought. *Better her than me.*

Sara finally agreed that moving to Seattle would be the best move she could make if she wanted to secure a future for her and her unborn child. She was already ashamed of what she had allowed to happen between her and Anthony.

Anthony hated the idea of Sara having to move away to Seattle, but he didn't have much say-so in the matter. He was no match for Brian Fullalove's influence over his daughter.

Raised by his father since his parents divorced, Anthony wanted to do more than take care of his child. He wanted to take care of Sara too. Now they were going to be hundreds of miles apart and he didn't know what he would do without her.

Sara loved Anthony, and so she could never allow him to marry her just because she was pregnant. She had dreams of marrying him one day, but not under these circumstances. She wanted it to be in the right way—a lavish church wedding with bridesmaids, a knockout white wedding dress and a sit-down dinner that would be to die for. But now, look at her. She was pregnant. All she could hear was her daddy's words replaying in her mind. She could never live down the fact that she had become pregnant outside of marriage, not in Broknfield anyway.

Anthony pleaded with her to remain in Broknfield and make things work for the sake of their baby, but she refused. When she gave birth to a chubby moon-faced little boy with skin the color of brown crayon, unconditional love replaced the disappointment felt by her parents, especially her father.

When Anthony saw him through the nursery window, he beamed with pride and love for his newborn son, whom Sara named Andrew.

9

Fresh Start

Fantasia's dreams of leaving Broknfield behind became a reality when she left home for college. She barely returned home during breaks, instead, she always managed to find a job or some excuse to keep her away from Broknfield. She couldn't believe how quickly time had passed. She was a first semester junior at Montserrat College of Arts. Soon she would be traveling abroad to study art in Italy during the summer. God and religion were a thing of the past for her and she liked her life the way it was just fine.

"Hey, how'd you do on your exam?" her roommate asked. "I got a low B and I can definitely live with that."

Fantasia responded proudly. "I aced mine. You know I won't have it any other way."

"Why am I not surprised? her roommate responded. "I'm headed to the University Center. Do you wanna come along?"

"No thanks. I have some more studying to do, and then I have to get my clothes packed. I'm going to try to get out of here tomorrow for my brother's high school graduation, remember?"

"Oh, yeah, I forgot about that. I'll catch up with you later," the girl replied as her blonde locks bounced up and down like a rubber ball.

I'd better call and check with Momma to see if everything is all set for Prodigal's graduation. Fantasia pushed the speed dial button on her phone. Ruth picked up on the first ring.

"Hello," Ruth said into the phone receiver.

"Hi, Momma. How's everything coming along?" Fantasia asked.

"Hi, baby. Everything is fine."

"Does Prodigal have everything he's going to need for the ceremony Saturday? You know how absent-minded that brother of mine is. I don't know where he got that trait from." Fantasia grinned.

"I don't know where he got it from either. But, anyway, I've been keeping tabs on him. I gave birth to that boy, so I know him inside out. I have his cap and gown, his black suit pants, and I just picked up his white shirt from the cleaners."

"Good. I'm glad all of that's taken care of."

"When will you be home?" Ruth inquired.

"I'll be there a couple of days early so I can spend some time with everyone, but I have to leave the day after his graduation since I have that job at the art gallery. I had a choice to be off a few days before the graduation or a few days after, so I chose before."

"Are you coming alone?"

"Momma, please don't start. If I ever decide to bring someone home, you'll be the first to know."

"Uh-hum."

For the life of her, Ruth couldn't understand why Fantasia shied away from relationships. No matter when she talked to her oldest child, there was never any mention of a boyfriend.

"I told you, Momma, I don't have time for a relationship right now. I have bigger and better things on my agenda. For one, I have to finish college. For two, I have to make a career and a name for myself—those are my priorities—and it takes time. So let me tell you again—I don't have time to be involved with anyone."

"Okay, okay," Ruth said in defeat. "But it would be nice to know that you have a friend or someone in your life. Your daddy and I . . . well . . . what we had was special. I want all of my children to find that same kind of happiness and love."

"Momma, I know you do," Fantasia replied tenderly. "And maybe I will one day, but not right now, okay?"

"Okay."

"Anyway, I'm happy. I have plenty of friends, and we have a great time hanging out and doing our thing. I don't need a man to be complete, and I don't have to be in a relationship like you and Daddy were."

"I said, 'Okay,' Fantasia—Forget I even mentioned it."

But Fantasia was on a roll. She wasn't about to let her mother off the hook just yet. "That's just not me. Plus, look at me—I'm doing great in school; I've studied abroad and met all kinds of interesting and important people; I'm at the top of my class; and some of my paintings are already selling for big bucks—Why can't you be proud and happy about that?"

"I am proud of you, but I still worry about you. I won't apologize for that, because that's not going to change. It's part of being a mother." Ruth quickly changed the conversation, so as not to alienate her daughter. "When did you say you would be here?"

"In a couple of days, Momma. I'll see you. I gotta go."

"Bye, baby."

Ruth felt defeated in her efforts to convince Fantasia that it wouldn't hurt to have a man in her life. This time Ruth may not have succeeded, but she believed there would always be a next time to persuade her daughter to take her advice. Somehow she wanted to drive home to Fantasia how much happier her life could be if she had someone wonderful to share it with.

"Life can still be quite lonely, no matter how successful a person becomes," Ruth said out loud.

10

Truth Be Told

Victory is mine, victory is mine, victory today is mine.

The one-hundred-year-old grey-stoned church was full of spirit. The choir sang out in full force. The shouts of "Amen," "Hallelujah," and "Praise the Lord" resonated through the stain-glassed windows.

The deacon stood up, motioning with his hands for the congregation and choir to stop singing. "Don't you know who woke you up this morning? Started you on your way?" He flailed his hands and moved his feet like he was on a dance floor, his glistening baldhead tilted toward the sky. "God loves to inhabit the praises of His people. He wants to be honored and magnified!" he shouted. "And that old sly one, y'all know who I'm talking about. He's known by many names—Lucifer, the Devil, Satan. Yeah, he sits beside some of you so-called God-fearing people that are lining these very pews."

"That's right. Go ahead. Tell it like it is, Deacon," several members of the congregation yelled with one or more of their hands outstretched toward him.

Pastor Grace sat perched in his chair in the raised pulpit.

"Pastor, you know what the Devil does?" the fired-up deacon asked.

"What does he do, Deacon?"

"He disguises himself as a saint, full of the spirit."

Pastor Grace nodded his head up and down in agreement. "Amen, Deacon. Tell 'em."

"But I'm here this morning to let you know that it's not the Spirit of God. And it's hard sometimes to tell the real Christian folk from the ones that are full of hell. Oh, now if you love the Lord, you better show some sign! Now sing. Sing unto the Lord as we prepare to end Sunday school and enter into our morning worship service."

Members of the congregation jumped to their feet. They clapped and waved their hands. The choir started singing again, their burgundy-and-gray choir robes sashaying back and forth.

Victory is mine, Victory is mine, Victory today is mine, they sang over and over again.

The sound of the blaring alarm startled Prodigal. He bolted upright in his twin bed. Still dazed, he glanced at the clock—8:30 a.m. He hadn't woken up that early on a Sunday in a very long time. But today was special. Not only was he going to church, but he was also going to meet Faith and her family at the morning service.

Hope was the only one in the Runsome family that attended church regularly. Of the three Runsome children, she was the one who wore her faith proudly. She was quite active in the youth group programs and faithfully attended Wednesday night youth bible study. Church meant everything to Hope. Ruth guessed it was a way of escape for her youngest child.

Most of Hope's friends and their families were regular churchgoers too. Like her father in many ways, Hope loved worshipping and serving God. Ruth was often amazed at the wisdom Hope possessed, though young in years.

Fantasia never entertained the thought of going to anybody's church, whether she was in Broknfield or away at school. Prodigal went every so often. As for Ruth, she rarely graced the doors of

Deliverance Temple anymore. She chose, instead, to watch the televangelists that flooded the television every Sunday.

Slipping each foot into his brown "pleather" slippers, Prodigal ambled toward his closet. He rubbed his eyes and yawned. He pushed his everyday clothes to the side and reached far in the back of his closet in search of his black trousers and white button-down cotton shirt. Next, he lazily moved toward his chest of drawers, pulled open the drawer that held everything from his socks to his underwear. At last, his black and white striped tie.

After laying his clothes out, he started the search for his black penny loafers but didn't see them in his closet, nor underneath the pile of laundry that sat comfortably in the corner.

"Ah, hah," he said out loud. He stooped down on his knees, raised the blanket on the side of his bed, and peered underneath the dark area of his bed. He couldn't see a thing, so he used his hand to sweep underneath the bed. "Bingo." He pulled the dusty, worn loafers from its hiding place. Now that he had his attire laid out, he could take care of some important business that he couldn't put off any longer. He ran into the hall bathroom, barely closing the door behind him, and took a much-needed leak. Next, he grabbed the jar of Vaseline from the medicine cabinet, picked up a face towel off the towel rack, and headed back to his room. He took the towel and dipped it into the Vaseline, coming up with just the right amount to put a dapper shine on his loafers.

Hey, these look pretty good, if I must say so myself.

When Prodigal finished ironing, he glanced over at his clock radio—9:15 a.m. Church started at eleven. He promised Faith the night before that he would be there and that he would be on time.

Man, I've got to get out of here.

"Prodigal, sweetheart," his mother called out.

Prodigal looked up and saw her heading down the hall toward his room. Still in her robe, she stopped just inside his bedroom door.

"Good morning, Momma."

"Good morning, baby. Where are you off to?"

Though it had been years since Solumun's death, Ruth still wore that same sad, lifeless expression she'd worn since his death.

"To church. Has the church van picked up Hope already?"

"Yes, sweetheart. Your sister left almost an hour ago. That girl reminds me of your daddy—she's not going to miss church, no matter what. You're going to church?"

"Yes, ma'am."

"That's nice, baby. Pray for me. I can't make it today." She turned and walked back down the hall to her room and shut her door.

Prodigal jumped in and out of the shower. He put his clothes on and headed for the door, not even taking time to eat. He could have sworn he heard his mother crying again, but he couldn't stop to find out for sure, not now.

Rushing out of the house, he ran across the street to Teary's house.

Ring, ring.

No answer.

Ring.

There was still no answer at the Fullalove residence.

"Dang! They must already be gone. I should have told Teary I wanted to ride to church with them this morning. Now I have to walk." Prodigal put one hand in his pocket and rubbed his head with the other. He drew in a deep breath and then started walking the three and a half blocks to Deliverance Temple of Praises.

When he arrived, he took a moment to catch his breath and regain his composure. It had been months since he'd been inside the church walls. He scanned the outside of the church. If he had to admit it to anyone, he really did miss it. He walked up the church steps.

Pastor Grace stood in the entrance greeting his members. When he saw Prodigal, he lifted his hands toward Heaven. "Hallelujah. Thank you, Jesus. Prodigal, my son, it's so good to see you. Thank you, Jesus. Come on in, son. Did your Momma come with you?

"No, sir, she couldn't make it today."

"I know Hope will be here, if she isn't already. How's Fantasia doing in college? I haven't seen that girl in God knows when."

"That's because she rarely gets the chance to come home, sir. But she's doing great. The church van picked up Hope." Prodigal spoke intentionally in a low, almost inaudible, voice.

He hurried quickly on past, just in case Pastor Grace wanted to say anything more. Once inside, he quickly spotted Faith sitting on the young people's side of the church. It wasn't really the young people's side by design. It was just that all the teenagers and young adults happened to gravitate to the left side of the church, and the adults gravitated to the right. So everybody started calling them the young people's side and the adult side.

Prodigal walked quickly toward Faith. "Hi," he said, admiring Faith's pretty, yellow dress.

She patted her manicured hands on the cushioned pew for him to take a seat beside her. "Hey, come on, I saved you a seat."

Prodigal sat down next to her.

"Ooh, you look handsome." A grin spread across her dimpled face.

He tried not to blush, but she made stuff come out of him that, at one time, only Teary could make him feel. Prodigal smiled and whispered in her ear, "You know you look beautiful, Faith."

This time Faith was the one who blushed. Her round cheeks turned beet-red, and another big grin moved across her moon-shaped face.

The keyboard player interrupted the constant chatter of the congregation. Church was about to start. The same opening praise hymn they sung at the close of Sunday school started up again.

Prodigal sang along and thought to himself, *Yes, victory today is mine.*

Prodigal felt someone tapping him on his shoulder. He turned around and met Teary's face as she eased in the pew behind him, along with Debra and Chelsia. He almost gasped when he saw how pretty she looked.

"Hi," she whispered to him. "I can't believe you're here. All the times I've tried to persuade you to come with me and you refused . . . must be something hot and heavy going on. You didn't even tell me you were coming."

"I know. I forgot. I went over to your house this morning, but you all had already left." Then he mumbled, "I had to walk."

Teary gasped. "That's what you get for leaving your best friend in the dark."

Faith turned around. "Hi, y'all."

"Hi, Faith," each of the girls responded softly.

Teary pinched him on the back of the neck before she leaned back against the cushioned pew.

"Will you cut it out. We're in the House of the Lord, or have you forgotten?"

"Whatever." Teary giggled.

Pastor Grace preached about, of all things, fornication. "Turn your Bibles to the fifth chapter of Ephesians," he instructed. "This is what the Word of God has placed on my spirit to share with his people." Pastor Grace didn't need to read from his Bible. The words of the passage rolled freely from his lips. "Be imitators of God. Among you there must not be even a hint of sexual immorality, or any kind of impurity, or greed, because these are improper for God's people."

Prodigal was mesmerized as he listened to Pastor Grace. He became somewhat uneasy. He thought about Teary. He hoped that she wasn't feeling uncomfortable. He didn't dare take a chance and look back to see her reaction. He continued to listen to Pastor Grace. Just because he was still a virgin physically, Prodigal knew that he was no better than Teary. He'd fallen to sleep night after night, dreaming and fantasizing about making love to her. He often longed to know her in an intimate way, but it was a dream that he believed would never come true, so he turned his thoughts to the pretty girl sitting next to him.

Quite a few of the kids from church attended Believers Academy, the church's privately run Christian school. Hope often wished her momma could afford to send her there.

David Peters, president of the youth group was one of the reasons Hope liked attending youth night. The middle child in a family of five, David was a sophomore at the Academy. He was smart, bright, and quite the popular young man. His magnetic charm naturally drew people to him, especially Hope. He carried his lanky body well.

Much like Hope, his face displayed the invasion of acne, and the braces that filled his mouth only served to make his blotched skin stand out even more, but David seemed not to be bothered by it at all. He was a cheery, fun-loving young man, a true comedian in his own way.

And he liked himself some Hope. He thought she was stunning. Hope's oval-shaped glasses matched her mahogany skin. She often wore her thin black braided hair in a ponytail, revealing the cluster of acne taking full residence on her otherwise pleasingly symmetrical face. Her plump nose and wide lips stood out, when she flashed a smile. She was pencil-thin, and there were times Ruth worried that she might be anorexic. But David Peters thought she looked perfect in every way.

He looked forward to seeing her at Sunday services and on Wednesday nights. He could put a smile on Hope's face, when everything else around her felt like it was about to cave in.

Unknowingly, Hope and David were sitting a few pews behind her brother. She saw Prodigal turn around and say something to Teary. Hope smiled in surprise, bowed her head, and mouthed a prayer of thanks to God for bringing her brother to church.

After church service, Faith's parents invited Prodigal to dinner at their house. He eagerly accepted the invitation and climbed in the back seat of their silver Buick.

For the first time in a long time, he felt a part of something good and positive. He felt like he belonged, that he mattered to someone other than his family. No more being on the outside looking in, no more wishing and hoping that he would have love in his life, a faint smile filled his face.

He phoned home to let his mother know about his invitation from the Meadows.

Mrs. Meadows must have prepared Sunday dinner the night before or early that morning before church. Whenever she did it, it sure was good. It had been ages since he'd tasted a delicious meal like turnip greens, fried corn, fresh tomatoes, hot water cornbread and home-made macaroni and cheese. To top it all off, Mrs. Meadows had prepared buttery peach cobbler à la mode for dessert.

When he finally pushed away from the table, Prodigal was as full as a tick. "Mrs. Meadows, everything was delicious. I haven't had a meal like that in a long, long time. I sure appreciate the invitation."

"You're so polite, Prodigal. I like that."

"Thank you, ma'am, but the truth is the truth. I'll help you with the dishes if you'd like me to."

"Boy, you know you're all right with me." Mr. Meadows pat Prodigal hard on the back. "Just don't you mistreat my girl, and you and I will be just fine."

"Of course not, Mr. Meadows. I wouldn't dare dream of hurting her. You'll never have to worry about that—that's a promise, sir."

"Come on, Prodigal. It's time to bust some suds." Hope stood up and grabbed Prodigal by the hand.

They gathered the dishes together and headed for the kitchen.

While Faith washed the dishes, and Prodigal rinsed, the couple laughed and talked about their future together.

"Do you think we'll always be together and that we'll stay happy like this?" Faith asked.

"Girl, I don't have to think—I know we will. We care about

each other, don't we? And we've been together for some months already, right?"

"Right."

"Then nothing should separate us." He looked deep into her soft hazel eyes. He leaned in close to her.

Without warning, she scooped a handful of soapy water in her hands and threw it at Prodigal and rushed to the other side of the kitchen.

"Oh, it's on now. Yeah, I'm going to get you now." He laughed, filled a glass with cold water and raced after her.

They laughed and played until they both were practically soaked.

Prodigal removed the last dish from Faith's hand and laid it in the dish rack. Then he turned her toward him, pulled her close, and bent his head down to kiss her firmly on the lips.

When she tasted the sweetness of his tongue, she allowed it to caress hers before pulling away.

"I'm sorry."

"No, don't be sorry. It's just that you know we can't let things get out of hand, Prodigal. Remember Pastor Grace's message today?

"Yes, and you're right, Faith."

"We've done good not to go all the way," Faith added. "I don't want anything to spoil what we have. Do you really understand, Prodigal?"

"Of course, I understand; I feel the same way." But his young manhood didn't agree. It had a mind of its own because he felt it keeping up a fuss inside his Sunday trousers.

11

Sheep's Clothing

Twenty-one-year-old womanizer Skyler Jenkins had been casing the mall for several hours before he spotted the three girls coming out of The Gap. Immediately his bluish-gray eyes zeroed in on Teary like a radar screen.

"Man, check out that female," Skyler told his friends. "If she ain't a dime piece then I don't know who is; with all that hair going down her back. Oooh, wee! I bet she's a wild one. And if she isn't, then I bet you under my expert tutelage she will be before you can say, 'Abracadabra.' "

Skyler and his boys released a loud round of laughter.

"Y'all talk to her friends if you want to, but leave her to me." He pointed at Teary as she and her friends headed unknowingly in his direction.

He stepped confidently to her and said, "Excuse me."

Teary liked what she saw. His naturally wavy hair was neat. The small gold hoop earring in his left ear further added to his appeal. His thick eyebrows arched upwards in a devilish manner, almost connecting across the center of his face.

"Can I have a word with you for a minute?"

She took a moment to look him up and down. He was strikingly handsome indeed. Skyler carried his slender, creamy-colored body on a six-foot frame. His designer jeans and matching jersey fit his body loosely, and a cluster of chest hairs pushed out from underneath his gold link necklace

"You don't know me. So why do you want to have a word with me?"

"Because you look like someone I'd like to get to know."

"Well," Teary said, "looks can be quite deceiving, don't you agree?"

"Yes, I agree. That's why I'd like to get to know you. I want to find out if my eyes are fooling me." His eyes shifted slightly in the direction of his friends. When he saw them busy delivering their own pick-up lines to the other girls, he figured he had a little more time to talk to her. He extended his hand to her. "Look, my name is Skyler. What's yours?"

"Teary," she responded, shaking his hand.

"Hey, I'm going to make a long story short—you're attractive to me, and I was just wondering if we could get to know each other a little bit better."

Teary started walking slowly along the mall, passing each store, peering inside like she was really interested in the items she saw, instead of the game he was throwing her way.

"Skyler, I may not want to get to know you." Teary stole a quick peek into his dazzling eyes.

"That may be true, but I hope that's not the case. Are you still in school?"

"Yep. I attend Fairley High. I'm a senior this year, and you?"

"I graduated a couple of years ago."

"What do you do now then?" she asked, fascinated at being pulled by an older boy.

"I work at Club Ecstasy, and I'm a full-time college student."

Her mind hadn't moved past the Club Ecstasy part yet. "Isn't Ecstasy a male strip club?" She raised one eyebrow and looked up at him suspiciously.

"Hey, it's a job, and it pays well. I do it for the money until I can graduate from college. I don't take all of my clothes off. You're welcome to come and see for yourself."

"Boy, you know I can't get into Club Ecstasy. I still have a few more months before I turn eighteen. Anyway, I don't care to go into that den of ill repute."

"Hey, I wouldn't exactly call it that. But I do know how you feel. Like I said, it's good money, and right now I need the money to take care of myself and to pay for my education. It's not like I plan to make stripping a life-long career or anything like that. I have my own apartment, well, me and a roommate, so that means bills." Skyler thought for a minute. "I tell you what—Why don't you give me a ring sometime so we can really talk?" He thumbed through his wallet and his jean pockets until he found a crumpled piece of paper. He borrowed a pen from Teary long enough to scribble his number down and then pushed it toward her. "Here's my number. Call me some time."

"I'll think about it." Teary hesitated before taking hold of the piece of paper. She was not going to let this fine-looking boy believe for one minute that she was falling for his pick-up line. The last thing she needed was another guy taking advantage of her. Langston Silverman had taught her a lot about trust. She had learned the hard way that all that glitters certainly isn't gold.

When Chelsia called her a few months after she and Langston broke up and told her that Langston was moving, Teary was ecstatic. Her prayers had been an answered. Langston's family moved to the other side of town, which meant he had to transfer to another school. Teary no longer had to face the humiliation of seeing him at school every day. Since Langston, she'd shied away from any boy that tried to talk to her. She didn't know if Langston had bad-mouthed her to the other boys at school or not. She didn't want to find out either.

She focused her thoughts back on the boy standing next to her. *He seems like he might be a pretty nice guy.*

"I definitely want to talk to you again, Teary. Don't make me wait too long."

When Skyler flashed his perfect set of pearly whites, Teary thought she would lose it.

"Well, look, Skyler, I have to go. I've been here most of the afternoon, and I still have some other things to do, so I'll talk to you later."

"Hey, sounds good to me. I can't wait."

She turned and walked toward Debra and Chelsia. "You guys ready?"

They giggled and shared their stories.

What a day, Teary thought. *What a day.*

Since her traumatic experience with Langston, she was determined not to be suckered by a boy again. So far she had remained true to her word, but Skyler was turning out to be different. Since their meeting at the mall, they had spent quite a bit of time talking on the phone. When he wasn't working or going to class, they would sometimes talk on the phone for hours. She liked talking to Skyler and listening to him. She was quite impressed. He made her laugh. Unlike Langston, he respected her opinion and seemed to care about what she wanted to do in life.

"What's your major?" Teary asked him during one of their phone conversations.

"Physical therapy. I'll be starting my clinicals after a couple more semesters."

Skyler enjoyed talking to Teary too. She was the first girl that he hadn't tried to jump into bed with right away. He had been a playa so long that he was even surprised at this turn of events. Women propositioned him all the time at the club, and before he met Teary, he often accepted their invitations. But since Teary had come into his life, he found himself losing his desire to jump from one female to the next. He didn't want to take a chance of ruining what obviously was turning out to be a pretty cool relationship, so he decided he would take things slow.

"Skyler, can I ask you something?"

"Yeah, go ahead," he answered one night when they were on the phone.

"Why haven't you asked me out? I mean, don't get me wrong, I like talking to you on the phone and all. And you've come over here a couple of times. But I still don't understand why we haven't gone on a real date, you know what I mean?" She didn't wait for a response. "We don't have to do a lot. We could just go out to eat or to a movie."

"I hear you, and you're right. But you know I work six days a week plus go to school. But I want to hang out with you too. What if I try to take off Saturday night and we can go out? You think that will be all right with your folks?"

"Sure. I don't see why not."

"It won't be all right if they find out I'm twenty-one years old, which, I guess, is another reason I've been playing it safe. I mean, you aren't eighteen yet. I could get in a lot of trouble."

"I know that, but it won't be much longer; plus you're only a few years older than me."

"But we still have to be cautious, Teary."

"I can't wait until my birthday in May. I'm glad it's only a few months away. I'll be eighteen, and we won't have to worry about anything like that. Until then, it's our secret. Agreed?"

"Agreed," he said with a sigh of relief.

Teary shared her excitement about her upcoming date with Debra, Chelsia, and Faith. She had purposely held back from telling Prodigal anything about Skyler and had sworn Faith to secrecy. When it came to Prodigal, she had to tread lightly. He sometimes acted like her father instead of her best friend.

Teary took a trip to the mall to find the perfect outfit for her date with Skyler. Her babysitting jobs were paying off. They kept her with enough money in her pocket to buy herself some of the things she wanted. She picked out a baby-blue, above-the-knee, knit dress with a short-sleeved matching waist-length jacket that flattered her size eight figure. She went to Kara's Shoes and found a pair of red flats. She didn't want to overdress, but she did want to look extra nice for her first date with Skyler.

"Hey, Johnny, are you hanging around the crib tonight or what?" Skyler asked his roommate.

"Don't think so. I'm thinking about stepping out to my girl's crib. Why? What's up?"

"I'm off work tonight, man, and I'm going to pick up Teary. We might hit the crib a little later, that's all."

"That's on you, man. I won't be in the way, if that's what you mean. It'll probably be late when I get back, if I make it back at all." Johnny laughed.

"I heard that. Maybe I'll be so lucky myself."

"Ahh," Teary screamed, shutting her eyes tightly. The gory horror scene on the giant drive-in screen was too yucky for her. She buried her head in Skyler's chest. In between the bloody scenes, the two of them nibbled on popcorn and gulped cherry cola. They laughed and talked, and then watched the movie some more.

"What are you going to do after you graduate from school, Teary?" Skyler shoved a handful of popcorn in his mouth.

"I'm going to college and major in English or journalism. I love to write."

"You never told me that you liked writing."

"I guess it never came up. Anyway, I want to see how far I can go with it. I'm not sure if I'll go out of town to college, or if I'm going to stay here and go to the university. I guess I'll have to make my decision soon, huh?"

"I think you should. It takes a while to get everything together for college."

"I've been accepted at a couple of universities, including Broknfield."

"Oh, that's great. I'm always talking about my dreams and stuff. There's still a lot about you that I don't know, but can I assume one thing?"

"It depends on what it is you want to assume." Teary took a sip of her soda.

"Can I assume that you like me?"

Her eyes met his. She was quiet for a moment. "I think it's safe to assume that," she said softly and smiled.

When he tilted her chin toward him, she met his kiss without resistance. He wasn't forceful or overpowering—she liked that about Skyler. His broad lips were sweet like the taste of bubblegum. His hands traveled along the course of her tiny waist, but not once did he try to invade her body.

She hoped he would never find out that she wasn't a virgin and definitely not the innocent girl he seemed to think she was. She wanted their relationship to be different.

The movie credits were rolling by the time their lips parted.

Skyler looked at the screen and pointed. "Can you believe that we sat here all this time and now look—the movie's over, and we have no idea how it ended. I guess we have to sit through the whole thing again, so we can see the end."

"Oh, no. I can't take another blood-curdling scream or see another person get butchered by Jason the fourth, fifth, or whatever Jason he is." Teary laughed.

"What now? We can go and get something to eat."

"No, I don't think I can eat another bite." Teary rubbed her stomach and shook her head.

"I tell you what. Do you want to go and see where I lay my head? I promise I won't try anything out of line. He made a V-shape with two fingers. "Scout's honor."

"So you were a Boy Scout, huh?"

"Not exactly. I learned that from some of my scout friends. Surely, that counts for something." He poked out his mouth and gave her a pleading look.

"Oh, all right. Since you put it like that, I guess my answer is yes. We can go by there for a minute; I'd like to see your bachelor's pad." She giggled.

They left the drive-in, talking all the way to Skyler's apartment.

Skyler pulled into the apartment complex and drove all the way to the back, pulling up at the last unit. He opened the door for Teary, reached for her hand, and led her to the second door of the downstairs units.

Teary was quiet and reserved as she entered the two-bedroom apartment. It was sparsely furnished with a chocolate-brown love seat, sofa, and recliner in the living room. A deck of cards was sprawled across the table, along with a few of Skyler's schoolbooks. Teary viewed the kitchen from the front room and didn't spot a single dish in the sink.

"Come on, I want you to see where I spend my lonely days and nights." Skyler grabbed her by the hand again like she was a little schoolgirl.

"Of course, why not." She zeroed in on her surroundings. The queen-size bed was expertly made. Books about physical therapy and anatomy rested on a bookshelf in the corner of his bedroom. Scented candles were on his dresser, along with several video cartridges and pictures.

Teary picked up one of the pictures. "Your parents?"

"Yep."

"They live here?"

"I'm actually from Charlotte. And to answer your question—no, my parents don't live here. They were killed when I was sixteen."

"Oh, I'm so sorry, Skyler. What happened . . . if you don't mind me asking?"

"No, I don't mind. A drunk driver ran a red light and hit them head-on. My little brother and sister were in the car too. They had just dropped me off at a friend's house and were on their way home, when it happened. There's a picture of my sister and brother over there on the other side of the dresser."

Teary held the picture of his brother and sister and stared at their innocent-looking faces. She was reeling from what he had just told her. "Skyler, that's awful. Who took care of you?"

"Basically, I've been taking care of myself ever since it happened. My momma and daddy didn't have sisters or brothers. My maternal grandparents died when I was four, and my daddy's parents aren't in the best of health. The reason I'm in Broknfield is because of my roommate, Johnny. We've been best friends since kindergarten. That's whose house I was over when the accident happened; they're like a second family to me."

"How did you end up in Broknfield?"

"Johnny's daddy is from here. When Johnny's grandfather was diagnosed with Alzheimer's, his parents decided to move back here to take care of him. They asked me to come along. So here I am."

Her heart overflowed with compassion for him. This was a part of Skyler she didn't know. She wished she could do something to help him. Teary sat the pictures back down on the dresser and walked into his arms and kissed him passionately.

He returned her kiss with an urgency of his own then pushed her away from him.

Looking bewildered and lost she asked, "What's wrong?"

"We'd better go before things get out of hand. Plus, it's late and I don't want to mess up with your people, especially on our first date. It won't be long before you're eighteen. We can wait. I want you to be sure about us."

Teary sulked, but she didn't say a word. She walked slowly back into the living room and picked up her jacket. Skyler was indeed different. That was one thing she was sure of.

Reluctantly she said, "I'm ready."

He led the way to the door without saying a word. *Man, what am I thinking? I can't believe I'm doing this . . . bad as I want this girl.*

The drive home was filled with silence. She nestled closely to him, resting her head on his shoulder while he drove. Teary felt safe and secure with him and believed this time around things would be different.

12

Time to Move On

Teary was about to let the cordless phone ring one more time before hanging up, when Prodigal picked up the other end.

"Hello. Whuzzup witch ya?" Prodigal said into the phone receiver.

"It's about time you answered the phone. I want to know if you and Faith are still going with me and Skyler to Chili's after our commencement."

"What's going on at Chili's?"

"I told you yesterday that we were going to go somewhere and celebrate. It's not every day we march down the aisle to receive our high school diploma. Can you believe it?" Teary didn't give him a chance to respond to her initial question.

"Girl, slow down. You're talking a mile a minute. I can't be hanging around with you too long 'cause I don't want to be around dude, you know that."

Teary was determined to keep things upbeat on their graduation night. "Prodigal, we've come a long way to get to this day, so please lay your ill feelings for my man aside just for tonight. Shucks, we actually made it, Prodigal." She laughed out loud. "I'm sure glad Faith came into your mixed-up, messed-up life and saved you."

"You're saying it like it's a joke, but I'm serious when I say I'm glad she did too. There's not a girl out there who can outdo her," he said rather proudly. "Not even you, Teary Fullalove—now what do you have to say about that?"

"Boy, please . . . whatever! Just answer my question—Are you two going or not?" Teary pranced around in her bedroom.

He pushed his bifocals back up against the bridge of his narrow nose. "Probably, but let me check with Faith. I'll call you back, but I bet she's going to say yes."

"Okay, but if you don't call me back in a few minutes, I'll just see you at the Convention Center, and you can let me know what you're going to do then. You're still riding with your family, right? Or do you need to catch a ride with me?"

"No, I'm cool. The king of the Runsome household is riding with the ladies—Momma, Fantasia, and Hope—my royal subjects." Prodigal laughed.

"*Funny*, Prodigal. You wish you were somebody's king. But seriously, though, remember to bring everything you're supposed to have," Teary told him. "You know how forgetful you are, especially since you're so in *luv*."

He rambled off the list of things he was supposed to take with him to the Convention Center. "Let's see . . . I have my gown, my tassel, my cap and uh, uh, and that's it, right?"

"Yeah, that sounds like everything."

"And as for being in love, you can't talk because if anyone's sprung, it's you. I haven't seen you this crazy about anyone since that bum, Langston." Nothingness traveled between the lines.

Prodigal visualized her on the other end with an awkward expression on her face. "Sorry about that, Teary. I didn't mean to drudge up bad memories. But now as for the present, I can say that Mr. Jenkins, even though I don't particularly like him, he has your nose so wide open, a train could run straight through it."

Both of them were laughing hard by this time.

"But seriously, Teary, thanks for looking out for me. I have everything, and I'll see you this afternoon."

"Bye, boy. I'll talk to you later."

After hanging up the phone, Prodigal leaned back on his bed, thinking about all he and Teary had gone through over the years. He reminisced about the fun times they shared when they were little kids—pulling her pigtails, riding their bikes to Willow Lake, exchanging blood vows. *Those were some good times. But I have Faith and she's completely different from Teary, and I'm crazy about her. But Teary will always be my special girl. If only she knew just how special she really is to me. I've never been able to tell her how I feel. Now, here we are on the verge of being adults. We're high school seniors preparing to march down the aisle and into our futures—together, yet apart. She's got her life with her new boyfriend, and I have Faith. Maybe it's best this way.*

The sound of his mother's voice startled him, breaking into his private thoughts. "Prodigal, are you getting your things ready? It won't be long before it's time for us to leave. You don't want to be late for your own graduation do you?" Ruth asked from his bedroom doorway.

"Yes, ma'am—I mean, no, ma'am. I don't want to be late. I'm going to start getting ready shortly."

After an hour or so of daydreaming, Prodigal called Faith to tell her he would see her at the Convention Center. They talked for a few minutes then he hung up and started getting ready. He could hear Fantasia and Hope downstairs shuffling around. It felt like old times with all of them in the house. If only his daddy was here to share this day with them, then the family would be complete.

Ruth looked at the clock on the wall in the kitchen. She yelled upstairs, "Prodigal, it's time to leave."

He rushed downstairs, his gown draped over his arm.

At that moment, Ruth had to fight back the tears—he looked just like Solumun.

Most of the time people told her that Prodigal was the spitting image of her, but not today. Today, she saw a replica of Solumun Runsome bolting down the stairs. She managed to smile as

Prodigal walked straight into her arms and hugged her, as if he could read her thoughts.

Fantasia and Hope interrupted the mother and son moment, perhaps not a minute too soon; Ruth didn't know if she could hold her tears back much longer.

"You look so handsome," Hope told her brother.

"He does, doesn't he?" Fantasia surveyed Prodigal from head to toe.

"Well, time to go." Ruth made a final check to be sure that Prodigal hadn't forgotten anything and hurried everyone to the car.

They pulled up at the front of the Convention Center, and Prodigal jumped out of the car. Ruth proceeded to the parking garage.

Proud parents and boasting relatives were quickly filing into the Broknfield Convention Center. The Runsome and Fullalove families boldly claimed seats front row and center. Ruth was quite proud of all her children. She remembered when Fantasia walked across the same stage as valedictorian of her class.

The program got underway. Prodigal's chest was bursting with excitement as he looked out at the crowd. He beamed when he saw his family on the front row. A sense of accomplishment and pride consumed him.

The moment had arrived for them to pass out the diplomas. Prodigal looked at Teary the same time she was looking back at him. The two of them smiled at each other, and Prodigal's heart fluttered.

Name after name was called. Prodigal clapped as hard as he could when he heard them say, "Teary Fullalove."

Teary held her head high when her name was called and strolled confidently across the stage. She reached out and shook Principal King's hand, and with her other hand she reached for the piece of paper that symbolized her freedom to move forward to the next stage in her life. The Fullalove clan, including Sara and Aunt Vashti who'd flown in from Seattle the night before, clapped their hands loudly and screamed as Teary pranced across the stage.

Aunt Vashti held on to Sara's little boy, Andrew, while he tried unsuccessfully to ease himself out of her lap.

Teary nervously peeked out in the audience. Her eyes scoped the crowd like a radar screen for Skyler. He has to be here. He promised he would. In the back of her mind, she heard Principal King calling the other students' names—*"Debra Mason, Faith Meadows, Chelsia Patterson, Prodigal Runsome."*

She looked up from her daydream just in time to see Prodigal strolling proudly across the stage. She joined in on the clapping and yelling. She felt especially happy for him, the one person who had been, and was her dearest and closest friend. She thought of their futures. What would happen to them now? Prodigal and Faith would probably one day get married. She and Skyler had their own plans too. But what would life hold for their friendship? She couldn't stand the thought of Prodigal not being part of her life. Even though he didn't like Skyler, she hoped that it wouldn't destroy the love and friendship she and Prodigal had for one another. She could make it in life without a lot of things and a lot of people, but Prodigal Runsome wasn't one of them.

"Teary," Prodigal said.

"What?"

"Faith said that Chili's sounds fine to her."

"Good. It's settled. Come on. Let's get out of these gowns." Teary took Prodigal by the hand and pulled him along.

Faith stood off to the side and saw Prodigal hand in hand with Teary, leaving the area that had been reserved for the graduates. She couldn't help feeling somewhat jealous. Instead of seeking her out, as usual, it was always Teary that Prodigal put first. Faith trailed several feet behind them to see where they were going.

She continued watching as the two of them turned in their gowns at the designated drop-off and walked down the corridor leading out of the auditorium.

"Teary, I can't stay at Chili's too long. Fantasia has to leave to-morrow, so I really want to spend some time with her."

"As long as you remember that midnight tonight I'm going to be eighteen years old." She squealed and jumped up and down. "Can you believe it? I graduated today, and tomorrow I'll offi-cially become an adult—Can it get any better than that?" She screamed again.

"Hold it down, crazy girl. I know tomorrow is your birthday. We're going to do something special, just you and me. Teary, all I'm saying is that it won't be tonight. I have to go to Faith's house later this evening. Her parents are having her a get-together. You know you're welcome to come; Faith told me that she invited you."

Faith stood quietly behind a wall at the end of the corridor, so they wouldn't see her. She listened, as they talked innocently about the plans they had for later that evening. She walked off and went to find her parents and relatives. She began to feel stu-pid for being jealous and distrustful of Prodigal. One day she was going to be Mrs. Prodigal Runsome, so she convinced herself there was nothing for her to be concerned about. Nothing at all.

"Prodigal, you're right—Faith did invite me—but I can't come tonight. After we leave Chili's, Skyler and I are going to hang out and celebrate my birthday."

"That's cool." He hesitated before he continued. "Teary, there's something I want to say, and since I don't know when we'll have the chance to be alone again, I want to say it now."

"Prodigal, if it's about Skyler, don't worry about me. Things are going to be fine, you'll see."

"This has nothing to do with him—this has to do with us. Come on." Prodigal grabbed hold of her shoulders and gave her a push into the empty dressing room.

"What are you doing?"

"Will you be quiet for a minute and listen?" He reached inside his pant pocket and pulled out a silver box.

"What is that? Is it something for Faith?"

"No, it's something for you." Prodigal opened the box, revealing a sterling silver bracelet with breakaway heart charms dangling from it. "Happy birthday, Teary."

Teary was speechless. She shifted her glistening eyes to the bracelet, pulling it out of its box. Holding it in her hands, she saw the dangling broken hearts. One half of the heart had the initial *P* engraved on it; the other half of the heart, *T*.

"Oh, Prodigal, it's beautiful. I love it."

Prodigal removed the bracelet from her hands and placed it on her tiny wrist. "Teary, I want you to promise me something, okay?"

"Sure. Anything. You know that."

"Teary . . ." He paused for a few seconds. "Promise me that we'll always be here for each other. Promise me that we'll never let anything or anyone come between our friendship."

"Is that all you wanted to say? You know nothing can come between us, not ever. That should go without saying."

"Wait, listen to me, Teary. I'm serious. You're the only person who knows everything there is about me. You're the only one who I trust completely. I mean, don't get me wrong, I care deeply for Faith. I might ask her to marry me one day. And I know you love Skyler, but—"

"Say no more—I'll always be here for you always. Do you remember when we were little and we pricked our fingers to pledge our bond of friendship?"

"Yes, I remember." A smile came across his face as he recalled that afternoon at Willow Lake.

"Well, that bond is still intact, Prodigal, and I'll never ever breach it. You've never judged me, you've never put me down. You're the one person I can truly be myself around, and I love you for that."

Prodigal was transfixed by what Teary had just said to him. For a moment, nothing and no one else mattered except the two of them.

"No matter where I travel in life, no matter what I do, or who

I'm with, you'll always be my best friend. You'll always know where I am, and whenever you need me, I promise to come running." He pulled her into his arms and embraced her as tight as he could. He wanted to tell her that he not only loved her but that he was in love with her, but he didn't want to ruin what they had.

He inhaled the sweet fragrance of her hair and gently twirled one of her locks between his fingers. "Girl, you're something else." Prodigal fixed his gaze on her. "It's no wonder I love your silly butt. By the way, don't think just because you're eighteen and a high school graduate that you're grown. You still have to answer to me." He yanked her hair like he used to do when they were kids.

"Boy, puhleeze. Don't you start no mess, or I'll whip your butt and send you running home to your momma." She smiled.

"Yeah, right." Prodigal laughed.

His face took on a serious look again. "Look at us—Today is the first day of the rest of our lives."

"Yes, it is, Prodigal." A tear formed in the crest of her eyes.

He reached out and hugged her again, only this time when he pulled back from her, their eyes locked, and he did what he'd longed to do for such a long time. He kissed her full on the lips, unable to bridle his passion. Their hot tongues explored the inside of each other's mouths. His arms embraced her shoulders before traveling to her delicate waist and landing on her thighs.

Teary wrapped her arms easily around his neck, holding on to him, pulling him toward her, never wanting to let him go. She heard his heavy breathing and felt his heart pounding. Or was it hers?

He hungered for her. He couldn't believe he was finally holding the girl he'd loved for all these years in his arms. Her body was soft, yielding to him. He heard himself groan and became aroused for her and only her. Oblivious to everything, he was where he'd always wanted to be, longed to be. He couldn't resist, as he explored the sweetness between her legs.

"Ahhh," he said as he thrust against her.

She put up no resistance, but answered with pleasurable moans of her own. Her hand touched him where he'd dreamed of her touching him, and he rose to meet her.

Suddenly, as if someone had prodded him with a hot poker, he pulled back, being careful not to allow himself to think he felt anything but true friendship for her.

She didn't fully comprehend what had just happened between the two of them or how she felt about it. She told herself it was just a kiss between friends, an innocent kiss. She stole one last look at her best friend before both of them pretended that what had just happened didn't.

"Does seven sound good for you and Faith?" Teary asked, her face still flush.

"Seven sounds fine." Prodigal cleared his throat.

They walked out hand in hand, in silence, down the long, winding corridor.

Teary rushed out of the auditorium and darted past her family in search of Skyler. She didn't see him anywhere, even though he had promised her he would be there.

Skyler, where are you?

She ran until she reached the double doors leading to the outside of the huge Convention Center. Just as she reached out to open one of the doors, Skyler yanked it open.

"Skyler, where have you been?" Her eyebrows arched in a frown.

"Listen, baby, I couldn't bring myself to come up front, so I just stayed in the back of the auditorium until the whole thing was over."

"But why?" she asked, not knowing whether to be angry or feel sad. "Look, you knew that today was an important chapter in my life. I wanted to share it with you and see your face when I walked across the stage." Her voice was high, and her body twitched.

"You are sharing it with me. I just didn't want any confusion. You know your parents don't like me much. And as for your boy, well, let's just say, you know how much he hates me. I just didn't want to mess up anything for you. I love you too much. I wanted this day to be special for you, girl. You looked good up there, baby. I'm proud of you." He drew her close to him and kissed her on the lips, holding her tight and caressing her.

"Please . . . not here."

"As you say, madam." He bowed his head toward her. "Look, I'll make it up to you, I promise. Now come on, let me see that pretty smile of yours." He moved a lock of hair back from her face and rubbed his hands across her cheek.

She forced a smile. She couldn't stay mad at him for very long. He just had that kind of effect on her.

"Hey, are we still going to Chili's?" he asked.

"Yes, but first I have to go back inside and let my parents and family fawn over me and all that stuff first, you know what I mean."

"No, I don't. I've never had that. I wish my parents had been alive to fawn over me and all."

She could have crawled up in a corner. She hated it when she made senseless, stupid remarks like she just did.

"I'm sorry. Look, it won't take me long to say my goodbyes to them. Are you going to wait on me, or do you want me to meet you there?"

"No, I'll wait." He gave her a kiss on her cheek and a tap on her butt. "Now go on and hurry back."

"Okay." She giggled and ran back into the auditorium.

Back in the auditorium, Prodigal and Faith's families were busy taking snapshots of the two of them.

"Stand over there by the fountain, Prodigal," Fantasia said as she took several shots with her digital camera. "Now, the both of you get together and give me one of those 'I'm-so-glad-to-be-out-of-school' kind of poses." She took more pictures.

Faith's parents captured their share too.

"Hey, you guys, that's a wrap," Mrs. Meadows finally announced. "I think we've taken enough pictures to fill an entire photo album."

Fantasia looped her arm inside the arm of her brothers. "Faith, mind if I steal your man for just a minute?"

"Sure. Take your time with him. He knows where to come when you're finished."

"Come on, bro, let me talk to you for a minute."

"What's up, sis?" Prodigal walked off arm in arm with his big sister.

"I just wanted to tell you how proud I am of you. You have a promising future ahead of you and a good girl by your side. I know you're going to do well out in the real world. Daddy would be proud of you too, you know."

The admiration Fantasia felt for her brother was overpowering. Of all people, she understood how difficult living without their daddy had been for Prodigal. Out of the three of them, she believed he was the one who suffered the worst.

"Thanks, Fantasia." Prodigal hugged his sister. "You've always believed in me. You've never put me down in any way; and I love you for that."

"I love you too, Prodigal."

They hugged each other.

"What time are we supposed to go over to Faith's for the cookout?"

"Around eight-thirty."

"What else do you have going on?"

"Faith and I are going to meet Teary and her boyfriend at Chili's. We aren't going to stay very long. I already told Teary that I want to spend some time with you before you leave."

"Sounds good to me. Now go and say your goodbyes to everybody until later. I'm going to take Hope to the mall. She wants to get an outfit for the 'youth lock-in' the church is having next weekend. By the time we finish doing that, you and Faith will probably be heading back from Chili's."

"Sounds like a great game plan to me, big sis. I'll see you later then." Prodigal turned and headed back inside to search for Faith.

Before he could make it any distance, she walked up.

Fantasia leaned over and kissed Faith on her cheek. "I'm proud of you too, but you know that already." She reached out to give her soon-to-be sister-in-law a hug and a kiss.

"Thanks, Fantasia. That means a lot to me. I heard that you're going to be taking your second march across the stage in a few months."

Fantasia raised her hand in a high-five motion. "You got that right, and I can't wait either. Are you going to be able to come with Prodigal?"

"I wouldn't miss it for anything in the world."

"Great. Well, look, don't let me be the one to hold y'all up. I know you're supposed to be meeting Teary, so let me get out of here and go find Momma and Hope. I'll see you later tonight."

"Okay," the both of them said.

Faith then turned her attention to Prodigal. "Prodigal, have you seen Teary?"

"Naw. The last I saw of her she was going to look for Skyler. She's probably outside with him somewhere."

Just as he finished his sentence, Teary appeared. She gave Prodigal an awkward look.

He returned her gaze with an uneasy one of his own. Sensations from their earlier encounter remained fresh in their minds.

"Have you said all of your good-byes?" Teary asked Faith.

"Sure have."

Prodigal nervously rubbed his hands across his forehead. "Yeah, we're ready." He began to look around. "Where's Skyler?"

Faith noticed that Prodigal was rather fidgety. "Are you all right?"

"Sure. Just still excited about today, that's all." Prodigal stole a quick glance in Teary's direction.

She immediately looked away. *I've got to keep it together. It was just a kiss between friends, nothing more.*

A chill moved up and down his spine. *Got to be cool.* "What did you say, Teary?"

"I said, 'He's outside waiting on us,'" Teary repeated. "Are y'all going to follow us or ride with us?"

"Faith is driving. We'll follow you," Prodigal answered.

A white Chevy Malibu was a surprise graduation gift to Faith from her parents. Prodigal disliked the fact that she always had to be the one to drive them from place to place. Before her parents bought her the car, they often let her use their Park Avenue from time to time. Prodigal wasn't angry with his mother for not being able to buy him a car. He was angry with his father. Why did his daddy have die? Why and how could he just check out on life like he did?

"We'll see you there then," Teary said.

"Yeah, sure," Prodigal responded without the least bit of excitement in his voice.

When they arrived at Chili's, Prodigal excused himself and dashed straight to the back of the restaurant. He went into the recreation area to try his hand at a game of pool.

Skyler made his way to the bar and ordered himself a beer.

Teary and Faith had the hostess seat them at a table in the non-smoking section. The two girls chatted most of the time about their plans for the future now that they had graduated.

"Now that we're officially free to conquer the world, what's your next move, Teary?" Faith placed the straw to her lips and sipped on her cherry cola.

Teary bent over and whispered, "Marriage, but don't tell anyone yet."

"Did you say 'marriage'?—You and Skyler?

"Yes, me and Skyler."

Faith was shocked to hear her talk about marriage. "When are you two getting married?"

"It's going to be soon. Real soon."

"Fill me in on everything—How and when did this come about?—and don't leave out any of the juicy details either."

"Girl, you're crazy." Teary took a swallow of her diet Cola. "But okay, here's how it happened—Skyler popped the big question one evening after we returned from seeing a movie. We were at his place listening to music and gulping down tacos. He started out by telling me, 'We've been together for almost a year. Everything is right between us, baby. You know that, don't you?' I told him, 'Yeah, of course, I do.' I didn't know exactly where he was going with the conversation."

"You had no idea what he was talking about?" Faith rested her chin in her hands and leaned in closer.

"Nope. But he looked serious and acted like he was searching for the right words or something. That's when I started getting a little nervous." Teary squirmed in her chair.

" 'Nervous'?—Why?"

"Because I thought he was about to break up or that something bad had happened. I didn't know what to think."

"I feel you on that," Faith said. "Keep on."

"Then he said, 'I want you to know that I love you, girl. I think I fell in love with you the first time I laid eyes on you in that mall. I know I don't have a lot, but you know I'm trying. You know that I do have a lot of love for you.' "

Faith shrieked, "What did you say? Did you just about fall out or what?" She took another gulp from her soda until there was a loud slurp, letting her know nothing else was in her glass.

"I didn't have time to react, because that's when he said, 'I want you to marry me, Teary. Tell me you will.' "

"Oh, no!" Faith hit her hands up and down on the wood table.

"Oh, yes, girl. I started boo-hooing and then I said, 'Yes, I'll marry you.' He grabbed my hand and put this on it." Teary reached inside her purse and pulled out a diamond cluster engagement ring.

Faith's eyes grew as big as marbles. "No, he did not." Faith gasped at the sight of the ring.

"Oh yes, he did," Teary countered. "Then he said, 'Teary, I'll make you happy, you'll see.'"

"Why don't you have it on your finger?"

"Because, I told you—I haven't told anyone, not even Prodigal. You're the first one who I've confided in."

"I can't believe you haven't told him." Faith looked over her shoulder, in Prodigal's direction.

"He's the main one that I don't want to tell. You of all people know how he is."

Faith felt a rush of satisfaction at hearing Teary say she and Skyler were going to get married. It removed some of Faith's insecurity when it came to Teary and Prodigal. Teary being married to Skyler would pave the way for her to have Prodigal completely. No more sharing him with Teary. She exhaled and continued to listen to Teary.

"Dang, Faith! I wish Prodigal and Skyler could get along."

"Me too, but I don't see that happening any time soon."

"Yeah, I know. Anyway, we've been looking for an apartment for a few weeks now. I think we're going to get a townhouse in the same complex where he and his roommate, Johnny, live."

"When are you going to tell your family?"

"Skyler said he thinks that the best thing would be for us to go ahead and get married before we tell them. I think he's right."

Faith sighed. "Teary, I don't know if that's the best thing to do."

The waitress came and refilled each of their glasses. "Are you ready to place your orders or do you want more time?"

Faith told her, "Yes, we're ready."

The girls ordered a couple of appetizers. They didn't want much to eat, since they all had other plans for later. They waited until the waitress turned and left to resume their conversation.

"Teary, you know your parents are going to be heartbroken if you don't tell them."

"You know for yourself if they find out that we want to get married, they're going to hit the ceiling. I don't want to hear the story about the two of us being unequally yoked. I don't want Daddy to start preaching about Skyler not being in church—So what if Skyler doesn't go to church?—He's still trying to make a difference in his life."

"Still, Teary, don't you think you should at least tell them before you get married?"

"No, I don't. Like I said, Skyler's had a really hard life, and I don't want to hear their mouths. I don't need the drama in my life. I love him just as much as you love Prodigal, and that's all that matters." Teary hoped that Faith would see her side of it. "I know you understand, don't you?"

"I know you love him. But I also think that the two of you should make sure that this is what you're ready to do. You're so young. Does he even have a steady job yet? I mean, one that can support the two of you? What about his education? Is he going to stay in college? What if you get pregnant? There's just a lot to think about, and I don't want to see you get hurt."

"I hear everything you're saying, but I can't worry about being scared. And I'm not too young to know that I love him. Everything has to work out for us. As for getting pregnant, I'm on the pill. But Skyler wants to have children right away, so I'm not worried about that either. I can't let him slip through my fingers. He needs me. He doesn't have any one in his life but me. I won't let him down."

"And you say you haven't mentioned any of this to Prodigal?"

Teary hesitated. "No, I haven't, and please, don't you breathe a word to him either. I'll tell him when the time is right."

"Whatever you say. But he's going to be crushed when he hears, and you know it. I hope we don't have to pull the two of them apart when you tell him."

"I hope not either. Anyway Prodigal has you, and he has his own life. I can't worry about him right now or what he thinks, Faith, I just can't."

"Suit yourself, but look, let me ask you this and then I'm through with it."

"Go ahead. Ask away."

"Have you prayed about this? You know that's what you're supposed to do. You, of all people, should know that neither of us can afford to walk into our future without seeking God, not after all we've been taught about him. I mean, we can't afford to abandon our faith, especially now."

"Look, I hear what you're saying, but I don't have to pray about it, Faith. I know Skyler is the one for me. If nobody else can see that, then so be it."

"Okay, whatever." Faith looked down at her Mickey Mouse watch.

The waitress brought the two overstuffed appetizer trays and sat them on a table beside them. While she unloaded their order, Faith thought of an excuse to get out of the conversation. She didn't want to tear her friend down, but she believed Teary was about to make a huge mistake.

"I better go and get Prodigal, so we can eat. It won't be long before it's time for us to go. But before I do, I just want you to know that I hope you and Skyler will be happy together."

"Too bad your future husband won't feel the same way."

"He just wants the best for you, that's all. You can't blame him for that, Teary. And you can't say too much about Prodigal anyway, because Skyler doesn't like him either, if I might remind you."

"I think they're jealous of one another. I was hoping tonight we could just hang out, enjoy each other, and maybe the two of them could begin to get along. But you see how that's turned out—your man's on one side of the restaurant, and Skyler's at the bar."

"Just give them time," Faith said. "Everything will work out."

Prodigal swallowed the last portion of hot wings. Without mouthing a word, he pounced up from the table like a kitten after a ball of yarn, almost knocking over the almost-empty glasses of soda. He politely took hold of Faith's elbow, and forced her to stand.

"Hey, can't I at least finish this last mozzarella cheese stick?" Faith asked.

Prodigal didn't answer her. Instead, he walked around to the other side of the table where Teary sat. "Look, we have to leave. I told Fantasia we wouldn't be gone long. You sure you don't want to come with us?"

"I'm sure. I already told you, Skyler and I are going to celebrate tonight, just the two of us. We're going to hang out here for a little while, and then go do a little something." Teary smiled coyly.

Skyler spoke up with an evil glint in his eye. "Anyway, man, my lady and I have a lot to celebrate tonight. We actually have three things, don't we, baby?" Skyler leaned over the table, propped his elbow on the edge, and started to outline Teary's lips with butterfly kisses.

Underneath the table she hit her knee against his for him to shut up, but he ignored her gesture.

"Tell me about it, man." Prodigal's jawbone flexed.

"Let's see . . . where do I start? First, my lady just graduated from high school."

"Yeah, keep on." Prodigal's voice conveyed his frustration with Skyler.

"Second, she just turned eighteen."

Prodigal stood rigid as a statue.

Faith didn't make as sound. She eyed Teary nervously.

You worthless punk, Prodigal thought to himself. "And the third?"

With a look of revenge plastered across his face and an uplifted eyebrow, Skyler stood up. "Yes, yes, yes, the third, the best out of the three—*da, dah*—may I present to you the soon-to-be Mrs. Skyler Jenkins. Right, baby?" He watched Prodigal's face turn from chocolate-brown to beet-red, adding insult to injury by kissing Teary passionately.

Faith was stunned. How could Skyler do something like this?

Prodigal lunged toward Skyler.

Faith managed to grab him before he landed a blow. "Prodigal, honey, don't do this. You should be glad for Teary. The two obviously love each other."

Teary stood up. "Prodigal, don't—Like Faith said, I love Skyler, and he loves me."

Prodigal couldn't believe what he'd just heard. *Married? How could she even think about doing such a stupid thing?* He gave Teary an ice-cold stare. *How could she do something like this without telling me? I'm sick of her messing her life up with one jerk after another.*

"Hey, I don't know what to say," Prodigal responded, his jaw flinching in anger even more than before.

"You can start by saying, 'Congratulations.' " Skyler stood up and planted another juicy kiss on Teary's open mouth.

Prodigal shrugged his shoulders and grabbed Faith's hand. "Congratulations. See yah, Teary."

"See yah, Prodigal. Bye, Faith," Teary said sadly.

Prodigal hurriedly left the restaurant.

Skyler and Teary watched as the couple exited the restaurant. Skyler smirked. He placed his arm around Teary. "Baby, don't look so down. You and I have the whole night to be together. Come on, sit back down."

Teary sat down quietly. She didn't want Prodigal to find out like this.

"Tell me something, sweetheart—would you rather be with them or with your man?" Skyler asked her in a pleading voice.

Teary looked into his searching eyes. "You know there's nobody in this world but you that I'd rather be with. It's just that I wasn't planning on Prodigal finding out about our marriage like this. I wanted to be the one to tell him. God, I wish the two of you could get along."

"Forget him. Let's have a toast—to sharing the rest of our lives together."

They sipped on their drinks while underneath the table Skyler rubbed his hands up and down her thighs.

"How about going to the club with me tonight? You'll be eighteen in about an hour and a half." Skyler chuckled. "So you can come and see where your fiancé performs."

"Okay," she answered hesitantly. "But I hope before we get married that you find something better to do than working at that club. How are we going to get our lives together and do the right thing if you keep working there? I know you make good money, but I still don't want my husband dancing half-naked in front of a bunch of wild, horny, desperate women—it just isn't right. What you're doing is not pleasing to God, Skyler, don't you agree?"

He evaded her probing question. "Don't worry, baby, I'll find something else. This is just for now, to help us get an apartment and some of the stuff we're going to need to start out. Come on, let's get out of here."

13

VIP

"Baby, this will be your special spot. Every time you come to see me perform, this is where I want your fine little butt parked, you hear me?" Skyler led Teary to a seat near the stage inside Club Ecstasy.

"Sure." She blushed.

Skyler pulled out the chair for her.

"Aren't you going to sit down?" Teary asked.

"No, baby. No sitting for me tonight."

"What are you getting ready to do?" Teary looked pleadingly up at him. It was her first time in a club, and a male strip club at that. She was nervous and apprehensive about Skyler leaving her alone.

He sensed her uneasiness. "I'm going in the back to get dressed. You don't have to worry about a thing. My act starts in about half an hour, and I need to freshen up. See you in a little bit, you sweet sexy woman of mine." He kissed her cheek and hurried to the back of the club.

Club Ecstasy was filled to capacity with women of all sizes, colors, and ages—overdressed, underdressed, well-dressed, and poorly dressed. Teary couldn't imagine where all the females came from. To her it seemed like this was something they were used to doing. The music was loud. Waiters strutted around decked out in colorful G-strings with matching bowties. They had triceps and biceps for days. Teary had never seen anything like it before in her life. The waiters piled the drinks on the females, nonstop. She saw many of the women who ordered drinks sliding money down the front of the waiters' G-strings.

A dark, well-built gentleman strode over to Teary's table. "May I get you a drink, pretty lady?"

She glanced up at him. Much to her amazement there stood Langston. "Langston. Langston Silverman?" She was shocked beyond belief. She hadn't run into Langston since he'd moved from the neighborhood, which was more than all right with her. *If fine was a crime, he sho' 'nuff would be doing time, with his no-good tail.* He looked like he'd been lifting weights. His body was perfectly chiseled and shining like he had just stepped out of a bath filled with body oil. His black G-string left very little to the imagination, not that Teary needed to be reminded of his assets.

"Hey, uh, didn't we go to school together?" he remarked sarcastically.

"You know doggone well we did more than go to school together, so don't even go there." *I can't believe this good-for-nothing punk is acting like he doesn't remember me.* She was furious, and she didn't want Skyler to find out anything about this.

"Yeah, right. What brings you down here?" he asked, a hopeful glint in his eye. "Looking for a little action? If you are, I'm sure I can arrange a little something for old times' sake."

"Don't flatter yourself, Langston. Anyway, if you must know, it's my birthday, so my man and I thought we'd do a little partying."

"Your man? And who might that be?"

"His name is Skyler," Teary remarked proudly.

"Skyler? Skyler Jenkins?"

She nodded. "You know him?" Her brow wrinkled, and a look of concern replaced her smile. "Yeah, you better believe I know that fool. He good people, you know. Well, I wish you two the best. See ya, wild girl." He winked, blew a kiss at her, and started to walk off. He paused. "Oh, and don't you worry your pretty little head about nothing, cause your secret's safe with me. I just hope you're as good to him as you were to me."

The smirk on his face made Teary sick to her stomach.

Winking again, he continued teasing her, "I'm sure since our time together you've gained a lot of experience in how to treat a man, haven't you? Glad I was the one who paved the way for you. See you around, lady."

"To hell with you, Langston." Teary wished she could crawl up in a hidden space out of sight from everybody and die. She felt humiliated and disgusted. Just when she made up in her mind to get up and leave, her eyes zeroed in on the dancer coming out in a red cape, which he used to shield his face and upper body. He wore a black Zorro mask that made it difficult to see his true features. Even though she couldn't make out his face and upper body, what she saw below was more than enough. His taut, shiny muscular legs gyrated in perfect rhythm to the beat of the song playing.

Women yelled, "The Sheik, the Sheik, the Sheik ain't no geek."

The Sheik gyrated and moved, his cape swerving around in the air.

The music was bumping, and Teary had begun to relax from the vodka and cranberry juice Langston had brought over to her. With her head spinning lightly, she swayed to the beat of the music.

The Sheik began to peel his cape away from his face.

She quickly sobered up, when she saw the man behind the cape was none other than Skyler. He looked so different. She had never seen him move the way he moved tonight.

He came closer to her table and began to gyrate his sexy, sinuous body all around her. He danced close to her face, taking one leg and placing it over the back of her chair. He bent forward, leaned in, and brushed his thick lips against hers.

The women went crazy. They were obviously quite jealous that she was getting all the attention.

Finally, Skyler danced around Teary and went on to the next table and did his oh-so-perfect gyrations, allowing the old wrinkled white woman to fill his pants with dead presidents. From table to table he danced, and more and more money was stuffed inside his red G-string.

Teary saw the women's reaction to her man. It was her turn to be jealous that Skyler was getting attention from all these females. She didn't know if she would be coming back to Club Ecstasy. What she did know was that Skyler would definitely have to find himself another career once they were married.

14

Standing on Your Own Two Feet

Prodigal couldn't believe that he was now a full-fledged high school graduate. He stared at himself in the mirror, carefully shaving the overnight stubble from his chin. *I can't believe I'm a grown man*, he thought. *It seemed like yesterday that I was a nappy-headed little boy running around playing hide-and-seek with Teary.* Immediately his thoughts turned to Teary's and Skyler's plans to marry. *Teary, why are you determined to screw up your life? I don't know what's up with you.*

Everything was going just like Prodigal had planned. He had been accepted for EMT school, which would put him just that much closer to fulfilling his dream to become a firefighter. He had already taken the pre-entrance physical examination along with the civil service exam. He was ecstatic that Fairley High had implemented a pre-graduate testing program in his sophomore year of high school. If a student had a C average or above, they were eligible to take a series of civil service exams for jobs throughout the city, which fell right in line with Prodigal's plans. He was also glad that Faith had decided to remain in Broknfield and attend the University, so they wouldn't be apart.

Suddenly, thoughts of his and Faith's future together took a back seat to thoughts of Teary again. *All these years I've loved that girl. But she couldn't love me in the same way, or could she? Didn't graduation day prove that we felt more than friendship for each other? The kiss we shared had to have stood for something. But I guess I need to move on from there. She loves that trick, Skyler. And what about her dreams of a writing career? Guess that's been thrown out with the bath water too. Why can't she see that if Skyler really loved her like he professed, then he would encourage her to pursue her dreams, not give them up? But I can't make her see that, and I certainly can't tell her how I really feel about her. I have to let go and concentrate on giving my all to living my own life.*

Prodigal hadn't fully accepted that he had to move on with his life, until the incident at the restaurant with Skyler. He was still reeling from the fact that she was going to marry that jerk. On top of that, she hadn't thought enough of their friendship to let him know. Hearing Skyler tell it made him want to pound the sucker. That night at Chili's, Prodigal was forced to accept that he would never have a chance to love Teary like he desperately wanted.

Several weeks after completing the EMT class, Prodigal received a call from the City Personnel office.

"Momma, I've been accepted at the Fire Academy," Prodigal said after he hung up the phone. He burst with uncontrollable joy when he heard the news.

"Prodigal, that's great," his mother said proudly. "I didn't doubt one moment that they would call. You're going to make a great firefighter, son." Ruth was elated that things were going well for her boy. There were times he missed his daddy so much that Ruth became worried about the direction he would take in life. Growing up without a father was hard enough for him, but to have a father who was such an important part of his children's lives suddenly disappear forever caused Ruth a great deal of worry about how their futures would turn out. So far, so good.

"What's the next step, baby?"

"The personnel director told me to come in next week for my

physical. I'm going to have to take some more tests too. If I pass my physical and the other tests, then they'll bring me on as an official city employee."

"Honey, I'm so proud of you." Tears gathered in Ruth's eyes.

"Thank you, Momma. I'm going to call Faith and tell her the news."

Ruth stopped him from dashing off upstairs. "Wait a minute before you do that, Prodigal. I wanted to ask about you and Faith."

"What about us?" Prodigal asked with a puzzled look on his face.

"I don't get a chance to talk to you as much as I'd like to, with my crazy work shift and all. I just want to know what's on your mind when it comes to Faith."

"Momma, I really care about her. I'm going to marry her one day—if she'll have me, that is." Prodigal grinned.

"Oh, she'll have you, baby, no doubt about that. That girl is crazy about you. You're such a good child, and Faith is such a sweet girl. I believe she'll make you a good wife too."

"And I'm going to be a good husband to her. She's going to start college in a couple of months. Hopefully by that time I'll be in full swing at the Fire Academy. I figure in about two years we'll be ready to walk down the aisle."

Ruth knew her son's heart really belonged to Teary. Always did. She couldn't understand why Teary couldn't see it or refused to see it. Ruth looked at it as a blessing from God when Faith came into Prodigal's life. Ruth hoped and prayed that Prodigal would learn to love Faith as much as he loved Teary.

"Good, I'm glad you have a plan," Ruth stated. "I wish Teary would think things through before she runs off and does something crazy with that boy Sky, or whatever his name is."

Prodigal had been so upset when Skyler told him about his plans to marry Teary that he confided in his mother. Other than Teary, his mother was the only other person he trusted. That was one of the things he loved about his mother—whenever he had a problem, he could always come to her and she would listen without being judgmental or critical.

"I wish she would too, Momma. But Teary is bullheaded. Sometimes she just won't listen. Who knows, maybe things will work out for her. I sure hope so, for her sake."

"I do too. But you and Faith are different, honey. You know what I told you—Love takes work and total commitment to each other. You can't run away every time you find yourself facing troubles or problems. You hear what I'm telling you, Prodigal?"

"I'm listening, Momma, and don't worry, things are going to work out for me and Faith. Just wait and see what I tell you." He winked. "You finished talking, Momma? I want to call Faith before she leaves for work."

" 'For work'? Where does Faith work?—I didn't even know she had a job."

"Yep, she started working at the Board of Education as an office assistant, right after we graduated."

"Good for her." Ruth smiled and nodded her head in approval.

"She's going to work there part-time and go to school. She said working at the Board will help her with her career as a teacher or guidance counselor."

"Whatever she decides to do, teach or counsel, she's going to make a good one."

"I agree. Well, gotta go. I'll talk to you later, Momma." Prodigal hurried up the stairs, climbing them two at a time.

Seconds later, Ruth heard Prodigal's bedroom door shut loudly behind him. She kicked off her furry blue slippers, swung her legs around, and plopped them on the den sofa. She grabbed the remote from the sofa table behind her and flipped until she found Soap Network.

Watching the actors and actresses flash across the screen pulled Ruth into her own private soap opera. The past years living without her soul mate had been tough. Not only did she suffer over Solumun's death, but the children suffered through their own private hell as well.

Ruth watched Prodigal grow from a scrawny little boy to the handsome, strong young man he was today. She prayed every day that he would be the kind of man that would make some woman proud to have him as a husband. She had hoped and prayed that someone would have been Teary. However, Teary had another agenda all of her own. Teary couldn't see the forest for the trees, Ruth believed. Ruth felt that Teary, in many ways, had taken Prodigal for granted. But Faith would make up for all that Prodigal had hoped to have with Teary.

Ruth was often worried about Fantasia and her lack of interest in the opposite sex. How could an ambitious, bright, beautiful young woman like Fantasia be so bitter about men and about God? If Solumun were still alive, Ruth believed that Fantasia's opinions and beliefs would've been totally different. Sometimes Ruth thought she understood the reason for Fantasia's self-imposed shell.

Other times, Ruth blamed God for allowing such pain to be inflicted upon her family. Then there was Hope. Hope was the most unscathed of all the Runsome children. Being but a toddler at the time, Hope had escaped much of the trauma Solumun's death had caused. Hope was content with her life, and for that Ruth was grateful.

Glancing at the screen again, Ruth meditated on life and its meaning. Into each person's life, including her children, there would be many roads to travel. Ruth understood that now. Some of those roads would lead to happy times, and some would take them down the path of pain and heartache. Her heart's desire was for her children to be spared from being hit by many of the sharp arrows of life. At the same time, she prayed that they would love and find love the way she and Solumun found each other.

The deep, familiar voice booming from the TV snapped Ruth

out of her daydream. She listened as Victor on *The Young and the Restless* told Nikki that he wanted out of their marriage for the third time.

Ruth sighed heavily. "Life is indeed a journey," she said out loud.

15

Secrets

Three months after graduating, and without her parents' knowledge, Teary and Skyler signed the lease on a two bedroom townhouse. She spent most of her free time getting things fixed up and ready for their upcoming marriage. She used babysitting money she'd saved and funds left over from her college Pell grant to pay the rent up for six months. They rented living room furniture, a pine veneer king-sized bedroom set, a dinette set, and a computer.

Skyler owned a stereo system, along with some other items he had accumulated while living out on his own. His steel blue Ford pickup was still in tip-top shape, thanks to his friend, Johnny, who was an excellent mechanic.

Teary and Debra sat on the floor of Debra's bedroom, flipping the remote back and forth from MTV to BET. "Debra, it won't be long before I'll be Mrs. Skyler Jenkins. We almost have everything we need for our apartment."

"You told your parents?"

"Nope. I told you that I'm going to tell them after everything is all over with."

Debra rubbed her forehead. "Are you sure that's a good idea? Something tells me that you need to just be up front."

"I can't be up front. I don't want to go through all the hoopla."

"Well, have you at least told Prodigal that you have an apartment?"

Teary popped her neck around, quickly focusing on Debra and ignoring the half-dressed rapper on the tube. "Are you crazy or what? What planet have you been on? You know doggone well he already flipped out that night in Chili's when Skyler told him about us getting married. I refuse to tell him anything else until it's done."

Debra released a long sigh. "I guess you know what you're doing. But I thought at least you would have told your boy. And I don't know why the two of you couldn't get together. The both of you got some real deep flavor for each other and you know it."

"Me and Prodigal? Girl, puhleeze . . . I do love him, but not like you're insinuating. I love him like a brother; that's the way it's always been." Teary refused to think about their shared kiss and the sensations it had stirred inside of her.

Debra flicked the channel to Comedy Central. "Suit yourself. All I can say is I'm here for you."

"Thanks, now let's get something to snack on. I'm starving."

Teary was at the townhouse unpacking toiletries, when Skyler walked in and grabbed her around the waist. He nibbled lightly on her neck. "Hey, baby, when are you going to tell your mom and dad that we're getting married? I don't understand what you're waiting for."

"You do know what I'm waiting for—I have to find the right time. You said so yourself."

Skyler turned her loose and moved around to face her. "Right time? Are you ashamed of me or what? You're a grown woman now. What's the big deal?"

"The big deal is that I want to handle this in the right way." Teary raised her voice. "And you know I'm not ashamed of you."

Skyler paced back and forth around their cramped kitchen. "I'm tired of sneaking around and having to be careful of what I say around them."

"I know it, baby. But when my sister got knocked up, everything became uneasy on the home front. My parents were really upset when they found that out. Ever since then, they've been uptight about me. Now you want me to spring this on them?—I don't think so." Teary brushed up against him and rubbed the back of her hand against his chiseled check.

"That's precisely why I think you should tell them—We're getting married, and you're not pregnant, so what's the big deal? You're going to college, so they can't say anything about that, so just tell 'em." Becoming irritated, Skyler pulled away from her.

"Let's just stick to the plan. When they leave to go visit Sara and my nephew, we'll get married. We'll tell them after they get back home."

He grabbed a set of pots and shoved them in the bottom cabinet. "Whatever, Teary."

Sara was thrilled when her mother called and told her they were coming to visit her and Andrew. They invited Teary to come along, but she managed to convince them that she had too much going on. Scheduled to start college in a couple of weeks, her parents didn't put up much of a fuss when she turned down their invitation.

Aunt Vashti had kept her word and helped Sara land a job at the University of Seattle in student affairs. Her job as a transcription records clerk enabled Sara to adequately support herself and little Andrew.

Anthony made sure child support payments were taken directly from his paycheck for his son, who he adored. He also sent Sara extra money for her and Andrew whenever he could. He never gave her any flack, when it came to their son. Whenever he could get time off from his job at FedEx, he'd take a jump seat flight to Seattle. His love for Sara was still strong, and he hoped one day she would finally agree to marry him.

Sara and Andrew lived in a two-bedroom bungalow in the back of her Aunt Vashti's house. It was small, cozy, and just the right size for Sara and her son.

Whenever Anthony came to visit he spent the weekend at a nearby hotel. Sara arranged her schedule to take Andrew to see him, not letting on that she wanted to see him just as bad. The three of them often went to the zoo, out to eat, or strolling in a nearby park.

Discussing the future of their relationship, marriage, or anything real serious was taboo for Sara. Whenever Anthony tried to approach the subject, Sara would shut down like a shell, so he feigned contentment with the way things were.

The three of them often lay in the hard, double bed at the hotel. Anthony and Sara would snuggle until little Andrew drifted off to sleep. Sara was careful this time. She took her birth control pills without fail and made sure Anthony used protection. On the weekends that he visited, she laid aside her Christian values and succumbed to her emotions and carnal desires. She knew she was doing wrong, but she found it impossible to say no to Anthony's touch.

This particular Saturday evening, after Anthony's departure, Sara sat in her bungalow and daydreamed about the wonderful time they had while he was there. She smiled as she recalled his gentle lovemaking. Then, unexpectedly, she felt convicted within her spirit for continuing to fornicate with him.

The following Sunday, when she went to church, she felt even worse listening to the preacher's message regarding temptation.

"We waltz around here, my people, talking about, 'The devil made me do it,'" the fiery preacher said. "But I'm here to tell you that if you're a child of the most high king, praise the Lord, then His word tells us that 'Greater is he that is in me than he that is in the world.' Hallelujah. Oh, I know the story you tell, talking about the flesh is weak. God tells us there is nothing too hard for Him. Praise the Lord. First Corinthians, chapter ten, verse thirteen states, 'No temptation has seized you except what is common to man.' And God is faithful. He will not let you be tempted beyond what you can bear. But when you are tempted, He will also provide a way out so that you can stand up under it."

Sara replayed the sermon over and over in her head, like a scratched record. *'A way out'? Lord, why can't I take you up on your word? Why do I allow my flesh to control me?*

No matter how bad she felt, whenever Anthony came to town, she'd follow the same routine. After kissing Anthony goodbye, she would climb into her Tercel and head back to her own private world, a world that included only her and little Andrew. Once she arrived at home, Sara would bathe Andrew, put him to bed, then get down on her knees and pray to God for His forgiveness, vowing never to fornicate again.

She faithfully attended church every Sunday, except when Anthony was in town. No one had any inkling of an idea that Andrew's father was a part of his life or Sara's, for that matter. They looked at Sara as a quiet, sweet, young girl who had been taken advantage of. They accepted her and little Andrew without judgment or condemnation. That was one of the things that had drawn her to this particular church. The members were genuinely loving and warm. If they only knew that in the midst of her serving the Lord she was fornicating, what would they think of her then? But she refused to focus on *what if*. All she knew was that Anthony was a part of her and Andrew's life. She was thankful that he was always there for the child they had conceived in love. She had even thought about inviting him to church when he came into town, and maybe she would one day.

Sara's parents would be arriving at the airport in a couple of hours. She carefully cleaned her bungalow, bathed and fed Andrew, then put him down for a short nap until it was time to pick them up. She took a steaming hot bath herself while he was napping.

Before she knew it, it was time to go and get her parents. She treaded through the ice and snow until she reached her Aunt Vashti's back porch.

"Aunt Vashti," Sara yelled through the back door, "you ready?"

"Yes, here I come." Aunt Vashti grabbed her navy cashmere overcoat and purse. "Let's go. Did you remember to put Andrew's car seat in my car?"

"Sure did."

They drove the eleven miles to the airport full of chatter. Aunt Vashti loved the fact that Sara and Andrew were part of her life. She, herself, had chosen to be on her own when she was a young girl about Sara's age. She'd opted out of the "married-with-children" thing and chose, instead, to invest her life in establishing a career for herself, and she had done just that. She'd graduated summa cum laude from the prestigious Xavier University with a master's degree in communications. She was one of the top-notch professors in the North, and her students adored her.

Aunt Vashti wished Sara would allow her to do more for her and Andrew. She didn't want to see them struggle for anything in life, not when she was able to help. She made a mental note to herself to check on getting Sara and little Andrew a larger place. It wasn't that she didn't enjoy having them live in the guest-house of her spacious home and grounds, she simply wanted more for her niece. She wanted the same for Teary as well. She wanted to see them prosper and succeed in life. If there was any way she could help them achieve success, she was willing to do it.

They arrived at the airport and didn't have to wait at all. As soon as they drove up to the passenger unloading area, they saw Mr. and Mrs. Fullalove standing there.

"Mom, Dad," Sara screamed while hanging out the passenger side window of Aunt Vashti's black on black Deville. Aunt Vashti expertly maneuvered the luxury car close to the curb, popped the trunk button, and then jumped out of the car to greet her brother and sister-in-law.

"Andrew, you're so handsome and precious." Sara's mom peeked inside the spacious Cadillac. "Grandma is glad to see her baby."

Andrew turned away shyly.

The week was chock full of excitement as Sara's parents exercised the role of loving grandparents. Shy at first, it didn't take Andrew long before he started soaking in every bit of the extra love and affection. Sara was pleased that her parents had finally come to accept what they had once called "her awful mistake." She realized she had hurt them deeply when she became pregnant out of wedlock. They had raised her and Teary up in the church so they'd know right from wrong; just so this kind of incident wouldn't happen.

But having Andrew made Sara and her parents realize that people often make mistakes and life's journey can be tough at times. In every person's life, there are lessons to be learned. Sara had come to understand herself that sometimes the very things in life her parents wanted to protect her from had to be experienced nonetheless. She'd made some unwise choices in life, but they had been her choices. She would have to face God for herself. Sara understood that.

As for Brian and Cynthia Fullalove, they adored their grandson. The joy little Andrew brought into their lives far outweighed their daughter's sinful act. Andrew had closed the gap between Sara and her parents. Through him, they had learned how to forgive.

Two days after her parents left for Seattle, Teary and Skyler arose early. Teary was especially excited because today was her wedding day. Now that her parents were away, things could go as planned. She gazed outside at the rain pounding fiercely against the windowpane. The sun was hidden from view, and dark clouds hung heavy and low.

"Dang, why did it have to rain, Skyler?" Teary asked.

"Don't worry, sweetheart. It's not raining in my heart." Skyler yawned.

"I wanted it to be lovely outside for my wedding day, though," Teary complained, her voice filled with dread. She wanted things to be perfect.

They were going to be married at the downtown courthouse, but she still wanted everything just right, including her wedding attire. Teary instructed Skyler to go to the other bathroom to get ready since she needed time to pamper herself.

Teary and Debra had stalked the mall day after day for weeks, until Teary finally settled on a two-piece cream-and-gold linen outfit. She found the perfect gold pumps to set it off.

Teary took her time preparing herself for her special day. After bathing, she rubbed scented lotion all over her body. The fragrance of Ellen Tracy cologne filled the bathroom. Her beautifully shaped legs and picture-perfect body made her look striking. She was careful to pull her thick braids up in a seductive French braid that flowed down the middle of her spine. She put a dab of powder on her face, to remove any signs of shine, and a tint of caramel lipstick.

Skyler almost drooled, when he saw her in the living room waiting on him to finish getting dressed. "Don't you look like an expensive piece of art." He leaned over to kiss her, but she stepped back.

"Don't, baby. You'll mess up my make-up." She smiled. "We'll have plenty of time for kisses, once we say, 'I do.'"

They climbed in the truck and drove along Commercial Street. Teary had coordinated her and Skyler's outfits perfectly. Skyler's cream-colored silk leisure suit graced his body in just the right way.

He pulled inside the courthouse garage and climbed out of the truck. As he made his way over to Teary's side, she inhaled at the sight of his handsome frame. His trousers were slightly baggy and swayed gently against the wind, showing off the muscular imprint of his calves. His cream kid leather loafers really made him stand out.

Dang! He has to be the finest man ever to walk the planet, and the best catch. I must be the luckiest girl alive. And even though the rain was coming down hard in Broknfield, there was nothing but sunshine and blue skies beaming in her heart.

Johnny and Debra met them at the courthouse. They came along as witnesses.

Teary really wanted Prodigal to be standing by her side, giving her his blessing. *But what the heck, he'll change his mind about Skyler once he sees how happy we are,* she thought. They weren't kids anymore, and as far as she was concerned, Prodigal had no right to begrudge her for wanting to be happy. They both had their lives to live. His included Faith, and hers was with Skyler. It wasn't often that she found herself upset with Prodigal, but this time he was dead wrong.

Debra leaned over and gave Teary a soft elbow nudge in the ribs. "Come on, snap out of your daydream. They just called your name."

Embracing each other, Skyler and Teary followed the court clerk into the judge's chambers. Johnny and Debra followed.

When the four of them walked in, the short, fat, out-of-breath judge mumbled a quick hello to the couple, without acknowledging Johnny or Debra. He told them he had only fifteen minutes before he had to be back in court. Teary didn't like his curtness, but she tried to put it out of her mind. She just wanted to become Mrs. Skyler Jenkins.

The judge didn't waste any time. He ordered Skyler and Teary to stand in front of his desk. He told Johnny to stand at the side of Skyler, and Debra was to take her place next to Teary.

"Do you, Teary Fullalove, take this man, Skyler Jenkins, to be your husband, through sickness and health, richer or poorer, 'til death do you part?"

Teary was hesitant in answering. Not because she was unsure of what she was doing, but because she always thought there was more to marriage vows. She always thought it was much longer and more involved. *Guess I'm wrong,* she thought. *What do I know anyway? I'm no judge or minister.* She proudly answered, "I do."

"And do you, Skyler, Skyler uh—" The judge looked down at the piece of paper he had on his desk—"Jenkins, take this woman, uh, Teary Fullalove, to be your lawfully wedded wife through sickness and health, richer or poorer, and 'til death do you part?" The judge glanced at his watch.

"I do," Skyler responded without any hesitation whatsoever.

"Then, by the power vested in me, you are now husband and wife. God bless your marriage and your new life together as husband and wife. You may kiss your bride."

Skyler looked down on his bride and kissed her passionately. Debra and Johnny embraced the newly married couple and extended their congratulations to them.

The judge, however, cut their celebration short when he said, "Follow me please, and hurry. I have to get back to court." He quickly led them back out into the hallway and gave them directions to the Marriage Records office.

Teary was floating. She was now Mrs. Skyler Jenkins. She couldn't wait to have some babies for her husband. She was going to be the perfect wife, the perfect mother, the perfect everything. Her parents would be angry when they came back from Seattle and found the two of them married, but she couldn't worry about that right now.

Images of Prodigal and her parents filtered through her mind. *He has Faith, and what's done is done. I've got to think about me for a change—Everybody will just have to understand that; plus they'll eventually get over it. And if they don't, then too bad . . . 'cause if they want me to be part of their lives, they'll have to accept the fact that I'm a married woman. Shucks! If they can forgive Sara, they can surely forgive me. At least what I've done is legal and not a sin and abomination. All I've done is marry the man I love.*

Teary never fully understood why it was Sara who got pregnant and not her. Of course, she wasn't complaining about it, but she just didn't understand it. She'd been on the pill for less than a year; now all of that was about to change. It had been six weeks since she'd swallowed a birth control pill. She wanted them out of her system so that as soon as she and Skyler were married, they could start working on having a family. It was time to give her husband a family of his own; a family that would never go anywhere, never leave him.

This time you're going to have a family that will be together forever and always. She released a smile as the very thought gave her soothing goose bumps.

That evening, at their apartment, they started their lives together as husband and wife. Skyler sat on the bed in anticipation. "Come on out of that bathroom, woman." Skyler's voice was gentle. This was their wedding night, their honeymoon. He had no idea how his wife would accept him. He had waited for this day, this moment, this very hour for such a long time. Now his dream was a reality. He had a chance to have a whole new life with a girl who loved him and who would give him plenty of children.

Teary was on the other side of the door shielding her body from her husband. During their courtship they had never gone completely all the way, though things had gotten pretty close to it. But tonight was going to be different. She felt like a virgin all over again. She didn't know if she would be able to please Skyler or not. It wasn't like she'd been promiscuous. She'd made a horrible mistake by giving her virginity to Langston, but that was a long time ago. Since then, she'd never been sexually active with anyone else.

Before she married Skyler, she resolved within herself to tell him that she was not a virgin. At first it was hard for her to face him, but she was glad she'd found the courage to confide in him about Langston. There was only one tiny detail that she purposely left out—She didn't tell him Langston's name. That part, Teary felt, was of no use. It was hard enough for her to admit to him that she was not exactly a virgin. Surprisingly, when she told Skyler the truth, he didn't act bothered by it at all. He said that he would have been surprised if she had been a virgin because girls were taking their virginity so lightly these days. He assured her that he loved her. She assured him that it happened one time, and one time only.

Nervously, Teary sat on the edge of the cold white toilet seat. She had purposely spent over an hour bathing and perfuming herself. Her thigh-length white silk gown showed her silky smooth thighs and majorette legs.

"Teary," he called out again, "are you okay in there?"

"Yes, I'm fine. I'll be out in just a minute." She took in one final breath, released it slowly, and then proceeded to turn the brass door handle.

Skyler stood up when he heard the door handle turning. He eagerly awaited his bride's entrance. When he saw the door slowly opening, he found himself becoming physically aroused. Skyler was instantly held captive by her exceptional beauty, as she made her way over to him. She felt her skin become flushed at the sight of her half-naked husband. Her body ached.

As she came close enough for him to touch her, his smooth, masculine hands gathered her close to him. The warmth of his chest made her private place tingle with desire.

Skyler moved his hands carefully, slowly up and down the length of her shoulders. The soft, silky feel of her gown rubbed gently back and forth against his body, bringing him to full excitement and exhilaration. The smell of her hair and the scent of her femininity drove him wild. His lips found hers, and his tongue parted her moist lips. He moved his hands carefully and ever so gently over her back and down to her buttocks before pulling her down on the bed beside him.

The anticipation they each had quickly gave way to full passion and unbridled desire, as they celebrated the beginning of their lives together.

Part Two

Twists and Turns

When I was a child, I talked like a child, I thought like a child, I reasoned like a child. When I became a man, I put childish ways behind me.
—1 Corinthians 13:11

16

The Future Is Now

Faith and Prodigal followed their plans for their future together almost to the letter. Faith obtained her college degree. She worked as an elementary teacher at All Believers Academy. Prodigal joined the Broknfield Fire Department. Now they were about to embark on the next phase of their future—holy matrimony.

"We are gathered here today to celebrate one of life's greatest moments," Pastor Grace announced, "to give recognition to the worth and beauty of love and to add our blessings to the words which shall unite Prodigal Runsome and Faith Meadows in marriage. Should there be anyone who has cause why this couple should not be united in marriage, they must speak now or forever hold their peace."

Teary stood nervously next to the other four bridesmaids. *The two of them look so happy. Faith is going to make him a good wife. Look at Prodigal—he really loves her. Too bad my marriage is a lie.* Teary scanned the guests that filled the church. Her eyes told her what her heart already knew—Skyler wasn't going to show up.

Her private thoughts were overpowered by Pastor Grace's loud boisterous voice.

"In Ephesians, the relationship between husband and wife is compared to the relationship between Christ and the church. Submit yourselves one to another as to the fear of God. Wives, show reverence for your own husbands, as unto the Lord. Husbands, love your wives, even as Christ also loved the church, and gave himself for it. He that loves his wife loves himself."

Several of the guests could be seen wiping away tears from their eyes.

"As the two of you enter a life together, remember these words from an old Apache proverb: Now you will feel no rain, for each will be shelter for the other. Now you will feel no cold, for each will be warmth for the other. Now there is no more loneliness. Now you are two persons, but there is only one life before you. Go now to your dwelling place to enter the days of your life together, and may your days be good and long upon this earth."

Pastor Grace made the sign of the cross over the heads of the bride and groom. "I now present to you Mr. and Mrs. Prodigal Runsome. Prodigal, you may salute your bride."

Prodigal kissed Faith passionately then stared lovingly into the eyes of his new bride. Thoughts of his father surfaced in his mind. *Daddy, look at this beautiful creature standing before me. How I wish you were here to celebrate with me. If you can see me and hear me from up there, then know this—I will cherish this girl until the day I die.*

The reception was just as grand as the wedding. Faith's parents had really gone all out for their daughter, and it showed in every facet of the wedding.

The DJ announced to the guests that it was time for the newlyweds to have their first dance together. Prodigal and Faith danced to one of their favorite songs, "Always and Forever." While Luther crooned in his one-of-a-kind voice, Prodigal held his bride close to him and thought about how blessed he was to have her as his wife.

Soon it was time for the newlyweds to leave for their honeymoon. As they prepared to leave, Prodigal turned from his new bride and looked anxiously through the crowd of people.

Faith didn't need anyone to tell her who Prodigal was searching for. She tried to hold back her anger. It was her wedding day, and she wasn't going to allow herself to become upset. She had him now. He was her husband. There was no way Teary could compete with that. The envy and jealousy she kept secretly tucked in her heart was still present, even on this her wedding day. What was so special about Teary? Why couldn't she stay out of their life for once?

"Wait here, baby. I promise, I'll be right back."

Prodigal pushed through the crowd of wedding guests until he saw her. Their eyes interlocked as he got closer to her. "Hey, you," Prodigal called out.

"Hey."

"You know I couldn't leave without telling you goodbye. You look beautiful in your bridesmaid dress."

"Thank you. You look pretty spiffy yourself."

"Well, look, I just wanted to tell you goodbye. I'll see you in a few days."

"Sure."

Prodigal looked around. "Where's—"

"Don't even go there—I don't know where Skyler is, and right now I don't care."

He leaned down and kissed her on the cheek and lovingly pushed the loose curl from her face.

Faith stood near the entrance of the church watching her husband, afraid to think what her heart tried to force her to admit.

Nervousness saturated Prodigal's mind on their way to Los Angeles. He wasn't worried about flying, although it was the first time the newlyweds had traveled by air. He was uneasy about spending his first night alone with Faith. *Man, what's going to hap-*

pen? Will I be able to perform the way a man is supposed to? I don't want to be a disappointment to her.

Faith sat quietly next to her husband. She refused to think about the scene she had witnessed at the reception earlier. Teary would not invade her thoughts tonight. She wanted to be with her husband and start her new life as Mrs. Runsome.

The bright lights of downtown Los Angeles ushered them closer to their destination.

I hope I can satisfy him, Faith thought. *Oh Lord, let me please my husband. I don't have a perfect figure like Teary. But, then again, I'm not her; I'm me. I just hope he sees that when he looks at me tonight. Maybe once we make love, he'll forget all about her. God, I sure hope so.*

"Please, fasten your seatbelts. We will be landing in the city of Los Angeles in fifteen minutes," the flight attendant announced.

"I think I can get used to this flying thing." Prodigal smiled as he held his wife's hand. "What about you, sweetheart?"

"As long as I'm with you, I can get used to anything." She lay her head on his arm as they walked through the busy airport terminal.

They retrieved their luggage from baggage claim and hailed a taxi to take them to their four-star hotel.

The driver pulled up to the front of the prestigious Biltmore Hotel, made his way to the passenger's side, and quickly opened the door for the newlyweds.

After checking into the hotel, they made their way to their fourth-floor honeymoon suite.

"Mrs. Prodigal Runsome, yeah, I like the sound of that, baby." Prodigal couldn't contain his happiness, married to a wonderful woman who loved him, and only him. "Come jump in these arms."

"Boy, you're so silly."

He lifted her into his strong arms and carried her over the threshold into room 436.

Faith marveled at the beauty and intricate detail of the suite.

"Wow! Look at this room. It's absolutely gorgeous." Her eyes lit up at the red and pink rose petals that lined the carpeted floor of the dimly lit room.

Prodigal put his new bride down and embraced her.

"Oh, Prodigal it's exquisite, absolutely luxurious. I feel like we're millionaires."

In the background Faith heard the voice of Michael Bolton singing, "You came to me like the dawn through the night."

"Prodigal, how did you pull this off without me knowing?" Her eyes perused the room. "You have Michael jamming, rose petals, candles, champagne, everything. Oh, baby, this is the happiest moment in my life." She couldn't hold back her tears.

"Come on over here, sweetheart. Stop crying." He reached over and pulled a tissue from an unusual-looking box setting on the table. Prodigal wiped her tears. "This is only the beginning of the happiness that's to come for both of us, Faith. I promise you that."

Prodigal gathered Faith in his arms. "Dance with me, Mrs. Runsome. This is our night. The beginning of our life together."

She laid her head against his chest.

The melody captured them as they slow danced. Prodigal kissed her hair. Inhaling the aroma of the rose petals and the sweet perfume enveloping his wife, he felt himself becoming aroused, but he wanted to take his time. This night was meant to last forever. He eased back from Faith, tilting her chin upward toward him. "I tell you what—let's get comfortable. We can have a glass of champagne."

"Okay, but I'd like to freshen up some first."

"Okay, come on."

He led her into the adjacent bedroom. More rose petals were strewn over the round king-sized bed. Lit, fragranced candles filled the room, transmitting a heavenly scent.

"Prodigal, did you plan all of this yourself? I'm shocked at how perfect everything is."

"Well, I can't lie. I had a little help. You like it?"

" *'Like it?'* I love it. Baby, I had no idea you were this romantic."

"You have a lot to learn about your husband, Mrs. Runsome." He kissed her again before opening the closet to retrieve their suitcases.

"You've thought of everything, haven't you?"

"I hope so, sweetheart."

Faith picked up a piece of her luggage and disappeared into the lavishly decorated bathroom. "I'll be back in just a few minutes."

After closing the door, Prodigal heard her. "Oh my God! Prodigal, you've really outdone yourself." She noticed the rose petals in the whirlpool tub and that candles were lit throughout the bathroom too.

"Baby, relax. Take as long as you need. We have the rest of our lives to spend together."

He listened to the next song on the track while he undressed. He put on his white silk robe. He zeroed in around the room to make sure the hotel had done everything he requested—*Candles, champagne, music. Okay, everything's just like I planned.*

Twenty minutes later, he heard the door as it slowly opened. He turned around, looked over his shoulder, and beheld the most striking sight he'd ever seen in his life.

Faith shyly entered the bedroom. The sheer white charmeuse gown clung to her body like it was part of her smooth, baby-soft skin. The cutout lace trim was adorned with tiny sequins and pearls cascading elegantly down the length of her body as it gracefully kissed the floor. He had never witnessed such beauty. He gasped, and his manhood took on a life of its own.

Hoarsely he finally spoke. "You are the most beautiful creature in the world." He rose from the side of the bed and extended his hand toward her.

She took hold of it, his hot breath against her neck igniting passion that covered her like a blanket.

"Here, have a glass of champagne." Prodigal planted the gold-trimmed flute in her trembling hand.

"Here's to us, sweetheart," he toasted. "May this night be the beginning of a perfect love. May I grow old beside you, may the love we share never die."

Their glasses met, and they slowly sipped on the champagne.

Seconds later, he removed the crystal flute from her hand and carefully placed it on the nightstand next to the bed. Leaning down toward her, Prodigal planted kisses along the side of his bride's neck. His tongue lightly flickered back and forth as he made himself familiar with the sweet taste of her body. His hands familiarized themselves with every inch of her.

In return, Faith kissed him hard.

He moved in closer to her, felt the soft silkiness of her gown and groaned loudly. He moved back closer to the bed, holding on to his bride. Leaning back, he pulled her down on top of him as he rested on the bed of rose petals.

The next track of Michael Bolton started, "Can I Touch You . . . There?"

Hungrily, he kissed her, caressed her, and explored every inch of her body. Lifting her gown for the first time, he witnessed the beauty of a woman's body—his woman. He stared in total awe of what lay beneath him.

"Faith," he groaned. "Oh, baby, you're beautiful."

If she wanted to respond, she couldn't.

His mouth covered hers. He moved his tongue along the length of her body, pausing only long enough to take in more of the view beneath him before their virgin bodies consumed each other in love.

17

Trouble in Paradise

"Skyler, where have you been?" Teary asked him, her voice revealing her disappointment. "You didn't show up at Prodigal's wedding like you promised. And you just got home; now you're going back out."

"Don't give me the third degree, Teary. I'm not having it tonight. Dude is your friend, not mine, so leave me alone. I'm going out, and that's that." He grabbed a beer out of the fridge and dashed toward the door before Teary could say another word.

The sound of Skyler slamming the door behind him made her jump. She fought back the tears that formed in the corners of her eyes. *Marriage wasn't supposed to be like this.*

Things between them were going from bad to worse with each passing day. In the beginning, everything was beautiful between her and Skyler. She smiled at the thought of how much time they used to spend making love that first year of their marriage. Now, Skyler barely even touched her.

She picked up the phone and called Debra, but there was no answer. *She probably went somewhere else after the reception.*

Next, she decided to call Sara. It had been a while since they last talked. Sara didn't answer either. Teary exhaled a heavy sigh of frustration before she fell back on the living room sofa.

The phone rang, and she quickly answered it. "Hello."

"Hi, honey."

"Oh, hi, Mom," she responded in a nonchalant voice.

"Well, don't sound too excited, dear."

"I'm sorry. I didn't mean to sound like that Momma. It's just one of those days, that's all."

"I just wanted to tell you how pretty you looked today."

"Thanks, Momma."

"What's wrong, baby? You want to talk about it?"

"I don't think so—You'll only say I told you so."

"Honey, please don't do this. Listen, I know you and Skyler have been dealing with some things."

Teary stood up, surprised to hear that her mother knew about her marriage problems. "How did you know, Momma?"

"Mothers just know these things. You haven't been happy in a long time. I know you want a child, honey." It was the first time her mother had addressed the fact that Teary hadn't conceived a child after being married for five and a half years.

Teary started to cry. "Momma, I want a baby so badly. What's wrong with me? Why haven't I gotten pregnant?"

"Sweetheart, you have to remember that everything is in God's hands. His timing is not always our timing."

"Momma, my marriage is falling apart. I can't give my husband the one thing he wants most and you're telling me it's not my time?" Teary screamed into the receiver. "Then tell me, Momma—when is my time then?"

"Calm down, baby."

"No, I won't calm down. You don't get it, do you, Mother?" she continued to yell. "My husband is staying away from home more and more. We argue and fight constantly, and it's always about the same thing—children." Teary's tears flooded down the side of her face, and teardrops leaked into the receiver.

"Oh, honey, I know it's hard. But please, don't give up. Have the two of you seen a doctor? Maybe one of those fertility specialists can help you."

"Skyler had himself checked out already. He's fine. As for me, at my last doctor's appointment the gynecologist gave me a clean bill of health. I don't know what else to do."

"First of all, as long as you're stressed out and worried about getting pregnant, you're probably not going to get pregnant. You have to calm down and try to relax."

"I hear you, Momma. Look, I have to hang up now. I have a couple of stories I need to finish for work tomorrow. Thanks for listening, Momma. Bye."

"Bye, honey. I'll check on you later."

"Bye, Mom." Teary hung up the phone, placed both hands over her face, and cried like the baby she desperately wanted to have but couldn't.

When she couldn't cry any longer, she trudged into their bedroom and pulled out a stack of papers she'd brought home from her job as assistant copy editor at *The Broknfield Gazette*. She was offered the position after working there as an intern during her senior year of college. In addition to a competitive salary, the demands of the job provided her with a fraction of relief from the tumultuous relationship she was having with Skyler. Flipping through the articles, she began to read each one, carefully looking for and notating any changes needed in style, tone, grammar, and punctuation. Tomorrow she would return the articles to the editor for final proofing.

Skyler sat in Club Ecstasy, nursing one beer after another.

"Anything I can get for you?" the sultry-looking woman asked as she eased up beside him.

Skyler's eyes grew large when he saw the less-than-tastefully-dressed woman leaning over in front of him, revealing her deep cleavage. "You new around here?"

"Yeah, I am. You?"

"Nope. Been coming around here for a long time."

"Tell me something—Why is a fine, sexy-looking brother like

you sitting here all alone? Someone must not be doing their job at home."

"Maybe I'm looking for that someone."

"Well, well, well . . . this might be your lucky day."

He took another swallow of beer. "Why is that?"

"Because you just may have found her." She rolled her tongue over her puckered lips.

"What's your name, sexy lady?"

"Geena."

"Geena, I'm Skyler. Why don't you sit here and keep me company for a while?"

"Certainly. It'll be my pleasure, Skyler."

18

The Harvest Is Plentiful

When a fellow minister informed Pastor Grace that he had an opening for a director of a church school in Bonsai Bay, Colorado, Pastor Grace felt the Holy Spirit speaking to him as he immediately thought of Faith Runsome. If she accepted the position, it would mean losing two of his favorite church members. Nevertheless, Pastor Grace believed that God had sent his minister friend to him for a reason. That reason was because Faith Runsome was being called to service somewhere else.

Three months later, Prodigal and Faith said goodbye to life in Broknfield.

Bonsai Bay, Colorado was more beautiful than Prodigal and Faith could ever have imagined. Much like Broknfield, there were spectacular mountain views with evergreen trees lining the immaculately kept lawns and neighborhoods. They were even more splendid during the winter when snow-covered trees nestled below an azure blue sky.

When Faith walked into her new office for the first time she felt, without a doubt, that this turn of events leading to their move to Bonsai Bay was truly a momentous gift orchestrated by God. Everything had fallen into its rightful place, without the tiniest problem.

When she first told Prodigal about the job offer and where it was, initially, he had secret reservations about making the move. He didn't want to leave Teary behind. Her marriage was on shaky ground, and he hated to leave her when things were going so badly for her. Each time he spoke to her she pretended things were marvelous, but Debra had told him that Teary suspected Skyler was cheating on her. But Prodigal had to think about his own wife and making sure she was happy. So when Faith approached him about a job as director of a new church school in Colorado he said, "We better start packing, don't you think, sweetheart?"

Prodigal sprung into action. He wanted Faith to know that he would support her in whatever dreams she wanted to fulfill in her life. As a firefighter, he didn't feel that he would have a problem getting on with a fire department in another state. He put in for a transfer and within weeks was offered a new station assignment in Bonsai Bay, Colorado.

Faith was excited about the chance to start her marriage in a new place. She didn't want to be selfish, but she was even more excited to know that Prodigal and Teary would be hundreds of miles apart.

Prodigal and Faith purchased their dream home—a single-level, 2,600-square-foot, four-bedroom house set close to the picturesque sandy beaches of Bonsai Bay. The dry climate and low humidity levels moderated temperatures throughout the year, and there was plenty of sunshine. The often cold, snowy Colorado winter was a slight adjustment for the two of them, but they didn't regret leaving Broknfield.

In addition to her job as director of Unity Church Academy, Faith willingly took on the job of teaching a group of seven- to ten-year-old mentally challenged students as well. She adored the kids, and they returned her adoration eagerly. She was full of energy and vibrancy, her love of God having grown tremendously over the years.

Everything about their life was good. They were active members in their new church, and Faith extended her gift of teaching even farther by teaching the three- and four-year-olds during Sunday school. Active in church again, Prodigal soon became one of the trustees at Unity Church. They had a solid marriage and an undying love for each other.

The relationship he and Faith shared often reminded Prodigal of the loving relationship his mother and father shared all those years. Each time he laid eyes on Faith, his heart flooded with desire. She was still just as beautiful as the first day he bumped into her. No man could ask for more.

19

Time to Be

Prodigal and Faith were ecstatic when Dr. Sampson confirmed that she was pregnant. When an ultrasound further revealed that they were having twins, both of their mouths dropped.

When they arrived home, Prodigal went straight into the study and dialed Teary's number. She would have to be the first to hear the exciting news.

"Hello, Teary Jenkins."

"Hey there," Prodigal said, trying to contain his excitement. "Are you busy? I know you're at work, but I wanted to call anyway."

"No, I can talk. It's good to hear from you. What's going on in Bonsai Bay? You still loving it?"

"Yep, sure do. Things couldn't be better. What about you? How are things going?"

She hesitated before answering. She was not about to confide in Prodigal this time. She couldn't let him know that her marriage was on the verge of breaking down. Instead, she continued her act. "Everything is great. Just keeping busy, that's all."

"I've got some exciting news for you."

"What? Tell me."

"Faith is pregnant."

"Prodigal, you've got to be kidding me. That's great."

On the one hand Teary was thrilled that Prodigal and Faith were going to be parents; on the other hand a feeling of disappointment surfaced in her mind at the thought that she still hadn't been able to get pregnant with Skyler's child.

"I know you two are ecstatic. I can't wait until the baby is here."

"I can't either. But there's one small correction I have to make."

" 'Correction'?—What are you talking about, Prodigal?"

"We're having twins!"

"Oh, my God!—twins—are you sure?"

"Yep, we went to the doctor earlier today. An ultrasound confirmed that Faith is carrying two babies."

"I don't know what to say, Prodigal. I'm in shock."

"You better come on and catch up with us. I thought you and Skyler would have had a little bundle of joy yourself by now."

"We're trying, and hopefully pretty soon I'll be calling you with some good news of my own."

"Well, listen, I know you're at work, so I'm going to let you go. I have to call the rest of the family, but you know you had to be the first to know."

"Yeah, you know it. Love you, and tell Faith I said congratulations too. Bye."

"Love you too. We'll talk later. Bye, Teary."

Teary stood at her desk in silence, phone still in hand. The dial tone sounded, and the tears flowed like a river.

Faith stood in the hallway. She had heard the conversation. This time she couldn't hold back her feelings. "Why is it that everything that goes on in this household you have to run and call Teary and tell her about it?"

Shocked, Prodigal looked over his shoulder in the direction of Faith's voice. "What did you just say?"

"You heard me—I don't stutter."

"What do you mean? You know that Teary is my best friend. What's wrong with you?"

"What's wrong with me is that I'm sick of competing against Teary. I thought when we moved to Bonsai Bay that things would be different, that we would have a chance to live our own lives without her being in the middle of our marriage."

"First of all, why were you even eavesdropping on my conversation?"

"Don't you even go there," she screamed. "Don't try to turn this around and put the blame on me."

His brow wrinkled, and he tried to maintain his composure. "Look, you're pregnant, and I know you're going to have mood swings. Why don't you just lie down for a minute and rest? You're not thinking rationally."

"Oh, quite the contrary, I am thinking quite rationally. I've wanted to say this for a long time. I won't have it any more, Prodigal. You will not tell that woman anything else about us. She has her own husband, so leave her alone." Faith abruptly turned around and walked out of the study.

Prodigal followed but went in the direction of the garage. Grabbing his keys from the key holster, he stormed out of the house. He needed to get a breath of fresh air before things got any worse. He thought about everything Faith had said. *How could she be jealous of me and Teary's friendship? She's never acted like this before. It has to be because she's pregnant and her hormones are running haywire.*

He went to the fire station and played a couple of games of basketball with some of his co-workers. Maybe by the time he returned home Faith would calm down.

Pulling his SUV into the garage, he noticed that the outside porch lights had not come on. Opening the door leading from the garage to the foyer, he flipped on the light switch. "Faith," he called out her name while he walked through the huge house. As he made his way to the master bedroom, he heard water running.

He opened the bathroom door and stood there for a few seconds, staring at the silhouette in the shower. He noticed the small mound of her stomach, and a smile broadened his face.

He tapped lightly on the shower door. "Hey, baby, are you still angry with me?"

She peeked out and stared at him without responding to his question.

He undressed without saying another word to her. He climbed into the shower and positioned himself behind her, allowing the warmth of her body and the water to caress him. He nibbled on the side of her neck and flickered his tongue back and forth around the small of her back.

She shivered from his touch and gave in to his demands.

"I love you, girl. Please don't be mad at me," he said in a low whisper, moving back and forth against her wet, soapy body.

"I love you too, Prodigal. I love you so much." She moaned as he made love to her.

"Forgiven?"

"Yeah, forgiven."

20

Joy and Pain

Faith stood sideways in front of the oval mirror and surveyed her huge, round stomach. The stretch marks coursing up and down her brown belly were barely noticeable. The twins weren't due for another two months, but because of the increased risk of complications associated with a multiple birth, Dr. Sampson placed Faith on bed rest after twenty-four weeks, telling the happy couple that everything looked fine.

Faith lay in the bed feeling exceptionally down about being away from the kids at the Academy. Prodigal, understanding how much she missed being away from Unity Academy and the students there, decided he would do something to lift her spirits. He contacted the assistant director of the Academy and arranged for some of the students to visit Faith.

When the nine girls and boys walked into the house, Faith's whole face beamed. They brought her pictures they had drawn and bracelets they had made just for her. The children sang songs and also ate lunch with Faith. By the time they left an hour and half later, she was exhausted, but she couldn't stop thanking Prodigal for his thoughtfulness.

"Sweetheart, I love you so much. I'm sorry I've been so edgy lately," she told him.

"Don't worry about it. I understand, Faith. I love you too." He climbed up in the bed beside her and began to gently rub her belly. Then he moved his head down to her belly and placed light kisses all over.

"Girl, you know I'm hooked on you," he told her between kisses. "You know you got me right where you want me." He lifted his head and moved up closer to her and began nibbling on her chin. He pecked her tenderly on the lips.

"I can't wait until you have our babies. I miss making love to you so much. I don't know how much longer I can wait. Shucks! Just looking at you makes me all excited."

"You old horny dog you, you better wait." She could barely contain her laughter. She leaned carefully over the side of the bed and picked up a paisley throw pillow and plopped him upside his head.

"Okay, woman, you better watch out. You're getting ready to start something. Just remember, I have the upper hand because it's going to take you a long time to get up out of this bed." He grinned.

"That's all right. You just wait until after the babies come. I'm going to get you good."

"I sure hope so," Prodigal said, a mannish grin etched across his face. "Faith Runsome, I love you, girl, you hear me?"

"Yeah, I hear you. And I love you more."

Faith's body contracted as she felt a sharp pain on the left side of her belly. Using both hands, she gently massaged her rotund belly, and talked to the babies. "What are you up to in there? Mommy can't get any sleep." Faith tried using her hands to reposition the babies, to no avail.

Another sharp pain hit her. Faith cried out in the dark empty house. She glanced over at the clock. It was 1:30 a.m. Prodigal's shift at the fire station wouldn't end for another six hours.

Moments later, Faith screamed out in pain. Another strong contraction stabbed her. Feeling around in the bed for the cordless phone, her hand trembled as it met up with the cold, hard phone. The next contraction was so strong that it almost rendered her speechless when Prodigal picked up.

"Faith, honey, are you all right?"

"I-I think it's time." She struggled to speak as a river of tears rolled down her face. "Send the ambulance, honey—" Another contraction forced her to drop the phone on the bed.

Faith arrived at the hospital with Prodigal running beside the stretcher. There was some concern about Faith and the babies, since the twins weren't due for another two months. After hours of strong contractions, the babies still refused to come. The doctor made the decision to perform a caesarean. The identical twin boys, Kevin and Kaleb, made their grand entrance into the world, weighing less than three pounds each.

Prodigal didn't chance calling Teary with the news of the twins' birth from Faith's hospital room. He opted to wait until Faith succumbed to sleep, and went to the hospital lobby to make the call. From the hospital pay phone he called Teary but didn't get an answer on her home phone. He left her a message then caught the hospital elevator and returned to his wife's bedside.

Teary and Skyler's relationship remained in trouble. The one thing Skyler wanted more than anything in the world, she was unable to give him. She had listened to Prodigal's message, telling her about the birth of his sons, and though happy for him, she couldn't fight the sense of depression she felt.

For the past two years she had tried every conceivable thing to get pregnant, from maintaining a healthy weight, eating the right foods, keeping up with her ovulation cycle, and taking her body temperature three times a day. Debra even told her that taking a tablespoon of Geritol daily could boost her chances of becoming pregnant, a theory Teary proved wrong.

Every day Skyler grew more on edge. Rather than support his

wife, he taunted Teary when she told him about the birth of Prodigal's twins. As weeks turned into months and months into years, he realized that it was highly unlikely that Teary could give him a child. To make matters even worse, their sex life dwindled quick, fast, and in a hurry because Teary often complained about experiencing pain whenever they did made love. She didn't know what was happening to her body, but she was scared to death. She decided to make an appointment to see a fertility specialist. She had to do whatever it took to give Skyler a child.

Debra and Chelsia accompanied Teary to the office of fertility specialist, Dr. Leland Spelding, who'd been highly recommended by a co-worker of Debra's.

"Mrs. Jenkins, you say that you've been experiencing painful sex for most of your marriage?"

"Yes, doctor." Teary held her head down.

"You've never discussed it with your regular doctor or gynecologist?"

"No, I haven't. Look, Dr. Spelding, I don't mean to sound rude, but I don't want to discuss my personal reasons for not going to a doctor about this. All I can say is that I'm here now talking to you about it. I need to know if you can help me."

Dr. Spelding couldn't believe what he was hearing. This lady was obviously desperate to have children but, on the other hand, she hadn't discussed her physical condition with her own doctor. He studied the classily dressed, attractive woman. "Let me ask you if you are experiencing unusual pain during your menstrual cycle."

"Yes, I am."

Teary was glad she had asked Debra and Chelsia to come along with her. She was too nervous and frightened to be alone. And she didn't want to tell Skyler just yet, not until she knew for sure whether or not there was something wrong with her.

"My periods are lasting longer too. I don't know what's going on with me, Dr. Spelding, but I need to get whatever it is diagnosed and then fixed. My biological clock is ticking, and my husband and I want children badly." Teary's voice was on the verge of breaking.

"I understand, Mrs. Jenkins. I'm going to do whatever I can to help you and your husband. By the way, is your husband also here with you today?"

"No, he's out of town on a business trip," she lied.

Debra and Chelsia looked at each other then over at Teary.

She cut her eyes slightly and arched her eyebrows as a signal for them to keep quiet.

Dr. Spelding asked her a series of questions, analyzed her urine, drew blood, and then decided he needed to perform more in-depth tests.

"Mrs. Jenkins, I can't tell you what's going on inside of your body without further tests. You said that your husband has already been tested for fertility and that everything is fine with him?"

"Yes, that's right."

"First, let me tell you that sometimes it can take years for a couple to conceive. Stress, anxiousness, diet, and exercise can all be contributing factors as to why you haven't become pregnant. It could be that it just isn't time for you and your husband. But having said all of that, I do want to perform a few more tests while you're here today."

"Why more tests?"

"Mrs. Jenkins, some of the symptoms you described are the same as those attributed to endometriosis, but without additional tests, I won't be able to tell you anything more."

Teary's eyes bulged, and her mouth flung open. She looked over at her friends and shook her head from side to side in shock and disbelief. " 'Endometriosis'? Doctor, I've heard of that disease. If I have endometriosis that means I won't be able to have children. It can't be. I know that it's not that." She fought back the teardrops that were trying to push themselves out the corner of her eyes.

Debra and Chelsia stood up and gathered around her. Debra took hold of Teary's hand, while Chelsia patted her on the back.

"That's not always the case," Dr. Spelding explained to Teary. "There are women who still conceive after being diagnosed with endometriosis. Plus, I didn't say that you have it. The symptoms you've explained to me can mimic a number of medical conditions—that's why I'd like to do an extensive pelvic exam. We'll talk more after that. Ladies"—He turned to Debra and Chelsia—"do you mind going into the waiting area for a few minutes please?"

Dr. Spelding opened the door and motioned with his hands for the ladies to follow him. "Mrs. Jenkins, my nurse will be in shortly to prep you."

"Thank you, doctor," Teary said, mentally preparing herself for whatever was next.

After the painful examination, an hour and a half later, Teary was called back into the doctor's office. She beckoned for Debra and Chelsia to come along with her.

"Mrs. Jenkins, the pelvic examination indicates some abnormalities in your womb," Dr. Spelding started. "I also felt some irregularity and inconsistencies in the tissue behind your uterus. We call that tissue the cul-de-sac. Based on my experience—I want to be up front with you—we might very well be looking at endometriosis. If you're prepared to stay, I'd like to do an ultrasound, which will allow me to make a concrete diagnosis one way or the other. If the ultrasound reveals endometriosis, then we'll talk about an in-hospital procedure called a laparoscopy. But let's take it one step at a time."

Dr. Spelding's pager buzzed. "If you'll excuse me . . . I'll be back shortly. I have to answer this page."

Teary's eyes began to water. "I don't believe I'm hearing this."

Debra and Chelsia were at her side, trying to keep her from breaking down."

"Teary, hold on, girl. Don't jump to conclusions. He's just trying to rule out anything serious."

"It's easy for you to say, Chelsia—You have two children already; Faith just gave birth to twins—And I can't even get pregnant with one."

"Teary, it'll happen, you'll see. Just hold on," Debra told her. "Look at me. I don't have kids, so we're both in the same boat."

"No, we aren't. It's different for you, Debra; you've never really wanted kids—I do. You know Skyler desperately wants children."

Dr. Spelding walked back into the room. "Sorry about that interruption. I've spoken with my nurse. We can do the ultrasound in about thirty minutes. Is that okay with you?"

"Thirty minutes will be fine." Teary then turned to her friends. "Why don't you all go and get you something to eat?—I'll call you when I'm ready, or I can just catch a cab home when I'm done."

"No way are we leaving you here. We can all get something to eat after this is over."

"We'll be in the waiting room if you need us," Chelsia explained.

"Okay, thanks. You guys are the best."

They turned and walked off, feeling sorry about Teary's situation.

The nurse came in and instructed Teary to follow her down the hallway. Lifting her office gown, the nurse rubbed the cold gel over Teary's belly.

Dr. Spelding began moving the ultrasound instrument slowly over her stomach, sides, and down to her pelvic area, talking to her to help her feel more at ease. "Have you had an ultrasound procedure done before, Mrs. Jenkins?"

"No, this is my first one. Please, Dr. Spelding. I want to get this over with as quickly as possible. And you'll see that I don't have endometriosis. I know it."

The procedure ended, and Teary got dressed. She returned to the waiting area, where Debra and Chelsia still sat patiently. The three of them waited until Teary was called back into his office yet again.

Dr. Spelding's suspicions were right—Teary Jenkins definitely had endometriosis. He felt sorry for the frightened woman and dreaded breaking the news to her.

Soon Teary's name was called. She cautiously went back into the exam room and sat down in the chair instead of the exam table.

Dr. Spelding entered Teary's examination room. "Mrs. Jenkins—"

"Please, doctor, no more formalities. Call me Teary."

"Okay, Teary. I'm sorry."

"No, don't say it. Don't tell me that I have it. Please don't tell me that."

Debra and Chelsia heard her screams from the waiting room. They both rushed into the exam room. Teary was hysterical.

"Please, Mrs. Jenkins, calm down, please," the doctor pleaded. "Nurse, administer a Valium intravenously to Mrs. Jenkins."

"Yes, doctor," his nurse answered. "Right away."

21

Some Things Are Meant to Be

D r. Spelding performed laser therapy, to destroy any traces of endometriotic implants without damaging any of Teary's surrounding tissue, and allowing Teary and her husband to attempt to conceive. However, almost a year after the procedure, Teary was still unable to get pregnant.

Dr. Spelding explained to the couple that if he performed hormonal therapy, it would take another nine months or so of treatment.

But Teary's time was running out, and Skyler's attitude toward her had changed for the worse. He started staying away from home for longer periods of time, sometimes not bothering to come home at all.

In the first years of their marriage, Skyler had focused his energies on getting his life together to start a family. He stopped stripping and instead managed to secure a job as a patient care representative at the Medical Center, going to school at night to complete his physical therapy degree.

When Teary told him the news about her closed womb, it didn't take long for him to return to his old ways. No matter how much Dr. Spelding told them that she might still be able to get pregnant and conceive a child, Skyler convinced himself that Teary would never be able to give him the family he longed for.

"Hi, Faith, how is everyone doing?" Teary said into the phone. She was trying to sound happy but was having a difficult time.

"We're fine, Teary. How are you? It's been a while since we've talked." Faith still found it somewhat difficult to erase her mind of the jealous emotions that Teary was able to stir up. She put on a front the best way she knew how by continuing to be as nice as she could whenever Teary called. "I hope you're calling with some good news—You're pregnant, aren't you?"

"Unfortunately, I'm not, Faith."

"Oh, I see. Are you all right? You sound a little down."

"Sure, I'm fine. I was wondering if Prodigal was home."

"Yes, he's in the garage tinkering around with something out there. Hold on, I'll get him."

"Thanks, Faith. It was good talking to you."

"You too, Teary." Faith stopped preparing dinner long enough to go to the garage door and tell Prodigal that Teary was on the phone.

Prodigal dashed inside and picked up the cordless phone, which Faith had purposely left lying on the kitchen counter. Faith pretended not to be bothered and started seasoning the chicken. Her ears however, were fine-tuned to what Prodigal was saying on his end. She could only guess Teary's part of the conversation.

"Hey, you, what's going on with you, woman? Long time no hear from."

Prodigal had stopped calling Teary from home like he used to do. He mostly e-mailed her or waited until he was at the station to call her. Though he hadn't come right out and told her about Faith's feelings concerning their relationship, Teary sensed that things weren't as peachy as they once were between him and Faith. She didn't want their friendship to cause a rift in his marriage, so she had eased up from calling him too. But today, she couldn't help herself. She had to talk to him.

"Hey, yourself. What were you doing out there in the garage— messing something up?" She laughed.

"Me? Naw, I'm putting together a couple of bikes for the boys."

"How are Kevin and Kaleb anyway?"

"They're great, growing like weeds, that's all, and eating us out of house and home."

"I heard that."

"What's up with you? You okay, Teary?"

"No, I'm not." Teary broke down and started to cry.

"Hey, hey, talk to me. What's going on?"

"Prodigal, I'm tired, I'm frustrated, and my marriage is falling apart."

"What?" Prodigal gasped, though he wasn't surprised. "What happened, Teary?"

"I can't have children, Prodigal. It's no use in believing that I can anymore. Look how long Skyler and I have been trying. He wants the one thing I can't give him. Now I think he's cheating on me."

"That low-down, dirty bastard."

"It's not his fault; it's mine, Prodigal. I can't give him what he wants most—a child."

"That doesn't give him a license to go out and cheat, Teary. And anyway, who says you can't have children? Didn't that doctor say there was still a chance that you could get pregnant?"

" 'A chance'? Look how long it's been, Prodigal. Don't you understand what I just said?" She screamed, "I'm barren," and cried hysterically into the phone.

"Please, baby, please, calm down. Look, why don't I fly to see you when I go on my four-day weekend? How does that sound?"

Faith almost lost it. She placed the seasoned chicken on to a baking tray and stuck it in the oven. She grabbed her forehead like she was about to faint. Gathering her composure and keeping her back toward Prodigal, she remained quiet and continued to listen. If it would keep their marriage intact, Faith was willing to bite her tongue and remain tight-lipped. *How dare he even make such an offer?*

"Prodigal, don't be ridiculous. You have a family. You can't come running every time I'm in trouble. I'll be okay. I just needed to hear your voice."

"Well, now you hear it. And I'm telling you, everything is going to be all right. Just hang in there, okay?"

"Okay. Look, I have to go. I'll talk to you later."

When Prodigal hung up the phone he was furious. How could Skyler be so insensitive and cruel? He wanted to go to Broknfield and crack his skull for being such a jerk. But Teary was right. He had his own family. As bad as he wanted to, he couldn't simply up and leave Bonsai Bay to go see about her.

Standing at the kitchen island, Faith stopped dicing the bell pepper. "Is everything all right with Teary?"

"Besides the fact that she can't have children and she's married to a worthless, insensitive fool, yeah, everything is just fine." Prodigal stormed out of the kitchen and went back into the garage.

When she heard the doorknob turn and the sudden thud in the kitchen, Teary's heart skipped a beat. Skyler was probably drunk again. Over the past couple of years, her marriage had deteriorated right before her very eyes. She prayed hard and long for God to make her marriage work. She wanted to be happy like Prodigal and Faith. She wanted that same kind of love.

Skyler stumbled into the dining room and tripped over the dining room chair. He yelled, "Teary, I have to talk to you. I can't deal with this anymore. If you can't give me what I want, I'm outta here." His words were slurred. The sound of his voice unveiled his anger and resentment toward his wife. Skyler entered the bedroom, staggering, his breath reeking of alcohol.

"Baby, I know we can make things work if you would just open up and talk to me. I need you, and you need me."

Skyler remained cold and detached. "I've tried to stick by you, tried to make this farce of a marriage work, but this whole marriage has been based on a lie. You tricked me. You deceived me. I can't believe I've wasted all of these years with you believing that one day we could be a real family." He looked at her in disgust as he swayed back and forth in the entrance to their bedroom.

Listening to his harsh, insensitive words, she felt herself getting sick to the stomach.

"We can be a real family, honey. And our marriage hasn't been a farce. I love you, and I know you love me too."

"Why can't I have a wife who can give me what I need, what I want most in the world—Tell me why?" He raised balled fists up in the air as he stumbled toward her.

She quickly moved away from him, afraid that his temper would lead to physical violence.

"Do you honestly think I want a barren, empty-womb woman for a wife? When my family died it almost destroyed me, Teary. Don't you understand that yet, girl?"

"Don't talk like that, Skyler."

"When I met you I thought I'd met a girl who I could settle down with and start a family of my own. Now look . . . you're no good to me. You're useless. Tell me you can give me a child, Teary, then we can work something out. If you can't tell me that, then I don't want anything else to do with you."

"I wish I could tell you different, but I can't. All I can tell you is that I love you."

Then I feel nothing but contempt and hate toward you. Of all the women for me to choose, I had to get one that can't give me the one thing I want in life. I want out of this marriage, you hear me?"

"You don't mean that, Skyler. You've had too much to drink, that's all. You'll feel better in the morning."

"I'm going to feel the same way in the morning, don't you see that? Time and time again, I've tried to convince myself that you could give me a child. All of this is your fault—that's why I've cheated on you."

"Don't tell me that, Skyler. How could you betray our marriage like that? How?" She fell on the bed and closed her hands over her ears, hoping somehow to block out the cruel things he'd said.

"You tricked me. You deceived me. That's why it was easy for me to lay down with someone else. Someone who could make me feel better about me."

"Please, Skyler, please don't talk like this," Teary said, sobbing uncontrollably. She walked over to him.

"Get away from me," he screamed.

"We can adopt children or maybe get one of those surrogate mothers. We can do something. But we can't give up. We love each other too much to do that, Skyler." She pulled his drunken frame down on the bed. It had been weeks since he had touched her, and she wanted him so badly. She wanted him to show her that he still loved her.

"Honey," she began again. This time she tried to kiss him, rubbing her shaking hands up and down his body.

He quickly snatched them away, moving from her quickly as if she bore a deadly, contagious disease. He looked at her with vacant eyes.

"Love? Did you say love? Woman, I don't love you. I loved what I thought you could do for me. I thought you'd make a nice baby-maker and mother. Haven't you realized that yet? If you haven't, you're more stupid than I imagined. I saw in you someone who would be a good mother to my children. I saw you as someone who I could have to depend on to be around the house when I needed them plus bring home a little of the bacon as well. But you aren't worth anything to me now. I've wasted all these years with you, and you still haven't given me what I wanted."

"Stop it! Don't say those things. You don't mean that, Skyler."

"I do mean it. You said you wanted to do things right. Well, I did things right. We waited until we were married to have sex. That's the way you wanted it. You said that your God wanted us to do it like that. You said we would be blessed. So I did it the way you wanted to. Well, where is your God now, huh? Where is He now that you really need Him to come through? Just forget it. I want a divorce. I want out of this." He jerked from the reach of her grasp and sprinted toward the door, grabbing a pair of trousers and a shirt from off the edge of the bed.

"Wait, please don't go. It's two o'clock in the morning. You just came home. Please don't do this, Skyler, puhleeze," she cried and begged.

He didn't say a word. Instead, he turned and looked at her with loathing. "I'm out of here. I've got a woman who can give me all I want and need, and it sure ain't you, baby, it sure ain't you." He slammed the front door behind him.

Teary fell across the bed, her tears coming out in full force. She was hurt, lonely, and alone.

Disregarding the time, she dialed Prodigal. Fortunately he hadn't fallen asleep yet. He answered the call on the first ring. He heard the familiar voice on the other end, sobbing uncontrollably.

"Teary, what is it?" He slowly got up from the bed and eased into the master bathroom, quietly closing the door behind him, so as not to wake up Faith, who lay on her side in a peaceful sleep.

"What have I done to deserve this, Prodigal? I would have been a good mother, and you know it. I've tried to be a good wife to Skyler. I don't know what else I can do?"

"Teary, please, don't cry," he whispered. Things between him and Faith were shaky still. He didn't want to jeopardize their marriage. He loved his wife, but he couldn't just turn a deaf ear to Teary, no matter what. He sat on the edge of the oversized bathtub. "What happened, Teary?"

Teary told him everything. He wanted to be by her side, to wipe her tears away. She needed a friend, but he couldn't be there for her.

"Teary, didn't I tell you that everything would work out? You'll see. You don't need Skyler. He doesn't deserve you, so stop crying. Please stop crying."

"Prodigal, I just don't know what to do anymore."

"I know. I know. But I'm here for you. You know that, don't you?"

"Yeah, I know. Thanks for listening to me. You're the only one I can talk to about this. You're the only one who understands."

"Look, it's late. I don't want to wake up Faith. I'll call you tomorrow, and we'll talk some more, I promise."

"I'm sorry I disturbed you, Prodigal. What was I thinking?" she asked between tears.

"There's no need to apologize. Remember our promise to always be there for each other?"

"Yes, I remember."

"Well then, I'll never break that promise, you hear?"

She sniffled. "Yes, I hear you."

"Now I want you to dry your tears. Try to get some rest. I'll call and check on you tomorrow."

"Okay." Teary hung up the phone. Without taking off her clothes, she climbed under the bed covers and cried until her eyes were swollen shut.

The knock on the door came hard.

"Hey, who is it out there?" the woman called out.

"Who do you think it is? Open up the door, Geena. I need a place to crash. Come on," Skyler ordered. "It's cold and wet out here."

Out of habit, Geena peeked through the peephole anyway. A sleepy smile spread across her face as she unlatched the door.

"What's going on with you? It's almost three o'clock in the morning. Your ol' lady must have thrown you out," she said sleepily.

"Naw, more like I walked out. I don't have time to listen to nagging and yelling from some lifeless, dried-up wench. I told you before that my marriage was over. I found out the broad lied to me about being able to have children, and you know how bad I want a family."

He watched as a sly, devilish smile appeared on the woman's face. The twenty-three-year-old biracial woman's golden locks were professionally cut to lay close against her neck. Her oval-shaped, blue-green eyes gave her the appearance of a porcelain doll. She sported a Barbie doll figure and more importantly, she was definitely able to conceive.

With a habit of sleeping around, she had already been pregnant twice, once at the tender age of sixteen, and again when she was eighteen. Both times she'd had an abortion. She'd come from a pretty well-to-do family and didn't worry about the consequences of her actions because she could always count on her dear old mother to whisk her off to get things taken care of. Her mother was a heart surgeon, and her father was the chief of staff at a Children's Hospital in upstate Oregon, so money was definitely not an issue. Her two brothers loved to spend their parents' money just as much as she did.

Geena spent her spare time watching television, listening to music, and partying. In addition to having a wild reputation, she stripped a little every now and then, which was how she met Skyler. They'd been fooling around on and off ever since she first met him, and she really liked him. When she found out he and his wife were having problems, she made sure she would be waiting for such a time as this. It was the same way Geena's mother had trapped her father. She'd caught him when things were going shaky with his first wife, and before you knew it she had stolen him right from underneath that pitiful ex-wife's very own nose.

"Bring yourself on in here." Geena pulled at Skyler's rain-soaked shirt. Her place was a three-bedroom condo, which her parents had purchased for her. They hoped that if she had her own place, somehow they might be able to fool themselves into believing that all was right with their only daughter. They gave her a weekly allowance that matched what some people earned after working for three or four months.

"Come on in. I want to get back to sleep," she said lazily.

Skyler began to tell her about the fight between him and Teary. "Geena, you know I've been going through some things with that woman almost from the start. I can't take it anymore. She knows how much I need some babies. My name has to be carried on somehow, someway."

Geena feigned sincerity. "I'm really sorry about you and Teresa. I know you don't believe me, but I really am."

"Her name is *Teary*."

"Yeah, Teary, whatever. Anyway, I hate to see you hurt like this, Skyler. Come on over here to me, baby. I'll make it all better."

It didn't take much for Skyler to forget his marriage vows and commitment to his wife. Geena played him like a fine-tuned piano. She knew exactly what he liked, what he needed, and most of all what Skyler Jenkins wanted, and she planned on giving it all to him.

22

Beyond Repair

"**Y**our Honor, I'm here today because I'd like to reassume my maiden name."

"The court would like to know your reasons for making this request, Mrs. Jenkins."

"Your Honor, I was recently granted a divorce. My ex-husband and I have no children, we have not purchased a home together, nor do we have a substantial amount of assets between the two of us. So in light of these things, I don't see why I should continue to bear his name. I want to be totally free from him and from all ties with him, so I can make a fresh start in my life."

"I see that your maiden name is Fullalove. Is that correct?"

"Yes, Your Honor, it is." Teary tried hard to conceal her nervousness. Even though her lawyer had told her that going before the judge was more of a formality rather than anything else, Teary was still a little on edge. She couldn't bear the thought of having to wear the name Jenkins one minute longer.

Humiliated and hurt at the failure of her marriage, Teary hated to admit it, but she still loved Skyler. Maybe if she went back to being a Fullalove, it would make it easier to forget him.

Over the years, Teary prayed that she and Skyler would be able to make their marriage work. But she had cried her last when she discovered that he was having an affair with a woman named Geena.

The night she begged him not to leave came to mind. Skyler had returned to the apartment only to get the rest of his things before moving in with Geena.

The ragged sound of the judge's voice pierced her thoughts.

"Your request has been granted. Please let the record show that Teary Jenkins is now returned to her maiden name of Fullalove. Miss Fullalove, the court clerk will draw up the order. Good day."

"Thank you, Your Honor." She exhaled. "Thank you, Lord," she mumbled underneath her breath.

The next thing on her agenda was making a move out of the city of Broknfield. She had to get away from everything. There was no way she could live here dodging Skyler, choosing the places she could or could not go to avoid running into him. Nor could she take the pitying stares from her friends who knew that she had been dumped because she couldn't have children. Yes, she definitely needed a fresh start, a second chance. Maybe she would find someone someday who would love her even though she would never be able to bear a child. But she didn't believe that person was in Broknfield.

"So it's all over, huh?" Prodigal asked through the phone.

"Yep. I'm officially Teary Fullalove again."

"How are you holding up?"

"So-so. They say time heals all wounds, but I don't know about that."

"The pain isn't going to disappear overnight, you know."

"I know that. But Skyler's been out of my life for some time now, Prodigal. I should be better, don't you think?"

"It still doesn't mean you can just turn your feelings off. You still love him, and to go through a divorce is traumatic. I just wish there was something I could do to make things easier."

"Having you listen to me is more than enough, Prodigal.

Knowing I can call on you is such a relief. You always come through for me."

"Hey, why don't you come here and visit for a while, relax your mind, have a change of scenery."

Faith cleared her throat as she entered the study.

Prodigal jerked around in time to see her, a look of disdain on her face.

She folded her arms and walked back out as quickly as she had come in. She used to accept the relationship he had with Teary, but now things were totally different.

He continued listening to Teary. *If only Faith could understand my relationship with Teary. Doesn't she know the woman needs someone to lean on?*

"I wish I could, but I'm in the middle of some big projects at work. Plus, I still have a few loose ends to tie up, now that my divorce is final."

"The sooner you handle the loose ends, the sooner you can move on with your life, you know?" He hated for her to be in pain. He longed to be there beside her to see her through this difficult time. He wished he could see Skyler so he could choke the life out of him for hurting Teary.

"You're right."

"I should be finished in a couple of weeks. Oh, by the way, I almost forgot . . ."

"Almost forgot what?"

"I'm thinking about relocating."

" 'Relocating'? Where?"

"I don't know just yet, but I need a change, you know what I mean? A chance to start over again—a new place, new town, new job."

"Maybe you're right. That might be exactly what you need, Teary. Hey, think about moving here. The twins would love to have you nearby all the time, not to mention me and Faith."

"I don't think that's such a good idea. Not that I don't want to be near you guys, but it's time for me to have a clean slate, Prodigal. I'm going to keep my options open and see what's out there. And you know that Faith definitely wouldn't be happy if I moved there, so be for real."

Prodigal hesitated. "I hear you. Well, don't dismiss Bonsai Bay altogether. I'd love to have you close to me."

"I won't. Well look, I have to go. I have a meeting with the rest of the news team in about fifteen minutes. I love you, and we'll talk soon. Kiss the boys for me too."

"Will do. I'll talk to you later." Prodigal hung up the phone, walked out of the study and into the family room to watch the basketball game. He refused to argue with Faith about Teary. She had her friends, and he had his, and no one was going to come between his friendship with Teary—no one.

When the basketball game ended, Prodigal took the boys to the neighborhood park. He invited Faith to come along, but she was still obviously upset with him and refused to go.

Later that night when he climbed in bed beside her, she asked him, "Do you want a divorce?"

" 'A divorce?'—Don't be ridiculous. Why would you ask me something like that?"

"You really don't know, do you?" She sat up in the bed and looked down on him.

"Know what, Faith?"

"Don't you see how your relationship with Teary affects our marriage—she's always running to you with her problems, and you're always the noble guy who just has to be there every time."

"Teary and I have been friends since we were kids, you know that, Faith. Why have you been constantly riding me about this? It's not like she's some female who just came up out of the blue; she's my best friend."

"That's the problem—I should be your best friend, Prodigal, not Teary. And how dare you ask her to move here to Bonsai Bay?"

"I knew she wasn't going to do that. Do you honestly think that I would have asked her if I thought she would move here?"

"I don't know what you'll do when it comes to her."

He grabbed her and pulled her down on top of him. "Look, I don't want to argue with you tonight or any night. And I certainly don't want a divorce. I love you, Faith. I know I get a little carried away sometimes when it comes to Teary, but the girl has been through so much."

"I know that, Prodigal. I just wish she had someone else's shoulder to cry on instead of yours, that's all."

"No one, not even Teary, can come between us, Faith. I love you with all of my heart. You've got to know that. And if you talk to her sometimes, maybe she won't feel the need to confide in me as much. She just needs someone, and she's used to me being there for her."

"Well, I want you to be here for me—I'm your wife."

"How can I ever forget that? You are my wife, you always will be. You have absolutely nothing to worry about because I'm not going anywhere and neither are you, Mrs. Runsome." He kissed and stroked her, squeezing her butt and running his fingers through her hair. She couldn't resist his touch. She never could, and tonight was no different.

23

Second Chances

Teary sat in her window office overlooking the muddy Mississippi and reminisced. Her life wasn't so bad right now. She could honestly say that she was contented with the way things had turned out for her since her divorce from Skyler. Moving to Memphis had been a good decision, one that so far she hadn't at all regretted. It seemed like only yesterday that she'd received the phone call from *The Commercial Appeal* newspaper in Memphis, Tennessee. She remembered the day quite well.

"Miss Fullalove, we'd like to fly you to Memphis for an interview, if you're still interested in the copy editor position," the human resources generalist said.

Teary couldn't believe her ears because she'd answered the ad on a whim. She didn't actually think she would get a response. And to think, only two weeks had passed since she e-mailed the Memphis newspaper her resume.

"Yes, I'm interested." *What am I doing?* Teary thought. She had never even visited Memphis. The only thing she knew about Memphis was that it was the home of Elvis Presley, the Memphis Grizzlies, and FedEx.

"Miss Fullalove, I'll be sending you your itinerary and flight information by FedEx. My contact information will be included, so if you have questions, or if your plans change and for some reason you cannot come as scheduled, please give me a call. "

"I sure will. Thank you and have a nice day." Teary hung up the phone, fell back against the swivel office chair, almost pushing it from underneath her. She scooted around in her matchbox cubicle, pulled herself closer to her workstation, and scribbled *MT* and the date in her desk planner.

She kept repeating the words, "Memphis, Tennessee . . . Memphis, Tennessee."

If she were offered the job as copy editor, it would be a positive step in her career, especially financially. Being an assistant copy editor in Broknfield was okay, but the money was meager, and Broknfield was such an uneventful place. It was time for her to do something different, and she wanted to do it somewhere other than in Broknfield.

She imagined someone asking her, *Where are you relocating?*

Oh, I've accepted a position in Memphis, Tennessee. The more she said it, the more she liked the sound of it. This was her chance, her opportunity, her blessing.

She flipped to one of her favorite passages of Scripture. "For I know the plans I have for you, declares the Lord," she read out loud, "plans to prosper you, not to harm you, plans to give you hope and a future."

There were times Teary couldn't bring herself to recite that bit of Scripture. She had been through so much in her life that it seemed like just the opposite. Maybe it was time for her to stop trying to second-guess God and instead just trust in Him. Deep down inside she knew that God loved her and that He would never leave her side. She just had a hard time trying to figure out His plans for her life. She kept revisiting her past. Somehow she couldn't let go of all the mistakes she'd made. She still thought about how she allowed Langston Silverman to rob her of her virginity. Prodigal always told her that she was way too trusting. She felt like she was stuck on stupid. She promised herself that if offered the job in Memphis, she would accept it and never look back. Broknfield would be a thing of the past.

Two months after being interviewed, Teary accepted the job at *The Commercial Appeal*, turned in her resignation to *The Broknfield Gazette*, and relocated to Memphis. For once, she felt like the storms had subsided and the sun was beginning to shine in her life again.

Now, here she was with a brand-new life, a nice home, new friends, and a great job. During the time she had been in Memphis, not once had she looked back.

"Prodigal, do you have everything?" Faith's voice radiated the love she had for her husband. For some reason, Teary's move to Memphis had a positive effect on Faith. Maybe it was because Teary's life had taken on a change for the better and she didn't call Prodigal as much.

"Yeah, I think so," he yelled back while standing in the doorway leading to the double garage.

The annual church picnic was something the entire congregation and community looked forward to. One of the many ways their pastor chose to reach out to the unchurched, every year it became better and larger.

Prodigal and Faith played an active role in the planning of the event. Prodigal commandeered everything that had to do with food, since he considered himself to be a master chef, especially when it came to grilling. He and a host of twenty-five other men from their church had been up since the break of dawn preparing everything from hot dogs to steaks. This was Prodigal's third year chairing the food committee, and he loved every single bit of his responsibilities.

Faith made sure the children attending this year's annual picnic would have plenty of fun-filled activities. There were going to be pony rides, a Ferris wheel, go-carts, a train ride, bumper cars and loads of other kiddy rides.

"Faith, I'm headed back to the church, sweetheart," Prodigal said, sneaking up behind her, pulling her closer to him, and stealing a kiss as she turned around to face him.

"Boy, you betta stop it." She giggled out loudly in a schoolgirl voice. She softly plopped him over the head with the empty paper towel roll she was holding.

"Ooooh, I love it when you get wild like that." Prodigal scooted from her reach and ran down the hallway laughing loudly.

The picnic turned out to be a blast. By the time six o'clock rolled around, the Runsome family was totally exhausted. As they drove home, Faith glanced in the back seat of the SUV, and a smile filled her face, when she saw her cherub-faced sons fast asleep.

She slid over as close to her husband as she could, without straddling the bucket seat. She kissed him on his stubbled cheek.

He allowed a heavy grunt to escape his lips as he felt himself becoming excited at the touch of his wife, her hands expertly caressing his groin. He could feel her sumptuous breasts pressed against the side of his arm, as he tried to maintain his composure while driving.

"Faith, the boys are—"

"Shhh! You just concentrate on driving. The boys are fine. They're asleep." She loved teasing Prodigal and bringing him to a fever pitch. He was her first and only lover, and she never regretted saving herself for marriage. She couldn't imagine ever having anyone do to her what Prodigal did to her.

"Look, girl, don't start anything you can't finish."

"I'm no quitter," she whispered hungrily in his ear. "You taught me to go after what I want, remember? And anything I start I can surely finish."

When she began nibbling on his ear, he thought he would lose total control of the vehicle. He was glad when he turned on to their street. He pulled up into the garage, turned off the ignition, and grabbed her, eagerly kissing and touching her in all the right places. Prodigal couldn't wait to get to their bedroom.

"Come on, baby, let's get the boys inside," she cooed seductively, "and I'll *show* you that I can finish what I start."

They carried the boys inside and put them in the bed. Neither of them woke up, which was perfect for Faith to carry out her plans of seducing her husband.

Their lovemaking left Prodigal spent, but the shrill ring of the phone awakened them from their twilight sleep. He didn't want to let go of his naked wife, as she lay cradled within the safety of his arms, her soft natural hair rubbing against his full chest of hair, creating a sensuous feeling that began to arouse him again.

"I'll get it, baby," she mumbled.

"No, let it ring."

"Sounds good to me." She snuggled against him closer.

Prodigal turned over on his side, using his arm to prop up his body, and looked down on his beautiful wife. He sucked in her beauty, and the aroma of their recent lovemaking aroused him again as they both satisfied each other's desires once more.

24

Choose This Day

"Prodigal, I forgot to tell you—Teary called earlier today while you were at the station." Faith turned over the fried chicken, so it could brown on the other side.

"Oh, she did? Was everything all right with her?"

"I guess so. She said she was just checking up on us. She wanted to make sure you were behaving yourself. I told her that I wouldn't have it any other way."

"I just bet you did. I don't know how you became so confident, Mrs. Runsome." Prodigal loved the fire in Faith, who seemed to always be in a good mood and full of spunk.

"I'm this way because I have a doggone good man, not to mention that I'm the only female in this household, so I deserve a little special treatment, don't you think?"

"I sure do."

"Anyway, Teary said you could give her a call later if you wanted to. She asked me if you retrieved her last e-mail. She said she sent you one of those stories that you like to read."

"I haven't checked my e-mail in a couple of days. I'll get to it a little later on. Did she really sound like she was doing okay?"

Here he goes again. Dang, why does this happen every single time?

Teary calls and he goes off in a warp zone of some kind. Lord, help me. I'm tired of sharing my husband with another woman. I'm tired.

"Yeah, she sounded fine to me, but of course you know she's not going to open up to me. You're the only one who can get her to say what's really going on inside of her."

"I guess you're right about that. It's always been that way with us."

"How well do I know. But, Prodigal . . ."

"What, baby?" He walked over and positioned himself next to her, lightly dipping his index finger into the steaming pot of spaghetti sauce.

Faith tapped his hand. "I mean, we have our own life here in Bonsai Bay. And there's already enough going on in our family without having to worry and guess what's going on with Teary. And before you get angry and uptight, I know your history with her, but you have me and the boys now—When are you going to put us first?"

"Why do you always have to do this?"

"Do what? What on earth are you talking about?" Faith threw the dishtowel on the cabinet and turned around to face Prodigal.

"You know what I'm talking about, Faith—How many times do I have to spoonfeed you like a baby, trying to reassure you every time Teary calls that she's just my friend? All the years we've been together, I can't believe I still have to put up with your insecurities."

"How dare you call me insecure." Faith's voice suddenly trembled. "Maybe if you would try paying more attention to me like you do her, then I wouldn't have to be insecure. She needs to get a life, find her own man."

"And she will. We just have to pray for her and lift her up before God. You know just as well as I do, everything she's been through. It's going to take time for her to come to terms with a lot of things in her life before God can send that person into her life. Not being able to have children has been hard for her to face too. And she's never really gotten over her breakup with Skyler.

Maybe things would have been easier if she had met someone halfway decent who could have taken her mind off of him, but that hasn't been the case. Where is your compassion? Where is the Faith I first met?"

"The Faith you first met is right here. The Faith you first met wants some time and attention too. I get sick of hearing about Teary and her problems. I thought when she moved to Memphis that she'd get a life, but dang! I guess I was wrong again."

"Things are better for her in Memphis. She has a great career, good friends, a great church, and a beautiful home. If you could find it in your so-called Christian heart to be more understanding, then things wouldn't be tense between us like they are whenever she calls here. Anyway, thanks for passing the message on to me. I'll give her a call later on and see what's up with her."

Faith was speechless. Her anger fumed to the point where she knew if she didn't get out of Prodigal's sight, she would say something she would live to regret. What she wanted to tell him was, 'To hell with Teary and her problems,' but that would only alienate him even more. She chose to leave him standing there defending the woman who was constantly invading what could have been a perfect marriage.

Teary answered the phone in her office on the second ring.

"Hello, Mizz Fullalove. Are you full of love this afternoon?" Prodigal laughed at the sound of his own corny remark.

Teary walked around the perimeter of her desk. She stood in front of the office window and gazed out over the Mississippi. "Prodigal Runsome, boy, I'm glad you didn't go into comedy because you would definitely suck at it." Teary laughed.

"Yeah, I know. Faith told me you called. You doing okay down there in Memphis? You haven't spotted Elvis running around there lately, have you?"

"Puhleeze . . . I'm fine, and as far as Elvis goes, I see some clown just about every day trying to impersonate him. They should let that poor man rest in peace."

"I know that's right. Well, what's up with you?"

"You've been on my mind. Since we hadn't talked in a while, I thought I'd give you a call. Things have been so busy here. Are you all right?"

"Yep. Me and the missus and those rowdy young kids of ours are great. I can't complain about anything. Anyway, it wouldn't do me any good; at least that's what Faith tells me." Prodigal laughed again.

"Man, that woman still has you whipped after all these years. I knew the first time you laid eyes on her that you were a lifer."

"I can't dispute you there. I am definitely a lifer. She's stuck with the likes of me. Now enough about me. Tell me, how are things going for you?"

"Prodigal, really, I'm fine. I just wanted to hear your voice. Sometimes when I'm feeling a little down, I need that picker-upper, and you're my picker-upper. You have that way of lifting my spirits and making me see things from a different perspective. I love you for that."

"I love you too. That's what friendship is all about—being there for one another."

Prodigal knew Teary far too well. When Faith told him that she had called, he surmised that Teary must have been going through a bout of depression. He was right.

Prodigal admitted to himself that he asked a lot of Faith when it came to accepting Teary. Faith tried to understand the depth of her husband's relationship with Teary. Other times, like earlier today, Faith was just the opposite. But he loved Faith. There had been times she doubted the depth of his love for her. Faith struggled to grasp why the love Prodigal and Teary shared was just as strong a bond as hers and Prodigal's. In a way, Teary did have something Faith didn't possess, and even though she would never admit it to Prodigal, there were times when Faith despised Teary. Prodigal would talk to Teary and tell her things that he wouldn't discuss with Faith. Prodigal wasn't aware that

Faith knew he still confided in Teary, but a woman always knows.

Slowly Faith began to make peace with the fact that Teary and Prodigal would always be close and she would just have to be fine with that. Maybe it was true that Teary knew a part of Prodigal that Faith probably would never know, but as his wife, Faith knew the part of him that satisfied her, that part that belonged to only her, that only she and Prodigal would share. In that she tried to remain content, confident, and secure.

"Look, I'm going to ask you for the umpteenth time—Why not come up for a visit?"

Teary was not about to agree to doing such a thing. She'd tried that before. The one time she actually went to visit them on her vacation turned out to be her first and last time. Faith treated her cordially. The two of them even did some shopping. Teary spent time getting to know the twins too, but she and Prodigal didn't get the chance to spend much time alone.

He talked to her about moving to Bonsai Bay, but she wouldn't even entertain the idea, knowing that could possibly destroy his otherwise great marriage.

"You haven't seen how much the boys have grown, Teary— Well, you have, but I'm not talking about through a computer photo. I mean, you should come and see 'em in person. How about it?"

"I would love to, but work is really hectic and probably will be for a while. I've been promoted to assistant editor. With that comes more responsibility, you know."

"Wow! Fantastic! I'm proud of you. I know who I can run to when I need to borrow some big bucks."

They both laughed.

"Now, do you see why I have to call on you, Prodigal?—You can always make me laugh and bring me up out of the dumps— Hold on a minute, will you? My admin just buzzed me."

"Sure."

A few seconds later, Teary returned to the phone. "Well, I've just received my cue. I'm needed in a meeting. We're getting in a big news story. I'll talk to you later. Kiss the boys for me and hug Faith. And thanks. Love you."

"Take care, Teary. I love you, too. Bye now."

25

Heart's Desire

After finishing art school, Fantasia opened Trinity Three Gallery and Museum. Selling for no less than $2,500 a whop, it wasn't unusual to find pieces of her art in the homes of the rich and famous. The girl was definitely a winner with anything and everything a bundle of money could buy. Her sprawling five-bedroom home was nestled in a private mountainside residence in Belleaf, Maryland. She rented a vacation home in southern California and a cottage in Massachusetts.

Fantasia persuaded her mother to retire and relocate to Belleaf. Under Fantasia's tutelage, Ruth learned much about the world of art. A lady of leisure and pleasure, Ruth didn't have to do a thing if she didn't want to, yet she loved spending her days at the gallery. Every morning, after carefully choosing one of her signature designer outfits, Ruth commandeered her black-on-black Jag through seven o'clock rush-hour traffic.

For some reason, people tended to gravitate toward Ruth and Fantasia. The mother-daughter duo was often recognized for their philanthropic work, in addition to Fantasia's exquisite artwork.

Despite Fantasia's success and good fortune, Ruth continued to be concerned about Fantasia's lack of interest in a relationship.

By no means did Ruth want to give Fantasia the impression that in order to be happy she had to have a man, but she did want each of her children to experience the kind of love she'd found with Solumun.

Fantasia was well aware that her mother was concerned about her lack of romantic involvement. She was always the bridesmaid, never the bride, and it suited her just fine. So what if she was a thirty-four-year-old virgin. It was definitely by choice. She'd had many an opportunity from many a man, but none could sway her to give up her heart or her body. And contrary to rumors that circulated in the tabloids from time to time, she wasn't a lesbian. She was, however, determined not to allow love to destroy her life as it did her mother's.

"Fantasia, sweetheart, are you going out this evening?"

"Nope. I have quite a bit of paperwork to finish up this weekend. Tonight's the perfect time to start, Mother."

"Fantasia, for goodness' sakes, it's Friday night. Don't you have something better to do?" Ruth asked in an irritated voice.

"Momma, you mean *someone* better to do, don't you? Look, let's not go there tonight. I don't have a date, and I don't want one. How many times do I have to tell you that I'm happy with things just like they are?" Fantasia sat on the edge of her office desk, her arms folded. The look of aggravation was evident in her wrinkled brow.

"I don't want to argue with you tonight, Fantasia. I just hate to see you working all the time. Life's too short not to enjoy it."

"I know that, Mother, and you see, that's where you're wrong—I *am* enjoying my life. You don't seem to think so, but I am. You equate loving someone with being fulfilled and happy."

"That's not true. I never said that. I understand what you're saying. Everything is not going to be a bed of roses in life, Fantasia; I never said it was."

" 'A bed of roses'?" Fantasia stood up and gave a fake laugh. "That's one thing you're right about. Life is nothing but a game to be played, Momma, and your God is the orchestrator of it all, including your sentimental view of love. What kind of love takes a father away from his children, Momma?"

"Oh, please, Fantasia." Ruth started to cry.

"Tell me that, Mother. Don't cry now. Why does God allow the things He does? And you want me to fall in love? You want me to do what you don't even do yourself because you know the consequences too?"

Ruth stared into her daughter's cold, callous, brown eyes.

Fantasia ran down the corridor to the sanctity of her office and stood at her office doorway, watching her mother until she disappeared into her office. *Sorry, Momma,* Fantasia thought to herself, *I didn't mean to hurt you, but I'm sick and tired of being made to feel like I'm wrong for not wanting a man in my life, or God for that matter. I don't see the sense in any of it, so what does it matter? God does what he wants to do, and I'm going to do my thing, live my life the way I want to. I'll help others when I can, and to hell with falling in love with anyone just to face heartbreak in the end.*

Turning around, she closed the door behind her. She dismissed what had just happened between her and Ruth, attending to the task before her. Taking a seat behind the walnut desk, Fantasia kicked off her Jay Cabachi heels and proceeded to leaf through the pile of neatly stacked papers.

Meanwhile, Ruth fell back into the arms of her plush office chair. She spied the box of Kleenex tissues resting on the end table and quickly grabbed one to wipe away her tears and clean her runny nose. She allowed her perfectly coiffed hair to lean against the high back of the chair. She needed answers before she could dish out any more advice.

Suave, debonair, and strikingly handsome, widower William Phillips was CEO of the multi-million-dollar Phillips Technology Corporation, which licensed and monitored Internet access, usage, and user name licensing. A great philanthropist and a lover of the arts, he had a special love for Fantasia Runsome's artistic flavor. Several of her art pieces lined the walls of his lavish office space in the Savoy Towers and in his mountaintop mansion. It was his normal routine to have his personal courier pick up pieces of Fantasia's art from her gallery for his perusal, before the public had a chance to purchase it.

Never having met her in person, William Phillips decided it was time to pay a personal visit to Fantasia. His assistant contacted her to make arrangements for him to visit the gallery. He wanted her to design a special piece for the waterfront mansion he had just built in Rhode Island. He also wanted to discuss the upcoming annual charity ball that Fantasia and her mother had agreed to chair.

When he arrived at the gallery, he was handsomely dressed in taupe Armani slacks and alligator loafers that displayed a splash of charcoal brown and perfectly matched his attire. The taupe and brown pinstriped silk shirt fit his muscular build to a *T*. The fifty-eight-year-old gray-haired bachelor with the matching thin mustache and goatee made Ruth skip a breath, when he strolled through the smoke glass double doors of the gallery.

Fantasia had told Ruth that she was expecting him. What she'd failed to mention to Ruth was just how handsome Mr. William Phillips was.

Even though he was a great philanthropist, he was rarely seen in public. Ruth had seen photos of him from time to time, but they did him no justice. And feelings that she had not felt since Solumun's death swelled in her.

As William approached the attractive woman with the flowing black tresses, he started to feel somewhat excited. She had long legs with curves in all the right places. *I wonder if this lovely vision of beauty is Fantasia's mother? Could this be her?*

William, still recovering emotionally from her death, hadn't been the least bit attracted to or concerned with any woman since the death of his wife, Lois, who'd died several years earlier from complications brought on by a stroke.

The black-and-white linen dress tastefully nestled against Ruth's full breasts. The black buttons that traced the back of her dress outlined her figure even more. Her legs were encased in sheer black pantyhose, and her size seven and a half feet were encased in two-inch black-and-white leather slingbacks. She wore her hair in curls that cascaded around her shoulders in a way that seemed to be calling William to her.

"Good afternoon, ma'am. I'm William Phillips. I'm here to see Fantasia Runsome," he said in a sexy Northern accent.

"Hello, Mr. Phillips. I'm Ruth Runsome, Fantasia's mother and the director of Trinity Three. We were expecting you." Ruth extended her perfectly manicured hand to him. "I must say that I'm glad we have finally had the opportunity to meet face-to-face."

When their hands intertwined in the shake, William felt the coolness and soft texture of her skin. She smelled good, like freshly cut flowers. It reminded him of Lois. His deceased wife loved cologne and expensive lotions. No matter where she went, what time of day or night, Lois smelled heavenly. When William thought of her, he imagined that she had Heaven smelling like a pasture of roses. God, did he miss her.

Since his sons were grown now and doing well for themselves, William spent his time involved in his church, business, and philanthropic works. When he laid eyes on Ruth, however, he felt something stirring inside. He didn't quite know what it was. All he knew was there was some attraction toward her. And now, the smell of her body and the touch of her hand made him know in no uncertain terms that he was still alive.

His hands feel so manly, so masculine. They feel like Solumun's hands used to feel, hands that played jazz with my body. No man had ever been able to move her like Solumun, and she had long since stopped trying to find one who did. Before she moved to Belleaf, she had been involved with only one man since Solumun's death, Ralph Gordon.

Ruth was working the second shift at Broknfield Medical Center, when she first met Ralph, who was at the hospital visiting his best friend who was recuperating from a diabetic-induced coma.

It didn't take long for Ruth to discover that Ralph Gordon loved to talk. Every day when she passed the room heading to nurse's station 707, he was there chattering away to his friend. She guessed they had to be rather close because she noticed Ralph never missed a day visiting the man. When she went in to check the patient's vitals, Ralph was always pleasant.

"Good afternoon, Nurse Runsome," Ralph said. "Did anyone tell you that you're like a breath of fresh spring flowers on a rainy day?"

Ruth tried to pretend she was offended. "I beg your pardon," she said in a stern voice. "Surely you aren't talking to me in such a way."

"Well, the name tag says your name is Nurse Ruth Runsome, and you're the only one in here who could possibly come close to smelling like fresh spring flowers. Old Country here sure doesn't, and I know I don't. So there, you have to accept it." He flashed a gold-toothed smile.

" 'Old Country'?" Ruth found herself blushing and looking confused at the same time.

"Well, I guess a thank you is in order, Old Country."

Ruth had played her defenses well over the years, daring a man to get near her. She wore a mean demeanor and came across as stuck-up and unapproachable. It was rumored that most of the hospital staff called her "the icemaker," but Ruth didn't care. As a matter of fact, she had come to love the nickname they had for her. That way, she didn't have to worry about any of the men there trying to hit on her.

Ralph allowed a hearty laugh to escape his lips, when she called him Old Country. "I'm not Old Country; that's what I call my buddy here." He reached out and touched the side of the hospital bed where his friend lay.

Ruth hid a subtle smile then turned and walked away. *He is sort of cute and a big flirt too.*

After a two-week hospital stay, Ralph's friend was about to be discharged from the hospital. Ruth arrived to work a few minutes early to take his vital signs and to say her good-byes.

"Hold on a minute," Ralph said as he stepped quickly toward her. "I hope you'll at least let me get your phone number. I'd like to call you sometime. Maybe we could go out and have a cup of coffee or even take in a movie."

Ruth hesitated before speaking. "Look, I don't know. I just don't see that I'll have time for anything like that. As a matter of fact, I'm sure I won't."

"Sure you will. I won't accept no for an answer. Anyway, it's not like I'm asking you to run off with me, woman. Just let me call you sometimes. I've enjoyed talking to you these last couple of weeks, and you seem to have liked talking to me too. I think we could be friends. Please, say yes. I promise I won't talk your ear off. Whaddaya say?"

"Well . . . I guess it'll be okay. And you are right. I have enjoyed talking to you." By this time Ruth was blushing from ear to ear. She wrote her number down and gave it to Ralph.

"It's settled. I'll give you a call this weekend, if not before."

"Okay. Goodbye, Mr. Gordon."

"What did I ask you to call me?"

"Oh, yeah. I'll be seeing you, Ralph."

Ralph turned and winked. "You can bank on that." He grinned.

Ralph and Ruth began to talk two or three times a week. She had to admit that having a man to talk to for a change felt kind of good. She still remembered and missed the long conversations she and Solumun used to share, so it was quite refreshing and revitalizing to talk to Ralph. She later found out that he had never been married and didn't have any children. They often met at Ruth's house for coffee, sometimes looking at rented videos and munching on popcorn.

The initial extent of their intimacy was a sweet, tender kiss they shared from time to time. However, three months into their relationship, Ralph and Ruth made love. She didn't remember sparks flying or firecrackers going off. The night was nice, though. Ralph invited her over to his place. Though it smelled like stale cigar smoke and beer, it was quite neat and clean. He had a mixed-breed terrier he called Puffy.

"What's on the menu this evening, Chef Ralph?"

"Let's see, I've prepared a meal of T-bone steak, baked potato, and Caesar salad. We're going to sip on white Zinfandel with dinner."

"Ahh, I see. I like the sound of this."

After a delicious meal and two glasses of wine, not only was Ruth full, she felt a little giddy. She hadn't drunk wine or any other alcoholic beverage for years.

They relaxed on the couch listening to a CD of the '70s best love songs. When he kissed her this time, he was more passionate. His tongue knowingly found his way to hers, and she found herself becoming quite aroused.

It had been twelve years since Solumun's death, twelve years since she had been touched, kissed, and caressed. Twelve years since she'd made love. She had come to trust Ralph, and she cared about him deeply, and he about her.

That night they made love slowly, gently, and passionately. Two people who were lonely and lost in a mean, evil world. Two people who were searching for some companionship, who wanted to belong to somebody. Two people who became one as they satisfied their wanton desire.

Over the next two years, they enjoyed each other's company without talk of commitment or the mention of love. Ruth welcomed Ralph's companionship. It was because of him she began to feel better about her life without Solumun. He erased some of the bouts of loneliness that used to attack her spirit from time to time.

She didn't want to accept, however, what was staring her dead in the face. She'd known for quite some time that Ralph was in love with her. She saw the way he watched her when he thought she wasn't looking. She felt it, when he kissed her and stroked her, but she could never love him in the way he deserved.

Ruth found herself in a dilemma, when Ralph asked her to marry him. Fifty years old, he was now ready to get hitched. She had to be careful because the last thing she wanted to do was hurt him. He meant a lot to her, but she couldn't accept his proposal of marriage. She would be cheating herself if she did.

"Ralph, I care about you, I really do. As a matter of fact, I care about you a lot, but I—"

"I know . . . you can't marry me. You don't love me in that way. I know that, Ruth. But we're not getting any younger. I mean, look here, woman, you know we're good for each other. I'll do whatever I can to make you happy for as long as we both live. You know that."

"I know you will, but you deserve more. You deserve someone who wants to make you happy too. That's not me, Ralph. I can't give my all to a man anymore. I just can't. Solumun will always have my all. Now maybe you don't understand that, since he's dead, but if you ever find that soul mate, that special one, then you'll know exactly what I'm talking about."

"Ruth, I do understand where you're coming from, but won't you just give me a chance? We can do this. I know we can."

"No, we can't. I know I haven't been true to my faith over the years, but that doesn't mean that I condone the kind of relationship we have. What we've done is a sin, Ralph. I know it, and you know it. How can I call myself a Christian, when I'm sleeping around with you? How can I keep on doing this?"

"Ruth, listen to me—"

"No, let me finish." She put two fingers against his thin lips. "We aren't children. Either we get married, or we don't. To be honest, I'm not ready to marry you or anyone for that matter, Ralph. I don't know if I'll ever be."

After what seemed liked an eternity of silence, Ralph finally spoke. "You're a heck of a woman." He kissed her gently and rose from the sofa. "I guess you're ready to leave now?"

"Yes, I think that would be best. Do you mind?" Ruth rose from the couch.

"I'm a big boy. I can't say that I'm not disappointed, because I am. But I respect you for being honest, and I really do understand."

Several minutes later, they pulled up at Ruth's house. "Can I at least walk you to your door?" Ralph smiled.

"Sure, you can, come on."

They moved down the trail in silence until they reached her front door. She turned to the side and looked over at him.

With a hint of sadness on his face, he returned her stare. "I'm leaving now. You know I won't be back, not after this. I just can't come back."

"I understand. Believe me, I do. But we'll both be all right, you'll see. You're a good man, Ralph Gordon. Your day will come. When it does, make sure you send me an invitation."

They hugged each other like the best of friends often do. He walked away, not once looking back.

Ruth unlocked the door, stepped inside, and closed the door behind her. Strolling to her bedroom, she grabbed her remote off the dresser, turned on the TV, and began to laugh when she saw the odd-looking couple on the Jerry Springer show.

Three months later, she took Fantasia up on her offer and retired from the hospital, packed her bags, and moved to Belleaf.

26

New Birth

"Come right this way, Mr. Phillips," Ruth said. "I'll show you to Fantasia's office."

"Please, call me William."

"This way then, William." Ruth led him down the long, winding corridor that was expertly lined with African-American art, abstracts, pastels, and Fantasia's famous heart pieces.

William prayed that Ruth could not hear the heavy pounding of his heart. *What's going on?* He didn't understand how this woman was having such a tantalizing effect on him.

God, I sure hope he doesn't notice how nervous he's making me, Ruth thought to herself. *I'm as excited as two toads on a lily pad with a pile full of June bugs.* She let out a soft giggle.

"Did you say something, Mrs. Runsome?" William asked her, as they continued down the corridor.

"Oh, no, I was just clearing my throat. It's a little scratchy." When they approached the entrance to Fantasia's office, she thought, *Thank God.* "Here we are, William, and by the way, please call me Ruth."

"My pleasure."

"Fantasia, William Phillips is here."

Fantasia immediately looked up from her desk, eyeing both

her mother and William Phillips. She could swear that the both of them had a flushed look about them, like they'd been caught with their hands in the cookie jar or something.

"Mr. Phillips, how nice it is to finally meet you in person. It's great to see the man behind the scenes, the one who loves my art, but who for some reason has refused to grace me with the pleasure of meeting him in person—until now."

"The pleasure is mine as well. And by all means, call me William," he said with a dashing smile.

"Okay, I shall, William." Fantasia smiled pleasantly. "Please, won't you have a seat." Gesturing with her hands, she directed him to another area of her office.

As he approached the round office table, William pulled out a chair for Fantasia then looked over his shoulder, as if beckoning for Ruth.

"No, I'm afraid I won't be joining you at this time." Ruth took this as the perfect opportunity to excuse herself. "I have tons of paperwork and phone calls to finish. I'm going to my office, Fantasia."

"All right, Mother."

"It was nice meeting you, Mr. Phillips—I mean, William."

"Surely, this won't be our last meeting." He paused a moment before mouthing under his breath so Ruth couldn't hear him, "You can rest assured of that, Miss Runsome."

Fantasia gave her mother a wink on the sly as if to say, *You go, girl.*

"Mrs. Runsome, Mr. Phillips on line two please," the gallery receptionist's voice echoed over the intercom.

"Good morning, William," Ruth said, politely, while smiling on the other end. "How are you this morning?"

"I'm doing great, and yourself?"

"I'm good. How can I help you?"

"I thought I should call to confirm that we're still on for this evening's planning session. You know the annual charity ball is only a few months away."

"It'll be here before we know it."

"Right you are, and we still have a long way to go before we finalize the plans about the roles both our companies are going to play."

"Yes, I know. So of course we're still on. You know you could have just had your assistant follow up with ours."

William paused momentarily. Her response made him feel somewhat awkward because she was right. What she didn't know was that he had made it a point to call her himself. Ever since he met her that day, he couldn't get her off his mind. Fantasia was the one who contacted him, asking if he would work with her mother on the charity ball, a suggestion he'd welcomed. But now, talking to Ruth this morning, William didn't want to do or say anything that would put this woman on the defensive. He didn't want to make any unwelcome moves. He missed his wife, but like his sons often told him, it was time to move on, to take the next step forward in his life. Lois would have wanted him to.

"William? William, are you still there?" Ruth called out, not hearing anything over the phone line.

"Yes, I'm still here. I was thinking about what you said. You're right—I could have asked my assistant to call the gallery, but I had some free time myself and she's going to be coming in late this morning, so I decided to go ahead and call. That's all right with you, isn't it?"

"Sure. I just know how busy you are, so I wouldn't want you to bother with matters that can be taken care of by someone else. You do understand what I mean, don't you?"

"Yes, but I have a confession to make."

"I'm all ears."

He hesitated. "I wanted to call personally."

She listened intently, her stomach churning.

"Ruth?"

"Yes."

"Did you hear me?"

"Yes, I heard you, William."

"Like I said, I thought I'd call personally." He treaded as cautiously as he knew how. "I wanted to know if, instead of meeting here at my office, if you'd like to discuss plans over dinner? I mean, I-I, uh, thought it would be something different." He shut his eyes real tight and said a prayer that Ruth would not think him too brassy or forward. *Just let her say yes,* he prayed.

"That's a great idea. Where do you want me to meet you?"

"I have an off-site meeting scheduled for later this afternoon. I should be finished with it by six. If you like, I can pick you up after that. I can come by the gallery or your place, or wherever you're going to be. Tell me where, and I'll be there, say, around seven?"

"Seven's fine. You can pick me up at my condo. My address is 3290 N. Guifford in Charles Village."

William responded while he wrote down her address. "Certainly. I'll be there at seven." His penmanship was somewhat shaky as he came to the realization that he had succeeded in making plans to have dinner with the most attractive woman he'd seen in a long time.

"Any ideas as to where we'll dine?"

"I thought we'd go to Hampton's."

" 'Hampton's'? My, I'm impressed. You couldn't have chosen a better place. Their food is simply heavenly. So I guess I'll see you later this evening. Bye for now."

"Goodbye, Ruth. Have a good day. I'll see you tonight."

When Ruth hung up the phone, she jumped from behind the oblong walnut desk and let out a low scream. "Ooohhh! I've met the man. Ooohhh!"

Throughout the course of the day, she could hardly keep her excitement hidden. She strolled proudly through the gallery all day, a big smile etched on her round face. With her deep-dimpled cheeks and flawless mocha-colored skin, Ruth was quite a looker.

The years had definitely been kind to her. Every strand of her thick, curly hair was in place.

She was usually somber-looking and pensive, but not today. No, today was a record-breaker for Ruth. Even Taiwan, the gallery receptionist, stared at Ruth in awe of her perky attitude. It wasn't that Ruth was mean or anything, but she was always about business, never showing that she had a personal side. She was friendly and courteous, but she never asked anyone about their personal affairs and no one was to ask about hers, an unspoken rule of thumb around the gallery.

"Yes!" William screeched. He raised his closed fist up and down in a swift motion, signifying he'd crossed over his first hurdle. He felt doggone good about it too. He let out another yelp and a laugh at the thought that he'd finally asked her out.

"Well, I mean I did tell her it was going to be a business meeting," he mumbled. "I don't guess that constitutes a date, but who cares? We're going to dinner so—what the heck—I'm calling it a date."

Unlike Ruth, William was a jovial boss who was personable with his staff and always concerned about what was going on in their lives.

"Mr. Phillips, is everything okay?" His assistant had a look of concern plastered across her face when she asked.

"Yes, everything is fine. Why—do I look like something's wrong?"

"I guess I'll have to answer yes to that question, Mr. Phillips. I've been standing here calling your name for about thirty seconds and not once did you look up. You've were sitting there staring out the window with a strange look on your face."

"Oh that. I guess I'm just thinking happy thoughts this morning," he jovially responded. He rose from his high-backed leather chair, strolled over to the table where coffee and water were always readily available, and poured himself a fresh cup of decaf. "Would you like some?" he asked his assistant.

"No, thank you, Mr. Phillips. I just wanted to let you know that I was here. Do you need anything, sir?"

"No, not at the moment." He paused. "On second thought, I do. Will you make sure I have the files pertaining to the charity gala before lunch? I need to look over them. Also, call Hampton's and make reservations for two, please. I'd like you to reserve one of their private dining rooms. I have an important engagement this evening with Mrs. Runsome from Trinity Three Art Gallery. Make the reservations for eight o'clock."

"I'll get on it right away, sir." She turned to walk away and smiled. She had an idea that her boss had a liking for Ruth Runsome, and she was happy for him. She'd witnessed the loneliness on his face from day to day. Women from his company were after him like a dog after a bone, but he wouldn't bite. He made a habit of attending galas like the charity ball solo. He'd arrive early and leave even earlier. Maybe this marked the beginning of something good in his life. He had certainly suffered his share of pain.

With the perfect blend of contemporary and classic design, richly lacquered panels, subtle ambiance and soft lights, Hampton's was nestled in the heart of downtown Belleaf. Its exquisite beauty complemented its reputation for excellent American cuisine. Ruth and William made their entrance into the restaurant and were greeted by a tuxedo-wearing host.

"Good evening, Mr. Phillips, Madam," the host remarked. "Right this way," he gestured with one hand, leading to the private dining room. "Your dining area is ready, sir."

"It's been some time since I've been here," Ruth told William as they entered the private area of the four-star restaurant. "Everything is lovely."

"I'm glad you approve of my choice." William smiled, his eyebrows perked, and his eyes seductively lingered on her. "I must tell you again, Ruth, that you look absolutely stunning this evening."

"Thank you." She smiled with added confidence and assurance.

Ruth was especially glad she'd chosen a wine-colored silk Badgley Mischka off-the-shoulder dress with capped sleeves. The delicate gathers around the top of the dress and along the hem formed a diamond like pattern, framing her curves perfectly. The sash around her waist further enhanced the ultimate femininity of Ruth Runsome, which showed in every step she took.

Ruth and William laughed and talked with ease while dining on roasted veal with ginger spiced apples and champagne.

"I like the ideas you've presented for the gala. Teaming up with you, I see, is really going to pay off," Ruth said.

William raised an eyebrow. "I have a sneaky suspicion that the pleasure of working alongside you is going to be all mine." William's smile highlighted his silvery mustache and porcelain veneers.

Ruth blushed. "What do you think our next step should be?"

"I think we should follow your suggestions and send out sponsorship letters right away. What I'd add to that is advertising the gala through TV and radio spots." William looked over at her empty glass. "Would you like more champagne, dessert, anything?"

"No, I can't eat another morsel, and I'm afraid if I drink any more champagne, I'll forget the reason we're here."

"Fine. No problem."

They chatted for almost two hours before Ruth brought their time together to an end. "William, it's been fun and informative too. I think we covered a lot of ground tonight, don't you?"

"Yes, I agree. Tomorrow morning I'll have my assistant type up our notes and courier them to you. We'll go from there after you've had a chance to review them."

The waiter approached the table. "Sir, is there anything else I can get for you?"

"No. Everything was fine. I'll have the check now please."

William paid the $185 check, leaving a generous tip. He proceeded to take Ruth home.

Seventeen minutes later they arrived at her tri-level condo.

"Thanks for a lovely evening." Ruth stared at William. She couldn't seem to take her eyes off of him. The physical attraction was far too strong. She cleared her throat and gathered her wine-colored sequined clutch bag as she readied herself to exit the car.

William zeroed in on her long, svelte legs. He hated that the evening had to end. *What I wouldn't give to taste those sensuous-looking lips of hers*, he thought to himself. *I bet she's soft as a ball of cotton. I'd better end this evening. I don't think I can continue acting like a gentleman; this woman is too fine and sexy.*

"Hold up, I'll get the door." William rushed over to her side of the car. Opening the door to the Lincoln, he stretched out his hand to help her. Her hands were smooth and soft, just like he knew they would be. "Let me walk you to your door."

"No, that won't be necessary, William."

"Please, allow me. The pleasure would be mine."

Ruth blushed again. *He sure knows the right words to say. Lord, have mercy. Control yourself, girl, control yourself.* "Goodnight," she said as she reached the door.

"Goodnight, Ruth."

When William turned and walked away, she let out a sigh, turned the key and went inside.

27

A Love That's Real

Twins, Kevin and Kaleb, were a handful indeed. They were smart, bright, and full of energy. Prodigal and Faith often told their friends that they couldn't ask for two lovelier and more highly favored children than Kevin and Kaleb, but Faith still wanted a little girl to add to their already happy family. She often chided Prodigal about having a little girl so that she could have someone on her side for a change. And, of course, Prodigal wanted to do whatever it took to keep his wife happy. He loved the thought of having a daughter as lovely as Faith.

Through the years, he'd tried to keep her assured of his love for her and the boys. His family meant the world to him, and he would never do anything to jeopardize that. But Teary meant the world to him too, and he could never break the vow he'd made to her all those many years ago. Some way, he had to make peace in his family. He couldn't lose Faith, and he couldn't lose Teary. But he couldn't take a chance on upsetting Faith again, not after the way their marriage had suffered.

Prodigal performed his nightly ritual of checking on the boys before retiring for the evening. As usual, his thoughts turned toward Teary. She was still having a difficult time in her life, and he wished there was something he could do to take her pain away.

When he'd first told Faith about Teary's health issue, Faith was understanding and tried more than once to talk to Teary, to console her and reassure her that God was still in control, but Teary didn't want to hear it. Teary couldn't understand how Faith, or Prodigal for that matter, could ever comprehend the emotional pain she was going through when they had been blessed with Kevin and Kaleb. She would never be able to have that same sense of joy, that feeling of being a mother.

Prodigal made a mental note to give Teary a call when he went out the next day, just to see how things were going. He would stop at the fire station and call from there. It had been a while since their last phone conversation. He had to admit that he was glad when Teary first told him she had been offered a job in Memphis. He had hoped that moving away from Broknfield would be the beginning of a new life for her. So far, things were working out for her, and for that he was grateful.

After the divorce, and with Prodigal's encouragement, Teary had returned to school and got her master's in journalism. Happier than she had been in a very long time, she was thankful to God for healing her heart. The job at the newspaper paid her a hefty five-figure salary. A good money manager, she invested in a beautiful, modest two-bedroom.

Prodigal gave the boys a final peck on the cheek, double-checked to make sure all the doors were locked, and then went into the bedroom.

Lying next to Faith, he felt warm and secure. He turned on his side, resting his body on one elbow. He traced her ear with his soft, warm breath.

She moaned softly.

He gently stroked her still slender, brown-skinned body and caressed her round, firm butt through her satin nightie. She wallowed in satisfaction as his hands moved the gown slowly along her body and up over her head. His hands touched her warm, bare skin, and she felt her desire reach a feverous pitch. He heard himself groan when he felt the moistness of her secret place.

She moaned out loud while he continued to caress her. The earlier tension Faith felt between them was forgotten and desire stepped in its place. His hard, rough hands moved with ease over her delicate body, touching her large, round mounds. He tenderly teased and manipulated every inch of her body between his fingers as his hands moved slowly, squeezing her in just the right places.

Suddenly he felt something unfamiliar. He knew every curve of her body, and something wasn't right. He manipulated her flesh again over the large, hard lump. He continued to move his hand over the familiar area of his wife's breast.

"Prod, ooh baby, that's tender," she screamed.

"I'm sorry, sweetheart." He raised himself up from over her and pulled her up toward him until she was lying back in his arms.

"Let me turn on the light. I want to see what's going on." He spotted the redness on her breast. He reached out and touched the hard area.

Once more she screamed again until tears formed in the corners of her eyes. She moved to the side of the bed, slipped her feet into her slippers, then went and stood in front of the mirror. She examined her breasts and discovered another lump underneath her left breast. She swallowed hard, and sweat broke out on her forehead.

"Hey," Prodigal said, moving his naked body off the bed, "it's probably just a couple of benign cysts. Remember if it were something more serious, I don't think it would be sore like that. Why don't you call the doctor's office tomorrow and make an appointment to see him. Let me know when you get the appointment set, so I can be sure to go with you, all right?"

"All right."

"Now, where were we?" he whispered in her ear. His hands encircled her waist again, and she relaxed back in his arms, against the hardness of his body. When he kissed her this time, her screams were not from pain, but from pleasure. He hoisted her body up on the dresser, and they showered each other with their love.

Two days later Faith and Prodigal sat in the doctor's office listening as the doctor told Faith, "We're going to schedule a mammogram."

"When will that be?" Prodigal asked.

"I'd like to have it done as quickly as possible. Let me check with my nurse so she can check to see if we can get you in this afternoon. I'll be right back," the doctor told them.

"Baby, don't start worrying." Prodigal stroked Faith's hair. He saw her furrowed brows and knew that she was trying to hold back her fear.

She responded by slightly nodding her head.

"Is three o'clock a good time?" the doctor asked when he returned to the room minutes later.

Prodigal responded for his wife, "Yes, we can do that."

"Fine. Be at the Women's Center this afternoon."

"Doctor, how can this be possible? I do a breast self-exam every month. I didn't notice anything last month that was different nor when I took a shower just a few days ago. I don't understand."

"It doesn't take long for a lump to surface, Mrs. Runsome," the doctor told her. "Don't worry yourself. Let's get the mammogram done first. After that, we'll more than likely do a diagnostic ultrasound as well. Then we'll arrange for you to talk to a specialist."

" 'A specialist'? God, no." Faith squirmed on the exam table.

"Don't let that scare you. A specialist can read the mammogram and ultrasound far more extensively."

"Thanks, doctor. We appreciate that." Prodigal placed his arm around his wife's shoulders.

"Honey, I'm scared," Faith said as they walked toward their car.

"There's nothing to worry about," Prodigal replied tenderly, trying not to show how worried he was. "Anyway, you heard what the doctor said, sweetheart—it's probably nothing. Come on, let's go have some lunch and do a little window-shopping until it's time to go over to the hospital. If you're a good girl, I might even buy you a little something." He laughed, and patted her on the butt.

Faith tried to let out a light laugh, but fear quickly welled up inside of her.

They went to have lunch at Houston's, a popular restaurant located on the strip that served everything from steak to cod.

"I don't know what I want to eat. I can't even think about food right now. I have too much on my mind," Faith said anxiously.

"Look, this is one of those times where we have to put our total trust in God." Prodigal looked deep into her worried face. "He's always brought us through, honey. I mean, look at us—we've been through your pregnancy with the twins, and you know how rough that was. Remember, the doctor didn't think you were going to be able to carry the boys to term? He put you on bed rest three months into your pregnancy, remember?"

"Yes, I remember, and you're right. Look at Kevin and Kaleb now—they came out healthy, handsome, and perfect, didn't they? And look at all we have. You're right, God has been good to us."

"He sure has, and now is not the time to lose our trust in Him. No matter what, you know I'll always be by your side. You have to know that, Faith. You have to believe that I love you with everything inside of me."

"I love you too, and we're going to make it through this. Anyway, it's probably like you said, just a cyst. I'm not claiming a malignancy or anything, right?"

"Right, baby." He shook his head, relieved that she wasn't going to give up. "Now let's get something to eat!"

The waitress approached the table and asked if they were ready to order.

"Yes, I'm ready. I'll have the grilled chicken platter with a baked potato and a large iced tea with lemon," Faith told the waitress.

"Now that's what I'm talking about." Prodigal smiled. "I'll have the same, but with a Dr. Pepper instead."

They sat in silence eating their lunch.

Prodigal didn't know what he would do if anything ever happened to Faith. He couldn't imagine life without her. The boys needed their mother, and he needed his wife. He wanted to call Teary to tell her what was happening but changed his mind. It was time he started being more considerate of his wife's feelings. He rubbed his hand over the top of his head, and his eyebrows furrowed. This was going to be tougher than he thought.

Teary paced back and forth outside of the restaurant, juggling in her mind whether to go inside and meet the guy from the gym. They'd talked several times when they'd run into each other after their exercise routines. He certainly seemed nice enough, had more than a little pocket change, wasn't hard on the eyes, and was quite articulate. So what was holding her back? Her life had been tumultuous, riddled with one too many bad relationship experiences. She couldn't seem to ever shake the remnants of her past. Smoothing down her white linen skirt with the palms of her hands, she made a step closer to the restaurant entrance, took a deep breath, and walked inside.

He was standing on the other side, waiting on her. With a single flower in his hands, he kissed her on the cheek, pushed the flower toward her, and led her to their table.

Teary enjoyed the dinner, but hearing him talk non-stop about his ex-wife and his baby mama was a tad too much for her. She savored the taste of the salmon with mixed vegetables. While he continued to talk, Teary ordered a molten chocolate brownie for dessert. His words had become jumbled in her mind to the point that she had to eat to keep from bursting into laughter. *This could happen to nobody but me*, she said to herself. *How hilarious.*

Being in Memphis had helped give her somewhat of a better

outlook on her life. The Southern hospitality, affordable housing, and a great job had lured her, and she had learned to love the city as her own. There were still moments of loneliness, and she missed being close to Prodigal. But if she was ever going to make it in the big bad world, she had to do what she had to do.

Maybe one day she would enjoy the kind of life Prodigal and Faith had together, including their rifts. Prodigal had never admitted it to Teary, but Teary sensed that even his perfect marriage was less than perfect and that she was somewhat to blame. Every now and then, Teary detected annoyance in Faith's voice, when she would call and ask for Prodigal. She'd tried to make her calls less frequent over the years so as not to alienate Faith, but it was hard. For Teary, excluding Prodigal from her life was virtually impossible to do.

Teary curled up on the sofa, thinking about her horrific date. She reached over for the phone to call Prodigal. He would get a kick out of what she was about to tell him about her latest dating adventure. Pausing for a moment, she dialed Sara's number instead of Prodigal's. This was one of those times when she longed to talk to him, but she reminded herself that she had to back off a little.

Sara was glad to hear from Teary and told her so. It wasn't often that they talked, but when they did, they tried to make up for lost time.

Sara laughed when Teary told her that at one point during dinner the guy actually started crying, talking about his baby mama. Talking to Sara proved to be like a dose of good medicine for Teary.

"Sara, it's been good talking to you," Teary told her sister. "I guess I'll call it a night."

"You know you have tripped me out tonight." Sara chuckled. "You sure know how to pick 'em, sis."

"Tell me about it." Teary laughed at herself. "I stand a better chance of winning the lottery than getting a good man."

"But you don't even gamble."

"Exactly. And that's what I'm talking about."

"Now I wouldn't go to that extent. Your day will come, and when it does, you'll know it. Until then, have fun. Enjoy the single life!"

The two sisters talked for several more minutes before saying goodbye.

Teary smiled again at herself, as she got ready for bed. After she showered, she knelt down beside her bed and prayed. She asked God to bring someone into her life who would love her for her. She asked Him to bless Prodigal and his family. "And, Lord, don't let me bring confusion or tension into Prodigal's life. You know I love him too much to do anything like that. Amen." She climbed up off her knees, slid between the covers, and drifted into dreamland.

Ruth was in awe at the turnout for the charity gala. It had turned out to be better than she could have hoped for, and then some. News teams, complete with their camera equipment and all the trappings, followed every minute of the event. The classic Diamante Ballroom and Convention Center was the perfect setting. Trinity Three Art Gallery and Museum brought in a select group of some of its most expensive pieces for a silent auction, while several other corporations donated items, everything from jewelry to round-trip tickets to Aruba and Venice.

"Isn't everything absolutely fabulous, William?" Ruth surveyed the crowded ballroom.

"Absolutely. This wouldn't have been possible without your hard work."

"No, no, no. I'm not going to let you give me all of the credit. It was the two of us. You're the one with all of the big connections, remember?" She sipped on her champagne and looked into his eyes, her head tilted slightly backward, allowing her hair to caress her neck.

He couldn't take his eyes off her. *She is breathtaking.*

Her velvet dress trimmed in black beaded fringe was accented with sparkling glass beads, and her revealing plunging neckline hinted at her intriguing sexiness.

Over 500 guests paid $750 per plate to dine on crunchy vegetable vermicelli with seared ahi appetizers. The entree included salmon grilled with fresh vegetables, avocados, and tomatoes.

"Mother, this is the best charity gala ever to be held in Belleaf, and it's all because of you two." Fantasia turned and looked at William with total satisfaction and admiration. "I don't know how to thank you. Not only have you managed to raise more money than any of the other charity galas over the last few years, but you've pushed Trinity Three a couple of notches up on the scales of the elite. People are going to leave here tonight with nothing but good things to say."

Ruth kissed her daughter on the forehead. "Sweetie, I'm glad everything turned out so well. William and I enjoyed pulling everything together. Now enough has been said. You've sung our praises long enough. Go have some fun, make some contacts. Strut your stuff."

"And you, Miss Runsome, won't you strut your stuff with me on the dance floor?" William extended his arm out to Ruth and then led her to the palatial dance area.

William was an excellent dancer, and Ruth found it easy to follow his lead. He held her in his arms as they slow-danced gracefully across the floor. She rested her head against his chest and listened to the band playing a sensuous jazz tune. She felt like she was Cinderella and he was her Prince Charming. He brought out a side of her that had lain dormant for all these years. He restored a smile to her entire spirit. She was living again.

Lying on the soft pillows of her king-sized bed at night she would often look at her picture of Solumun and talk to him as if he were right beside her. "Solumun, I never thought there would ever be anyone in my life again, sweetheart, not ever. I don't know how things are going to turn out between William and I. All I know is that I feel safe with this man. He'll never be able to replace you, no one will. But he does make me laugh. He makes me feel good inside. He makes me happy. I just want you to know that I'll always love you—always." She kissed his picture and clutched it tightly to her bosom, and closed her eyes in a peaceful sleep.

Fantasia loved the change that she witnessed in her mother. She adored William because not only was he a good man, he was a good man for her mom.

Ruth was responsible for her share of glad tidings to William as well. In Ruth, William found someone he could trust, confide in, and open up to. He found in her what he once believed no one but Lois could ever possess. The two of them were like lovesick puppy dogs. They often behaved like star-struck teenage lovers, walking hand in hand, stealing butterfly kisses from each other. Life and love were grand.

28

Fear Not

Faith was referred to an oncologist for additional tests. Today she would get the results of those tests. During the past couple of days, she had prayed constantly. Like Prodigal told her, this was the time to rely on her faith in God. Besides God, her two healthy, rambunctious boys and, of course, Prodigal, was the core of her life.

Thinking about the years she spent jealous and angry about Prodigal and Teary, she was determined to push her insecure feelings about their relationship aside. Life was far too short, and she wanted to live it to the fullest with the three men she loved most in the world. She made a pledge to herself to stop sweating the small stuff, and like she'd read somewhere—All of it was small stuff. Beginning today, she would embrace her life and her family. No more jealousy and envy over Teary. If anything, she needed to pray harder for Teary to find the same happiness she'd found with Prodigal.

"Mrs. Runsome, please come in." The oncologist gestured for Faith to sit down.

To Faith, the woman doctor sounded almost too polite.

"Please have a seat, and we'll go over your test results."

"Can you wait for just a few minutes? My husband went to call the sitter and check on our boys, and I would prefer that he be here with me."

"Certainly. That's no problem."

Prodigal suddenly burst through the door. "I'm sorry," he said, out of breath. "Baby, the boys are fine—Did I miss anything?"

"No. As a matter of fact, we just came in here. Have a seat." The doctor pointed to a corner chair. "Mrs. Runsome, the mammogram and ultrasound revealed two lumps in the left breast area, one at the three o'clock spot, and the other one at the nine o'clock area of your breast. What I'd like to do next is arrange for you to have a biopsy to determine whether the lumps are malignant or not.

"I must tell you that I would like to go on and make arrangements before you leave this afternoon to have the biopsy done this week. Is that okay with you?"

Faith stared straight ahead. She couldn't bear to look at the hurt and bewilderment that she knew must've been on her husband's face. She nodded yes to the doctor. "Do what you have to do. I want to get this over and done with as quickly as possible."

Prodigal reached over to squeeze her hand. "Faith, are you sure?"

"Yes, I'm sure."

"Mrs. Runsome, have you undergone a breast biopsy before?"

"No."

"Let me tell you some of the things you should expect. First, I will perform what is called an open surgical biopsy, which is done in an operating room. The biopsy will not require general anesthesia. Instead, you will be given a local anesthetic to the breast only. In some cases it might be necessary to use a combination of intravenous sedation along with a local anesthetic, but that will be determined the day of your biopsy. I'll make a one-half to two-inch incision in the breast. Once the incision is made, I will completely remove both lumps, along with the surrounding tissue. Are you with me so far?"

"Yes, I understand." Faith nodded.

"You'll require a few stitches. After the procedure is complete, most patients require at least a full day of recovery. Any questions?"

Faith spoke up right away. "Yes. How accurate is this biopsy, doctor?"

"Close to one hundred percent. I can also tell you that sixty-five to eighty percent of breast biopsies turn out to be non-cancerous. However, if the biopsy results do indicate a malignancy, I must ask you to please think seriously about whether you want me to proceed with removing the malignancy, which oftentimes includes the removal of the entire breast, or if we go in and see a malignancy and it is localized, we may be able to perform a lumpectomy."

Confused and dazed, Prodigal asked, "What exactly is a lumpectomy?"

"Instead of removing the entire breast, we surgically remove the malignant lump in the breast, along with a small margin of the surrounding normal breast tissue. If this procedure has to be done, it will allow your wife to maintain most of her breast after surgery. If the biopsy reveals a malignancy, I want to assure you that the earlier breast cancer is diagnosed, the greater the chances for survival. I know this sounds frightening, Mr. and Mrs. Runsome, but I want to be as candid with you as possible. I also encourage you to seek a second opinion."

"Sure. Thanks, doctor," Prodigal said as he and Faith sat there stunned.

"I tell you what I'm going to do." The doctor stood up. "I'm going to leave you two alone for a few minutes, while I go and get everything scheduled and get back with you. Feel free to sit here in my office, and as hard as it might be, try to relax. Here are some brochures you can take with you when you leave that will give you a more in-depth explanation of the biopsy procedure. Do you have other questions, before I leave?"

Neither of them replied.

The doctor took this as a no and quickly exited through the oak door.

"Mrs. Runsome, please try to calm down. I know this is hard for you, but I must re-emphasize that when breast cancer is detected early, such as the case with you, there is a greater chance that you can overcome this disease. Please, take a little time to calm down, so you can think rationally about what you want to do from here, not what other people want."

Faith could only hear the doctor's initial words ringing throughout her mind, *The biopsy showed cancerous cells in the breast area and also in the lymph nodes.*

Prodigal vaguely heard the specialist himself. He thought he heard her say something like, "Think about what you want to do, what you're willing to do, and what you are able to do."

'*Able to do*'? Prodigal thought. *What is the doctor saying?* Prodigal's anger raged within. He tried to calm his wife as best he could by holding her tight against his chest, caressing her hair, and sharing in her sorrow.

"Faith, we're going to make it through this," he assured her. "We're going to fight against this thing tooth and nail, you hear me?"

"Yes, I hear you, and you're right," she said in-between deep sobs. "I'm going to keep my trust in God because He doesn't give us any more than we can bear. I'll beat this disease. We will beat it, right?" She looked into Prodigal's eyes for confirmation.

"Right, sweetheart."

They clung to each other in silence.

The specialist continued talking. "This is the beginning of a difficult journey, a critical juncture in your life. I must tell you that some women give up without even trying. Instead they become hopeless, even though they may end up going through treatment steps; they refuse to fight against it. That's what it's going to take, Mrs. Runsome. Breast cancer is a war, a war that is trying to steal away your dreams, your hopes, your life. You have

INTO EACH LIFE 219

to fight the war by taking on one battle at a time. You and your husband seem to have faith in a higher power, so re-direct your anger and hurt to tuning in to that higher power. You have to be strong for the battle ahead, Mrs. Runsome. And Mr. Runsome, she's going to need your total support."

"You don't have to tell me that, doctor. I'm going to stick by my wife, no matter what. I'm going to help her to win this battle. And as far as a higher power goes, we don't believe in a 'higher power,' doctor. We believe in God, our Savior. He'll see us through this, won't he, Faith?"

"Yes, Prodigal. God will see us through this," she whispered softly.

Soon after the devastating news, Faith's health took a sudden turn for the worse. A mastectomy was performed on her breast, but chemotherapy and radiation proved to be of no real value because the cancer had spread not only to her lymph nodes, but also basically all over her body. In fact, the doctor gave her less than six months to live.

Faith and Prodigal tried to make life as seamless as possible, when it came to the boys. There was just no use in telling them the seriousness of their mother's illness. More as a source of comfort for herself, Faith began making tapes of different events that she believed the boys would experience throughout their lives. She gave them a mother's point of view. One thing she knew that she would be able to rely on even after she was dead and gone was that Prodigal would take good care of their sons. She wasn't worried about that at all. She was saddened by the fact that she would not be a part of the everyday lives of her boys for much longer to provide a mother's love and guidance.

She hung on to God, clinging to Him in prayer, asking Him to watch over her man and her sons throughout their lives. If it was her time to die, she was ready because she had come to know the Lord when she about the same age as Kevin and Kaleb were now.

Immediately upon learning of Faith's grave illness, their church family went into action and provided the Runsome family with plenty of loving support. They held a prayer vigil on their behalf as well, and claimed total healing and deliverance for her. Church members and neighbors provided home-cooked meals for the Runsome family around the clock. The men saw to it that the lawn was maintained, and the church helped pitch in on paying some of the family's mounting medical bills. Their neighbors and friends often volunteered to help with the twins. The women and young people took turns coming to clean the house and taking Kevin and Kaleb on outings. They didn't have to worry about a thing, except her getting well. She insisted that Prodigal take her to church whenever she felt like she could put up with the pain long enough to sit through a sermon. The closer she came to death, the more she wanted to be at church.

Just as the doctor had warned, each day the pain became more unbearable as the cancer savagely attacked her body, yet Faith refused to remain in the hospital. She wanted to be with her family. Though her speech had become nearly inaudible, she continued to try to make a tape of all the things she wanted to share with her sons. She talked to them about girls, about treating them with love and respect. She talked to them about the dangers of sex outside of marriage; about drugs and wild living. She told them about standing tall and about being the head of the household when they entered marriage.

Most of all, she told them about accepting Christ and being at peace even during her time of death. She loved her family and was so grateful to God for blessing her with such a divine love.

Prodigal, on the other hand, became quite bitter about the fact that he was losing his wife, the precious mother of his children, right before his very eyes. He reflected on the early death of his father and believed somehow that a curse of some kind must be on him. *Why are you doing this? What's going on? First my father and now Faith?* More and more anger consumed him every day as he pushed the morphine pump into her tender skin.

Faith noticed the change in him and confronted him about it.

"Prodigal, you can't go on like this. You have to know that God does love us. He blessed us with each other. Though we won't grow old together, know that I will always be with you in spirit. Maybe you won't be able to see me physically any more, but baby, don't you know that nothing can separate our love?"

"Stop it, Faith. Don't talk like that."

"No! I won't stop it. You have to listen to me." Faith sat up in her bed. "Nothing can tear us apart, not even this. You have to believe in God, no matter what. You have to believe in Him for Kevin and Kaleb's sake, baby, and for your own sanity and survival. Please, when it's time for me to go, I want to go in peace. I'm going to Heaven, and I'm not afraid anymore," she said in a weak voice.

Warm tears streamed quietly down Prodigal's tear-stained face. He looked into the eyes of the girl he had loved since high school. And he couldn't bear the thought of living the rest of his life without her.

"Prodigal, listen to me—I know Heaven will be grand and beautiful; I'll be there waiting on you."

Tears flowed heavily from Prodigal's eyes. He held on to her thin, fragile body as best he could. He looked deep into her brown eyes.

She reached up with her pain-streaked fingers and brushed the tears from his eyes. "Prod, I love you," she whispered. "I love you, boy. I've loved you from the first moment I laid eyes on you. But I love God too, and He loves me. He loves us with a love we can't even begin to conceive. You know that, don't you?"

Prodigal nodded his head slowly up and down.

"Now, listen. You let this anger in your heart go. Let the bitterness leave you now. I have to know that you're going to be all right, you hear me?"

"Yes, I hear you, Faith. I love you. I love you so much." He wept uncontrollably.

Faith screamed out, her body wracked with pain.

Prodigal took hold of the morphine pump and squeezed the handle hard. Within a matter of seconds, she had drifted off into a deep sleep.

He pulled the covers up underneath her chin, leaving her to rest. Looking back over his shoulder, she looked so peaceful to him. He went into the living room and stood before the triple-wide living room window and watched with intensity the huge snowflakes as they fell silently to the ground. He thought of how quiet and serene the snow appeared.

He watched as their neighbors, the Richards, pulled into their driveway across the street. They were in their late seventies and had been married for over fifty years! *What's so different about them? What have they done that's so right? Why do they deserve to be together all of these years and me and Faith's time together is swiftly coming to an end after only ten years of marriage? What do they have that we don't? God, I don't understand any of this.* He slammed his fist hard against the wall. He hated them for having the chance to spend their entire lives together while his family was being ripped apart.

29

A Faith So Strong

Christmas was a few weeks away, and Prodigal didn't know if Faith would make it until then. He hoped that she would be able to spend one more Christmas with him and the boys. Surely God would allow them that much. His spirit being sapped away with each shallow breath she took, he was too distraught, too angry, and too hurt to pray.

He tried to be strong for the boys, waiting until they were asleep before he allowed himself to break down and cry. He certainly couldn't let Faith or the boys know he was hurting so badly. After all, she told him that he had to be strong for Kevin and Kaleb, but who would be strong for him?

He thought of Teary. She had been his confidante, the one he could always count on. They could talk about anything. How he wished he could call on her now, but on the other hand, he didn't want to tell her what was going on just yet. There was no one he could really confide in at the fire station. Just like when he was a young boy, he still had a difficult time forming deep friendships.

Of course, there was always his church family, but he didn't want to keep loading them down with his problems on top of all that they were helping them with already. He was basically the same person he was back then—a loner, except when it came to him and Teary.

He looked in on Faith and saw that she was sleeping soundly. Then he peeped in the boys' bedroom. They were asleep too. He went in the kitchen and poured himself a glass of plum wine, something he rarely did. He swished a little around in his mouth, then went into the family room and lay back on the cold leather couch.

Everything was cold to him. He knew it was only a matter of time—"A matter of days," the doctor said—before his world would completely crumble. His dear beloved wife would be gone. He didn't know how he would live without her. He didn't know how he would breathe without her. How would he and the boys survive without their tower of strength and love?

Piercing moans coming from the bedroom jarred him from his sleep. He didn't know how long he had been asleep, but he clumsily leaped up from the sofa, stumbled over the floor pillows, and barely missed the gifts scattered around the base of the Christmas tree.

"Baby, I'm here. Shhh! Everything is going to be fine." He pushed the button to release another injection of morphine into her weak body. Placing her head on his chest, he cradled her like a newborn baby, while she drifted into unconsciousness. He lay down beside her for a few minutes, studying her, remembering her, locking her into his memory.

Afraid that he might roll over and hurt her, he'd been sleeping on the sofa in the family room. Facing another night of tossing and turning, he went into the study. Aimlessly, he shuffled around the papers on his desk. Prodigal rubbed both hands back and forth through his hair. He felt totally alone and helpless.

He needed someone to talk to, but not just anyone, he wanted to talk to Teary. It had been months since they last talked, when she told him she'd received another promotion. After that, their phone conversations had become few and far between. Their schedules never could quite get into sync, especially since she would often go away on some new assignment. Maybe it was for the best. But now, he needed her.

He shuffled through the mahogany and oak desk in his study. "Where's my blue address book?" *I don't remember the last time I saw it. Darn it! I don't remember a lot of things since Faith's illness.*

Everything and every day seemed to be running together. Prodigal had been on family medical leave ever since Faith was first diagnosed, and he had no intentions of returning to the fire station until she was back to her normal self. He refused to believe that her life was over.

"God, You've got to heal her," he prayed. "You've got to do it, God. I just need to be patient and trust You, that's all."

Aha! Here it is. He pulled out the book from beneath the pile of papers stuffed in the back of the drawer. He flipped through the worn pages until he ran across her number. He eagerly dialed.

The phone rang one time . . . two times . . . three times. Teary's familiar voice began to speak—"Hi, you've called at a time when I'm unable to answer your call, but your call is important to me. So please leave a message, and I'll call you back. Bye now." *Beep.*

For the first time in a long time he allowed himself to smile.

He left a message, "Hi, bet you'll never guess who this is. I know. We haven't talked in a while. I really miss you, so I thought I'd give you a call. Wait—part of what I just said is a lie. I do miss you; that part is true—but I need you too.

"Faith is sick, I mean, real sick. I don't know what to do. I'm losing it. We said we'd be there for each other no matter what. Well, this is one of those no-matter-what times, so call me." Prodigal hung up the phone.

He stood up and shuffled into the kitchen, poured himself another glass of wine, then went back into the family room and lay on the couch. Prodigal fell asleep there. The wine had served its intended purpose.

"Hello," he answered, his voice groggy. Prodigal didn't know how long the phone had been ringing.

"Prodigal, is that you?" the familiar voice on the other end asked.

"Hey, yeah, it's me." He sat up on the couch. "Woman, am I glad to hear your voice."

His heart raced. He didn't know if it was from the three—or was it four—glasses of wine he drank earlier, or if it was because Teary was on the other end.

"How are you? It's been a while."

"Yeah, too long," Teary responded.

"Tell me what's going on with you, Miss Fullalove."

"Actually things are going pretty good. I'm still one of the editors at *The Commercial Appeal*. I'm loving every minute of it too."

He could see her smile as he listened to her. "I'm glad you got something you love—that's important you know."

"Guess what?"

"What?"

"Can you believe I have a dog and two cats? Who would have thought that, huh?"

"You must be crazy. What are you running—an animal sanctuary or something?" Prodigal was overcome with laughter.

"Nope, I just fell for these adorable creatures. One of my coworkers got me hooked on cats. They keep me from feeling so lonely. When I get home, they run and greet me, you know."

"Well, that's good. Whatever works for you. Still involved in church?"

"Yep, and I still attend the same church."

"Met Mr. Right yet?"

"I wish, but nope, I'm still not married, engaged, or anything like that. Don't have any prospects either. But such is my life. Now, that's enough about me. What's going on? What's wrong with Faith? You said it was serious, but I know your idea of serious; you just wanted to make sure I called you back, huh? One of your practical jokes."

"I wish I could say it was a practical joke, but it's not. Faith was diagnosed with breast cancer several months ago. We've been through the surgery thing, chemo, radiation, the whole works. The doctors say it's practically all over her body now." He burst into tears. "Oh, Teary, they say she won't make it but a few more days. I'm going crazy. I don't know what to do."

"Hey, listen to me. Faith is a strong woman. She always has been, and you know it. She won't let this get the best of her. She just won't. And you can't let it get the best of you either. Look, do you want me to come up there? I have a few days I can take off anyway because of the holidays. Why don't I do that, okay?" She knew he needed her, and she wanted to be there for him.

"Naw, don't come here now. I just wanted to hear your voice. I needed to hear your voice."

She could still hear him sniffling. "Why haven't you called me before now? You know I would have come a long time ago, if only I had known."

"Let's just talk, okay."

"Okay."

And the two of them did just that. Teary quickly took his mind off his present circumstances. They talked about everything, from her divorce to his sister, Hope, and her clan of children. They talked about Teary's job as well.

By the time they ended their conversation some two and a half hours later, he felt a bit of pressure lifted off him. He almost felt like things were normal . . . until he heard Faith's voice.

"Hey, I'll talk to you later. Faith's calling me."

"Okay, I'll call you tomorrow."

He abruptly hung up the phone.

"Baby, here I come," he yelled. With two giant steps he was by her side. "What is it, sweetheart?" His voice was etched with worry. "Are you in pain?" He stroked her head and kissed her hair.

"Yes," she whispered hoarsely, "but don't push the button just yet, I want to tell you something."

"What is it? Talk to me." He leaned in close to her parched lips.

"Prod," she whispered, raising her frail and bony fingers to his face.

He couldn't hold the tears back any longer. They were warm, running down his cheeks across her fingers.

"Prod, I love you." She struggled to release each word.

He leaned down even closer until she could feel his tears dripping down upon her face.

"This thing called death will never separate our love—remember what I'm saying, okay?"

"Of course, I will." He kissed her hot, feverish lips ever so softly. He wanted to lie in her chest, rest in the comfort of her arms like he used to do, but he knew he could not. Her body was far too weak and fragile. He saw her ribs and the print of her pelvis through her white cotton gown. He loved this woman. He was going to lose her any moment now and didn't know what he would do.

Her breathing became labored. "Take me to the boys. I want to see them."

"Baby, you need your rest. You can see them in the morning. It's almost daylight. I'll bring them in first thing."

"No, take me to them now. I won't be here at daylight."

"Sure, you will. Remember, it's almost Christmas, Faith." He kept trying to fight back his tears. "You're going to make it. You're going to be here for the boys and me. You can't leave us like this. We have a lifetime of living left."

"Please, take me to my boys," she begged softly, flinching from the piercing pain pounding her body.

Without another word being said, he obeyed her request and gently lifted her small body from the bed, carrying her into the boys' bedroom. He placed her down gently beside Kevin.

She reached over and stroked his sandy brown hair. "I love you, Kevin."

Kevin didn't move a muscle.

She looked at him, and a tear rolled down her sunken cheek. She motioned for Prodigal to take her over to Kaleb.

"Kaleb, my dear, sweet Kaleb," she cried. "My two precious gifts from God. Leaving the two of you is going to be so hard." She bent over and kissed him, and like his brother, he didn't flinch.

Prodigal then carried her back into the bedroom.

"Come, Prodigal," she said. "Lie beside me. I want you to hold me. Hold me like you used to hold me."

He climbed in the bed next to her.

"Take off your clothes. Take all of them off," she whispered. "I want to feel you, the real you, next to me. I want to sleep my life away wrapped in your arms. You have been the best husband a woman could ever hope for. You've been my gift, my knight in shining armor. You have given me what people are in search of— true love. Some people are together a lifetime and never experience the kind of love we have."

She looked into his eyes, and he into hers.

"I love you."

"I love you back," she said softly. Then a faint smile of love etched across her face and her eyes locked into his as she took her final breath.

30

I'll Be There

Teary finished some last-minute packing. Hearing about Faith's death was taking a toll on her. She was devastated. Placing the last of her things in her suitcase, Teary rolled two pieces of luggage to the kitchen door, hoping she had packed enough clothes. Moving to the kitchen window, she peeped outside just in time to see Patricia pulling up in her driveway.

Her co-worker, Patricia, had become a close friend and volunteered to drive Teary to the airport. Patricia had never been married, but she had gone through several unhealthy relationships. Whenever she met a guy, she would fall instantly for him and put her all into making the relationship permanent. She scared guys off with her "head-over-heels" emotions. It wasn't that any of the guys Patricia met were bummers either. They were mostly good, decent men with a lot to offer, but of course, the thought of commitment to someone too soon caused the icing on the cake to melt quick and fast.

"Patricia, take good care of my babies," Teary said, referring to her pets.

"Don't I always take care of them when you have to travel?"

"Yes, you do. But this time is a little different because I don't know exactly how long I'll be gone. I asked for a thirty-day leave of absence. I'm going to stay as long as Prodigal needs me. I told you, we go way back, and I have to be there for him."

"I know that," Patricia said. "Just take your time. Everything here will be fine. I sure hate this happened during the holidays—I mean, I hate that it's happened at all—I didn't mean that the way it came out."

"I know what you mean, and I agree with you. I know it must be hard for him and the boys. I mean, right before Christmas too. Instead of opening presents and singing Christmas carols, they're burying their momma, and he's saying goodbye to his one and only true love. I just can't even imagine the pain he is going through, Patricia. I don't know what I'm going to say to him when I see him. I just don't know."

"It's going to mean a lot to him just to have you there."

"There's no other way. I have to go to him. And there's something else I'm thinking about."

"What?"

"I know I shouldn't be thinking about my ex-husband right now. But I know I can tell you what's on my mind."

"You know it."

"I'm wondering if he's going to be at Faith's funeral. I talked to Prodigal's youngest sister, Hope, not long ago. She told me the last she heard, Skyler was still with that home-wrecker, Geena. They're married now."

"That's pitiful. I guess they both deserve each other, huh?"

"Yeah, but she also said they were doing pretty good for themselves."

"I wouldn't give a cahoots about them, Teary. He is a thing of the past, so I say forget him."

"You're right, but I can't help but wonder about him. What if he comes to the funeral and brings her with him, Patricia? They have two kids now too."

"Good for that fool. Maybe he's learned a thing or two about being a man."

"I doubt it, but she also said Geena opened a boutique that's doing really well. He's supposed to be helping her operate that. He also finally got his degree in physical therapy, and you know what kind of money PTs make."

"I hope that money goes through his hands like water. I can't believe you hadn't told me any of this stuff—What else did she say?" Patricia tried to hide the slight attitude from Teary holding out on her.

"I hadn't had a chance to tell you, with everything that's been going on with Prodigal. Anyway, you're really going to trip on this last thing."

"What is it?"

"I know I should be happy and thankful."

"Forget all that. Come on, tell me."

"He and Geena got saved. Hope said he's walking around spouting Scripture verses all over the place. Can you believe it? Why couldn't that have been me and him?"

Patricia looked up at her friend with a glint of sadness pouring from her blue eyes.

Teary seemed to know what she was thinking. "I guess you're saying that Skyler and I couldn't be like that because I still wouldn't be able to give him what he wanted most in the world."

Patricia remained silent for a moment. "Teary, it doesn't matter anyway. He's out of your life for good. The past is gone and can never be brought back again. Live for today. Remember that *all things*, not *some* things, but *all* things work out for good to those that love the Lord and are called according to His purpose—not our purpose, God's purpose, Teary."

"I know, but sometimes I just think, what if."

"Yeah, I know what you mean. But so be it; let it go. Now come on, stop thinking about the past and remember that your best friend needs you. It's not about you right now. It's about him and those two precious little boys of his."

"You're absolutely right." Teary smiled as they continued the drive to the airport.

Patricia quickly pulled up to the passenger drop-off lane of the busy Memphis International Airport. She flicked on her flashers, jumped out of the car, and helped Teary get her luggage out of the back of her steel-gray Saturn.

"Girl, you be strong now. That man is going to need you. I know he has family and all, but sometimes the shoulder of a good friend is better."

"Yeah, I know. One of the reasons I love you is because you will tell me the truth, even if it does hurt sometimes to hear it."

"The feeling is mutual. Now go on. Get going. Your flight leaves in less than an hour."

They hugged each other, while the baggage carrier tagged Teary's bags and carried them to the ticket counter.

"Bye, I'll call you."

Teary checked in then rushed through the busy terminal to catch her flight.

Gazing out the window of the airplane, Teary thought about all the years of friendship she and Prodigal shared. She envisioned him watching her, Sara, and their friends playing hopscotch from across the street in his front yard. In all the years she'd known him, there wasn't a time he'd judged her or teased her.

She rested her head against the leather seat and reflected on their friendship. A half-smile formed on her lips, when she relived the intimate kiss they shared as teenagers after their high school graduation. She could feel his lips touch hers and his hands roaming over her body. She opened her eyes to stop that thought. This surely wasn't the time to be thinking about something like that.

She was on her way to share with him the greatest pain of all—grief. Sure, it hurt him real bad when his daddy died, but he was a young boy then, and he was worried more about his momma. Losing Faith would be a totally different kind of grieving for him, because it was a different kind of love. If only she could know for a moment the kind of love Prodigal and Faith shared.

She thought she had it, when Langston slithered into her

life—wrong. Then she just knew she had found it when she met Skyler—wrong again. Now thirty-two, she'd only seen love through the eyes of another, never knowing or having it herself.

The mechanical voice of the stewardess brought her back to the present. "Please buckle your seat belts. We'll be landing in Bonsai Bay in approximately fifteen minutes."

31

Afraid to Love

Sara was doing quite well for herself and Andrew. The two of them lived in a gated, middle-class community. She and Anthony continued their relationship, but still remained unmarried. Anthony had decided several years earlier to move to Seattle to be closer to Sara and his son. It was hard to figure out the two of them. They appeared to have a good relationship. Like always, Andrew never wanted for anything. He had the love of both parents.

Anthony, however, wanted more. He didn't want just a baby mama. He wanted Sara to be his wife. Anthony had popped the question many times over the years, yet Sara's answer was always the same.

Today was another such time. Andrew was attending an out-of-town basketball clinic, and Anthony decided he'd take Sara to dinner.

After a pleasant dinner at one of her favorite restaurants, the two of them returned to Sara's apartment, where Anthony pleaded with her once again to marry him.

"I'm just not ready to marry you, Anthony. Don't you see that everything is all right just the way it is? I mean, we get along. We're both doing well for ourselves; plus you know you're free to walk out that door at any time—as long as you don't you walk out of Andrew's life, that is."

"Girl, why do you talk so crazy? I'm not going anywhere. All I'm trying to do is make things right between us, Sara. It's not right for us to deprive Andrew of having a real family. And here you are calling yourself a child of God, but the two of us are living in sin."

" 'Living in sin'?" Sara whirled around and gave him a stare that bore straight through him. "We're not living in sin. You have your own place, and I have mine—How is that living in sin, Anthony? Tell me that!" shouted Sara.

"Hold up. Just because we don't live together doesn't mean we aren't sinning just the same. I may not go to church like you do, but even I know that much. We might as well be living together as much as I'm over here. And oh yeah, I guess you forgot another important factor—we are sleeping together. I'm not trying to sound sanctimonious because I'm far from it, which is one of the reasons that I don't go to church with you."

"Don't try to use our relationship as the reason you don't go to church." Sara paced around the family room, her temper rising to a boiling point. "You don't go to church because you don't want to commit your life to God. I know that I'm not perfect, Anthony—that's why I do go to church. The two or three times that you have gone to church with me and Andrew, everyone welcomed you there with open arms. So your faith or, should I say, your lack of faith, is all on you, not me."

Anthony walked over to where Sara stood and wrapped his football-size arms around her full-figured frame. "Baby, I don't want to argue with you." He nibbled on her neck. "All I'm trying to say is that we have to do better, if not for us, then for our son. Have you really taken a good look at Andrew lately? He's not a baby anymore, Sara. The boy is sixteen years old, do you hear me?—sixteen years old."

"But, Anthony, that's just it—We aren't depriving him of anything. He has your name. He has the love of both of us. So why can't you just be content with the way things are?" Sara's voice resonated the uneasiness she felt inside. She didn't want to face what she knew was true and right.

"Didn't you hear anything I just said, Sara? It just isn't right!" He pulled away from her, his anger evident. "I want you to have my last name too—What kind of example are we setting for Andrew, huh? Answer that."

"Well, if things aren't good enough for you the way they are, maybe we should just . . . just do something else, because I can't marry you."

"Sara, you know what—maybe you're right. Maybe we do need to 'just do something else,' as you put it," he mocked. "I tell you what—while you're on the way to Faith's funeral, why don't you do this?" Anthony didn't flinch a muscle as he spoke.

Sara remained still as a statue.

"You think about us. Think about what you want for our future. Think about what Faith and Prodigal had and about what we have now. When you get back, we'll settle things between us once and for all. No more playing games, Sara, no more."

Sara was shocked. She didn't expect an ultimatum. She didn't know what she was going to do. She nodded her head as if in agreement. Turning away from him, she went in her bedroom to start packing, without saying another word to Anthony.

Faith's death opened Sara's eyes to how temporary life truly is. She thought of the mistake, or rather the accident, she'd made with Anthony. She loved her son, but if she admitted it to herself, she just didn't know if she was in love with the man who helped to produce such a loving child as Andrew.

Anthony expected her to give him an answer about their future together when she returned. She would be back in a day or two, and she hated the fact that she had to have her entire future planned in such a short span of time.

She analyzed the situation on the flight to Bonsai Bay. She was comfortable with Anthony. He was a good man, definitely a good father and a great provider. After thinking about all of his great qualities, she still didn't believe she was actually in love with him. But they had been a part of each other's lives since high school, so there must be something she felt for him, she reasoned.

There had never been another man in her life to compare Anthony with. She had thought about the possibility of dating someone else but was too afraid to act on any of her mixed-up feelings. Sara was determined not to make another mistake like she did with Anthony.

Still a fairly attractive, busty woman, Sara sported a short, bleached blonde, natural hairstyle. She was a stylish dresser too, a trait she'd picked up from her Aunt Vashti. Some of the people at work labeled her a flirt. She had to admit that she did like to see if men were still attracted to her, so she knew that she could be a big flirt whenever she wanted.

Maybe, just maybe, she said to herself while staring out the window of the plane, *that's how I've survived all these years with Anthony.*

Had she not had her fantasy world of men, she probably would have left him long ago. But this was the real world, and Anthony was insisting that she make a decision. She didn't see any way she would be able to avoid giving him an answer.

She had to think of how her decision would affect Andrew too. She dared not do anything that she thought would ruin his happiness. He loved his father dearly, and he loved the idea of his parents getting married. Anthony had continually impressed that upon his son's mind, every chance he had.

When she arrived in Bonsai Bay, Sara's thoughts yielded to her reason for being there. Of all the couples in the world, why did this have to happen to destroy Prodigal and Faith's lives together? God had his reasons for everything, but she just couldn't see it in this sad occasion.

Teary steered the rent-a-car into the passenger pick-up area of the airport and parked. Looking down at her watch to check the time, she waited patiently for fifteen minutes before seeing Sara come through the outside double doors of the massive airport.

Jumping out of the car, Teary squealed, "Sara!" loud enough for several people, including Sara, to look in the direction of the voice.

Running into each other's arms, the two sisters embraced each other tightly. It had been almost two years since they'd seen each other. Their main means of communication was via e-mail or a phone call once a month. They lived totally different lives on separate sides of the U.S., which made it difficult for them to hook up with each other as much as they may have wanted to.

"How are you, girl?" Teary looked around the outside airport area as she helped Sara put her luggage in the trunk of the rent-a-car. "I thought Anthony and Andrew were coming with you."

"They were, but Andrew had a basketball camp to attend. Plus Anthony and I decided that it would be better if Andrew didn't have to see this. It's so terrible about Faith, Teary. We didn't want to interrupt his school and his sports with something so sad, so Anthony stayed home."

They climbed inside the car and resumed their conversation.

"I already know what you're thinking."

"What am I thinking, sis?" Teary looked over at Sara.

"You're thinking that since Andrew's a young man, he can stay home and take care of himself. But you know me, I believe in guidance twenty-four, seven. It helps to keep our young people on the straight and narrow. You know there's so much going on out there in the streets, Teary."

"See, I wasn't going to say anything like that. I think it's great that you, Anthony, and Andrew are as close as you are. It's good to be loved and share love like the three of you do. I'm proud of the fine job you've done raising Andrew. I can only imagine that it hasn't always been easy for you.

"Now, tell me about you and Anthony—Have you decided to tie the knot yet?"

"Actually, he's given me an ultimatum. Can you believe that?"

Sara flailed her arms. "When I get back home he expects me to tell him where we stand in our relationship. I don't know what I'm going to do, Teary. I don't know if I want to spend the rest of my life with him."

Teary eyed the look of utter confusion on her sister's face. She believed that deep inside, Sara did love Anthony. There was no doubt in her mind that Anthony loved Sara. She didn't know what was holding Sara back from making a total commitment to him. "Have you prayed about it, Sara?"

"A little, but not like I should. I don't think I've really ever turned it over to God. I think I'm scared that things won't last between us if we get married. I don't know why I feel like this, Teary. I just do, that's all."

"Look, don't think about it right now." Teary pulled into the circular drive of the hotel where Sara would be staying. "While you check in, I'll get a luggage carrier to put your bags on."

"Thanks, sis. I'll meet you in the lobby."

Sara checked into her hotel room.

The sisters talked non-stop. When Sara went inside the bathroom to take a shower, Teary talked to her from the other side of the bathroom door.

"I told Prodigal I wouldn't be gone too long. When you finish your shower, we'll leave. I know you want to visit with everyone before the funeral tomorrow."

"Teary, you're really a good friend to him. He's blessed to have you in his life."

"We're blessed to have each other."

Sara came out of the bathroom, a hotel towel wrapped around her hair and her body. "How is he holding up? How are his boys doing?"

"He's having a really hard time, girl. He and Faith were the perfect couple. Then something like this happens. And to think, it happened so fast. As for the boys, they're doing okay. Prodigal's neighbors and his church family have been keeping them occupied. I helped Prodigal with the arrangements. Fantasia and Mrs. Runsome are here, so that helps too. There's nothing like the presence of family during a time like this."

"Yeah, you're right about that. My heart goes out to him, Teary. I can't begin to imagine how he feels. I hope I never have to experience it."

William was taken aback, when he heard the hysterical voice over the telephone. It took him a moment to realize that the frantic voice belonged to Ruth. *What's going on?* His heart raced wildly as her penetrating cries saturated the air.

"William," Ruth cried into the phone receiver.

"Ruth, please . . . what's going on?" He could barely understand what she was saying. "Wait a minute, calm down. Tell me what's wrong."

" 'Calm down'? I can't calm down. My daughter-in-law just died. Oh, William, how I hurt for him. She was such a lovely, beautiful, and strong Christian woman. She was so good, for not only Prodigal, but all of us in the family. Ohhh, William . . ."

"Ruth, I'll be right over, sweetheart." He abruptly hung up the phone, changed into his blue velour jogging suit, grabbed his jacket, and rushed out the door.

He must have driven his Lincoln Navigator every bit of ninety miles an hour, trying to get to Ruth as fast as he could. What was normally a forty-five minute drive took William less than twenty minutes.

Fantasia met him at the door, eyes puffy and red, obviously from crying herself.

He reached out and grabbed her, pulling her close to his chest.

She couldn't hold back any longer. Her tears fell freely, as if his arrival allowed her to release her full devastation.

"Yes, yes. There now, everything will be all right, Fantasia. Shhh, baby. You'll see, everything will be just fine."

"Thank you for coming," Fantasia said between sobs. "I'll be fine, but I don't know about my mother. I don't know if she can take this again, William, I just don't know."

"Where is she?"

"She's upstairs. Go on up. I just made her some warm spiced tea. Would you like some?" Fantasia sniffled.

"No, no, I'm fine. I know how to go in the kitchen and get some if I decide to a little later. You just try to take it easy. I'll let you know when I leave."

"Okay. I'm going to go and lay down. I have to try to make some sense of all this." Fantasia turned and left William to go to her mother's rescue.

William leaped up the spiral staircase two at a time. He tapped lightly on the oak door, simultaneously turning the knob and entering her room.

Ruth sat with her head in her folded hands and pressed against the back of the teal sofa. She was staring aimlessly out the window.

William couldn't tell if she even heard him enter. "Ruth," he called out softly to her. When she didn't make a stir, he cautiously walked over to her, taking a seat beside her.

She turned and glanced at him with a look of pain that he knew only too well. "William." She fell into the warmth of his embrace.

He held her tight, like he would never let her go. Gently stroking her hair, he kissed her tears as they streamed down her cheeks then cradled her in his arms until sleep overtook her.

William sat and held her, as she slept underneath the curl of his arms.

Bright and early the next morning, a white Cadillac limo pulled up in front of Ruth's luxury condo.

"William, thank you. Your friendship means the world to me. I don't know what Fantasia and I would do if you weren't here."

"Hey, don't even go there. You two mean a lot to me too.

There's nothing I wouldn't do for you. Now you just take care of yourself, and I'll see you when you get back, okay? Has the driver arrived yet?" William stirred around in the room, drinking a cup of strong black coffee. It had been a long night for him. Even after convincing Ruth to get in her bed, he had remained awake, watching her as she slept.

"I think that's him pulling up in the drive now," she answered sadly, as she stood looking out of the second-floor window.

"Look, go on and be with your family. I'll be praying for your strength and for your son's strength too." William rested a hand on her shoulder. "Whether you want to hear this or not, God is with you and your family, Ruth. Believe me, He really is."

"I think I have everything packed and ready." Ruth moved away from the window. Refusing to look at William, she retreated downstairs to greet the driver. She couldn't bear to hear any well-meaning words about God. She felt betrayed by Him, and now was not the time.

William remained with Ruth and Fantasia until it was time for them to leave. Walking outside with them, William hugged Ruth before kissing her tenderly. He walked over to Fantasia and hugged her too and kissed her forehead.

"If you need anything, I mean anything, you call me," William told them.

"I will, William," Fantasia said. "Thank you for everything."

"I'll call you when we get there," Ruth said, the deep, dark circles underneath her eyes revealing her pain.

Hope and David, along with their five "stair-step" children, arrived the day before the funeral. Their first child, David, Jr., was six years old, followed by five-year-old twins, Elizabeth and Mary, three-year-old Daniel, and eight-month old Noah. Hope was a full-time mom and loving wife. Their relationship was solid, and their love was complete with true, unconditional love and devotion for one another.

Upon graduating from high school, David Peters had attended

the seminary. Throughout his seminary days, he gained further spiritual guidance and knowledge under the tutelage of none other than Pastor Grace. David was welcomed with open arms as the pastor of Mount Sinai Christian Church. The small congregation loved their new, young, energetic pastor and his lovely wife, "first lady" Hope Peters.

When Hope and David first arrived at Prodigal's house, Kevin and Kaleb dashed toward the sound of the chattering Peters brood. The cousins didn't see each other often, but they acted like they played together every day.

"Prodigal, I'm so sorry to hear about Faith." Hope hugged her brother.

David held his youngest child. "I know this is hard. I can't imagine your pain. But I do want you to know that God *does* know your pain. He's not going to forsake, you. He'll help you through this," David tried to assure him.

"I don't want to talk about God right now," Prodigal said sharply. "I feel like I've been pushed aside and stepped on, like my heart has been snatched from me." Prodigal's body shook, and his tears poured. "I don't want to be preached to right now, I'm sorry, I just don't."

"It's okay, brother. It's okay," Hope said in a soothing voice. "We're here for you."

Baby Noah reached for his mother.

Hope took him from David's arms and kissed his chubby cheeks. "I'm going to feed Noah, and then I'll check on the other children."

David nodded. "Okay, sweetheart. I'm going to stay in here with Prodigal. If you need me, just holler."

The following day, having returned home from laying Faith to rest, Prodigal did his best to put on a brave front for the many guests who came to pay their last respects to her. Their church had seen to it once again that there was an abundance of food and drink at the repast. While guests nibbled on the vast variety of food, Prodigal Runsome tried to hold back the attacks of grief that pounded away at his very soul.

Passing through the hallway, David spotted Prodigal in his study. He tapped lightly on the slightly opened door. "May I come in?"

Prodigal quickly lifted his head from his hands. "Sure, brother-in-law."

David took a seat on the matching brown high-back leather chair across from Prodigal. "Prodigal, my brother, I know you are going to grieve for Faith. You're going to cry for her. You're going to miss her, something awful. And you will never stop missing her or loving her. But God wants me to remind you that Faith is now in His presence. When grief stages its attack on you, my brother, cling to this very fact—those who belong to Him, well let me say this. The word tells us that to be absent from the body is to be present with the Lord, which means we can rest assured that Faith is definitely with the Master now. You know how much she loved God, don't you, Prodigal?" David asked in a soft tone.

"Yeah, Pas—David, I know, man." Prodigal almost called his brother-in-law *Pastor*. "Hey, man, thanks for your words of encouragement. I can't tell you how grateful I am to have you and Hope here."

"We wouldn't have it any other way, Prodigal. By the way, the last of the guests were leaving when I came in here. Would you care to go out into the family room now?"

"Sure. I should at least come out and say goodbye and thanks to everyone."

The two of them talked for a couple more minutes and then headed out of the study. Walking into the family room, they spotted the kids playing. David and Hope's small tribe definitely helped take the twins minds off everything that was going on in their young lives right now. Prodigal didn't have to worry too much about Kevin and Kaleb, as long as the Peters brood was around.

Hope was excited to see everyone together, even though it

wasn't under pleasant circumstances. But for Hope, it could be the darkest of days, and she would still be smiling and praising the Lord.

Teary reached out to him and pulled him close to her on the sofa.

Everyone was gone and they were alone now. Prodigal and Faith's families went to their hotels to try to escape the weight of grief they had experienced during Faith's funeral. Seeing her lowered in the grave forced them to realize that everything was final. She was gone, never to return.

Christmas Eve was three days away. Prodigal's neighbors, Mr. and Mrs. Richards, graciously volunteered to take the boys to see Christmas lights, to give them some sense of normalcy in the midst of their grief. They were brave little boys. But that was all because of their mother.

She prepared them for this moment. She told them she wanted them to know she would always be with them. "There'll be times when you'll miss Mommy," she told them, "but it's only temporary, because one day we'll all be together again. Until then, Mommy wants you to be good boys . . . godly boys. Be obedient and always do your best in everything you do. I'll be looking down on you from up in Heaven, and I'll be smiling. Always remember that you must keep God first."

"Hey, thanks for coming," Prodigal said to Teary, his voice weak and drawn. "I didn't know if you would be able to get here or not, but I'm sure glad you did."

"I'll stay for as long as you and the boys need me." Teary rubbed his hands.

He responded with teardrops in the corner of his brown, puppy-dog eyes. "Thanks. You know what, Teary?"

"What?"

"I can't describe the pain. It's something I can't put into words. All I know is that I never want to experience this kind of hurt again." Without warning, cries erupted from him, his body shaking with each deafening sob.

Teary held him close, and together they cried.

Ruth and Fantasia remained in Bonsai Bay for a week after the funeral. Ruth was prepared to stay longer to help him out with the house and the boys, but he was adamant about her going back to Belleaf with Fantasia.

"Momma, Teary already made plans to stay with me and the boys for a few weeks."

"Honey, I know, but I don't want to leave you, not now."

"We'll be fine, I promise."

"If you say so, son, but you know I'm only a phone call away. Say the word, and I'm on my way."

The fact that Teary would be staying with Prodigal for a few weeks gave Ruth some sense of relief. She didn't know how much help she would have been to Prodigal anyway. Faith's death was far too painful for her and brought back sad memories of her own.

As Ruth pondered Faith's death, tears crested in the corners of her eyes. *I still can't believe she's really dead.*

Fantasia was also glad that Teary had decided to stay with Prodigal for a while. She wanted to get back to the gallery as quickly as possible herself and couldn't stand to see her brother in pain. By submerging herself in her work she could mask the true sense of hurt she felt inside.

Faith's death reinforced Fantasia's feelings about God, religion, and the whole gamut of stuff she had been brought up to believe in when she was a little girl. She was determined to live her life just like she was doing—without God. She'd witnessed only heartache and heartbreak. If this was what having faith and believing in God was all about, she didn't want any part of it. She was doing fine on her own. Fantasia was also anxious to get her mother away from this pain as much as possible.

Ruth was somewhat reluctant to board the plane and had second thoughts about leaving her son so soon after Faith's death.

"Look, Momma, I know you'll be more than happy to stay, but believe me, I'll be fine." Prodigal handed his mother her carry-on bag. "The Richards are more than happy to help with the twins; plus several church members have agreed to help out too. And remember, Teary's here too, you know. So please go home and take some time to get yourself together. I know this is just as hard on you as it is on me. You loved Faith too."

"Sweetheart, I'll respect your wishes." Ruth hugged him. "It does give me some peace to see all the wonderful friends you and Faith have made here. I'm proud of you, Prodigal. You're so much like your father—strong, handsome, stubborn." She spoke to him softly and slowly stroked the side of his face with the back of her hand. "Call me if there's anything you need, and I'll come running, you know that, don't you?"

"Of course, I do, Mom, but I'll be okay." Prodigal turned toward Fantasia. "You be good, sis. Take care of Momma and yourself too." He hugged her tightly.

Fantasia reciprocated with an even tighter squeeze. "You know I will. And like Momma said, call if you need anything."

"Will do. Now hurry before you two miss your plane. Call when you make it home. Is your friend going to pick you up from the airport, Momma?"

"Yes, he'll be there. Bye sweetheart." Ruth blew a kiss in the air at her son and then headed toward the plane.

When they arrived in Belleaf, William was there to greet them at the airport.

Ruth raced to the arms of William Phillips, her love, her second chance at happiness.

32

Woman in the Mirror

Sara approached the entrance to Surrey Hills, where she and Andrew had lived for the past five and a half years. When she swirled up in the drive leading to her condo, she still hadn't made a decision about her future with Anthony. She would have to play it by ear and not allow him to continue to unduly pressure her. This was a time in her life when she longed for her Aunt Vashti. She would have been able to go to her aunt for advice about Anthony and his ultimatum.

Unfortunately, like Faith, Aunt Vashti had answered God's call for her life too. It had been two years since Aunt Vashti died in her sleep of a heart attack. Her death had been hard on their family, especially because Aunt Vashti had barely a sick day in her life. She'd never even spent one day in a hospital.

When Aunt Vashti died, Sara remembered what the old folks used to say, "Your best day can be your dying day." Aunt Vashti proved that saying to be right.

Just as memories of her aunt flashed across her mind, so did Derrel Perkins, the director of finance at the University of Seattle. The two of them had been making goo-goo eyes at each other for the past year, and Sara was definitely attracted to him.

His perfectly formed stature made her blush at the sight of

him, while his rugged and reddish complexion only fed her lust. He strode along the halls of the university in perfectly tailored suits with a cocky sort of confidence. To Sara, this man was nothing but pure fineness, from the top of his head to the soles of his feet.

"Momma," Andrew yelled. He ran toward her, grabbed her in his long arms, and hugged her tight, planting sloppy kisses all over her face.

"Hi, baby." Sara smiled. "Don't you know you're getting too big to run at me like that? Shucks! I can hardly keep myself planted to the ground." She hugged him tightly in return and laughed heartily as he made her forget all about the illicit thoughts that were going through her mind seconds before.

"I'm glad you made it back home safely, Ma," Andrew said, excitedly.

"Thanks, baby. I am too. Where's your daddy?"

"Upstairs in the shower. I had a game today, so we haven't been home that long. How's Mr. Runsome?"

"Mr. Runsome is having a hard time, Andrew, so we have to keep praying for him and his sons. You know he and his wife had been together just as long as me and your daddy. As a matter of fact, your daddy and I met each other around the same time Mr. Runsome and his wife met each other."

"Wow! It's a bummer what happened to her. How is Auntie Teary?"

"She's fine, sweetie. She told me to give you a great, big bear hug. Oh, I almost forgot—she sent you some money too."

"Yeah, now that's what I'm talking about. Hand it over, Ma." Laughter spread across his brown, chiseled face. He looked so much like Anthony.

"Here you go." Sara pulled out the small wad of money and handed it to him. "Before you go running off to the mall to spend it, tell me what you've been up to since I've been gone. Didn't you say you had a game today?" Sara asked her son, as they walked inside the house and into the family room.

"Yes, ma'am."

"Great. My mind has been so consumed with the death of Faith. But I'm home now, and it's the best feeling in the world, Andrew." Sara reached over, hugged her son, and gave him a couple of kisses on each cheek.

Andrew had been playing basketball since he was four years old. He'd started out playing for the YMCA, and now this was his second year playing on a competitive basketball team sponsored by the community center. They had a game every Saturday morning. He also played point guard on his high school varsity team. Sometimes Sara thought that Anthony enjoyed the games even more than Andrew.

"Did y'all win today, honey?"

"Yep. By eight points. I shot twelve points today and had five assists."

Sara turned around and screamed for joy. "Andrew, I'm so proud of you. You are awesome, simply awesome. But you know that already, don't you?"

"Sho' you right,"

Anthony walked into the family room, where the two of them sat. "I'm glad you're back." He walked over to Sara and planted a kiss on her forehead.

"Hi there," Sara said. "You think we have a future NBA star here or what?"

"I believe we do. This son of ours is dangerous on a basketball court."

"Momma, you have to come and see me play more often."

"I do come out and see you play, Andrew. But you know how I feel about that. That's you and your father's private time. I don't like to interfere."

"Yeah, I know, but still you're going to have to come to the last game."

"I always do, don't I? And when I do, you tell me that I become too excited. But I can't help it. Those referees can act so stupid sometimes that it makes me furious."

Father and son laughed at Sara's remark.

Later that night, when Sara and Anthony prepared for bed, she somehow felt Anthony was going to ask her if she'd made a decision. She took extra time in the bathroom, hoping he would have fallen asleep by the time she stepped out or maybe he wouldn't stay over tonight.

"Come on in here, woman." He reached out for her to climb into the king-sized bed beside him. "You didn't think I was going to go home without so much as a kiss from you, did you? And you've been gone away too—Naw, you aren't going to get off that easy." Anthony grabbed Sara's thick body close to his, allowing his rough, enormous hands to travel their familiar course.

Sara looked at him, his eyes closed, and his mouth hungrily planting kisses along her face.

It had been almost two months since she and Anthony last made love. She didn't know why she didn't want to marry him. All she knew was that it was Anthony who changed the direction of her life when they did it that first time sixteen years ago. She couldn't forget the fact that she'd allowed him to take her virginity. She blamed him for robbing her of the future and kind of life she always wanted to live. She was thankful that she'd had Andrew, but she couldn't help thinking from time to time, *What if things had been different?*

With Anthony's lips covering hers, she allowed herself to imagine it was Derrel Perkins.

Anthony whispered in her ear, "I love you, Sara. Say you'll be my wife." He moaned heavy and panted hard, moving his firm 220-pound body slowly and carefully on top of her. "Talk to me. Talk to me, Sara. Tell me that you're mine. Tell me, Sara," he lovingly pleaded.

"Yes, Derrel, I'm yours. Yes, baby, yes, yes, yes," she screamed, releasing the pressure that she'd held back for the past few months.

Anthony pulled away from her. He jumped up and put on his

jogging pants and T-shirt. Then he bolted down the stairs and was out the door.

Sara heard the door slam hard behind him, as she lay there not believing what had just happened. She lay in silence, too shocked to move. How could she have done that? Just because she didn't want to marry Anthony didn't mean that she wanted to hurt him. He was too good to her and to their son. He had always been there for them. How could she have done such a stupid thing? What was she thinking?

Sara heard the sound of Anthony's Nissan leaving out the driveway. She jumped up and dashed to the window just in time to see him speeding down the street. For the first time, Sara realized that it wasn't other men she wanted. She enjoyed flirting, of course, but that was only to mask what was going on inside of her. That was to mask the true fact that she was afraid because of the mistakes she'd made in her life. She didn't want things to go wrong with her and Anthony. She truly did love him.

She sat on the edge of the bed and allowed the tears to flow, tears that had been penned up inside of her for many years. She cried, "Anthony, my dear, sweet Anthony."

Dawn quickly made its entrance, and Anthony had not answered any of Sara's numerous calls during the night. Sara was worried. She didn't know where he was or if he was okay. She realized that she didn't want to lose him. The thought of them being forever apart tore at her heart. She thought about all that they had been through—He was the one whose love for her had remained constant; he was the one who had shown Andrew what it was to be a man; he was the one who nursed her and Andrew back to health whenever they were sick; the one who moved to Seattle just to be closer to her and his son.

It was Anthony who comforted her when Aunt Vashti died. Anthony was such a part of her life that she had begun to not see him anymore. She was so accustomed to him being there; now he was gone.

"Aunt Vashti, tell me what love is," Sara remembered saying to her aunt, when Andrew was just a toddler. "How do I know what love looks like and feels like between a man and a woman? I know what it looks like between a mother and child. I know that each time I look at Andrew, each time I hold him in my arms, each time he cries, I know I love him, Aunt Vashti. But the love between a man and a woman, it's different, isn't it?"

"Why, of course, it's different, honey . . . but not in the way you might think. Love between a man and a woman oftentimes produces offspring like Andrew, sweetheart. But Andrew, you see, is the by-product of, or should have been, the by-product of the love you and Anthony shared for each other. Come here, my child," Vashti said. "Let me show you something."

Aunt Vashti led Sara into her lavishly furnished bedroom and walked over to her wooden, oriental print night table and pulled out a journal. She flipped the pages until she came to what Sara thought was a poem of some kind. "Listen to this—Love never gives up. Love cares more for others than for self. Love doesn't want what it doesn't have. Love doesn't strut, doesn't have a swelled head, doesn't force itself on others, isn't always 'me first,' doesn't fly off the handle, doesn't keep score of the sins of others, doesn't revel when others grovel, takes pleasure in the flowering of truth, trusts God always, always looks for the best, never looks back, but keeps going to the end—that, my child, is love."

"Aunt Vashti, that's beautiful. Where did you get that?"

"It came from a Bible translation called *The Message*. It's actually the thirteenth chapter of first Corinthians. Some call it the love chapter. I'm going to have it printed and framed for you, Sara. I want you to remember and know what love looks like, acts like, and talks like. It's not based on feelings. It's far from that. As a matter of fact, your feelings can lead you astray. You can feel excited about something or someone that has absolutely nothing to do with love. I don't know what you and that boy, Anthony, called yourself doing. Maybe you thought you loved each other. Maybe you do love each other, I don't know. All I can say is, time will tell. Believe me, one day you *will* know, honey. One day you'll know for sure."

Sara allowed her mind to come back to the present. She rose from her bed and walked over to the cedar chest she kept tucked away in her walk-in closet. She knelt down on her knees and ruffled through the piles of papers and sentimental items she'd collected over the years. She found what she was searching for. She carefully pulled out the gold frame that Aunt Vashti had given her years before. Aunt Vashti had the passage of Scripture printed and framed in a sterling silver frame, just like she had promised Sara she would.

Sara read the words again. She began to sense what she had known within her spirit all along but was afraid to admit—Anthony loved her. It was she who had been selfish and rude. It was she who had been unkind and walked around with a swelled head. She had hidden her true self from Anthony all of these years. She had walked around looking for love in all the wrong places, when she had it right underneath her very nose.

Sara held the framed words against her chest and prayed, "Lord, forgive me for being stupid and selfish. I hurt the man who loves me. I hurt the father of my child. I hurt the man I love.

"Give me a chance to show Anthony that I love him." She was still on her knees in the closet praying, when Anthony walked in the house.

The sun had come up.

He looked worn and haggard. He crept up the stairs, his face drawn and hurt. He loved Sara, but he didn't believe she loved him, and for the first time, was willing to accept that. He felt belittled, humiliated, and destroyed. As he entered her bedroom, he heard her pleading voice coming from the closet.

"O God," she continued, "please give me one more chance

with Anthony, please. You know I've never cheated on him. I know it was the devil that made me call out another man's name. Lord, I don't want that man. I want *my* man, not some figment of my imagination. Bring Anthony back, Father, I need him to forgive me. I want to be his wife." She looked up, suddenly startled by the sound coming toward her.

There stood Anthony, right outside the entrance of the closet.

Sara stood up and rushed out of the closet toward him. "Anthony, I'm so sorry. I love you. Won't you forgive me?" She wept uncontrollably. "I want to be your wife for the rest of my life. I want to grow old with you. I want to make love to you forever. I want to sleep with you, eat with you, laugh with you, and cry with you."

"I've waited all these years to hear you say those three words." He grabbed her and held her tight, squeezing her, tears flowing from both of their eyes.

Sara kissed him with fervor. Opening her eyes, she looked at the woman in the mirror—she was smiling.

33

In My Face

Teary's voice rang with excitement over the phone. "Debra, long time no hear from."

"Hey, girl. How is life treating you in the good old South, my friend?"

"All right, I guess. I'm working hard, but that's nothing unusual. When are you coming to visit me? All this time I've been down here, and you haven't been here, not once."

"Teary, be for real—You know how it is when you have someone else to answer to. This husband of mine is something else. Being married is great, but it's a lot of responsibility."

"You're happy, aren't you?"

"Yeah, of course. He's good to me, but hey, why shouldn't he be . . . because I'm good to him too."

"I heard that."

"What's up with your buddy? Have you heard from him lately?"

"I talk to him at least every couple of weeks. We e-mail each other a lot. I hated to leave him and come back to Memphis, but time is helping him heal."

"I was really sorry to hear about Faith. I wish I could have made it to the funeral, but things just didn't work out for me to get to Bonsai Bay."

"I'll tell him you asked about him the next time I talk to him," Teary promised. "So tell me, what is happening with you?"

"That's why I'm calling you."

"What do you mean by, that's why you're calling me? What's up?"

"I'm pregnant!" Debra exclaimed. "I couldn't wait to tell you."

Teary couldn't believe it. *Pregnant? She's been married for less than a year, and already she's pregnant?* Teary almost dropped the phone.

"Hey, are you still there?"

"Yeah, I'm still here. Congratulations. I'm happy for you. When is the baby due?" Teary asked, feigning excitement.

"I just came from seeing the doctor. I'm eight weeks. Can you see me with a big stomach, walking around all slow and stuff?" Debra giggled.

A smile formed on Teary's lips as she pictured the scene. "No. Frankly, I can't. You have definitely got to e-mail me some pictures, especially when that belly of yours starts swelling like a watermelon."

"You know I will."

Teary laughed out. "I never thought you of all people would be an at-home wife, playing the 'Miss Betty Crocker' role. And you're about to be a mother." Sarcastically she said, "Wow! I'm impressed."

"*Funny*. But to tell you the truth, neither did I. A desperate housewife, maybe. Seriously though, who knows what life is going to hold?"

"What else is going on around Broknfield, girl?"

"Not much. Same old, same old. But if you're asking about your boy on the sly, last I heard, he was doing pretty well. But I don't even want to go there with you. This call is not to depress you."

"I know that's right. I was just curious, that's all. I don't really care what Skyler is doing."

Debra couldn't understand why Teary still wanted to know what Skyler was up to. She deserved so much more than he could give her. She wished Teary could find someone she could love and trust. "Look, I better get off this phone. I have a million and one things to do around the house before the hubby gets home."

"Take care of yourself, Debra. Congratulations. We'll talk again soon."

"Sure, and I'll send you those pictures. Love ya. Bye."

34

Choke Hold

While Prodigal was busy getting his life back to some semblance of order, Teary was doing the same. She found herself thinking less of Skyler. So what if he was doing fine; so was she. There was more to life than love and relationships anyway, is what she kept telling herself. Yet somehow she knew she was only fooling herself. She was lonely, frightened, and quite unhappy. She tried to become involved in the "singles ministry" at the church she attended sporadically, but she felt out of place, as if she didn't really belong there either. She didn't know quite where she was supposed to be at this time in her life. She wasn't getting any younger, and she was still in search of that yellow brick road that leads to happiness.

After working a twelve-hour day, Teary arrived home from work, plopped down on the cushiony plum loveseat, and breathed a sigh of relief. She pulled off her black-leather Muse and dropped them to the floor. She then reached over the top of the loveseat and grabbed the cordless phone off the sofa table and hit the button to listen to her messages.

"Teary, just calling to see what's up for the weekend girl," was the message from one of the girls who lived a few houses away from her. The two of them sometimes hung out together. "Call and let me know what you have planned."

Beep. *"Ms. Fullalove, this is Bridget from The Furniture Store,"* was the next message. *"Please contact me at 333-1458. I want to know if you still plan on purchasing the living room set we have on hold for you."*

Several weeks had passed since Teary had picked out the suave Bradford lilac-and-cream living room suite she thought was to die for. *Oh, dang it! I forgot all about it,* she thought. She scribbled down the woman's name and number to remind herself to call and let her know that she still wanted the furniture.

Beep. *"Teary, it's your mother. I haven't heard from you in over a week. Give me a call. Let me know you're still in the land of the living. Love you, bye."*

Teary laughed at her mother's message.

Beep. *"Hey, girl,"* Patricia said. *"Just checking to see what's up with you. Give me a call when you can. Talk to you later."*

Beep. *"Teary, it's me,"* the voice on the other end said with little emotion.

Teary jumped straight up and listened.

"I was just thinking about you. Don't worry, everything is fine. I just wanted to talk." His voice quivered over the crackle of the answering machine. *"Call me when you get a chance."*

She rewound the answering machine to listen to the time of his call. The mechanical device said, *Caller number four, received at 12:45 a.m. Monday.*

"Monday . . . that was two days ago," Teary said to her cats and dog as they gathered around her feet. She couldn't believe she hadn't listened to her messages. Well, actually she didn't find it so unusual because she often went days before she listened to them. After all, it wasn't like anyone special would be calling or anything.

Every now and then Teary would meet a guy. The relationship would last a few weeks at the most. But they all turned out the same way. He would turn out to be married, a wannabe playa, divorced with four or five kids to support, an atheist, or just the opposite, a religious fanatic. Either he was too big or too skinny, too tall or too short, too dark or too light, too fine or too ugly, didn't make much money or didn't work at all. The list of no-no's was endless. There was always something she would find that was wrong. So most of her time was split between work, church, or cooped up in the house with her pets and a good novel. Sometimes she'd hang out with Patricia or a couple of other girlfriends she'd formed friendships with since living in Memphis. And once a month she attended a book club meeting at the local mall.

She glanced at the grandfather clock standing in the corner of the nearly bare living room. *Eight twenty-five. That means it's seven twenty-five in Bonsai Bay.* She picked up the phone and dialed his number.

"Runsome residence, may I help you?"

Teary was shocked to hear a female answer the phone. She hesitated a moment before she responded.

"Uh, yes, this is Teary. Teary Fullalove. Is Prodigal in, please?"

"No, ma'am. He should be here around nine thirty or ten. Would you like to leave a message?" she asked rather politely.

As Teary listened, she realized the voice on the other end belonged to a young girl, perhaps fifteen or sixteen at the most. *She must be babysitting the boys.* "Would you tell him that I called? My name again is Teary. By the way, are the boys there?" Teary asked, just to be certain she was indeed the babysitter.

"Yes, ma'am. They're upstairs playing their video games. I'll tell Mr. Runsome you called. Does he have your number?" The girl popped her chewing gum.

"Yes, he has it. May I ask your name, young lady?"

"Carrie."

"By chance, are you babysitting Kevin and Kaleb this evening?"

"Yes, ma'am. I keep them a lot for Mr. Runsome. We go to the same church. Well, if there's nothing else you want me to tell him, I better go and check on them."

"All right. Be sure to tell him that I called."

She responded, "Yes, ma'am," and quickly hung up the phone.

Teary had planned to spend a quiet evening at home alone with her pets. Originally she had planned to go home to Broknfield to visit her parents for Thanksgiving, but quickly decided against it. She had the time and the finances, but she lacked the enthusiasm that would be expected at the prospect of being around family and friends. Her parents missed her, and she missed them too. But Teary couldn't deal with going back to revisit her past.

When she called and told her mother that she wouldn't be coming home for the holidays, it didn't sit too well with Cynthia Fullalove. It was rare that Teary came home period, but for her not to come home for Thanksgiving or Christmas really upset Mrs. Fullalove. Cynthia would talk to Brian and see if he could convince his baby girl to come home for the holidays.

Prodigal couldn't believe that almost a year had passed since Faith's death. He didn't know how he would make it through the approaching holiday season. Thanksgiving and Christmas, once his two favorite holidays, were marred by memories of Faith's illness and her death. But he would do all he could to keep his spirits up, for the sake of his sons. He never really had time to completely grieve because he concentrated his efforts on making sure Kevin and Kaleb were happy and adjusting well to life without their mother. He didn't know if he would ever be able to fall in love again, but the boys needed a mother. "They need a woman in their lives. I don't have to be in love with her either, just as long as she loves my sons and treats them kindly," he told himself.

He missed Faith so much, and the time of year was proving to be devastating for him. He had to make sure that the boys had plenty to keep their little minds busy and active during this time.

"Look, boys, I have to leave for work. Mr. and Mrs. Richards are going to take you to church for the children's pre-Thanksgiving Day potluck," Prodigal explained to Kevin and Kaleb.

"Okay, Daddy," they both chimed together.

"When I get off work tomorrow morning, we'll start some of our Christmas shopping."

"Yeah, yeah," they squealed with joy.

"Come on. Bundle up, so we can get out of here."

He whisked them out the door to confront the cold, wintry day. It had been snowing most of the night, and Doppler radar said no let-up was in sight. They were expecting at least five to seven more inches of the white stuff.

While he walked the boys across the street to the Richards, the three of them grabbed the chance to play around in the snow. They chased after each other with giant snowballs in their hands, while the wind pushed them along at a rapid pace across the wide neighborhood street.

Mrs. Richards stood in the doorway watching them with a big grin on her face.

After playing for several minutes, Prodigal dropped the boys off at her doorstep.

"Thanks, Mrs. Richards. Have a good time, fellows." He gave each of them a hug before turning around and going back across the street.

Prodigal climbed into his champagne Lexus SUV and headed to the firehouse. As he drove, he allowed his eyes to occasionally roam up and down the icy-slick streets. People had already begun to put up Christmas decorations. He made a mental note to remind himself to put up some for Kevin and Kaleb.

With envy, he watched couples strolling along the slippery sidewalks. Some laughed, others snuggled. Children were laughing, jumping up and down, dodging snowballs and making snow people of different shapes and sizes. The scenes before him could have been placed on a greeting card. Looking at the carefully adorned preparations, Prodigal's heart filled with grief. Silent tears swelled. Inhaling deeply, he tried to avoid the pain that was determined to push itself out.

Why couldn't she be here with me? Life is so unfair.

His body shook hard as he tried to maintain control of the SUV. The sound of a blaring horn jarred him back to his senses. He slammed on his brakes. Swerving over the ice- and snow-filled street, he wrestled with the steering wheel until he regained control of his vehicle.

"Whew, that was a close one," he told himself.

After making it safe and sound, Prodigal strolled into the fire station. "Hey, guys, something smells awfully good."

"Glen has some of his homemade chili brewing, bro," one of the other firefighters said. "You know he thinks he's a chef instead of a firefighter."

"One thing's for sure—we're going to eat hearty today. We already have the crackers, chili peppers and our appetites," another firefighter added.

Prodigal nudged his fellow firefighter, Glen, in the ribs. "Hey, man, don't worry about them checking you. Let me tell you what I have to say about your cooking. I think it's great—for a pack of hungry wolves that is."

All the firefighters broke out in laughter.

"Naw, seriously, man, I definitely brought my appetite with me this evening." Prodigal laughed. "So you fellows better watch out."

After each of them ate their fill, several of the firefighters chose to relax by watching football on *ESPN*. A couple of them played checkers, and some of the others decided to take a nap. In the middle of the fourth quarter, the loud, almost deafening sound of the siren started to blast.

"Move it," the fire commander yelled to his team. "We've got a four-alarm on Fifth and Granger, about six and a half blocks out. Let's go!"

They moved with lightning speed, jumping into gear, and climbing aboard the fire engines.

In less than four minutes they arrived on the scene. A crowd of people stood outside of the complex. People were fleeing the burning building. The midnight wind blew and fueled the flames.

Prodigal heard screams. He tilted his firefighter's hat and veered his face upward. His well-trained eyes focused on a young girl and a little boy who looked to be about the same age as his sons. They stood in the window of an upstairs apartment unit, arms outstretched and flailing, screaming for help.

Prodigal and Glen rushed inside. They made it up to the second floor of the three-story building, battling the flames as they cautiously moved along. Searing heat scorched Prodigal's skin. He smelled the unpleasant aroma as the flames found their target. The fire was spreading rapidly.

From the amount of debris falling, years of experience had taught Prodigal, who'd made lieutenant two years before, that it wouldn't be much longer before the entire structure collapsed. They had to move fast. If they didn't, not only would the children stand to lose their lives, but they were in danger of losing theirs as well.

Prodigal was the one who first spotted the scorched clothes of the children and saw how quickly the flames were overtaking the room where they were trapped. The fire was already covering the stairwell, and the kids couldn't get out.

They huddled together, hoping someone would save them.

"We're coming. Everything is going to be fine," Prodigal shouted.

"We're going to get you out of here," Glen said, trying to reassure the terrified children.

Prodigal, being closest to the trapped children, moved even closer to them, escaping the blinding smoke and mounting flames by mere inches. He didn't know how many other victims there might be, but he definitely knew for sure that he had seen two screaming children in the window.

Glen screamed loudly through the blaze of fire. "Prodigal, can you reach them?"

"Yeah, I think I so." Prodigal moved carefully past the flames and the thick swirling black smoke to get to the children. "Come on now. I've gotcha." He grabbed hold of the little boy and swiftly pushed him safely into Glen's arms. "Hurry, get him out of here, Glen," Prodigal ordered.

Next, Prodigal went for the teenaged girl. There wasn't much time left. With the building threatening to collapse, Prodigal thought it best to find an alternate means of escape. Grabbing hold of her, he shielded her with his own body.

Meanwhile the second fire truck had already arrived and was positioning the ladder at the window where the frightened child stood.

The girl's long, sculptured nails dug deep, seeking Prodigal's flesh.

"You're safe, sweetheart. I've got you," Prodigal reassured her. "I want you to trust me, okay?"

Though frightened, she shook her head up and down. The young girl wore a look of utter terror on her face as she surveyed the crowd below, and Prodigal recognized right away her apprehension.

Two other firefighters were climbing the ladder toward Prodigal and the girl, a safety basket attached to the ladder.

"I can't do it. I'm scared," she cried, clinging to Prodigal.

"I know you are, but I have to get you out of here. Now I need you to do as I say," he said in a soothing voice.

She mumbled, "Yes, sir."

Prodigal pointed. "You see those guys coming up here?"

"Uh, huh."

"They won't let anything happen to you, you hear me?"

"Yes."

Prodigal glanced over his left shoulder. The flames were moving in closer. The room was black as midnight. He had to hurry. "When you step onto it, they're going to be right there to help you. I promise they won't let anything happen to you. Now, on the count of three, I want you to step out on the ledge. My buddies are going to help you get into the basket, you hear? Then they're going to lower you down, all right?"

"Okay."

"One . . . two . . . three."

She stepped out on the ledge hesitantly. The other firefighter guided her steps, and she climbed into the basket to safety.

Prodigal turned around to survey what was left of the burning room. Just as he turned to make his own escape, he heard a whimpering sound. He cautiously moved against the darkness that consumed the room, searching for the other victim.

Again, he heard the whimper. Then he saw a spotted puppy crouched in a corner of the burning room. He reached out toward the puppy, but the terrified pup ran out of his reach and out of sight. His heart said he needed to save 'em, but the heat was telling him he had to go.

"I hate to leave you, little fellow, but I have to get out of here," Prodigal said to himself. Flames licked hungrily at the tail of Prodigal's coat. It wouldn't be much longer before he would be the one trapped. Groping in the darkness, Prodigal tried to go back to the window where he'd let the girl down to safety, but he couldn't find it. The darkness outside had gelled with the darkness inside the smoke-filled building.

Trying to drop to the floor so he could see, Prodigal made a sudden move. His breathing apparatus got caught on something and hurled him to the floor, causing him to lose air. He removed his air mask to keep from choking to death. Huddling as low to the ground as he could so he could breathe, Prodigal landed on the hot, melting floor. Flames eagerly raced toward him. The blaze intensified, hurling huge planes of metal. Prodigal screamed in pain as one of the flaming hot pieces of metal bored deep into his leg, rendering him unable to move.

Glen saw that the girl had made it to safety but saw no sign of Prodigal. He alerted the other firefighters. Two of them, including Glen, went back inside to rescue Prodigal.

"Is somebody calling me?" Prodigal's thoughts were jumbled in a sea of confusion, as his eyes closed.

With a vengeance, Glen fought back racing flames, falling

chunks of wood, and steel beams, until he made it to where an unconscious Prodigal lay in a twisted fetal position near one of the exits.

"Prodigal, take my hand," Glen yelled when he saw Prodigal. Prodigal didn't respond.

The firefighter prayed that he wasn't dead. Calling his name again, he began to shake Prodigal savagely. As he was about to give up, Prodigal slowly opened his eyes.

"Prodigal, come on, man, we've gotta get outta here."

"No, leave me. Save yourself," Prodigal screamed in-between the stabbing pain shooting through his body. "Get those kids out of here. This place is going to blow any second."

"Are you crazy? I'm not leaving you, and the kids are safe, re-member? You got them out of here. Now come on. You have to help me, man."

"I can't. I'm going to be with Faith. This is my chance."

He shook Prodigal harder. "What about Kevin and Kaleb? Faith wouldn't want this, man. You can't run out on them like this. Now get up," he yelled in anger.

Like an electric jolt suddenly hitting him, Prodigal tried to move. "God, I want to live," he pleaded, and tried to move his badly injured body. Just as he shifted his legs to hoist himself up, indescribable pain traveled unmercifully up the length of his right leg. It felt like something was trying to squeeze the life out of it. He didn't know what was happening. Screaming in agony, again he tried to pull his body to freedom.

Several other firefighters raced to save Prodigal. They screamed, "Prodigal!"

The fire, by this time, raged out of control. Colossal chunks of wood fell, scalding the firefighters' bodies.

"My leg is stuck. Ohhh!" Prodigal wailed like a wounded ani-mal.

"Hold on, we're getting you out of here," Glen yelled.

They pried and pulled at the debris that held on to the lower half of Prodigal's body like vise grips. Moving with expert precision, they managed to free his mangled body before gigantic balls of fire hurled down around them.

They dragged him out of the apartment complex just before the flames exploded wildly.

Within minutes the three-story complex was reduced to a pile of smoking rubble.

Distressed, they wheeled Prodigal into the waiting ambulance. What was supposed to be his arms and legs were now encased in a thick, gooey, reddish-purple substance.

At first he didn't remember what had transpired. Then his mind began to slowly come back into focus. The deep-purple concoction was his own blood. A mist of smoke rose from his scorched clothes, and his lungs felt like they were about to burst. As he gasped for air, he was met with a fresh burst of air from the oxygen mask placed over his parched lips and nose. His eyes closed in unconsciousness, and he dreamed of Faith.

Prodigal woke up to his head pounding and his legs aching. He forced his heavy eyelids open to the blur of a pristine white room. *Am I dead?*

A burly, auburn-haired nurse walked into his room. "Mr. Runsome, you finally decided to wake up from your beauty sleep, huh?"

Before she could place the thermometer in his mouth, Prodigal asked, "Where, where am I?" Fear saturated his mind and spirit. Something was wrong. Terribly wrong. "Where are my sons? What am I doing here? What's going on?"

"Hold on, Mr. Runsome, one question at a time. You're in the Critical Care Unit of Mercy Trauma Center. You were injured while rescuing two very lucky children from an apartment fire several days ago. You've been hovering in and out of consciousness since then. As for your sons, they're doing just fine. They're with your neighbors."

The short, stubby-faced doctor entered the room. "Mr. Runsome, it's good to see that you're awake."

"How bad am I hurt, doctor?" Prodigal tried pulling himself up to a sitting position, but the pain in his legs was so excruciating that he was forced to lay back. "Ahh!" He looked down at the lower half of his body. The shrill echo of his deafening scream was heard all along the hospital corridor.

"Mr. Runsome, please let me explain what has happened."

"'Explain what's happened'? Hell, you don't have to explain what's happened. I can very well see what's happened. You've butchered me; that's what's happened. Why did you do this? Why didn't you just let me die?"

"Please, try to settle down, and I'll explain," the doctor urged. "You had life threatening complications from the accident. First, you gave us quite a scare with all of the smoke you inhaled. After finally getting you stable, we went to work to try and save your leg."

"No, oh, God nooo!"

The doctor looked up at the nurse still standing on the other side of Prodigal's bed. "Nurse, get a sedative in here, stat." Then he continued, "Mr. Runsome, we did everything we could, but the fact of the matter is, unfortunately your right leg was almost torn in half when it went through the floor of the building. By the time you made it to the Trauma Center, infection was already spreading into your bloodstream. The nerves in your leg had begun to die out. There wasn't enough blood circulating to keep your leg alive. I'm sorry, but there was no possible way for us to improve your blood supply or fight the infection. The only alternative was amputation."

Prodigal felt a tiny prick in his arm as he retreated into his own private dream world, a world devoid of pain. He drifted, drifted, drifted. *Into each life, some pain is going to fall.*

Six weeks after the fire, Prodigal was being fitted with his first artificial limb so that he could be sent home.

Home was one place Prodigal longed to return to. Day after day, lying in the hospital bed, he sunk deeper and deeper into a state of depression.

His mother flew to Bonsai Bay as soon as she'd received the terrible news from the Bonsai Bay Fire Department. Ruth, having been a nurse herself, visited him at the hospital every day. She understood the reason he had to have the amputation. This time the duty of telling her grandsons about their father fell on her. She explained to them how he was deemed a hero for saving the lives of two children. "In the process," she told them, "your father was badly injured. Doctors did everything to make your father better. And they did. But there's one thing they had to do so that he *would* get better."

Kaleb spoke up, "What did they do to Daddy, Grandma Ruth?"

"Well, your daddy hurt his right leg really, really bad. So bad that the doctor had to remove the part of his leg that was making him sick."

"Remove it how?" Kevin asked.

Ruth was quiet. Looking at her grandsons, she saw features of both Prodigal and Faith. "They had to remove your father's leg below the knee. He'll have to wear an artificial leg from now on to help him walk. But the good thing about it is, your daddy will be coming home real soon. He's going to be just fine. I'll even take you to the hospital to see him in a few days. Would you like that?"

"Yeah, I would," Kevin answered.

"Me too."

Knowing their father was going to be coming home soon was enough for Kevin and Kaleb not to be bothered by what Ruth had told them concerning their father's leg. Daddy was coming home—that's all that mattered.

The physiotherapist insisted that Prodigal start walking with help. "Mr. Runsome," the therapist said, "this isn't your permanent prosthesis. After you heal a little more, you'll be fitted with a permanent, below-knee prosthesis. The prosthetic leg will be barely noticeable with your clothes on."

Prodigal didn't have much to say. Depression had set in. He didn't care to hear about a temporary this or a permanent that. He wanted his leg back. *My life is over. What good will I be to anyone now? How are my sons going to deal with this? How am I going to deal with this?*

The therapist continued rambling, but Prodigal didn't hear a word.

At night he kept reaching for his leg. *What's wrong with me? Crazy or something. How can I reach for something and feel a leg that isn't there? I must be loony.* How could he tell Doctor Walker about the itching and funny sensation he was having in the very area where his leg was amputated?

As if on cue, he carefully reached his right hand over toward the left side of the hospital bed, until his long, cold fingers hugged the railing. He managed to turn his body until he faced the table next to the bed. Immediately his eyes met up with the brochure peeking out from under the water pitcher. He reached slowly toward the stand, barely able to grab hold of it.

The front of the brochure read: "Phantom Sensation Is Real." Prodigal opened it and began reading: "Fifty percent to a high of ninety percent of amputees experience what has come to be known as 'phantom sensation.' For most patients, this sensation is nothing more than a minor distraction such as a warm and tingly, itching sensation, much like that found in an intact limb. For others, there can be pain that requires treatment. The pain can range from cramping to burning and a shooting or stabbing pain. This is then known as phantom pain. Phantom pain can occur anytime and can be experienced periodically by the amputee for the rest of his or her life. Stress, fatigue, temperature, and humidity can contribute to this pain as well."

The pamphlet went on to list several things an amputee could do to help relieve phantom pain without medication.

Prodigal read the entire brochure before breaking down in sobs.

35

Missing You

Teary went outside to empty the litter boxes. She inhaled the fresh smell of spring flowers in the air. *I can't believe I haven't heard from that old knucklehead,* she thought to herself. *That joker hasn't answered my e-mails either.* She stooped down and rubbed her Weimaraner, Rocco, on the head. She spoke in a baby voice to her dog. "Hey, Mommy's sweet baby."

Rocco rolled over on his belly for a tummy massage.

"And I guess he must be screening his daggone calls too, huh, Rocco. Sorry, we can't take your call right now, but leave a message after the tone, and we'll get back to you as soon as possible," she mimicked.

Teary wondered who the "we" was that Prodigal was talking about. Could it be that he had remarried? Maybe he had someone living with him. Surely he would have told her something as important as that.

"Since I can't reach him, I guess I'll call Fantasia and find out what's up," she told Rocco. She picked up the clean litter boxes, and the two of them headed into the house.

Diamond and Sassy met her at the door and purred around her feet.

"Okay, okay, I know what you girls want. I've got something

for you. Be patient, and I'll get it as soon as I fill your litter boxes." She carried the litter boxes to the small space near the utility room. Sitting the litter boxes down, she filled them with fresh litter before returning to the kitchen and her purring cats. Teary went to the pantry, pulled kitty treats from the bottom cabinet, and scattered almost half of the can on the floor.

She then went to her bedroom. She looked in her telephone directory for the number for Trinity Three. "Hello, may I speak with Miss Runsome?" she asked.

"Which one?—Fantasia or Ruth?"

"Oh, I'm sorry. Fantasia, please."

"May I tell her who's calling?" the voice asked politely.

"Yes, tell her it's Teary Fullalove."

"Hold on please while I put your call through, Miss Fullalove."

A few seconds later, Fantasia answered. "Hi, Teary, what's going on, girl?"

"Hi, Fantasia. Nothing much, just the same ol', same ol'. What about with you? How's the art business going?"

"Business is booming hard and heavy. I'm not complaining one bit." Fantasia laughed.

"How is Miss Ruth?"

"She's doing fine too. She's still seeing William Phillips. He treats her like a queen. And what about you? Met anyone? Gotten married or anything?"

"Naw, I'm still playing the singles game. Finally, I can say that I believe I'm beginning to enjoy my singleness."

"I've been like that all along really. I don't think I can adjust to having a man in my life full-time, you know. I mean, I date every now and then. I've even had a couple of short-term relationships, but nothing that lasted past the six-month mark, which is definitely okay with me."

"I heard that."

"Well, enough of the small talk. I know you must be calling

about my brother. Maybe you can help him out because none of us can get through to him."

"What do you mean by 'get through to him'?"

"You know how he is, Teary. You know better than any of us."

"Yeah, I know he can be a butthole at times, but he doesn't have to shut me out. I haven't heard from him in months. His e-mail is full, and when I call him, all I get is his corny answering machine. Can you believe that?"

"Yeah, I can. Ever since they amputated his leg, he's shut himself off from just about everybody. Shucks! We can barely get him to answer our calls. He's become mean, irritable, and withdrawn. But, really, I can't say I blame him. He had to deal with Faith's death, and almost a year to the day of her death, he loses his leg. Can't work; can't run and play with the boys like he used to. Hell! Can you blame him?"

Teary didn't respond, and Fantasia kept right on talking.

"My brother's in a bad way. He's in a deep state of depression and rightfully so. Girl, my goodness, talking about tragedy, Prodigal has had more than his share. And folks wonder why I refuse to believe in some so-called higher power. Not me, honey, this chick is definitely too smart for that."

At this point, after what she'd just heard, Teary could care less about Fantasia's beliefs. "Fantasia," Teary said, finally able to get a word in.

"Huh?"

"Did you say Prodigal's leg was amputated? I don't believe what I just heard," she screamed.

"I thought you knew. I thought that's why you were calling— to check up on him, to see if we had talked to him."

"I was calling to check up on him because he hadn't answered any of my e-mails or phone calls. I thought he had gotten himself married again or something. Oh, my God! I can't believe this." Teary could barely control her tears.

"Well, unfortunately, it's true."

"How did it happen?"

"He was trapped in a really bad fire."

"What?"

"It was caused by a space heater. Prodigal always hated those things. The good thing that came out of the whole ordeal is that he saved the lives of two children. But that's my brother for you." Fantasia kept chattering nervously. "I've gone to see him a couple of times, so has Mother. When it first happened she flew out there. She stayed for a few weeks, helping with the boys, until Prodigal was able to come home. But he's just not himself anymore. It's like he's lost his will to live."

Too shocked to interrupt, Teary continued to listen.

"Kevin and Kaleb spend most of their time with the Richards or some of the other church members. You remember the Richards, don't you? They're the elderly couple who live across the street from him."

"Yeah, er, er, sure, I-I remember them," Teary stammered.

"Not long after he was discharged from the hospital, I flew to Bonsai Bay on my way to an art convention in Nevada. I was only able to stay with him overnight, but while I was there, all he did was sit in front of the television, flipping the remote. Kevin and Kaleb barely said a word either. They looked like they had lost both parents. Poor babies. When Momma was getting ready to come back home, she offered to bring the boys with her to stay here for a while, you know, until Prodigal was able to care for them like before. Of course, Prodigal wouldn't entertain that suggestion, not for one second. So she had no choice but to leave them in Bonsai Bay.

"Prodigal is just so stubborn. He even refuses to wear the prosthesis they made for him. If he would go to therapy, he could learn how to use it and do a lot of the things he used to do. He'll never be a firefighter again, but shucks!—he received a nice sum of money from his insurance since he was on the job when he lost his leg. I know that doesn't take the place of him losing his leg.

That's not what I'm trying to insinuate at all, but he can make the most of a terrible situation if he would allow—"

"Look, Fantasia, thanks for letting me know. I'm glad I called. I have to go now," Teary said, still in a daze.

"Okay, we'll talk again soon. And don't wait so long to let me hear from you. By the way, maybe you can reach Prodigal. You've always been able to get through to him when no one else could."

"Maybe. Bye, Fantasia."

In shock, and reeling from what she'd just heard, Teary hung up the phone and began to cry. She cried for all that Prodigal was going through. She cried for herself, for all the times she had been hurt, for not being able to make her marriage work, for not being able to bear children, for all the pain she and Prodigal had endured throughout their lives.

Tears streamed down her face until she began to resemble a puffed-up water balloon. When she finally stopped, the house was dark, and her pets were asleep. She looked over at the clock sitting on the mantel. It was 3:30 a.m. She turned over to the other side of her bed, picked up the phone from its cradle, and dialed Prodigal's number.

The phone rang until she heard the all-too-familiar sound of his answering machine. This time, she screamed incessantly into the receiver.

"Prodigal! Prodigal Runsome! I know you're there. Pick up the phone. Pick up the phone, I said. If you don't, I'm going to keep calling back until you either answer the darn phone, get your number changed or whatever; do you hear me?" she screamed.

Still there was no answer.

The incessant ringing of the phone had awakened Prodigal. He listened as Teary screamed into the answering machine. She would just have to keep on screaming because he wanted nothing to do with her or anyone else. *Why can't people just leave me alone?*

He listened to her ranting and raving but still had no desire to pick up the phone. *She must have found out. Dang! Who could have told her? I bet she called Fantasia or Hope. I don't need her pity; I don't need anybody's pity for that matter.*

He shifted his position in the bed, turning away from the voice booming over the answering machine. He started to turn off his ringer, but since the twins were sleeping over at a friend's house, he didn't want to do that. Anything could happen, and they would need to get in touch with him. *I should have signed up for memory call service. That way I could determine whether I wanted to play my messages or not.* He'd definitely have to call the phone company and look into doing just that.

Less than five minutes later, the phone rang again. It was Teary again. This time she yelled even louder.

She must be losing her mind or something. To avoid her incessant calling, Prodigal gave in and answered the phone. "You're full of it, you know."

"I told you I was going to keep calling until I reached you, or until you became sick of me calling and changed your number. I was worried about you. I've been e-mailing you and calling you, and I haven't heard a thing from you. I called Fantasia and she told me what happened. Prodigal, I am so sorry."

"See, that's exactly what I don't want. I don't need yours or anyone else's sympathy. It's just one of those things. I've come to the conclusion that life hates me and God hates me even more. You know what else I've come to realize?"

"No, but I'm sure you're going to tell me."

"I think God created me just to have someone he could tease and mock, you know, like a puppet or something. I mean, he took my daddy to test my reaction. Then he kept the first girl I ever loved always out of my reach," Prodigal said, referring to his friendship with Teary. "But that was only the beginning of the game. You see, next, he let me believe my life had changed for the better by giving me a wonderful woman who loved me and who I loved in return. What does 'the man upstairs' do?—Boom!—He takes her away from me too. I'm sure he got a kick outta that. Then he says to himself, 'Let me destroy him further by taking his leg and see how he does with that.'"

"Oh, come off it, Prodigal. Talking about somebody pitying you . . . you're doing enough of that yourself. You know good and well that God doesn't operate like that. You're just angry and hurt; you're still grieving, and you're lonely."

"Sure, you know everything—I guess that's why you're still alone, unmarried and barren."

His words cut her like a knife, but she refused to internalize what he was saying. The Prodigal she had come to know and love would never intentionally hurt her. He would never try to destroy her. It was the enemy talking through him, trying to keep her away from him. She couldn't listen to him, wouldn't listen to him. Instead, she stood up to him, and refused to be chased away from her best friend's life.

"Say what you want to say because you're right. I *am* alone, unmarried, and I'll never be able to give birth to a child of my own," she said as calmly as possible so as not to let him know how much his words stung her. "But, there's one thing I do have—I have you, Prodigal. You're my best friend. You always have been, and you always will be. You can try to be mean to me if you want to, you can try to use your words to hurt me and shut me out, but it's not going to work."

There was an agonizing silence. Then deafening sobs quickly took its place. Prodigal couldn't hold back any longer the tears, which rushed forward like a mighty waterfall.

"Prodigal, I'm coming to see you," she said, hanging up before he could respond.

Entering her manager's office that same morning, Teary was prepared to resign if she didn't get what she wanted. She was quite thrifty and had accumulated a nice-sized nest egg over the years. After all, what else was she going to do with her money but save it for a rainy day?

"I have a family emergency and I need some time off," she explained. "I wish I could give more notice, but I can't."

"Do you know how long you'll be gone?" the stocky gentleman asked.

"I'm not sure. Probably a few weeks."

Without hesitation, he gave his approval.

She cleared up some last-minute assignments before heading home to pack. She went online when she got home and purchased an e-ticket to leave at 4:45 that same afternoon. She glanced at her watch. *Eleven forty-five. I don't have much time.*

She called Patricia and made arrangements for her to take care of her pets and her house. Sifting through the mountain of items in her hall closet, she found her luggage and hurriedly packed several pieces of clothing. *If this isn't enough, I'll just have to go shopping when I get there.*

She dialed his number, and the answering machine came on. "Prodigal, my flight will be arriving at 9:05 tonight. I expect you to be at the airport to pick me up. I'll be downstairs, right outside the baggage claim area. If you don't show up, I'll get a cab or whatever, but rest assured, I will be there one way or the other."

Prodigal glared at his clock. He didn't have much time. Hoisting himself out of the bed and into his electric scooter, he went into his specially equipped bathroom. To accommodate his new disability, the house had been remodeled to make things more accessible for him. He had also purchased a specially equipped Yukon XL with a custom-designed motorized wheelchair lift and hand control, so he could drive himself and the boys wherever he desired, though he very seldom drove or ventured outside anymore. He had taken the boys to a drive-in movie once or twice, and to McDonald's, but he refused to be seen out in his scooter. Shame and self-consciousness replaced his once self-assured, while not arrogant, disposition.

How is she going to react when she sees me? Why is she so determined to humiliate me even further by coming here?

"Kevin, Kaleb," he called out.

They came running from the direction of their playroom.

They're growing up fast, he thought. How he wished that Faith were here to see them. "Hey, you two, guess who's coming to visit?"

"Who, Daddy?" Kevin was the first to ask.

"My best friend, Teary, that's who. I have to go and pick her up from the airport tonight, okay?"

"Okay, Dad," they both said.

"Can we go with you?" Kaleb asked.

"Sure, you can. I was hoping the two of you could help get her luggage loaded, you know, be the fine gentlemen that you are." Prodigal laughed.

Kaleb said, "We sure will. Is that all, Daddy?"

"Our friends are in the playroom," Kevin told him. "We were playing the pinball machine."

"Yeah, go ahead." He was glad the boys had friends.

As they were getting older, their friends spent more time at the house. It was certainly a good idea to add the recreation room, when he had the house remodeled.

Prodigal and the twins sat in the SUV waiting for Teary's plane to arrive.

"Kevin and Kaleb, when Teary gets here, I want you to be on your best behavior."

"Dad, don't worry about us. We'll be good," Kevin said confidently.

The boys each played their handheld Game Boys, while he fidgeted with the steering wheel. Prodigal glanced at his watch every few seconds then strained his head forward to look toward the luggage area.

A raspy voice came over the outdoor intercom. "Flight 1289 arriving from Memphis is now unloading. Flight 1289 arriving from Memphis is now unloading."

"Okay, boys, that's her flight. Hurry. Go to the baggage claim area right through the automatic doors." Prodigal pointed at the doors.

The boys scurried out of the truck, while Prodigal opened his door, and then pushed the remote control button that operated his lift. He steered his scooter on to the lift, and within minutes, he was lowered to the pavement.

He proceeded in the direction of the baggage area. *Well here goes. I don't know how this is going to go, but I guess I'm about to find out.* When Prodigal saw Teary coming down the escalator, an automatic smile stretched wide across his weary, unkempt face. She was still as pretty as ever, full of laughter and life.

They spotted each other at the same time. She looked at him and at once ran to meet him. "Prodigal!" Teary reached out to hug him. "Am I glad to see you."

He drew her close to him, inhaling her familiar scent and welcoming her warm embrace. *God, she smells good.*

Kevin and Kaleb ran up. "Hi, Teary," they exclaimed.

"Hi, guys. Boy, have you two grown up."

Kevin and Kaleb giggled.

"Come on, sons, grab Teary's luggage, so we can get out of here."

"Sounds good to me."

They hurriedly loaded the three-piece vintage luggage into the SUV with ease.

"All aboard?" Prodigal teased.

Teary raced to his side. "What can I do to help you?"

He turned abruptly and shot her a deadly stare, like she had committed an unpardonable sin. In a frustrated voice he told her, "If you've come all this way because you feel sorry for me, then you can turn right back around and take your tail back to Memphis. I don't need or want your pity, Teary—don't give me that."

He swerved the electric scooter around so quickly that it almost went into a tailspin, missing her foot by a hair. He proceeded to press the button to the automated lift.

Teary skipped out of the line of fire at the same time, letting his words roll off her like water on a duck's back.

"My, my . . . don't we have our shorts in a wad this evening. Come on, boys. Climb in," she said, ignoring Prodigal's attitude. "Hey, I'm starving, Mr. Meany Weeny. Can we stop and grab something to eat on the way to the house?"

Kevin and Kaleb laughed out loud.

Prodigal, however, failed to see the humor. "Whatever," he grumbled.

Kaleb asked, "Teary, can we get pizza?"

"Pizza sounds good to me. What about you two?" She looked at Prodigal, then at Kevin.

"I'd like pizza too, with extra cheese and pepperoni," Kevin said.

"Whatever," Prodigal mumbled again.

"They do deliver pizza here, don't they?" Teary asked.

"Yeah, why?" Prodigal replied, his tension cooling down somewhat.

"I was thinking that we could call it in now, and by the time we get to the house and get settled, the pizza should be arriving. How about it, you guys?"

"Whatever." Prodigal pulled his cell phone from the side compartment on the door. "What kind do y'all want?"

Kevin, Kaleb, and Teary looked at each other. Right on cue they answered in unison, "Whatever."

Prodigal looked at the three of them, and they all broke out in laughter.

Once the pizza was delivered, they gathered around the kitchen table and devoured it. Afterwards, the boys took their baths and went to bed, leaving the house quiet.

"How long are you planning on hanging around my neck of the woods?" Prodigal asked Teary, as the two of them sat in the beautifully furnished family room.

"For as long as you need me or want me here, or until I'm sat-

isfied that you're doing okay." She lay back in the sandalwood recliner and sipped on her raspberry tea, savoring every delicious
drop. "Why didn't you answer my e-mails or my phone calls?
Why didn't you let me know about your accident?"

He remained quiet for a few seconds then said, "I just couldn't,
don't you see? The past two years have been like two years from
hell. I couldn't begin to tell you all the stuff that's been going on
inside my head. I mean, losing Faith and now losing my leg. I
just don't know. I'm still in a daze. I'm still hoping against hope
that one day I'll wake up and find that I've been living a bad
dream or something, that none of this is real. But you know what,
Teary . . . it is for real, isn't it? It really is for real."

"Yes, unfortunately it is, but we can make it. We'll face it together. I'll always be here for you, just like you've always been
here for me. Everything's going to work out just fine, you'll see. I
don't know why things happen the way they do. I've been told
repeatedly that everything is supposed to work out for good to
those who belong to the Lord—that's all I can say about this."

She reached for the lever on the side of the recliner, bringing
herself up to a full sitting position. She stood up and went toward
him, then knelt down at the foot of his scooter. She planted her
head on his thighs, as if doing so would make everything all right
in his world and in hers too.

The next few weeks moved at breakneck speed. The boys enjoyed Teary and quickly became accustomed to her being part of
their everyday lives. She made it a point to get up early every
morning and fix their breakfast before sending them off to school,
and dinner was always ready when they arrived home.

At night she tucked them in; she did all the things a mother
would do. Almost every Sunday morning, she gathered the boys
in the SUV and headed to church. Sometimes Prodigal would
join them; other times he stayed behind.

Lying alone in her bed at the close of each day, Teary thought
about how much she loved her role as surrogate mother. At times

a pinch of sadness would revisit her whenever she thought about not being able to have children of her own, but then she remembered how God was continually blessing and enriching her life.

Since Teary's arrival at Bonsai Bay, Prodigal attitude took on a change for the better as he felt some happiness slowly reclaiming his life. He started his physical therapy and gained new strength each day. He slowly began to use his prosthesis more. Most days, Teary accompanied him to therapy, and she made an effort to learn everything she could about his amputation and its effects.

Like always, the two of them proved to be good for each other. She had her own challenges in life, replete with battles that sometimes kept her feeling bound and saddened, but he was the one who could bring a smile to her face.

Teary still held that special place in Prodigal's heart; yet throughout their lives, they somehow found themselves seeking love, attention, and affection from someone other than each other. But when his world was cold and gray, he could count on her to add a sprinkle of sunlight. The two of them had seen each other through some rough times; with each other they waded through the storms of life.

From the first time he saw her all of those many years ago, she was destined to play a special role in his life. He could still vividly see her pigtails swinging back and forth underneath the bright, blue skies. His little eyes were mesmerized, as she looked over from the side of the moving van, waving as if she had already known him. He remembered waving back, and a smile spreading across his face. From that moment on, they were the best of friends.

He recalled the time he asked her to be his girlfriend. They were playing hide and seek with some of the other kids. They found a good hiding spot in the bushes behind Debra's house. While Debra counted, he and Teary tried hard to keep from laughing out loud.

From out of nowhere he suddenly said, "If you're my girlfriend and I'm your boyfriend, give me a kiss."

"Okey-dokey."

They kissed each other on the cheek and started giggling again.

Debra rushed into the bushes and tagged them both. "You're out, you're out!" she screamed.

"Teary, why do you have to leave?" Kevin asked the night before she planned on going back home.

"Honey, I have to go back home. I have a job, and I have two cats and a dog who I miss terribly and who I know miss me too."

"But you could bring your dog and cats here to live with us," Kaleb told her.

She knelt down next to his bed and stroked his hair. "But, baby, my home is in Memphis now."

"We'll help you take care of 'em, we promise. And Daddy likes animals too. Couldn't you get a job here?"

She hugged both Kaleb and Kevin. "Look, tell you what, I promise to come back real soon. Now come on, you two, it's time for bed. Get on your knees. It's prayer time."

In unison, they recited the Lord's Prayer. Then the twins said their own special prayers to God.

Teary tucked them in bed and kissed each of them on the forehead. "I love you, Kevin. I love you, Kaleb. Sleep tight and don't let the bed bugs bite." She pinched them lightly as if a bug was biting them.

They squealed out loud.

"Hey, what's going on in there?" Prodigal yelled. "Bedbugs must be biting tonight."

"Daddy, help us." They screamed with laughter.

Prodigal rolled in on his scooter and wheeled right up beside Teary. He grabbed her around her waist and pulled her onto his lap and held her so Kevin and Kaleb could tickle her.

"Hey, I give up. I've been outnumbered."

Prodigal and Teary hustled the boys into their beds.

"Goodnight, Teary. Goodnight, Daddy," Kevin and Kaleb told them.

"Goodnight, sons. I love you. Now get some sleep. See you in the morning."

"Yeah, see you guys in the morning." Teary blew a kiss at each of them before closing the door.

"Hey, do you want a nightcap before we call it a day? There's a pitcher of tea in the fridge, and I believe there's some leftover linguini too. How 'bout it?" Prodigal asked.

"Sounds good to me. Let's do it."

They went into the kitchen, and Prodigal pulled out the pitcher of raspberry tea and fixed each of them a glass.

Teary shuffled through the refrigerator until she found the white Chinese box filled with linguini.

"Hey, don't bother about warming it up." He smiled. "There's nothing better than cold linguini."

She grabbed the box and sat it on the kitchen island.

He moved close by her. "Are you sure you have to go? The boys are going to have a tough time when you leave."

"I wish that I didn't have to leave, but you know I do. I do have a job, house, and pets."

"Stop. There's no need to say more. I don't know how I could be so selfish. Of course, you have a life in Memphis. And me of all people should know better than to even think about asking you to stay. Forgive me?" He made a long face, stuck his lips out, and held his head to the side.

"Boy, you're so silly. Here, eat up." She dangled a long piece of linguini in front of his open mouth.

He tilted his head back to receive it.

"Get it, get it." She screamed with laughter, wiggling it back and forth out of his reach.

"So you want to play hard ball, huh?" He pulled himself up from the chair and strained to catch the swaying strands of linguini.

290 Shelia E. Lipsey

Still laughing, Teary inched closer to the edge of the granite countertop island. Within a split second she found herself tottering. Unable to steady herself in time, she fell forward, headed straight for Prodigal.

He reached up just in time to grab her by the waist. They were sheer inches from each other, face-to-face. He felt the warmth of her breath as she exhaled. He didn't let her go, and she didn't try to move from his grasp. Their eyes locked, and the chemistry between them permeated through the sounds of their beating hearts. This time he refused to give in to what he was afraid to admit. He was still attracted to her, but they weren't teenagers anymore; they were two sensible and responsible adults.

He gathered his thoughts quickly and eased her off him, helping her to regain her footing.

Teary nervously moved away from his scooter. "No more feeding you."

"Ha, ha, ha! Very funny—Give me that box, and I'll do it myself." Prodigal reached for the box.

She passed the box over to him and watched him gulp down the remaining strands of pasta. He slurped down the last strand and then wiped his mouth with the back of his hand. "Ahhh! That was pretty good."

"Come on, Mr. Greedy. Time for you to get to bed too."

"Oh, do I have to?" he asked, imitating a child's tone.

"Yes, we both do. It's been a long day."

Cutting the lights off in the kitchen and the hallway, they both headed to bed, telling each other goodnight along the way.

The following morning, everyone was quiet over breakfast. No one seemed to have much of an appetite.

"Come on, enough already with the long faces. Eat your pancakes and bacon," Teary ordered the boys.

"Hey, maybe we'll come to Memphis sometime to visit you and that fabulous zoo you say they have." Prodigal laughed.

"That would be great. I'd love that. I'll take you to Graceland too."

" 'Graceland'? Ugh." Kevin twisted his face. "I don't want to go to Graceland; I just want to come to Memphis and see your cats and dog."

"I want to go to Graceland, and I want to see your cats and dog, and I want to see where you live, and I want to see where you work and everything," Kaleb babbled.

"Well, that would be fine too." Teary smiled. "I can't wait. Come on now, eat up, you two. It's almost time for me to get to the airport. I don't want to miss my flight."

After breakfast, the boys helped Teary load her luggage in the SUV. Soon, it was time to leave. She checked the guest room, to make sure she wasn't leaving anything.

Teary and Prodigal made light conversation on the way to the airport. She felt a tug at her heart at the thought of leaving the twins. She wondered if this was how motherhood felt—never wanting to be apart from your children, and hurting when you have to leave them. She especially thought about having to leave Prodigal. She would miss him something fierce.

"Kevin, Kaleb, I'm going to miss you so much. I want you to be good while I'm gone." She hugged them as tight as she could. Then she turned to Prodigal, who was sitting in his scooter, quietly watching the tender love she displayed toward his sons. He felt something stir within his heart, but he didn't know exactly how to define the feeling. He just knew he saw her through different eyes.

She walked over to him and slowly bent down and kissed him lightly on the lips. "You better be a good boy too," she said as the two of them embraced. "I love you, man."

"Yeah, me too."

"Call me, and I'll do the same."

"Sure, now go on and get on the plane before you're stuck here."

36

Forever by Your Side

Prodigal, I miss you and the boys. I hope you've been going to therapy. Things are pretty much back to normal here. Work is hectic as usual. Tell me what's going on with you. Love ya, bye. Oh, yeah, kiss the boys for me.

Prodigal quickly replied to Teary's e-mail:

We miss you too. I'm being a good boy (lol). Going to therapy religiously twice a week (church too!). With each visit, I'm gaining more strength and stamina. You'll be proud to hear that I'm starting to use my prosthesis more and relying less on my scooter. I can even do some of the things that I used to do. I'm standing for longer periods of time, and I haven't fallen when I get out of the bed lately either. I guess my mind is catching up with my body. The twins are great and talk about you all the time. I'll call you later tonight. Got some news to tell you. Bye for now.

He pushed the send button, shut off his computer, and went to prepare dinner for Kevin and Kaleb.

I wonder what he has to tell me, Teary thought after reading Prodigal's e-mail. She couldn't wait to get home later that evening and hear what he had to say. She peeked at the clock on her desk—5:25 p.m. Another half hour or so and she was going to call it a day.

At six o'clock, Teary exited her office and headed home, making it there around 6:30. While she ran a hot bath, she let the cats and dog outside. *What a day—meetings, meetings, and more meetings. I feel like I spend half my life in meetings.*

She slowly stepped out of her designer shoes and slid off her pantyhose. She unzipped her teal blue straight-laced skirt and allowed it to kiss the sea-green ceramic bathroom tile. Next she unbuttoned the two pearl buttons on her jacket and hung it over the chair next to her vanity. After unhooking her bra and placing it on top of her jacket, she stepped into the warm, welcoming water, closed her eyes, and relaxed.

"Okay, you guys, time for bed," Prodigal told Kaleb and Kevin. They whined, "But, Daddy . . ."

"No 'but Daddy' tonight. It's bedtime."

"Can't we stay up a little longer and watch *Batman*, puh-leeze?" Kevin begged.

"Not tonight. You have school tomorrow, so don't even think about it. Now off to bed. Let's go." Prodigal's voice was stern. "And remember to say your prayers too."

Kevin pouted. "Yes, sir."

"Yes, sir."

Prodigal kissed the boys good night and tucked them in. He ambled into his bedroom, plopped down on the bed, and unbuckled the straps on his prosthesis. He tapped the button on his scooter and pushed the handle to guide it closer to him. Without so much as a grunt, he used his arms to lift himself over into his motorized chair and proceeded to the oversized master bath. With relative ease, he maneuvered his masculine body onto the shower bench the way he'd been taught in therapy. The warm jet stream of water refreshed his tired body.

He lingered in the shower until the soothing jet streams turned cold. After drying off and rubbing his body down with lotion, he climbed between the satin sheets, allowing the smooth fabric to gently massage his naked skin. *I can't imagine why anyone wants to sleep in pajamas.* From the time he was a little boy he hated the feel of clothing once he got into bed. Often his mother would come into the room to check on him, and there she'd find him lying in bed stark naked. He smiled at the thought.

"You sound a little tired," Prodigal said into the phone.

"Yeah, I am. I had one meeting after another today." Teary sighed. "How was your day?"

"Uneventful. I went to therapy, which is always a half-day ordeal, came back here and tidied up a little bit, and put on a green bean casserole for dinner."

"You cooked? Boy, I don't believe it. How did it turn out? It must have been one of Faith's recipes."

"Yeah, for sure. It turned out pretty good; the boys didn't complain, not one bit."

"I wish I was there. I'd love to sink my teeth into a good casserole. All I had for dinner was a tuna salad sub and some chips."

"That's not such a bad idea, you know?"

"What?—eating a tuna salad sub?"

"No, coming back to Bonsai Bay. Why don't you come back and, this time, plan on staying for more than a few weeks?"

The invitation took her by surprise. She had to admit, she did miss them. Since she would never have any of her own, she gloried in the time she was able to spend with them. "There's nothing I would love more than that, but I just can't up and leave everything I've worked hard for."

"Teary, the pets are welcome, and as far as your job—Wasn't it you who told me one time before that you could transfer just about anywhere you wanted to? Even if you couldn't, I have enough money to take care of you, me, and the boys three or four times over. And there's definitely plenty of room here, you know that. Plus, the boys need you, and they miss you."

"Is this what you had to tell me, or should I say *ask* me?"

"It's been on my mind for a while."

"I tell you what—I'll think about it. Let me research the job market out there and find out some other things. I'll let you know."

"I'm going to hold you to your word too. Tell me, how's your love life?"

"What love life? All I do is work like a hound dog. I haven't had a real date in ages. I probably wouldn't know how to act if a guy asked me out."

"Girl, what's wrong with the cats in Memphis? Don't they know a good woman when they see one?"

"I guess they don't want a good woman. They want a hoochie mama or something like the ones in the videos shaking their booties."

"Well, start shaking that booty of yours and bring 'em on in."

"You got me messed up," she grinned.

"I tell you what, when you come to Bonsai Bay, I'll introduce you to some of my partners at the fire station."

She released a yawn. "Don't worry about it. Things will work out in due time."

"Sounds like you're ready to call it a night."

"I think so. Like I told you, I'm exhausted."

"Well, I'll let you go. Sweet dreams," he whispered and hung up the phone. Pulling the covers up around his neck, he soon drifted off into a pleasant, dreamless sleep.

37

Second Chances

"*Lord God, these are Your people. I commit them back into your hands. Guide them, protect them, and keep them in your care, as they leave this place. Amen.*"

Prodigal talked with some of the church members as they made their way through the crowd.

"That was a great service, wasn't it?" one of the members said to him.

"Sure was. Pastor makes his messages so plain and clear."

"That's one of the main reasons I like Unity Church."

"I'll second that. Well, it was nice talking to you. Have a great week." Prodigal then went in the direction of children's church to pick up the boys.

Arriving home, the boys rushed inside. "Daddy, I'm hungry," Kaleb whined as they entered the house.

"Go look in the fridge and grab a fruit. We're going to Captain James Landing for dinner a little later."

"Yes, sir." Kaleb raced into the kitchen.

Several months had passed, and there was no further mention in conversation about Teary moving to Bonsai Bay. It wasn't that he had forgotten, he just didn't want her to think he was pushing her to make such a big move. Events, however, turned out so that the decision was made for both of them.

For the past several weeks, Prodigal had been having problems with his amputation. Excruciating pain, swelling, and redness ran from the point of amputation up to his hip, for no apparent reason. The doctors were afraid that infection might have had settled in his good tissue, because the skin around his hip area was discolored and it was difficult for him to wear his prosthesis.

Prodigal went to see an orthopedic doctor, and was advised to spend more time in his scooter, something he preferred to the heavy dose of painkillers always at his disposal.

When Prodigal's pain and swelling became unbearable, Dr. Walker, his orthopedist, decided to put him in the hospital and run some tests. When he made it home from the doctor's office, he sent Teary an e-mail and informed her about his situation.

Instead of e-mailing him back, she picked up the phone and called him instead. "Hey, what's going on? You all right?"

"Yeah, I'm fine. I just need to have some tests done."

She yelled, "What kind of tests? Why didn't you tell me you were having problems with your leg?"

"Whoa! Wait a minute, woman—one question at a time. I'm not going to tell you every time I have an ache or pain. I'm a big boy who's fully capable of taking care of himself. My doctor just wants to rule out some things, that's all. I don't think it's anything serious. I'll only be in the hospital a couple of days."

" 'The hospital'? Who's going to take care of the boys?"

"The Richards, so don't go worrying about us."

"Mr. and Mrs. Richards are too old to be trying to take care of two rambunctious boys, and you know it. When are they planning on doing the tests?"

"Let me see . . . how do I answer these third degree questions? Well, they want me to have the tests done right away, but I told Dr. Walker, there's no way I can do it right now, I have too much to get done. I just can't up and check into the hospital at the drop of a dime. I have my sons to think about. After all, I don't know what the tests are going to reveal, so I have to get things in order on the home front first. So, to make a long story short, I told him I'd do it in a couple of weeks. Why do you want to know all of this stuff, my nosy little friend?"

"Because I'll be there. I'll work things out with my job. This time I guess I'll probably have to bring my four-legged babies along, if you don't mind."

"I don't want you to do this. I'll be fine."

"It's not you that I'm worried about; it's the boys."

"I guess we'll see you in a couple of weeks then, huh? And since you've made up your mind to come, take my credit card information and book the flight for you and your mini-zoo."

"I'll talk to you later. I have plans to make," she said, excitedly.

The next day Teary went into her boss's office to ask for an extended leave of absence. Her boss hated the idea, because he had a strange feeling that she might not come back this time. Nevertheless, he approved a three-month leave of absence and gave her some connections at a couple of newspaper offices in Bonsai Bay, in case she wanted to do some freelance work.

Teary made arrangements for her pets to travel, and informed her friend Patricia of her plans. She went to the post office and had her mail forwarded to a post office box, which Patricia agreed to check once a week. Everything was working out just fine.

Prodigal pulled back the Velcro holding strap on his prosthesis and carefully placed it next to his scooter then eased himself into the king-sized bed. Though he hadn't had the tests done yet, the anti-inflammatory medications the doctor prescribed had helped to alleviate some of the discomfort he had experienced over the past few weeks. Knowing Teary would be arriving in a few days lifted his spirits too.

Repositioning his head on the pillow and placing his hands

underneath the back of his head, Prodigal laughed out loud suddenly. His thoughts were on the blind date he was about to go on
the following night. How could he have allowed Glen to convince him to go on a blind date, of all things? *Man, what was I
thinking when I agreed to meet his wife's cousin?* Prodigal laughed at
himself.

He called and told Teary about the blind date set-up, hoping
she would tell him that it wasn't such a good idea. But, much to
his surprise, she'd done just the opposite and encouraged him to
go, saying that she wished she were in Bonsai Bay to see him go
on his first date, as she put it.

But Prodigal was nervous enough already. This time tomorrow
night, he would be sitting across a dinner table from God knows
who just because Glen couldn't find a way to entertain his wife's
cousin, who'd recently moved to Bonsai Bay.

Teary gave him some ideas on how to dress fashionably, so he
wouldn't come off as a geek.

The following day arrived way too soon for Prodigal. He took
his shower then began to get ready for his date. He was never the
kind who loved to dress up, but if the occasion called for it, he
had no problems doing it. Tonight was one such time. Of course,
Teary had insisted that he buy something new.

After putting on his ensemble, he surveyed himself in the mirror and was quite pleased at what stared back at him—fresh hair-
cut, black-and-cream Sean John dress shirt, black, tailor-made
slacks, black square-toed Cole Haan shoes, spot of jewelry on the
left hand, Movado on the right wrist. *Definitely not bad, not bad at
all.* By the time he finished getting dressed, it was time to take
the boys to the sitter's.

Prodigal grabbed the boys' jackets, and they headed outside.

"Come on, hurry up. I'm going to be late." He led them across
the street.

Mrs. Richards stood in the doorway patiently waiting on them.

"Good evening, Mrs. Richards."

"Hello, Prodigal. Hi boys, come on in. I just made a batch of chocolate chip cookies."

Kaleb and Kevin ran inside without saying goodbye to their father.

"Have a good time, Prodigal," Mrs. Richards said in her always-pleasant voice.

"Thank you, Mrs. Richards. I'm going to try." He went back across the street and climbed into his SUV.

Twenty minutes after leaving home, he pulled up in front of his mystery date's house. Before he could get out of the SUV, he saw a woman standing in the doorway.

"Don't bother getting out because I'm ready," she said as she approached the vehicle. "I was looking out for you."

He leaned over and opened the door for her just in time to get a peek at the camisole she wore underneath her fringed bouclé blazer. He liked what he saw. Her fuchsia wide leg pants were accented with a satin sash, which highlighted her svelte figure.

When she eased into the car, he smelled the freshness of her skin. Leather, beaded slides revealed perfectly pedicured feet.

He allowed his eyes to visit the contours of her curvaceous body. "Hi, I'm Prodigal, and you must be my lovely blind date."

"Yes, I'm Sheerah Samuels." She smiled and extended her hand to him.

"You are a gorgeous blind date." Prodigal shook her hand gently.

"Thanks. What a nice thing to say!"

"I call it like I see it."

Sheerah blushed and closed the door.

"Ready?"

"Yep, I'm ready. Let's get this party started." Sheerah laughed.

The two of them laughed and talked with relative ease on their way to the restaurant.

When they arrived and were seated at their table, Prodigal said to her, "Tell me about yourself, Sheerah."

"I'm a recent divorcee with a daughter who'll be fifteen in a couple of weeks. She can't wait to get her first cell phone."

"I guess that's the latest fad for teenagers. At least I don't have to worry about that for a few years."

"How many children do you have?"

"Two—six-year-old twin boys who love action figures and video games."

Prodigal felt relaxed the more he talked to his date. It felt good to be out with a woman. He hadn't realized how much he missed the companionship of the opposite sex. In addition to being easy to talk to, Sheerah was definitely easy on the eyes.

"Your turn."

"Let's see . . . I'm a widow. My wife died a little over two years ago."

"Oh, I'm sorry to hear that."

"Thanks."

"What happened to your leg?"

"Wow! You're not shy, are you?"

Sheerah looked directly at him. "I believe the only way to find out what you want to know is to ask. And if you don't want to answer, then that's fine too."

"No, it's just that I'm not used to people being so up front. Usually they just stare at me when I walk. Now that's when I get pissed. But, to answer your question, I'm a firefighter. I had some complications, after getting injured in a pretty big blaze."

"I see." Sheerah nodded.

"Since we're asking all of these deep questions, now it's your turn."

Sheerah smiled. "Let her rip."

"What caused the breakup of your marriage?"

"Well, me and my husband had a great marriage for almost twenty years." Sheerah twitched in her chair. "We were high-school sweethearts and best friends. He worked hard, made a good home for me and our daughter, but somewhere along the way he got lost."

" 'Lost'?—What do you mean?"

"He's a trial lawyer, a good one at that. But with his career came long hours. As for me, I dabble in real estate a little bit, but mostly I was at home playing the part of the good wife and mother. I don't know when things changed. It's like I woke up one morning, and we had grown apart. I didn't know who he was any more."

Prodigal saw the pain envelop her face as she spoke. "If you can't go on, then don't. I didn't mean to dredge up unpleasant memories."

"No, it's okay. We were invited to the mayor's ball. We would attend every year. I was busy socializing at the ball, not really realizing that I hadn't seen him for at least an hour. When I finally did miss him, my initial thought was that maybe he was somewhere conducting business, which wasn't unusual for him. About thirty more minutes passed, and I still didn't see any sign of him anywhere. I walked to the outer lobby. He wasn't out there, so I walked down the corridor toward the balcony. As I approached the balcony, I heard muffled sounds. The voice became clearer as I got nearer. 'I love you.' The voice wasn't that of a stranger. I felt a sickening sensation in the pit of my stomach. I tiptoed closer until I could see both of them. He held her up against him the way he used to hold me. They were sharing a deep, passionate kiss. I watched as his hands took free reign over her body. I listened to her sounds of obvious pleasure."

Prodigal stopped her. "Don't go any further, Sheerah."

Sheerah met his gaze. "It's okay. It doesn't hurt so much now."

"I didn't mean to pry, really, I didn't. And I'm sorry you had to go through something like that. To see your husband in the arms of another woman had to be devastating."

"It was. And I knew her too. It was one of the partners in his law firm. I never suspected a thing."

"The two of you couldn't work things out?"

"We tried, but eventually I had to admit that he just didn't love me anymore, so we got a divorce. I needed to make a new start, and here I am." Sheerah smiled and raised her hands.

"I'm sorry about the divorce, but I'm glad you came to Bonsai Bay. Come on, let's have a toast."

They raised their glasses of red wine up in the air. Prodigal proposed the toast. "To the future and all good things in life."

They clinked their glasses together and laughed as they each took a sip.

"The halibut was good, wasn't it?" Sheerah remarked.

"It sure was. And the cheese biscuits . . . I could eat a dozen of them. "

"I think you did."

"Wait a minute now, are you trying to call me greedy?"

"If the shoe fits."

They laughed.

Deciding not to have dessert, the two of them left the restaurant after Prodigal paid the check.

Once inside the car, Prodigal began talking to Sheerah about Teary. "We've been friends since we were kids," he explained. "The woman has always been there for me. And I've tried to be there for her as well."

"It's good to have friends like that. My best friend is in Denver, though we haven't been friends as long as you and yours. But really, my best friend was my husband. Which is one of the reasons I could never hate him or dislike him. I was hurt by his act of betrayal, but once my heart began to heal, I realized that he and I would always share something special. Out of our love our daughter, Alexis, was born."

"Yeah, that's a blessing in and of itself." Prodigal stopped at the traffic light. "Anger and hate sap our strength and suck away at our lives. When Faith died, it took a while before I was able to let go of the anger and bitterness. Once I let go, then I felt my heart begin to heal."

"I'm sure Teary was there for you, huh?"

"Yeah, she was, and she still is. The woman is remarkable. She's going to be here in a few days; maybe you two will get a chance to meet."

"Yeah, maybe we will."

Arriving at Sheerah's house, he pulled up into her driveway and turned off the engine.

"Would you like to come in and have a cup of coffee before we say good night?"

"On one condition."

"What's that?"

"If you let me make it."

"You won't get a fight from me. Follow me."

Prodigal followed Sheerah inside. He complimented her taste in decorating her house.

Sheerah led him into the kitchen and showed him where everything was for the coffee. Then she sat down at the breakfast nook. When Prodigal finished making the coffee, Sheerah retrieved two mugs from the cabinet and brought them over to the table.

Prodigal took pleasure in Sheerah's company. Sitting down in the chair across from her, he sipped on his coffee before setting it on the table in front of him.

Slowly, Sheerah removed her manicured hands from around her cup and sat it down next to his.

Encircling her slender fingers between his, he brought them to his lips and kissed them lightly. Their eyes locked simultaneously.

Without resistance, she welcomed the warmth of his moist kiss before pulling back. "I think you'd better go," she said.

"I think you're right." Prodigal stood up.

Sheerah walked him to the door. For the first time since he picked her up, they remained quiet.

"Good night, Sheerah."

"Good night, Prodigal. And thanks for a wonderful evening."

38

Got Your Back

"Listen, Prodigal," Teary told him, "I don't want you to worry about a thing. The boys will be fine. All I want you to do is lay back, relax, and let the doctor run whatever tests he sees fit."

"Yes, ma'am," Prodigal answered sarcastically to the amusement of Kevin and Kaleb.

Just like before, Teary became the perfect surrogate mother.

Prodigal's tests turned out fine. He didn't have a bacterial infection in his tissues after all. His prosthesis had caused the swelling and abrasions and his doctor informed him that he would have to be fitted with a new prosthesis. Until then, he was to alternate between using his scooter and his prosthesis until the skin healed and the swelling went down.

Once his tests were done and he received his doctor's positive verdict, Prodigal arranged for Teary and Sheerah to meet. He believed it would be one of the best things for Sheerah and Teary to like each other. If there was anything about Sheerah that wasn't right, Teary would be the one to detect it and immediately let him know. But when she met Sheerah, she gave him her stamp of approval.

For some reason, Teary thought Sheerah would be a stuck-up little twit who had her mind set on snatching Prodigal from the world, and who would be jealous of Prodigal's relationship with her. But she soon found out that Sheerah was nothing like she pegged her to be. Teary understood fully why Prodigal was taken by her. Sheerah was an attractive, friendly woman, with a sparkling personality.

Teary enjoyed seeing Prodigal smile again. He and Sheerah were spending quite a bit of time together. Prodigal liked her well enough to take the next step and introduce her to his sons.

Kevin and Kaleb liked her so much that they started asking their father when Sheerah would be coming back to their house.

Teary witnessed the positive change in Prodigal, and the boys too, since he started dating Sheerah. So why did Teary start to feel bent out of shape, like she was intruding in their lives?

"Teary," Kevin said one night while she tucked him and his brother in.

"Yes, sweetheart."

"Are you going to stay here with us forever?" he asked innocently.

"Yeah, are you?" Kaleb asked.

Teary looked at the both of them. She had come to love them like they were her own flesh and blood. She watched them night after night when they closed their eyes in sleep and thought about how she longed for children of her own. Since she would never have any, she poured out all of her love on them. She didn't want to leave them either. But she couldn't just invade their lives like a permanent fixture. That wouldn't be fair to the boys or to Prodigal.

Kevin tugged on her shirt. "Aren't you going to answer us?"

"Let's not talk about that tonight. Let's just enjoy each other for the time I am here, okay? Now, the two of you, go to sleep. Maybe we'll catch a movie tomorrow or something since it's Saturday. I love you."

"Love you too. Good night," Kevin said.

"Good night, Teary," Kaleb whispered in a sleepy voice.

"Good night, my babies."

"Teary," Kevin called her as she was turning to leave.

"What is it, Kevin?"

"When is Daddy coming home?"

"He'll be here soon, don't worry. Now, it's time for sleeping, not talking."

"Good night."

"Sweet dreams." Teary turned out the light and walked slowly toward the guest room.

Prodigal was out again tonight with Sheerah, and she was left home alone. Not that she had a problem with taking care of the boys, because she adored them. But hearing the happiness in Prodigal's voice, seeing the sparkle in his eyes when he talked about Sheerah, was invoking a little jealousy in Teary.

Once again, she felt like she was being left out, high and dry, while everyone else's life was perfect. She closed her bedroom door, sat on the edge of the bed, and began slowly undressing.

Prodigal pulled the SUV up in the garage after another wonderful night of being with Sheerah. A fresh smile still covered his face as he thought about the good time they had together. Walking into the foyer, he saw that the rest of the house was dark. It was rather late, so Prodigal wasn't surprised that Teary and the boys had turned in for the night.

As Prodigal passed by Teary's door, heading to bed himself, he heard her whimpering. He knocked lightly on her door.

"Yes?"

"Hey, you all right in there?" he asked from the other side of the door.

"Yes, I'm fine. Just getting a cold, I think."

"You want me to bring you a Tylenol or something?"

"No, I'm fine. Really, I am. Did you have a good time tonight?" she asked, pretending everything was okay.

"Yeah, we had a great time. Teary, are you sure you're okay?"

"Yes, I told you. I'm fine. Just go to bed. That's what I'm going to do myself. Good night."

"Night, Teary. Call me if you need me."

If only he had an idea just how much I need him. God I want him so bad, but it's Sheerah he wants. And I don't blame him. I mean, we've been best friends since we were little. I don't want to do anything to fracture our relationship. I guess it took him being interested in someone else for me to realize that I care about him more than I've been admitting to myself.

Teary often thought about Faith and how she would feel if she knew her feelings toward Prodigal. Certainly Faith would be happy to know that the boys would be loved and well taken care of, and that she would love Prodigal with all of her heart.

But it didn't matter any longer what Faith might have wanted because someone other than Teary was about to fill the void that she had left.

After saying her prayers, Teary slowly, but tearfully, drifted off into a troubled sleep.

39

Left Out

"Prodigal, would you like to come over for coffee and cake?" Sheerah asked at the close of Sunday worship. Sheerah and her daughter had been attending Unity Church ever since Prodigal invited her soon after they first met.

"Sure. I wouldn't miss it for the world," was Prodigal's quick response.

"You come too, Teary," Sheerah told her.

"Thanks, but I'm tired. I think I'm going to go to the house and crash."

Prodigal eased his arm around Teary's shoulder. "Are you sure?"

"Yes, I'm sure. And since I'm going home, why don't I take the boys with me. That way you don't have to rush home."

"You're something else, Teary. Look, tell you what . . . we'll stop somewhere on the way home, and I'll pick up something for dinner. That way you don't have to worry about fixing anything for the boys."

"No, that's not necessary. I don't mind fixing the boys something to eat."

"But Teary—"

"But Teary nothing. I told you—there's no need to stop any-where; we have plenty of food at home."

"If you insist." Prodigal then turned his gaze toward Sheerah. "I promise, I won't be long, Sheerah. I'll see you in about half an hour."

"Sounds good. Bye, Teary."

"Goodbye, Sheerah," Teary answered without enthusiasm.

Sitting on the couch next to Sheerah and swallowing his last bite of pound cake, Prodigal asked, "How long have we known each other?"

"A couple of months, I guess."

"Feels longer than that. I feel comfortable and secure around you."

"I'm glad. You know how to make a girl feel special too."

"I try." He paused, twiddling his thumbs around. "There's something I want to say to you."

"What is it?"

"I like you. I like you a lot, Sheerah."

"I like you too."

"What I'm really trying to say is that you're good for me, and I think I'm good for you."

"Prodigal, I don't know what to say."

"I don't want you to say anything right now. I just want you to give us a chance, a real chance to make something lasting in this relationship. Just think about it, please."

He leaned over and kissed her, and she eased her arms around his neck and returned his kiss.

Teary liked Sheerah, and she could tell that Prodigal had deep feelings for her. Why else would he spend so much time with her? Part of her was ecstatic for him, and the other part . . . well, she didn't know what she honestly felt about his new relation-ship.

She tried psychoanalyzing herself while she prepared dinner.

Attractive, successful career, good salary, but look at me—I'm here at my best friend's house with no potential mate in sight, no one trying to even hit on me. What's up with that? And look at Prodigal—he's moving on with his life, and I'm stuck on stupid in mine.

The boiling water and milk spilled over the top of the pot and brought her back to the present. Teary prepared the boys favorite meal of mac n'cheese, fried chicken, and sweet peas.

After eating their dinner, they curled up in front of the television and watched *Shrek* on DVD. They must have watched *Shrek 1* and *2* at least ten times during the time she had been in Bonsai Bay; they never seemed to tire of it.

Ten minutes into the movie, Teary heard Prodigal coming inside. If Kevin and Kaleb heard their father, they didn't show it. Their eyes were glued to the screen.

"Hi," Prodigal said. He walked over and sat down in his recliner, while Teary and the boys continued to cuddle up on the couch, along with Rocco and the cats at their feet.

"Did you enjoy yourself today?" Teary asked.

"Sure. Sheerah and I talked, took a walk, and basically just enjoyed one another's company. Nothing serious."

"I see." Teary nodded. "That's nice."

Kevin recited his favorite lines in unison with the movie, followed by a constant tugging on Teary's shirt.

"Daddy, tell Kevin to be quiet. I can't hear the movie."

"I'm not talking loud. I was just saying what Shrek said and telling Teary to fix us some popcorn, that's all."

Prodigal glared at the both of them with a stern eye. "Hey, cut it out, you two. Don't give me any trouble. If you want to finish watching *Shrek*, I suggest you stop arguing and be quiet. And Kevin, you don't *tell* anyone to do anything, you ask."

"Prodigal, chill out. I know what he means. He wasn't telling me in the sense you're talking about. I was about to get up and fix something to snack on anyway. He was just trying to let me know that he wanted popcorn."

Prodigal mumbled, "Mm-hmm."

Teary always managed to find a way to take up for the boys. She couldn't stand to see them get into trouble with their dad or anyone else. She stood up and went into the kitchen and fixed the popcorn, along with some strawberry kiwi Kool-Aid. The boys loved it.

"You want some too?" Teary asked Prodigal.

"Yeah, I guess I'll have a little." He got up from the recliner, limped over to the sofa, and sat down on the opposite end.

By the time the movie came to an end, Kevin and Kaleb had fallen fast asleep.

"I'll take them to their rooms," Teary whispered, standing up and stepping over Rocco and the felines.

"No, don't bother. Let's make them a pallet here on the floor and let them sleep. They don't have school tomorrow because of the teachers' conference, so they can sleep in late if they like. Plus they'll think it's a big thing when they wake up and find themselves in the family room in front of the TV."

"Well, okay. I'm going to turn in myself after we make their pallets. I have a lot of packing to do before I leave Wednesday."

"Is it that time already?"

"Yeah, it's time for me to get back into the routine of work and paying bills. You know how that goes."

"The boys are going to miss you, Teary. You know that, don't you?"

"Yeah, but they'll be okay. They're young and full of life. Plus, we'll keep in touch. And they have Sheerah and Alexis now too. That's good for them. Anyway, you all owe me a visit, remember?" She didn't want to come off sounding jealous of his relationship with Sheerah. She wanted to be happy for him, but something kept nagging at her, and she didn't know what it was.

"Yeah, but that won't be until sometime in mid-summer."

"I know it, but you also know they're super at using e-mail. Remember when the only thing we had to look forward to was a letter every now and then from an aunt or uncle?"

"Yep, but not today. These kids have it made. Well, come on, let's call it a night. I'm beat too."

They headed toward their rooms.

"Teary," he spoke slowly.

"Yes?" Teary turned toward him and bumped into his chest. She didn't realize he was so close up on her. She smelled the buttery popcorn on his breath and found herself looking longingly into his eyes.

He tried not to look into her enticing eyes. "I just, well, I just want you to know that I appreciate all that you've done for the boys. I mean, being here and all, helping us out. Faith would be so grateful to you. You know you've sacrificed so much, put your life on hold for us. I can never thank you enough." He looked down at her slender body and felt his manly desire rising within. He didn't expect to feel this way. He and Teary were supposed to be like brothers and sisters, not lovers. But if that were true, why was he aroused? His eyes captured her chestnut brown skin, he took in the fragrance of her body, and he wanted her. For the first time since his wife's death, he found himself becoming fully aroused. Why did he have to get this way with Teary and not Sheerah?

Teary felt her own sense of heightened passion for this man who knew her so well. This man who accepted her for who she was. She looked at his broad chest and saw the fine black hairs peeking through his shirt.

A fiery energy surged between them. Neither of them knew when their lips met, as they were taken away by the passion of the moment, two lonely souls. They were two people who wanted to be loved and to love. Their fervor mounted.

Prodigal pushed her hard against the wall. His taut, firm body pressed against her thighs. His desire for her was overpowering. He hungrily planted tiny, delicate traces of kisses over her face, her neck, her ears, and her hair. His hands traveled swiftly and urgently up and down her yielding body. The sound of desire escaped from her lips. Or were they coming from his?

She met his demands and held him tightly. "Make love to me. Make love to me now." Teary's body was already in a sweat, and her heart throbbed from the need for his touch.

Abruptly, he yanked himself away and looked at her with uncertainty and confusion in his eyes.

"No, I'm sorry. I can't do this. We can't do this. It's not right. We shouldn't be doing this." Prodigal breathed heavily. "Look, I was planning on telling you earlier—"

"Telling me what?" Teary looked flushed, and her heart still raced.

"I'm going to ask Sheerah to marry me. I'm going to ask her to be my wife, so don't you see this is wrong? This whole thing between us is wrong, Teary, I'm sorry. I don't know what I was thinking and how I could ever let myself get out of control like this with you. You've been so good to me and the boys, and I love you for it, Teary. I never want to hurt you, you know that, so please forgive me." He rushed off, slamming the door to his room behind him and plopped down on the gingham recliner sitting in the corner of the oversized master bedroom.

My, Lord, what was I thinking? What just happened out there? I have to get a grip. I almost lost it. And why did I tell her I was going to ask Sheerah to marry me? Where did that lie surface from? God, I think I've hurt Teary, something I never wanted to do.

Teary rushed inside her room, slammed the door hard, and flung herself across the bed. *How could this have happened? He wanted me. I could feel it, see it, and sense it. I'm not that big of a fool. Or am I? Maybe it's because I'm the one who wants him. Maybe he was fantasizing, thinking of Sheerah. Oh my God—Sheerah . . . he's in love with her. He wants to marry her.*

Teary's mind was in a blur. Her heart was pounding, and her head was spinning. So much had happened in such a short span of time. Now things between her and Prodigal would never be the same. She finally had to admit to herself that she loved Prodigal Runsome. She couldn't stand the thought of him being with another woman. She wanted to be the one he loved, the one he wanted to marry, but now all that had changed. It would never happen.

She fell to her knees. "God, here I am again," she prayed. "Please hear me. I need Your strength. I need to hear a word from You. I love Prodigal. I probably always have, but I don't want to make any more mistakes when it comes to relationships, Lord. You know I've made enough, so help me to be strong. I need you to help me through this." She climbed in the bed and curled up against the down pillows and cried herself to sleep—again.

The following morning, Prodigal was awakened by the boys pounding up and down on his chest.

"Daddy, wake up!" they screamed in his ear.

"We want to eat. Daddy, how did we get on the floor last night? Daddy, come on, get up."

"Hey, you guys," Prodigal said, his brain still fuzzy, "give your old man a break. Slow down and hit me with one question at a time." He grabbed one and then the other, tickling them.

"Come on, Daddy, go fix breakfast." Kaleb pulled Prodigal by the hand.

"Oh, okay, if you insist. Let me get cleaned up, and I'll be there in a few minutes. You two, run off and get your teeth brushed and your face washed. I'll fix some of my special pecan pancakes."

"Yeah, yeah," they screamed in delight.

Prodigal thought back to the previous night. He didn't know how he could have allowed his emotions to spiral out of control like that. *What was I thinking? How could I even think that Teary and I could share anything intimate? I must have been crazy and living in some sort of make-believe world.*

While shaving in the bathroom he cried out, "God, please forgive me. I don't know what came over me. I looked at Teary, and she looked so beautiful, so sweet. I wanted her so bad. How could I betray you, and how could I betray Faith with these lustful thoughts of mine?"

Suddenly, the enemy planted thoughts in his mind, reminding

Prodigal of how soft Teary felt underneath his powerful hands, of how good she tasted when he kissed her.

The enemy taunted him, *Don't be a fool.*

It was almost as if Prodigal could feel him standing beside him. Prodigal recognized that the things going on in his mind were definitely not from God, but he listened anyway. As quickly as he had appeared, the enemy vanished from his thoughts, when the boys burst into the bathroom.

"Daddy, come on, you're not through yet?" Kaleb asked quite impatiently. "I'm hungry."

"Me too," Kevin chimed in. "Hurry up. If you don't come on, Teary might try to fix the pancakes. "And, Daddy . . . ?"

"What, son?"

"Teary's pancakes just don't taste as good as yours."

"Yeah, Daddy, we like how she cooks," Kaleb added, "but you fix pancakes better. So hurry up before she starts on 'em."

Prodigal looked at his sons and laughed. "Okay," he whispered back, "I'll be right there. And don't worry, we won't say a thing to Teary about it. I'll just go in there and tell her to sit back and relax and let me do the cooking. So come on, you two."

Teary woke up to the smell of coffee percolating and bacon frying. She'd momentarily erased in her mind what happened the night before. She stumbled out of bed and walked slowly into the bathroom, still with the same clothes on from last night. She removed her sticky underwear and climbed into the steaming hot shower. How would she face Prodigal after what transpired last night?

What am I going to say? she pondered, the piping hot water streaming over her body. Shivers ran up and down her spine at the thought of the previous night's encounter. *I have to get a grip on this. I can't let him know just how hurt I really am. Maybe I'm just not attractive to him. Maybe he really does see me as only that little girl from across the street of a long time ago. Maybe he really does love Sheerah. Whatever it is he's thinking, I can't let him know that I'm hurt.*

She showered for a few minutes longer before climbing out of the shower to get dressed. Then she lotioned her body until it was silky smooth. She stepped into a pair of pink khakis and a cotton pullover, bumped a few curls in her hair, and proceeded out to the breakfast room.

Muffled sounds of Kevin and Kaleb's laughter spilled from the kitchen.

She walked into the kitchen, being careful not to look directly into Prodigal's eyes.

"Good morning," Prodigal said.

"Good morning," she mumbled back at him.

"I want you to sit back and relax. I'm doing the cooking this morning."

"No problem. I'm going to go outside and get the paper."

"Sure."

If the boys were a little older, they would have been able to detect the tension between them. Prodigal didn't think he could ever look at Teary the same way. He looked out the window while cooking, watching her going down the driveway, seeing her in a totally new light. *I've always had the hots for her.* But it went without saying, he loved Faith. Faith had been his lifeline, his be all and end all, his "all in all," his once-in-a-lifetime love. Yet, he knew that there had been times during his marriage that he sometimes thought of how it might have been if he had married Teary instead. He was careful not to entertain the thought for long, but he admitted to himself that it happened.

He had no idea what Teary would do now. But he didn't want her to leave, couldn't let her leave. He had to make things right, or did he? Then again, maybe he should just leave well enough alone and try to make things work between him and Sheerah. They could be a real family; he knew it.

At any rate, Teary deserved someone who would always be able to take care of her. He had plenty of money and all, but could he really fulfill all of her needs? He was confused, his mind boggled.

Teary strolled out to the end of the landscaped lawn and retrieved the paper. *I've got to get myself together.* Her body was still on fire from the passion that emanated between the two of them. Each of their lives had taken a different road. Hers led down a pathway of mess-ups. She couldn't seem to ever get things right or do things right, at least not for long. Was God punishing her for something? Had she been that awful? She didn't know any more. What she did know was that last night felt right. Last night felt good. She visualized the two of them going all the way. She felt his hands traveling to the secret places that would bring her to ecstasy. She felt his kisses, felt his passion and desire.

She heard a light moan escaping her lips even then. *Oh, Prodigal.* The tingle went from the top of her head to the bottom of her feet. She stood out in the warmth of the sunshine, allowing the tall oak trees to bathe her. She tilted her head up toward the sky. *I should try to forget about everything. I don't want to interfere with his happiness, or the boys' for that matter. He must love Sheerah if he's going to ask her to marry him.* The only thing left for her to do was leave. She couldn't stay another day.

She turned and ran back inside, being careful to plant a smile on her face in front of Kevin and Kaleb.

Everything was rather quiet at the breakfast table. Prodigal hurriedly ate his pancakes and drank his coffee.

Kevin finally broke the silence between big bites of pancakes and bacon. "Teary, are you still taking us to the picnic at church?"

She looked stunned. She had totally forgotten. "Boys, I'm sorry, but I won't be able to take you," she said, full of regret. "I'm sure your daddy will take you. And remember Sheerah and Alexis will be there."

Prodigal stopped drinking his coffee and pulled the newspaper down from his face.

"And remember what I told you guys? I have a home and a job that's waiting on me. I have to go home. Don't you think that Diamond and Sassy miss their home too? And surely you know that Rocco wants to go home. They have cat and dog friends they miss, you know."

"But you promised to take us to the children's day picnic," Kaleb said. "I don't like you any more. You broke your promise. You told Kevin and me that you loved us. I thought you loved us." He ran out of the kitchen, crying his heart out.

Now it was Kevin's turn. "That's right, you promised, you promised. Mommy!" he screamed. "I want my mommy." He took off running too.

The silence was so thick, you could cut the air with it.

"Why are you doing this? I could understand if it was just me and you decided to run, but it's the boys too. They need you."

"Oh, is that right?" she responded angrily. "I know they do; tell me something I don't know . . . like, do you need me?—Answer that. Tell me why you turned away from me last night. Tell me that, Prodigal. I can't take it any longer. I don't know what to do. I don't know what to feel any more. I have to leave."

It was Teary who ran out this time, leaving Prodigal alone at the breakfast table. She dashed to her room and phoned the airline to confirm reservations for her and her pets to leave later that afternoon. At first she thought she should stay for the picnic, but doing that was only going to prolong the situation that much longer. And she didn't want to face Sheerah either. The boys would hate her for walking out on them, but she believed in time they would come to understand and forgive her. After all, Prodigal obviously found in Sheerah someone he could freely love again and who in turn loved him and the twins. She had no right to be angry with him, and tried to convince herself that she should be ecstatic about him having someone special in his life.

Prodigal went into the study and closed the heavy oak door behind him. He looked at Faith's portrait over the mantle of the fireplace and began to cry. "Faith, what do I do? I want to live again. I want to love again. I want to laugh again. I don't know which direction I'm headed in. Everything is just so different without you." His tears flowed hard and freely. He wept from deep within his spirit.

He didn't know how long he had been crying, when he began

to think back to the night Faith died. He could see the beautiful aura around her. He saw the tender smile stretch softly and peacefully across her face. He could still feel the touch of her hand as she gingerly touched his lips, his eyes. He planted his head in his hands and stared at the picture of her sitting on his desk, and pondered over the last words she had spoken to him.

"Prodigal," she'd whispered faintly, "I'll always love you. Take good care of the boys and yourself."

He remembered the tears streaming down his face as he listened carefully to his dying love.

"I want you to go on with your life. I want you to love again and laugh again. Promise me you will, sweetheart."

He heard himself tell his beloved Faith, "I promise." He kissed her lips softly, as the last breath escaped her body.

He realized that God had allowed the memory of that night to resurface in his mind at this very moment for a reason. He couldn't lose Teary. He couldn't let her go. He loved her.

He moved as swiftly as he could on his prosthesis toward her room. The knock on the door came softly. "Teary, may I come in?"

"I'm-I'm busy packing right now. My flight leaves in a few hours, and I have a lot to get done."

"Teary, please . . . it'll only take a few minutes."

"No, I don't think so. Not right now anyway. There's really nothing more for the two of us to talk about. Will you just tell the twins I'll be out a little later to tell them goodbye?"

"The Richards just came over and picked them up to carry them to the picnic."

She yanked open the door. "You mean to tell me that you're so angry at me that you would let the boys leave without telling me goodbye? You despise me that much? How dare you!" She slammed the door shut and hurriedly turned the lock.

"Wait. Listen to me, Teary. I would never do that to you. I just didn't know what time you were leaving. I guess I just didn't want to believe that you really were leaving. I can get the boys back home before you go. I promise, I will. But please let me in. You have to listen to what I have to say. We have to talk. We can't part like this. Teary, please . . ."

Still there was silence. Just as he turned to walk away, he heard the door open.

Before he could say a word, she lashed out. "Look, last night was wrong," she cried, the hurt evident on her face, in her voice. "I know that; you know that. I've thought about it, and you did right to pull away from me. I don't know what I was thinking. I have no right to be angry with you at all. I want you and Sheerah to be happy. She'll make you a good wife, and she'll be a good mother to Kevin and Kaleb. So let's put what happened in the past and leave it there. And right now, I just want to finish my packing and have a chance to say goodbye to the boys before I go."

"But-but, Teary, I—"

"Please, don't," she said, cutting him off. "Let's not mess this up any more than we already have. I think we should just try to say a civil goodbye to each other. I've already arranged for a taxi to pick me up. That way I can run by the church to tell the boys goodbye." After saying that, she closed the door—and her heart.

Sheerah dialed Prodigal's phone number. "Prodigal, what's going on? Teary just left here, and she looked quite upset."

"It's a long story, one I don't have time to explain."

"The twins are in an uproar too." Sheerah didn't know what to think. "She said she was on her way to the airport. She mumbled something about having to get back to Memphis. I thought she wasn't leaving until Sunday."

"She wasn't, but something came up. We'll talk later, Sheerah." Prodigal hung up the phone and began pacing. He couldn't let Teary leave this way. He just couldn't.

Before Prodigal knew it, he hopped in his truck and was speeding to the airport. When he arrived, he immediately spotted Teary standing at the curbside ticket counter. He got out of his truck as quickly as he could, walked up and positioned himself beside her.

She looked up at him. The hurt he'd brought into her life remained visible on her face.

"Teary, don't go. Don't leave," he pleaded.

"You know that I have to." Teary barely looked at him. Retrieving her boarding pass from the ticket agent, she swiftly turned away from him.

"Teary, listen, don't let things end like this."

"Prodigal, things are ending exactly the way they need to end—for your sake and for mine. Now, look, I have to go. Tell the boys I love them," she said, fighting back the tears.

"Goodbye, Prodigal." Teary began walking through the airport terminal in the direction of her boarding gate.

Prodigal hung his head down, and his eyes filled with water. He stood in the middle of the terminal, people passing him on all sides. He stood until Teary disappeared from his view. Not once did she look back.

"Goodbye, Teary Fullalove," he said to himself. "Goodbye."

40

Sorry Isn't Enough

Months had passed since that ill-fated night. Upon returning to Memphis, Teary spoke to Prodigal and the boys only briefly over the next few months, preferring to e-mail the twins instead. Her conversations with Prodigal were strained, to say the least.

Prodigal hated the way things had played out between them. But if Teary was going to ever have a chance at love, he felt that he needed to be out of her way. She'd already put her career, her way of life, everything, on hold for him and the boys, and he wasn't going to be selfish any longer. How could he have crossed over their boundary of friendship like he did that night? Time and time again, he asked himself that question. He definitely had to keep some space between them. It was the right thing to do, for Teary's sake.

On top of everything that occurred in Bonsai Bay, nothing had changed for Teary when she returned to Memphis as far as a relationship, and she liked it that way. When she wasn't working, she was at church. She became an active part of the Greeter's Ministry. Most Sundays and Wednesday nights she welcomed members as they came to church. Because of her increased involvement with the church, Teary felt herself regaining spiritual strength.

She often thought about Prodigal, but she refused to be the one to complicate his life again. She wanted Kevin and Kaleb to have a chance to really get to know Sheerah, since she was going to be their stepmother. She wanted Prodigal to have a chance at loving again, something he couldn't do as long as she was around. As for what had transpired between her and Prodigal, she tried to block it out of her mind.

Teary and Patricia attended the Singles Ministry meetings faithfully, instead of doing the club scene. She especially liked the fact that in the Singles Ministry no one was concerned about her past. They accepted her for who she was—nothing more, nothing less. She and Patricia volunteered to be planning coordinators for the Singles Ministry. They hosted Single Parents Night Out, weekend retreats, seminars, movie nights, and a load of other delightful events. The ministry began to see significant growth.

Teary had other girlfriends, but they were either too busy or involved with someone. She occasionally talked to Debra. As for Chelsia, she hadn't seen or heard from her in ages. Along with church, Patricia and Teary's friendship provided a much-needed outlet for the both of them. They confided in each other, without being judgmental or putting the other one down.

Prodigal soon began thinking long and hard about his relationship with Sheerah. He liked her; he liked her a lot. She was a great woman, a good mother, and a fine Christian. Any man in his right mind would be crazy not to want her. So why hadn't their relationship evolved past friendship? He knew why but didn't want to face what was really going on inside of his head and heart. He pulled back the heavy tangerine comforter and pushed himself up in the bed. It was time for him to be true to himself.

His thoughts turned toward Teary. While he cared deeply for Sheerah, with Teary things were different. He loved Teary. He didn't know what he would do without her. She was one of the very few people he could still be himself with. She would never look down on him or think any less of him, no matter what. He enjoyed having her in his life, and the boys loved her too. There were many times he used to think about asking her to live with them, to actually quit her job and move to Bonsai Bay. *That would have been totally selfish on my part.* Prodigal pulled the down comforter up close around his chest. *It wouldn't have been fair anyway for me to ask her to give up her career, her home, or her life just because of me and the boys. But God, she's so good with them.*

Prodigal tossed and turned. It was time he made a decision. And he had to make it soon. He couldn't expect Sheerah to wait around on him to get his life in order. She had already gone out with a couple of other guys, and the fact remained that he wanted her to be sure about her future as well. She'd spent nineteen years in a marriage that went sour, and she often reminded him that, when and if she walked down the aisle again, it would be with the Lord's blessings or not at all.

Lord, I've managed to put myself in a jam once again, and I need you to pull me out. He reached over his right side, flicked the light off on the nightstand, and closed his eyes, entering into what would be a fitful sleep.

41

Making Up Is Hard to Do

One night while they were at Red Lobster preparing to dine on the all-you-can-eat shrimp special, Teary said to Patricia, "It's been months since I've heard from Prodigal and the boys. I really miss Kevin and Kaleb. Do you think he and Sheerah are married now?"

"I know you miss Kevin and Kaleb. From what you've told me, they're wonderful boys. But let's be for real here. Face the music—you know who you really miss?—Prodigal. I know you say the Sheerah chick is nice and all. That's well and fine, but *nice* doesn't cut it, if the man doesn't love her. So why don't you just pick up the phone and call him? The two of you have been friends far too long to throw it away because of something that *almost* happened."

"I can't, Patricia. I'm still too embarrassed. Anyway, he probably hates me. I behaved like a fool." Teary turned beet-red in the face at the thought. "Plus, he hasn't bothered to call me either."

"Fool or no fool, you said he was a man that doesn't hold grudges. From what you told me about him, he's not the type that will look down on you. And another thing, you said he was the one who actually made the first move on you that night, so imagine how he must feel. He's probably just as embarrassed as you are."

The waitress interrupted their conversation. "Hi, my name is Canton. I'll be your server this evening."

Teary spoke up first. "We know what we'd like. We want the all-you-can-eat shrimp special. I'd like mine fried."

"And I'd like mine grilled."

"Anything else? Can I get you something to drink?"

"A large sweet tea."

Patricia glanced over the beverage side of the menu. "I'd like a virgin strawberry daiquiri, please."

"I'll be back shortly with your orders." The waitress collected their menus and walked away.

"I'm still going to wait it out," Teary said. "I'm going to see if he's going to call."

A few minutes later the waitress returned with their drink orders.

Patricia swirled the stirrer around in her glass and sipped on her daiquiri. "One of y'all needs to make a move, but suit yourself."

When the waitress brought their food, their vibrant conversation was replaced with the sound of satisfaction in the form of smacking lips.

After sending the waitress back for seconds and thirds, Teary wiped her mouth with the white cloth napkin and made a grunting sound. "Ooh, I'm full. That was so good."

"Yes, it was. And this bread will make you run home and slap your momma, daddy, and baby sister." Patricia laughed.

Teary laughed too.

"Now let's get back to the subject at hand—What are you going to do about Prodigal?"

"I'm not going to worry about him any more—That's what I'm going to do. What God has for me is for me."

"Whatever, Teary. Come on, let's get out of here. I'm stuffed. Now I'm ready to go home and hit the sack."

"Ditto on that." Teary took the last sip from her drink and then grabbed her purse and jacket.

Patricia eyed the check. "It's my turn to pay." She pulled out a twenty, a ten, and a five and placed it on top of the check.

"Here's the money for the tip." Teary laid ten dollars on top of the thirty-five. "Now let's get out of here."

Prodigal started working out at the gym quite frequently. He used his prosthesis continually and even had one of those that enabled him to run again. He had run a few short marathons and had actually won a couple of trophies too.

His relationship with Sheerah was going pretty good too. Like him, Sheerah loved running, and both of them ran 5k and 10k races. He was feeling good about himself again. Occasionally he would meet some of the guys from the fire station or church for a movie or join them at a football game.

Prodigal found himself closer to God and calling on Him for guidance and direction. His sense of self-worth returned. The anger and bitterness he once felt for the situations in his life were quickly dissipating. He no longer lashed out at God. Instead, he thanked God for keeping him sane through all the tragedy and sorrow he had experienced throughout his life; he felt stronger for it. Prodigal recalled 2 Corinthians 12:9, a passage he had come to claim as his own: "But he said to me: My grace is sufficient for you, for my power is made perfect in weakness. Therefore I will boast all the more gladly about my weaknesses, so that Christ's power may rest on me."

He had mixed emotions and was torn between starting something serious with Sheerah and submitting to the love he had for Teary. *I've just got to bite the bullet and do it . . . be up front with her about everything.* He paced back and forth in his study. *I've got to talk to Sheerah.*

He nervously dialed her number.

"Sheerah, can you meet me at Starbucks for coffee later this afternoon, say around four?"

"I think four will be okay. I have to show a house at two-thirty, so I'll meet you after that."

"Good. I want to talk to you about something."

"Is everything all right?"

"Yeah, of course. I'll see you then."

A few minutes past four o'clock, when Sheerah strolled into the Starbucks, Prodigal couldn't conceal his delight at seeing her. She moved with the ease of a cat, her lavender pinstripe pantsuit complementing her frame perfectly.

He pulled out the chair for her as she approached. "Hey, how's it going with you this afternoon?"

She took her seat. "Good. The couple I showed the house to decided to make an offer on it."

"That's great, Sheerah. What are you going to have? I'll go and order it."

"I'll have a tall Chai latte."

"One tall Chai latte coming up." He moved cautiously through the crowd of customers, inching slowly to the counter.

He returned several minutes later with the Chai and a Mocha Valencia.

"Sheerah, I don't want to lead you on about anything, especially my feelings . . . when it comes to you."

"Listen, Prodigal, you've done no such thing. I like you, and I know you like me too."

"But I don't think I've been fair to you. Especially lately."

"How is that? And what do you mean?"

"Things have changed so fast for me. Ever since Teary left, I've been forced to face my feelings. I don't know how to tell you this."

"Tell me what?"

He took another sip of his Valencia. "I think I'm in love with

Teary—I'm sorry, Sheerah. I didn't want to do this to you . . . to our relationship. We had something special, I know, but I can't deny what I feel for Teary any longer."

"Prodigal, there's no need to feel like you've betrayed me. To be honest, I had no idea that you were this serious about us. I like you a lot, but I'm not in love with you."

"You aren't?"

"No, and you've never given me the impression that you were in love with me either."

"But I had serious intentions about you and me," he said, surprised and relieved at the same time. "I thought about taking our relationship to the next level."

"Maybe you *thought* you wanted to take it to the next level."

"What do you mean by that?"

"When I first met Teary, maybe even before I met her, I heard it in your voice."

"Heard what in my voice?"

"Love—It was quite obvious to me that she meant a lot to you."

"Is that right?"

"That's right. Then when I met her in person, I could tell that she cared just as deeply for you too. Only, it wasn't like a sisterly type of caring. The girl loves you. I guess the two of you are the only ones who can't see it."

"Sheerah, this is all so surprising coming from you. Here I was ready to beg you to not hate me for telling you how I felt about Teary. Instead, you've read me like an open book." He laughed, shook his head, took another sip of his Mocha Valencia, and leaned back in his chair.

"Don't get me wrong, I care about you and the boys, but I've said it time and time again—I'm not ready to commit myself to any one person right now, especially so soon after a divorce. I want to take my time and enjoy me for a change and spend time with Alexis, watch her mature into a young lady, you know what I mean?"

"Yeah, I know. You're quite a woman, Sheerah. Your ex was a fool to let you get away."

"Thanks, Prodigal. I'm enjoying my freedom. I feel like a new person since my divorce, and I'm determined to enjoy my new life. As for you and me, I hope we'll remain friends."

"I understand where you're coming from. And you can always count on my friendship." Prodigal reached across the table and held on to her hand. He could now breathe a sigh of relief, knowing that his relationship with Sheerah was not broken but, instead, strengthened.

He was now left to face his true feelings for Teary. He went on to confide in Sheerah about what had transpired between him and Teary, and the real reason she had left Bonsai Bay so hastily.

"You should call her and try to make things right. Don't let love slip through your fingers because you're too stubborn to admit you made a mistake."

Sheerah was special, and Prodigal respected her for being truthful and real with him. He would take her advice. He had to work it out with Teary, but he had to do it face-to-face.

42

To See You Again

"Daddy, can we call Teary?" Kaleb asked.

"Yeah, can we, Dad? We want her to come to our birthday party. We never get a chance to talk to her any more," Kaleb said, a sad expression on his face.

"I tell you what," Prodigal responded without thinking, "why don't we do better than that? Why don't we fly to Memphis and see her? We might even celebrate your birthdays there."

Prodigal couldn't believe what he'd just said. *Go and see Teary? Without talking to her? With no warning?* How could he even entertain such an idea as popping up on Teary? "I'd better call her," he said out loud. *I sure wouldn't want to pop up on her, only to find that she has someone in her life. I wouldn't know how to handle that.*

"I tell you what . . . let's go out and grab something to eat first. When we come back home, we can get on the computer and check out some tickets. Then we'll call Teary."

"Wow! Daddy that would be great," Kevin said.

"All right. Come on, let's go."

Teary turned the lock to the side door entrance of her house just in time to hear her phone ringing. *Who could that be?* She hurried to get the door unlocked. Her phone was programmed to ring three times before rolling over into her memory call service. Just as she opened the door, the final ring sounded. "Oh, well," she mumbled.

She sat her purse down on the kitchen counter, and Diamond and Sassy gathered around her feet, meowing loudly.

"Oh, you sweet babies. Momma's here now, and I'm going to pet you in just a few minutes," she cooed to them.

Before she could take another step, Rocco came racing toward her, jumping up and down like a horse.

"Hi ya, boy," she said, using baby talk. "You big, old, sweet thing, you." She stooped down and loved on all of them a few minutes.

She then went to the back door to get Rocco's leash from off the hanger so she could take him out to relieve himself. She would check the caller ID and her messages when she returned.

The air was still. Other than a couple of dogs barking somewhere else in the safely guarded neighborhood, all was quiet. Rocco led her over toward the playground area and then down the walking trail by the lake. There was only one other person walking his dog, and a couple of teenyboppers holding hands and smooching on one of the benches.

Teary slipped into her own world. She thought about her life. She went all the way back to when she was a teenager and Langston Silverman deceived her. She couldn't believe she had been so stupid and naïve. She should have known better. And not only that, she kept on allowing him to use and misuse her.

When she'd married Skyler, she faced the same thing, but just in a different form. He wasn't a Christian when she met him, but being young at the time, she thought that he would come around eventually. He did go to church with her a few times, but he never accepted Christ, that is, until much later in his life and after she was long gone out of the picture. If only she had listened and taken heed to her parents, to her upbringing, and married someone who'd shared her beliefs, things probably would have worked out differently for her.

Rocco finally relieved himself, and she turned and did a light jog back home. She gave him some fresh water, fed the cats, and then went in her bedroom to check her messages before running her bath. She looked at her caller ID. At first she didn't recognize the number. She looked more closely and read the name on the box—*Prodigal Runs*, the rest of his name cut off. Her heart picked up its pace.

She grabbed her cordless phone and heard the quick, quiet beeps indicating she had a message. She dialed her pass code and listened.

"Hello, Teary." She heard the all-too-familiar voice of not only Prodigal, but Kevin and Kaleb who were talking in the background as well. Then she heard him say, "Pipe down, you guys."

"Hi, Teary," he said more slowly this time, "it's me, Prodigal, and the boys. Give us a call when you can. Kevin and Kaleb have been riding me about calling you. They really miss you, and so I was thinking about bringing them to Memphis to see you. Well, sorry we missed you. Just call me when you get a chance and let me know what you think about us visiting you for a few days. Talk to you later."

He actually wants to come to Memphis? She didn't know what to think or how she was going to respond. She really wanted to see the twins again, and him too, for that matter, but she didn't know how she would face him after all this time.

She decided to take a nice long bath before returning the call. The feel of the warm, bubbly water helped her to think and relax. She leaned back against the soft purple bath pillow, closed her eyes, and whispered a prayer. "Lord, I'm going to really need Your help on this one. I want to do the right thing. More important than that, I want to do Your will. Guide each step I make. And whatever You want for Prodigal and me, I will accept it. I know You don't make any mistakes, so I'm placing my total trust in You. Amen."

Her eyes remained closed as she visualized Prodigal and the

boys coming to Memphis. When she climbed out the tub, an hour and a half had passed.

She found herself dialing the number. The phone rang about four times. She was just getting ready to hang up, when she heard his voice.

"Hello," he answered.

"Hi, Prodigal." Teary tried to sound nonchalant.

"Hey, it's good to hear your voice. I'm glad you called back."

"Why wouldn't I call back?" she asked, knowing full well why he made that statement.

"I didn't say you wouldn't call back. I just wasn't sure. Look, let me say this before I lose my nerve—I'm sorry about what happened the last time you were here; I really crossed the line, I know that. But I want you to know that I would never intentionally do anything to jeopardize our friendship. You mean too much to me, girl, and the boys too, for that matter. So, please, won't you forgive me?"

"The same here, Prodigal. And there's nothing to forgive. Anyway, that was a long time ago. We just got caught up in the moment."

Both of them were lying to each other. They had crossed the line, and there was no turning back. They just couldn't admit that their feelings toward each other were deeper than mere friendship.

"Look, like I said on your answering machine, I was thinking about bringing the boys your way. They've been missing you like crazy. And since their birthday is next week, we thought we could come and celebrate with you."

"And you?"

"What did you say?"

"I said, 'And you?'—have you missed me too?"

"Of course, I miss you—What kind of question is that?" Prodigal squirmed in his La-Z-Boy recliner. He only wished he could tell her just how much he missed her. He ached for her like a dope fiend for a hit. He still replayed that last night she was in Bonsai Bay in his mind. He loved her, plain and simple. He just didn't know how to tell her. But he would. He was going to do it, that is, if she would allow him to come and see her. He wasn't going to let love pass him by, not after God allowed him another chance to love again. Some folks didn't even get a chance to know the God-sent kind of love one time, and here he was being allowed to experience it yet again. He had prayed long and hard about his decision.

She interrupted his thoughts. "When were you planning on coming?"

"As soon as you give me the go-ahead. I don't have anything holding me down here, and the boys are out of school right now. So just say when, and we'll be on our way."

"When." She jumped up and down, unable to contain her excitement.

"Huh?"

"You said to say when, and I just said it—when—silly, that means come right now if you want to. My place isn't as large as yours, but what's mine is yours still."

"That's no problem. It doesn't take much for us. We just want to see you. Let me finalize our flight, and I'll give you a call back. It'll probably be as soon as the end of the week."

"Okay, no problem. I'll talk to you later."

Teary hung up the phone and immediately picked it back up and dialed Patricia's number. As soon as Patricia answered, Teary started telling her about her call from Prodigal. "Girl, guess who just called me—Prodigal." Teary squealed.

Patricia's voice was full of lazy excitement. "No, he didn't, girl." She had just turned over in her bed and was in the first stages of getting her sleep on. She bolted straight up in her queen-size canopied bed when she heard this. "What did he say?"

"He's coming to Memphis," Teary screamed. "He and the boys are coming sometime this week. You have to help me get things cleaned up and ready. I cannot believe it."

"Will you please stop screaming in my ear? Look, I'll be over there first thing after work tomorrow, and we'll get everything fixed up. But you don't have much to do anyway. Shucks! You keep that doggone place of yours so clean, it's like being in a hospital operating room. Did you ask him about Sheerah?"

"No, and he didn't mention her either. I'm not thinking about her right now anyway. If things were that tight between them, he would have said so. He's not one who'd mess over somebody. He's going to be truthful and honest. I'm excited and nervous at the same time. He said he was sorry about what happened between us and that he would never do anything to jeopardize our friendship. Oh, Patricia, I'm so glad I heard from him."

"I am too. I can't wait to meet him. Look, calm yourself down and try to get some sleep because you won't be getting much when they get here, you know."

"Okay, talk to you later."

Teary snuggled up against Rocco and her cats; by this time they had all jumped in the bed with her. She closed her eyes in sleep but not before saying happily, "Thank you Jesus."

Not wanting to inconvenience Teary, Prodigal rented a car. The trip was sudden enough already. But he had something to say—It was time he told her how he felt once and for all.

Teary paced nervously back and forth across the lacquered hardwood floor, checking her watch every few minutes. It was approaching one o'clock, meaning Prodigal's flight had landed almost forty minutes earlier. They should be arriving at her place any moment. She had his cell number, but she wasn't going to call it right now. She would give him about fifteen more minutes. The airport was about thirty minutes away, so she realized it would take time, since he had to get their luggage, the rental car, and find his way to her place. But she was anxious and didn't know how much longer she could wait.

At one-thirty she dialed his cell phone.

He answered on the first ring. "Hello."

"Hi, where are you?"

"I'm standing in the Hertz line. We should be leaving here in about fifteen minutes or so. I'll call you when I'm headed your way."

"Okay, I'll see you soon."

After getting the rental car, Prodigal followed the directions Teary had given him over the phone. By two-fifteen he and the boys were driving up to her gated neighborhood. He dialed the access code she had given him and proceeded to maneuver the rented black-and-gray Yukon XL through the somewhat narrow gates.

The boys loved the idea of staying at Teary's instead of a hotel. Once inside the community, they passed by a monstrous man-made lake, which was meticulously designed and landscaped. They yelled in excitement, when they saw a family of ducks waddling across the perfectly manicured grounds.

"Daddy, Daddy, look! Look at the ducks," Kaleb squealed in excitement.

"Kaleb, look on this side. There's a playground with slides and a monkey bar and swings and stuff too. Daddy, can we go over there?"

"We'll go, but not now. The first thing we're going to do is find Teary's place. Then we'll plan what we're going to do next."

Reading the directions, he made a left turn, took another left onto Plum, and then a right onto Wheeler Drive.

"Boys, help me look for 2378 Wheeler Drive."

"2370," Kaleb read.

"2375." Kevin pointed his finger at the same time.

"Look, there it is—2378," Kevin yelled out, before his brother could get another word in edgewise.

Prodigal tapped the horn.

Teary heard the blare of a horn and raced to the front entrance. "Hey, you guys," she yelled, running to the car with Rocco, Diamond, and Sassy trailing behind her. "Boy, am I glad to see you. You're a sight for sore eyes!"

The boys jumped down out of the SUV and dashed straight

for her outstretched arms. She stooped down to welcome their embrace then she kissed their faces.

Kevin and Kaleb knelt down, allowing Rocco to welcome them with sloppy dog kisses, while the felines raced back into the safety of the house.

Next Teary sprinted toward Prodigal.

He lifted his prosthesis-clad leg out of the SUV and prepared to stand up.

Teary didn't give him a chance. She climbed up on the running board of the Yukon XL and dashed straight toward him and gave him a tight hug before he could get out and steady himself. He fell back against the tan leather seat, with her almost on top of him. Tears rested in the corner of her eyes until they refused to stay back any longer. She held on tight to her best friend in the entire world.

He welcomed her warmth and inhaled her fragrance, his heart pounding wildly for the woman he loved with all of his heart.

She soaked in the handsome dark frame of the man who had been part of her life for all of her life. Only, this time when she looked at him, she saw him through the eyes of someone she loved deeply.

Prodigal's plans were for him and the boys to stay in Memphis from Wednesday through Sunday. He respected the fact that Teary had to work, and he didn't want to do anything to get her off track, especially since she had been on and off work so much during the past two and a half years and mostly because of him.

They celebrated the boys' eighth birthday by going to Chucky Cheese's Pizza Parlor. Teary invited Patricia's nephew, who was the same age as the twins, to come along. While the boys wolfed down several helpings of pizza, and played arcade games, Teary and Prodigal caught up on what was happening in their respective lives. They laughed and talked like old times.

"What have Sara and Anthony been up to these days?" he asked.

"I talked to Sara a couple of weeks ago. They're renovating Aunt Vashti's house. They had been renting it out since Aunt Vashti died, but the tenants were doing more damage than anything. Anthony said they might as well fix it up, and then they're going to move in it themselves. That way they'll have more money for Andrew's needs when he goes off to college in the fall."

"That's a smart idea," Prodigal told her. "What about your mom and dad? How are they doing?"

"Oh, they're doing super too. Momma said she was thinking about coming here sometime in early fall. She retired a couple of months ago. And you know Daddy has been retired for some time now, so they're both getting used to being under each other's feet every day. But they're in good health and sound mind, and that's a lot to be thankful for. I still talk to them once or twice a week—What about your folks? It's been a while since I've talked to Fantasia."

"Fantasia is just fine, but you know her—she's all about those dead presidents. She focuses all of her energy into that gallery. Maybe she'll succumb to the call of love one day, who knows? But as long as she's happy, then I'm happy for her."

"I've learned that a person can be contented and at peace even in their singleness. I'm a living witness to that," Teary said.

"I agree with you, but that's not what bothers me about her."

"What is it then?"

"What bothers me more than anything else about her is that she still hasn't accepted Christ into her life. You and I both know that Satan disguises himself as an angel of light. I'm not saying that she wouldn't be any less successful if she was saved, but what I am saying is that I've learned that only what we do for Christ lasts. I just don't know what else to do about it or what else to say to her."

"There's nothing more you can do. Just keep on praying for her."

"Well, I do that."

"How is Mrs. Runsome? Is she still dating the same man?"

"Yep, she most definitely is. Something tells me that we might be hearing the sound of wedding bells real soon."

"What! Are they that serious?"

"From what Fantasia tells me, yes, they are. And every time I talk to Momma, she sounds like she's in a world that involves only the two of them. She's been going with him to his church almost every Sunday too. I'm glad for that because her faith was always something sacred to her. It was really tested when Daddy died. It took a long time for Momma to start living again, but she's happy now. Her faith is strong, and she's opened her heart again."

Prodigal smiled warmly.

"You know, we all fall off the wagon at some time in our lives. You and I are proof of that, aren't we?" Teary laughed.

"You got that right."

"How are Hope and David and their small village of children doing?"

"They couldn't be any better. Most of their energy is put into their church. From what David tells me, their congregation is growing. Hope is amazing with the kids. I don't understand how she manages five little ones under her feet twenty-four seven. For me, it's more than a handful taking care of two boys."

"She has that gift of patience; not everyone can do what she does. David is truly blessed to have her as his wife."

Their conversation was interrupted by the boys begging for more game tokens.

Prodigal spoke up after the boys returned a third time for more tokens. "Hold up, guys, it's time to sing happy birthday and dig into this delicious-looking superhero cake. Come on, let's do it."

Together they sang, "Happy birthday to you, happy birthday, dear Kevin and Kaleb, happy birthday to you."

Prodigal added in a crazy voice, "And many more."

Once the boys returned to play, Teary asked the question that had been lingering in the back of her mind the whole time. She desperately wanted to know the answer, but at the same time she was afraid to hear his response. "How are Sheerah and her daughter?—Did she accept your proposal?"

"She's great. Sweet as ever. She's really something else. But I guess I don't have to tell you that, huh?"

"No, you don't. She *is* a kindhearted person—You didn't answer all of my question."

"I know it. Alexis is fine. She has a crush on one of the boys in her class at Unity. As for Sheerah and I, marriage is definitely not in the picture. She wants to take her time and do what God directs her to do. And I agree with her. We're still friends; we see each other from time to time. We do a lot of things with the kids too, but there's no marriage in the forecast for us. Now tell me about you—What have you been up to, and who have you been up to it with?" Prodigal grinned.

"I've been great. I'm quite active in the Singles Ministry and the Greeters Ministry at church. I've been doing quite a bit of freelance work, and I'm beginning to build up quite a nice client list. I might even be able to freelance full-time in a few more months."

"Teary, that's good to hear. I'm happy things are working so well for you."

"As for someone special in my life, there's no one, but you know what?"

"What's that?"

"I'm quite contented. I'm enjoying my work, I make good money, I love my church, and I love working in the church. I've truly grown in the Lord over these past couple of years, even more so over these last few months. God's been good to me. He's sustained me through all the situations I've had to face in my life. For that, I am truly thankful to Him, Prodigal."

"I heard that. You go on with your bad self."

Both of them laughed and locked hands across the table.

Teary was elated to have Prodigal and the boys at her house. During the time they were there, she kept their schedule full of things to do. They had fun at Libertyland, visited Graceland, the National Civil Rights Museum, and watched the sunset at Tom Lee Park. Patricia scooped them up for a day at the Fire Museum and Stax Academy, and Teary showed them where she worked and introduced them to just about everyone at the newspaper.

At night, after the boys were tucked in and fast asleep, Teary and Prodigal sat up till the wee hours of the morning, drinking raspberry tea and reminiscing about their high-school days. They were careful not to mention the events of the past that caused the rift in their friendship.

When Prodigal and Teary said goodnight and retreated to their bedrooms, Prodigal lay in the king-sized bed, thinking about Teary in the next room. He was sharing the guestroom with the boys. What he really wanted was to lie next to Teary and cradle her underneath his arms. He felt good about his decision to come to Memphis. It only confirmed what his heart was trying to tell him—Teary made him happy; Teary made him feel complete.

Time zoomed by way too fast for the both of them, and before either of them realized, Prodigal found himself gathering up his and the boys' things.

Teary laughed at the sight of Kevin, Kaleb, Rocco, and the cats snuggled up on the living room floor. Like always, the boys had fallen asleep while watching a movie. This time, it was *X-Men* that lulled them to sleep. She went into the closet and pulled down a couple of blankets to cover them with and then proceeded to go help Prodigal pack. This was their last night together, and she was missing him already.

She knocked on the door of the guestroom. "May I come in?" She snuck a look inside.

"Of course, after all, it's your house."

"I thought you might like some help."

"Yeah, sure."

"Hey, move over." She gave him a gentle shove.

He inched over toward the head of the bed.

She began picking up some of the boys' clothes and started

folding them neatly. "So what are your plans when you get back home?"

"Kevin and Kaleb are enrolled in a summer camp program sponsored by our church. It starts next Wednesday. They'll be going to the mountains for the first two weeks of camp, and then spending another week at a retreat center about two hours outside of Denver. As for me, I recently joined a sports group at the Center for Independent Living. They teach people like me how to engage in sports even with their physical challenges. There's also a special group that counsels newly injured individuals by educating them concerning their disability, the trauma a major injury causes, and then presents options for the individual to get back in the swing of things, especially those who love sports, like me. I'm going to be one of the counselors."

"Prodigal, that's fabulous. I knew you could do it."

"And I know you won't believe this next thing I'm going to tell you."

"What?—Don't keep me in suspense."

"I've been elected to serve as a deacon at my church—can you believe it?"

She was astounded. These were exactly the kinds of things she hoped he would get involved with. She believed that he could do whatever he set his mind to. "That's great, Prodigal. I'm glad to know you've decided to get back to living. I don't think I ever told you this, but I know it's been extremely hard for you. So much has happened in so little time. I can't begin to understand what you must be feeling. But I've learned that God is in control of every single situation in our lives. That includes those situations and times when we mess up. It means He's in control of the good things and the bad things that enter into our lives. I've had to remind myself of this often, so I'm not trying to lecture you or anything. But you know we were brought up to believe in God and to trust in Him, right?"

"Right. It's just that life gets hard sometimes. You know this. And after Faith's death, it was like that was the last straw. I mean,

I saw my father die and then Faith. I just didn't understand why God was allowing all of this to happen to me. When I lost my leg, I just knew my life was over. When that happened, I thought about ending it all, but something within kept me thinking about my sons. I couldn't leave them. I couldn't let them grow up without any parents. It was hard enough for me when Daddy died, so I realized that I just couldn't give up, no matter what."

Tears swelled up in both of their eyes. Prodigal stopped packing. "I know God's ways are not our ways, Teary, and His thoughts are not our thoughts. But I just wish sometimes that I could understand some of the stuff He allows in our lives. Look at you—you're such a sweet, kind, and compassionate woman. But then you get some scumbag like Skyler who all but destroys your life. You didn't deserve that kind of treatment.

"And then I look at my mom. You know she loved my dad with all of her heart, yet God called him home and left my momma to raise us all alone. She grieved for that man for so many years. I know that she's finally found some happiness, and I'm glad. But I also know that no one will ever replace Solumun Runsome in her heart.

"And then there's Faith, my darling Faith. Who would have thought that she would go to be with God at such an early age and leave me and the boys longing for her and missing her? I always thought we would grow old together, you know. There isn't a day that goes by when I don't think about her and wish that she was here with the boys and me; I still miss her, Teary." The tears refused to stay back any longer.

Teary stroked his back gently. "Prodigal, we'll probably never know the answers to all the questions we have, but we do know the one who holds the answers. That's what keeps me going. That's what keeps me moving and striving. You know that, don't you?"

"Yeah, I know."

They sat on the bed in silence, holding each other as if they were afraid that if they let go, they would both fall apart. They were two people whose lives had been designed from the beginning to intertwine, to connect, to be united forever. And so they sat and allowed the silence to satisfy them.

Prodigal penetrated the wall of silence. "Teary . . . about that night . . . I have to tell you something about that night."

"No, shhh. It's all right. We don't have to go there." She brushed her fingers gently across his lips to hush him.

"Oh, yes, we do." His wrinkled brow revealed his desperate need to speak. His words came out slowly. "I wanted you so bad that night. I wanted to hold you close to me, to feel your body surrender underneath my touch." As he spoke, he weaved his fingers in and out of the locks of her hair nestled along the side of her face. "I wanted to inhale the soft fragrance of your hair." He leaned forward and breathed in the fragrance of her hair. "I wanted to taste your sweet lips and feel the warmth of your body next to mine." Prodigal grazed his fingers seductively over the curve of her lips. "I wanted you, Teary. I believed I've wanted you since I was that little four-eyed, dusty boy from Broknfield. I've loved you all along." He moved himself from Teary, afraid even at that moment that the love he felt for her would overtake him. He reached out and stroked her soft, baby-smooth face. His fingers traced her eyes, and then moved to her nose. He traced the outline of her lips.

She closed her eyes. She felt the same trembling envelop her body just like that night they had both tried so hard to forget. She knew he was right. She always knew there was something special about their relationship. She loved Prodigal Runsome like a woman loves a man. She wanted him just as much as he wanted her.

"Prodigal," she whispered to him, breathing heavily, "I love you too. I love you too," she repeated. "I was afraid that I had ruined everything for us. I was afraid that you didn't feel the same way I felt about you. I didn't want our friendship destroyed because of my foolish thoughts and desires."

"No. Don't you see? Through everything that has happened

in our lives, we've survived, and we've survived together. I know there will never be another Faith, but I also know there'll never be another Teary Fullalove either. We can do this. We can make it together."

" 'Together'?"

"Yes, together. I came here to set the record straight. I want to tell you how I really feel, to tell you that I'm in love with you. You see, I want to be the one who lies beside you every night and wakes up beside you every morning."

"Prodigal—"

He placed two fingers against her lips. "Shhh. Listen, baby, I want to be the one to take care of you, to be that man you've always deserved. I want to love you, Teary, for the rest of our lives."

Teary was speechless. *Surely I didn't hear what I just heard. I must be dreaming. But if I'm dreaming, then I don't want to wake up. I want to live this dream forever.*

"Teary," he said nervously, "did you hear what I just said?"

"Oh yes, I heard every word. And I want to lie beside *you* every night and wake up beside *you* every morning. I want to be the one to take care of *you*, to love *you* totally and completely."

This time when their lips met there was no hesitancy. There was no feeling of wrongdoing; everything felt right; everything felt good.

43

Set Free

Ruth curled up on the loveseat in her luxurious master bedroom suite on the third floor of the gallery. She spent a lot of her downtime in this two-bedroom suite, especially when the weather was bad or when she was just plain too tired to go home. The suite was tastefully decorated in soothing, earth tone colors, with dashes of lavender accessories. The interior designer had done an excellent job. Ruth's king-sized bed faced a bank of curved glass windows overlooking a panoramic view of Belleaf. The mantled fireplace and seating area gave the room a warm, inviting aura.

While she sipped on her club soda, gazing out at the captivating scenic view, she reminisced. She dreamed of how much she longed to have Solumun beside her. The two of them could be enjoying life and living together. Fantasia had been good to her. If Solumun was alive, things would only have been that much better. She would be with the man who stole a young teenage girl's heart all those many years ago.

Then her mind drifted to thoughts of William Phillips, her rescuer, the one who breathed life into her existence again. The one who proved to her that she had room in her heart to love someone again. She never thought in a million years that she would ever feel love for another man, not after Solumun. But not only did she love William; for the first time since Solumun's death, she felt a genuine sense of peace. It was like Solumun was with her, giving her his blessings, his approval. She had found a good man in William, and she wasn't going to let him go.

She dropped to the side of the loveseat and knelt down on her knees. Hot tears rolled down the length of her face. *Lord, forgive me.* Ruth released all of the hurt, the anger, the bitterness, the pain, and the grief that she had kept bottled up inside her for the past twenty-seven years. *God, I've been angry with you for so long that my anger turned to bitterness. I've been full of heartache, but I'm tired of being bitter. I'm tired of questioning you. Bring me back into your fold where I belong.*

An indescribable peace rose up inside Ruth. She felt released. She felt free. She felt alive. But most of all, Ruth Runsome felt the forgiveness and mercy of God.

Epilogue

September-October 2006

Fantasia and her staff were busy finalizing plans for the wedding of the year. There was a lot to do, and being the perfectionist that she was, she insisted that everything be perfect. After all, this was not going to be an ordinary wedding, but the talk of the town for the socialites of Belleaf, Maryland.

They scurried around meeting with caterers, making sure they chose the perfect wedding dress, the perfect colors for the wedding, and the best food.

The delicately embossed wedding invitations were outlined with Japanese characters signifying peace, love, and happiness. An intricate pearl foil border added to their elegance and further signified the importance of this event. The invitations expressed the love the couple had for each other and for God.

Desiring God's perfect will for their lives and believing that includes each other, Ruth Diane Runsome and William Garner Phillips invite you to share in their joy, As they are united to each other in the name of the Lord Jesus Christ, The twenty-ninth day of October at half past after three o'clock, At Trinity Three Art Gallery, 377 Stance Avenue, Belleaf, Maryland. Reception to be held at the Fantasy Room of Trinity Three Art Gallery.

* * *

"I'm so happy for Momma, aren't you?" Hope said to her big brother.

"Hope, I can't think of anyone who deserves happiness more than Momma." Prodigal smiled at his sister.

"Well, I can think of two other people myself." Hope adjusted the newest addition to the Peters family higher up on her left hip.

"And who could those two people possibly be?"

"Why, you of course, big brother. You and your wife. David and I were ecstatic to hear the news of your marriage. It feels good when you not only listen to God, but when you actually listen and then *obey* Him. Don't you think so, Prodigal?"

"Sis, I couldn't agree more."

Just then, Kevin and Kaleb came dashing across the marble floor in their cream-colored tuxedos.

"Whoa, stop clowning around, you two. And anyway, where's your mother? I bet she has no idea that you guys are running around the church like this."

The woman walked up, hearing Prodigal chastising the boys. "Sweetheart, you're right. I was just looking for them. Kevin and Kaleb, go back in the parlor and wait until it's time for you to take your places; your cousins are in there already. And I don't want to catch you running through here again, do you hear me?" Her voice never moved above a gentle tone.

"Yes, ma'am," they replied.

She then turned toward Hope. "Hope, this little girl is just as precious as she can be. How old did you say she is?"

"She'll be ten months next Monday."

"Oh, I just can't wait until we have our little one. Can you, Prodigal?"

"No, I'm on pins and needles."

"You'll do fine," Hope assured him. "If David and I can manage six, then you two can manage three. How much longer will it be anyway?"

"We have two more days before the papers are finalized. You should see her, Hope. She is such a precious little princess."

"Oh, my! I think some little lady is going to be spoiled." Hope smiled.

"Oh, I know she is; she's going to be a daddy's girl. God is just so good. He's blessed us in so many ways. We have two handsome sons and now a precious baby girl. Did I tell you what we decided to name her?"

"No, you didn't. And you didn't tell me how old she is either. I guess y'all were just too excited about the news."

"Yeah, you know we only received the final call two days ago. Her name is Elisabeth Faith Runsome. Our precious little China doll is just two weeks old." Prodigal's voice bubbled over with fatherly pride, his hand comfortably nestled around his wife's waist.

Teary couldn't remember a time when she was any happier than at this moment. She was Mrs. Prodigal Runsome. And now she was finally free to be all that God would have her to be. The two of them walked hand in hand around the gallery, greeting old and new friends.

The organ music flowed. Teary sat next to Sara, Anthony, their son Andrew, and the new addition to their family, two-year-old little Bethany. Everyone rose to their feet as the radiant bride made her entrance.

Prodigal stood handsomely and proudly at his mother's side. Teary was mesmerized by the sight of her husband, and unconditional love overflowed in her heart.

Ruth turned to face the man who had shown her how to love again. She could hardly hold back the tears forming in the corners of her eyes, when she heard William's baritone voice reciting his vows. When he finished, she felt the love she had for him swelling inside, and she thanked God for giving her another chance.

She began to recite her vows. "I, Ruth Dianne Runsome, take you, William Garner Phillips, to be my husband, my partner in life and my true love. I shall cherish our friendship and will love you always, now and forever. I will trust you and honor you. I will laugh with you and cry with you. I promise to love you completely. Through the best of times and the worst of times. Through the storms and through the sunshine, I will love you. I will always be there for you, my love. As I give you my hand to hold, I give you all of me. All of my love is yours for as long as we both shall live, so help me God."

"Will both of you now repeat after me," David said.

William looked at his lovely bride, and she at him. They began to speak in unison, tears now flowing freely from their eyes.

"Entreat me not to leave you, or to return from following after you, for where you go, I will go, and where you stay, I will stay. Your people will be my people, and your God will be my God. And where you die, I will die, and there I will be buried. May the Lord do with me and more if anything but death parts you from me."

"May God bless this union, may His countenance of love shine upon you as long as you both shall live," David said. "By the powers vested in me, I now pronounce you Mr. and Mrs. William Garner Phillips. You may now salute your lovely bride."

William leaned forward and passionately kissed Ruth.

The guests clapped loudly as the newlyweds turned toward them, and William kissed his blushing bride again.

Prodigal lightly tapped the crystal flute filled with champagne. "Everyone, please, may I have your attention. I'd like to make a toast to the newlyweds."

The room became silent. The guests focused their attention on the handsome tuxedoed man standing at the front of the room.

"To my mother, a woman of strength, a woman who showed her children the meaning of hope, faith, perseverance, and most of all love. And to her husband, William Phillips, a man of good character, high morals, and truly a man of God, may the two of you always have the kind of love you have now—unconditional love that always gives. Unconditional love that loves just because. May you keep God first in all that you do. And may His blessings continually be showered upon you for all the days of your lives. I love you. We love you."

The music began to play.

William and Ruth were the first on the floor.

After a few minutes couples quickly filled the spacious dance floor.

Prodigal found his way to the arms of his loving wife and his dearest friend. He reached out for her and pulled her close to him. She felt his heart beat in tune with hers, as they danced to an old but familiar song by the Beatles, "There Are Places I Remember."

The End

Reading Group Discussion Guide

Prodigal Runsome

1. Prodigal is a young boy when he first experiences tragedy. Do you think this colors the way he lives his life? If so, in what ways? How does it affect him spiritually and emotionally?

2. Why do you think God allows such things to happen in Prodigal's life?

3. Do people today really face the types of problems Prodigal faced?

4. Can Prodigal be likened to any Bible character? If so, who and why?

Teary Fullalove

1. Teary is raised in the church, yet at an early age she gives up her precious gift of virginity outside of marriage to Langston. How could she do this after being raised in church?

2. How can what Teary experienced as a young teen apply to the lives of young adolescent girls and boys today who take fornication so lightly?

3. What can we, as adults, whether Christians or non-Christians, do to encourage today's youth to make proper and wise decisions?

4. Can Christians truly profess to be Christians when they fornicate and shack up with one another? Why? Why not?

5. Much like Prodigal, Teary faces her own battles in life. Do you
see any similarities in their characters and/or personalities?
What are they?

6. Why are Langston and Skyler able to get next to Teary?

7. Did Skyler love Teary?

PRODIGAL AND FAITH

1. Did Prodigal truly love Fath?

2. Is Faith justified in feeling the way she does about Prodigal
and Teary's friendship?

RUTH RUNSOME

1. Ruth takes the death of her husband as a terrible blow that affects her for over twenty years. It often appears as if she has
given up on her faith and trust in God. Why didn't she lean toward her faith instead of falling away from her faith?

2. Why couldn't she love Ralph Gordon, obviously a good man
who loved her deeply?

3. How is William Phillips able to penetrate her shell?

4. What are some of the ways people react to tragedy, sorrow, and
disappointment in their lives? Is it natural to be angry and bitter when faced with tragedy, hurt, and disappointment?

FAITH MEADOWS

1. How does what happens to Faith fall in line with God's purpose and design for Prodigal's life? For Teary's life?

FANTASIA RUNSOME

1. What was the significance, if any, of Fantasia's heart pieces of art?

2. Did Fantasia believe in God?

3. What is your opinion about Fantasia's sexuality?

4. Fantasia's vast wealth, power, and success is something that Christians and non-Christians alike often only dream of. How can Christians steer clear of getting caught up in feelings of jealousy and envy, when non-Christians seem to prosper at every turn?

5. What kind of man, if any, will it take to break through Fantasia's mindset about love and relationships?

HOPE AND MINISTER DAVID PETERS

1. Why did they have so many children? What was the significance of this, if any?

SARA FULLALOVE

1. Why do you think Sara waited so long to marry Anthony?

2. What role did Aunt Vashti play in Sara's life?

BRIAN AND CYNTHIA FULLALOVE

1. After all the teaching of Brian Fullalove, why did Sara and Teary do the opposite of what he taught them?

2. Very little is mentioned about Mrs. Fullalove. What type of role do you think she played in the Fullalove household? How do you think it affected the way Sara and Teary grew up?

SHEERAH SAMUELS

1. What role, if any, do you think Sheerah plays in Prodigal and Teary's relationship?

INTO EACH LIFE RATING

1. How do you rate this novel, and why?

2. Would you read a sequel to *Into Each Life*? If so, what characters would you want to see included in the sequel? Why? What characters wouldn't you want included? Why not?

Author's Note

Prodigal and Teary came to realize that life is a journey that everyone must travel. Into each person's life there will be times of sadness and gladness, sunshine and rain, tragedy and sorrow, ups and downs, troubles and triumphs. But the greatest gift that any person can be blessed to receive in life is love. Though Prodigal and Teary found themselves being tested and tried throughout their lives, they ultimately came out victorious because they were blessed to have a lasting friendship and an undying love for each other that overcame the adversities they faced.

No matter how much one acquires in life, it is all fruitless if you have no one to share it with, no one to love and to love you in return, and no faith in the Creator who makes it all possible. We are not of our own making. We are intricately designed by God to fulfill His purpose for our lives.

Each of us will travel the amazing journey of life with all of its adventures, some good and some not so good. Yet, life is for living, and love is for giving and *Into Each Life* some_____will fall. (*You* fill in the blank.)

About the Author

Shelia E. Lipsey, resides in Memphis, Tennessee. She self-published two other works before signing on with Kensington/Urban Books. Shelia's mission is to write real-life situational stories about Christian people. *Into Each Life* is her first book with Kensington/Urban. She hopes to write many more stories that will touch the lives of people and bring about change in the world. She is the mother of two adult sons, and she has three grandchildren (many more grandchildren by love).

A Personal Invitation from the Author

If you have never made a decision to accept Jesus Christ as your personal Lord and Savior, God himself extends this invitation to you.

If you have not trusted Him and believed Him to be the giver of eternal life, you can do so right now. We do not know the second, the minute, the hour, the moment, or day that God will come to claim us. Will you be ready?

Romans 10: 9-10 (NIV) says, "If you confess with your mouth, Jesus is Lord, and believe in your heart that God raised Jesus from the dead, you will be saved. For it is with your heart that you believe and are justified, and it is with your mouth that you confess and are SAVED."